Prais
The Three Kin   D1552648

...A fantastic adventure and James Morris is a prince of an author. Family is who fights with and for you... and writes a book you want to reread. Props, Brother James!
— Nancy Holder, *New York Times* bestselling author of THE WICKED SAGA.

Sam Cutter's adventures in the Three Kingdoms come to a crash-bang climax, as the just-turned 16-year-old and his allies confront the forces of the New Power... Sam struggles with issues of loss, the costs of fighting, even for a just cause, and relationships with friends, peers, and adversaries -- including a well-depicted blooming romance. A rousing end to an epic journey.
- Maryelizabeth Hart, Mysterious Galaxy

A world ripped into three kingdoms... A terrifying imbalance of power... A clever young adventurer with a streak of reluctant heroism... pure white-knuckle adventure at its very best.
— William H. McDonald, film maker and author of *PURPLE HEARTS*, and *A SPIRITUAL WARRIOR'S JOURNEY*

Samuel Cutter and his artificially intelligent sidekick, Dac, take the reader on an adventure that will leave them hanging onto every word in sheer anticipation.
— Kerry Frey, author of *BURIED LIE*

...A masterful blend of action, intrigue, and edge-of-your-seat excitement that will keep you flipping the pages long into the night. James Morris combines the world-building ingenuity of Philip K. Dick with a raw-edged creativity that I've never seen in such a young author. Remember this kid's name, because you're going to be asking for his autograph.
— Jeff Edwards, award-winning author of *THE SEVENTH ANGEL*, and *SWORD OF SHIVA*

Books by James Morris

Three Kingdoms

Sky Bound
Water Tower
Surface

SURFACE

JAMES MORRIS

Mitchell—
Thanks
for reading!

2/23/19

Edited by Eric Donica
Cover illustration by Analise Hanna
Digital painting and design by Jonathan Nowinski

ISBN 978-0-9838844-5-3

Typography by James Morris
10 9 8 7 6 5 4 3 2 1

First Edition: April 2015

If I thanked everybody individually that needed to be thanked, the book would probably be twice as long. Thank you to everybody that has supported me and believed in me and to all of you who have ever picked up a copy of the book. You guys are half the joy of writing. It has been amazing sharing Sam's story with you and I can't wait until our next adventure.

Prologue

"So, yet again, the Cutter boy has bested you?" a shadowed figure asks Steven.

"Master, forgive me," Steven pleads, "It is not for lack of trying." His master looks at him from his throne with disdain. "I guarantee you he perished in the Water Tower. Cutter was paralyzed." Steven himself is still injured from his battle with the boy. Even here the injuries won't seem to fade. The Red Elixir that he drank took a real toll on his body. If the punishment that Sam gave him wasn't enough, that was the topping on the cake. As expected with Red Elixir, Steven kept some of the strength that was gifted to him after its effects wore off, but it's barely a fraction of what he commanded at the time of ingestion.

"Your failures are beginning to become countless," Steven's master says. "And your delay in getting me this report does *not* amuse me." If it were possible to gracefully snarl, the master just pulled it off. It's enough to intimidate Steven who visibly flinches at his master's words. He falls to a knee, even that much motion hurting him. He should be further healed, but his mind can't seem to be rid of the phantom pain.

"I have good reason for the delay, master," Steven says, not chancing a look up from the floor. The monochromatic floor's color is only disrupted by the light provided by the torches on either side of the great hall. The floor reflects their dancing flames in a way that, while beautiful, is more off-putting to Steven than not. Still, the shifting reflections of flames are more than an ample distraction to avoid having to see the rage that Steven knows is in his master's face. Twice now he has been told to directly intervene in taking control of a nation. Twice he has failed.

"I'm sure you do," Steven's master mocks. "But it will not be 'good' enough." A foreboding energy swarms into the room as Steven's master pushes himself up out of his throne. The man himself is still cloaked in shadows, too dark to see. He seems to be the type that can take the darkness and wreath it around himself and wear it as a cape. That is the man he is. He is the one who can even control the darkness, for it is too afraid to do anything else.

Steven's master takes but one step down from his throne. He places a foot on the step beneath the level his throne is on, and a howling wind rushes throughout the entire hall. It's powerful enough that it stings Steven's skin as it rushes by. The gust seems to pick up the shadows that Steven's master is wearing, but they are too stubborn to leave his body. The shadows extend out from where the master stands as all the torches are blown out by this wind, and the entire hall turns pitch black.

Steven blinks hard, hoping that something was only wrong with his eyes and that the light is still there. There's no way that his master can do *this*. Right?

The wind dies down as suddenly as it started. The only sound echoing through this haunting hall is the ragged sound of Steven's breathing as he fails to calm himself. He breaks out into a cold sweat that spreads all over his body. In no time, it's enough that Steven's shirt is sticking to his body uncomfortably. The silence becomes deafening.

Second after second ticks by with Steven hoping beyond hope that his master still hasn't moved, that he will say something.

"Are you scared?" Steven's master asks, his voice coming from everywhere all at the same time. Surprised by the voice, Steven jumps and ducks his head in, shrugging his shoulders high. If there was enough light to see, it would look as if Steven is trying to make himself as small as possible. That's how he feels right now. A whimper escapes his lips, and a small chuckle comes echoing from all directions. A man that he knows can end his life in less than a second, the man he serves, is toying with him. Nearly a year ago, this would never have been the case.

Nearly a year ago, the Sky Nation was almost his! Everything was going to plan. They were broken. The resistance became the entertainment in the arena. The greatest of them became the new recruits, a brilliant idea that Steven takes credit for. Even then, he had his agents infiltrated within the Ravens in case things didn't go according to plan.

And then it all changed.

Steven attended the arena fight that day. A new shipment of gladiators had just come in. He got the call and rushed over immediately. It was bound to be a good show. After all, they had some exotic combatants that day: two of a shamefully rare breed. They had caught one years before, but he became so dull that they didn't even bother making him fight anymore. If these two Surface dwellers were anywhere near as entertaining as the last one they caught was, then it would've been one of the best matches they had in a long while.

The match was entertaining, yes, but not in the way Steven was expecting. Not at all. One of the Surface dwellers could fight. It was... intriguing. The other wasn't as funny as Steven had hoped. Neither was funny. One of them was ferocious. He fought as a desperate animal would. Even though he wasn't the best in the arena, Steven had ordered that he be made a new recruit. He wanted that ferocity among his rank. And besides, he needed a new toy.

Unfortunately, word had reached Steven's ears that the last of the remaining Ravens launched an assault against the transports that were taking the fighters to the prison. Of course, the attack was lead by that damnable Jinn Grant, the unofficial leader of the Ravens. Steven never could get close enough to get control of him. How unfortunate. There's another talent that he would've loved to get his hands on. He had heard that the boy died in the attack.

Oh how Steven wishes that were true today. Looking back at it all, he should've killed the lot of them. He thought that the Surface rats would be good playthings, but no. One of them changed everything. Sam Cutter, the demon sent from the darkest depths of Hell, Satan made incarnate, came to ruin everything. He didn't die then. No, that would've been too easy.

Again, months down the road, Steven attended a match at the arena. The resistance was fighting back harder than ever. Before, they were bugs just waiting to be squashed. Now they were animals with teeth. Or so it seemed. They became reinspired by some unknown force and were a thorn in his side. It was no matter, though, because the Sky would still be his. It would just take longer. He went to the arena to unwind. Multiple squads of his troops were viciously attacked in the streets, and he needed to clear his head.

That's when he saw a ghost.

The same boy as before was again in the arena. So he didn't die after all. This time, when the boy fought, he was even more fearsome. Beyond the ferocity he showed last time, he showed experience, knowledge, skill. He had been trained. He knew how to fight now. Who would've trained him? The Surface rat could even go against Armando, one of Steven's previous play-things. The rat beat him! Still, he didn't win the fight. He was taken out by a girl stabbing him in the back. He was rather dumb, but a powerful fool. This time the boy will be his! Nothing can stop him.

Patrols were arranged along the transport's route in case any Ravens thought it would be fun to attack again. Steven's greatest asset was at hand. And then everything went wrong.

The boy led an escape. He took control of the transport and hijacked the train. With that, he led a prison break and revitalized the Ravens further. Steven sent close to a fleet to get them back. The boy defeated them all. The reports said that he flew from bike to bike, using tactics no one in the Sky Nation had ever seen before. Beyond that, he flew without the aid of a jetpack or a Sky Bike!

This must be it, Steven thought to himself at the time. The weapon that he had so sought after was turned against him. And its blade was more lethal than any other.

Sam Cutter defeated everything Steven threw at him. He was even suicidal enough to crash the warship that Steven had brought to fight against him. He was hopeful then that Cutter died. But hope holds no place for him.

"Well?" Steven's master asks him, his voice a hiss circling around him. "Be honest now. I'll know if you're lying."

"Terrified," Steven says weakly, answering his master's previous question.

"Now tell me again," Steven's master says. This time sounding as if he's whispering right into Steven's ear. Steven can even feel the hot breath of another human being on his neck. "What happened to Lynch?"

Lynch was another servant of the master's that was in charge of taking the Water Nation. As Steven was in charge of the Sky, Lynch was in charge of the Water. Emphasis on the *was*. In that final battle in the Water Tower, Lynch had been slain.

"Cutter happened," Steven says between clenched teeth, his fear turning to anger.

Even there, in essentially another world than the Sky, the Cutter boy haunted Steven. He burned down one of their warehouses, freed his new recruits *again*, and slayed Lynch.

Steven personally called Cutter to the Tower. He had complete control of Kane, the king of the Water Nation. He thought victory was a sure win. How wrong he was. His greatest banes, old and new, both showed up to challenge him atop the Water Tower. Due to some special training he received, Steven was a match for Jinn as Cutter battled Kane. Then, they switched. Jinn kidnapped Kane while Cutter stayed behind to battle Steven. Steven wasted no time in pulling out all the stops to remove this nuisance from his life. Permanently. At the end of their duel, both of them were so injured that neither could move. The only way Steven was able to stand and escape from the drowning tower was by relying even more heavily on the power the Red Elixir granted him. Cutter perished in that tower. There is no way he can cheat death to such an extent twice. But still, a nagging little voice in the back of Steven's mind is telling him that Cutter made it. Samuel Cutter, the greatest threat to the New Power, may still be out there.

"I see," Steven's master says. Steven feels something brush against his skin and freezes up. "And yet you return."

"Yes, sir," Steven says automatically. He was never very fond of Lynch, but that didn't make him glad that he had died. He was a brother. Not a biological one, but he was the same rank as Steven within the New Power, acting directly under their master. Steven and Lynch are the only two that speak with the master directly. Or so Steven believes anyway.

"I may have preferred him," Steven's master says as the torches burst to life. It's like there's a small explosion atop each and every one of them before the fires return to their normal burning. Steven is initially blinded by the return of light. "I could've sworn that I ordered you to bring me the head of Samuel Cutter, and yet I see no head. Lynch did not return having failed not one, but *two* assignments." As Steven's eyes readjust to the light, he sees that his master is firmly seated in his throne, still wearing his layer of shadows.

"My deepest apologies, Master," Steven says, bowing his head but standing up straight. As afraid as he is of his master, he's starting to develop a healthy fear of the Cutter boy. He has been much harder to kill than anything else that the New Power, than Steven, has ever encountered. He wonders if that's how they're all bred on the Surface, or if Cutter's an exception. All the others he has encountered from there, with the exception of his master, have been cowards unlike any other. The kings were all raised on the Surface, so Steven supposes he can include them in Cutter's category, but he's not quite sure if they count. When one walks the Earth for more than a millennium, the personality tends to shift to something unprecedented. Yet Cutter is the same as them and he's just a child. Steven doesn't know how old the Royals are. Nobody knows exactly. No stories say.

"Hmph," Steven's master grunts angrily, squeezing the arms of his throne so hard that their ends explode in his hand. Steven gulps and takes an involuntary step back. "Is there anything else you wish to say, you useless creature?" His master asks him dismissively.

Steven opens his mouth to respond, but I cut him off by yelling, "Yeah!" over to the brooding guy on a big fancy chair. I bet it's not even comfortable. I walk up out of the shadows on the opposite end of the room. Dac and I have been listening in on their little conversation, and I only now decided that I should probably add my two cents. The clack of my footsteps echo throughout the massive hall. They're the only noise there at all. Steven slowly turns in horror to see me step from the shadows. I pause a good ten, fifteen paces away from him and jab a finger at his mysterious master. "I'm going to kick your ass."

Chapter
One

My eyes snap open and I take a second to control my ragged breathing. My chest rises and falls unevenly. My mind plays back over what I just did. At least I know that Steven's master actually exists now... and that I just challenged him. Without thinking about it, I bring a hand up and full on slap myself in the face. What the hell was I thinking?

"I'm such an idiot," I mumble to myself.

You're only getting that now? Dac, my ever-faithful pain in the butt, constant companion asks. *You've done dumber stuff than that.*

Have I? I ask him right back. I've done some things that can't necessarily be called smart by any stretch of the imagination, but this is something else. I just told the head of the New Power that I'm coming for him. I don't even know who he is!

Eh, maybe. Honesty is such an annoying quality sometimes. I lift the blankets off of me and take a good look at myself. I'm still good and wrapped up in bandages. My torso is wrapped tightly, as is my left shoulder. I got a nasty gash back there in the Water Tower, and my ribs were mostly crushed thanks to an overly excited giant squid that actually saved my life...

long story. Initially, Jinn and the others wanted to force feed me Blue Elixir, but there was no way that I was going to do that again. After getting myself beaten up in my first big fight against Steven, here at Jinn's house, they gave me an almost lethal amount of the stuff so that I would heal up by the next morning.

First problem was that Jinn only brought so much with him down to the Water Nation, and we had used up most of it making sure that he, Mark, and I didn't die before that fight even started. I had to have a couple doses due to a series of rather unfortunate events. I look at the silver sliver on my left palm that I got when I stupidly ran right into a burning building. Still, I'd saved a good amount of people there. One of them later lost an eye fighting the New Power, but that's beside the point. Eli's fine now. When we left the Water Nation he was putting his Sprinters together so that Hub Fourteen, and actually all of the Water Nation, could have a fighting force if the New Power ever showed their ugly heads again. He was well into the process of putting them together when I first woke up from the fight at the Water Tower. Apparently, I was asleep for a long while. I believe it. I wasn't in a good place when I passed out. I also learned that apparently the tower's name was changed to the Drowned Tower.

Okay, so we broke it a little bit. That doesn't mean you can't fix it.

A little bit?

Fine, we mostly destroyed it and put a lot of holes in the thing. I let a genuinely terrifying eight-year-old shoot a massive cannon at it and, well, the cannon did what cannons do.

There was a big boom. It was aimed at me. I don't plan a repeat performance. Sorry kids.

I try and look out my window, but the blinds are

closed. I think I can see daylight peaking through them, but that might just be my imagination. With how late I've been sleeping lately, though, I don't have any problems believing that it could be the middle of the day. I got too used to having Blue Elixir patch me up nice and fast. Healing the old fashioned way sucks. Well, it's nice at times, but it takes forever. I've always been a fast healer, but you can't beat a sixty-second recovery.

I swing my legs over the side of the bed and wiggle my toes. Somehow, I'm surprised that I still have all ten of them. Ten toes and ten fingers. Doesn't get much better than that.

You could have four arms, Dac corrects me.

As cool as that would be, I'm working with what I have here. I stand up and try to stretch, raising my arms over my head. A sharp pain in my chest quickly gets me doubled over though. I grunt at the pain without meaning to. Yeah, a couple of my ribs got more than a little broken. Between Billy and a Red Elixir juiced Steven, I took a lot of punishment.

I head into the bathroom and turn the shower on. I carefully unwrap myself, set the bandages aside, and hop in. The water stings initially, but then it starts to feel really good. The water trails down my necklace before going back to my body. It's funny how such small things can change your life so much. I go through my normal shower routine before getting out. Then comes the drying myself off, re-bandaging myself, and finally throwing on a pair of jeans and whatever shirt is on the top of my drawer.

It's really quiet here in Jinn's house, but then again it usually is. It's such a big place and, for the most part, only Jinn, Dac, and I live here. All the guest rooms have come in handy over the past few months though. More than a couple people have stayed in them, and John's still living in one right now.

I leave my room and head down stairs, guided by my stomach. I wonder if we have any hot dogs?

I look out the window at the top of the stairs as I'm passing and notice a transport and a couple Sky Bikes parked on Jinn's lawn. We have company? Why isn't there any noise then? I'll ask Jinn when I see him. He's usually down stairs. Oh, maybe they're all in the back yard. The house is crazy sound proof.

I move down the stairs slowly, not wanting to bounce myself around very much. Being sore sucks. Jinn even insisted on us training while I was hurt. He was just trying to push me to drink some Blue Elixir, but I don't want any. Sometimes you have to heal the old fashion way. And besides, I still won most of our sparring matches.

I get to the bottom of the stairs after a lifetime of traveling down them—which is oddly harder than going up right now—and head into the kitchen.

"*SURPRISE!*" a horde of people scream at the top of their lungs. I'm so surprised that I actually jump at the sound. My hand dives into my pocket to grab my sword and… and then… what is that?

Pretty much everyone that I know and have met over the past year is gathered in Jinn's kitchen and living room under a giant banner that reads "Happy Sixteenth Birthday, Sam!"

"Uuuuuh," I start to say before people start swarming me and giving me hugs. Face after face goes by and I recognize each of them. I recognize them, but I don't really pay attention. I'm in a bit of a daze right now. They all wish me a happy birthday and give me well wishes as they pass by me, and even after.

"Well, what do you think?" I'm fairly certain Jinn asks me.

I try to take everything in and very gracefully say, "Uuuuuuuh."

Say thank you, Dac prompts me.

"Th-thank you," I say, following instructions without really thinking about it. Oh boy. If they think this is a surprise, just wait until they find out what mine is.

Yeah, you may want to save that till later. We've been planning this for weeks.

We?

Well, my job was to make sure that I warned everyone when you got down here. They didn't want you knowing what was going on because you can read my thoughts. Razzle. Frazzle. Ugh.

"Wait, what day is it?" I ask them all. I never told anyone what day my birthday is.

"Well, we are celebrating your birthday, so it's pretty obviously December twenty-first." Who said that? I look around and see Rose walking towards me, so I'm guessing it was her. "Happy birthday," she says, wrapping her arms around me. I'll be honest, I don't mind. I hug her back tightly, but not so much that it hurts my ribs. She's painfully aware of how bad they were when I got hurt. "You're finally as old as me."

"Yeah," I say, still only half paying attention, this time for an altogether different reason.

Who told them? I ask Dac. The only ones here that know my birthday are Dac and John so...

It was John. I knew it. I'm so getting him back for this later. *Why? It seems nice to me. You've never had a party like this before.*

Did you not notice that I almost attacked you guys? I remind him.

You would've lost, he says certainly. *There are too many of us and you're hurt.* He pauses a moment before adding, *Just shut up and hug your girlfriend.*

I can do that.

"Get a room," John yells over at us. Rose glares in his direction, which is how I find out where he is, sticks her tongue out, and kisses me on the cheek before letting go.

You sure know how to pick 'em, Dac says.

Tell me about it, I say. There's a rather loud, obnoxious whistle that snaps me out of my mental conversation with Dac and trip down memory lane of meeting Rose. I have to say it's not the best way to meet someone, but hey, it works. I look over at where the noise is coming from and see two people I really didn't expect to see.

"Rick? Fred?" I say, looking at them.

"SAM!" they both shout at me, pushing their way through the crowd of people. There's actually a crowd of people at my birthday party... weird. They push Rose aside and take up her position of hugging me. Rick even goes the extra mile and plants one on my cheek. Gross.

"I thought you two were in the Water Nation?" I say, hugging them back in a way. After the fight at the Water Tower, Rick and Fred decided to stay down in the Water Nation. They said they liked it. I was sad to see them go, but hey, that's why we left the Surface to begin with, so that all of us could find a new place to belong. A better place to call home. And they found theirs on the bottom of the ocean.

John was out of there like a bat out of hell. Turns out he's extremely claustrophobic. Living on the bottom of the ocean is a terrible place for claustrophobic people. We learned this very quickly.

"We couldn't miss your birthday," they tell me. I don't think they even knew that my birthday is today other than *John* probably telling them. Still, it's good to see them. Been a while. We basically left the Water Nation after I woke up. And speaking of people I haven't seen in

14

a while.

I look around to try and spot Gabriel, Nathan, Kane, or Sarah. I don't see any of them. Damn. There's something I really need to ask Nathan about. Right before I blacked out after the fight at the Water Tower, he dropped a pretty big bomb on me. He was long gone by the time I woke up. Apparently he came back up here to, you know, actually rule his kingdom. Kings are generally supposed to do that. But he was gone for more than ten years. Couldn't he have waited just a few more days? You don't tell a person that they're the most important man in existence and then just disappear. It's not cool!

"Well, thanks," I tell them as they pull away.

They step back towards the crowd as Mark says, "Well this is a party isn't it? Let's get it started!" almost exactly when he finishes talking, somebody hits the play button on some stereo and loud music starts blaring. The others can do what they want, but at the moment, I freeze up. I don't dance. Especially when it hurts to move.

"Come on dorkle," Rose teases, grabbing my wrist. "Dance a bit," she tries to make it sound like a friendly suggestion, but she basically drags me into the next room where people I know are dancing so terribly that I'm on the verge of laughing. They're enthusiastic, but terrible. Mark's leading the charge with dance moves that would put even the worst dancer to shame. On the other hand, Arthur actually has some moves. Who would've thought that a big, gruff blacksmith could dance?

Rose takes my attention when she starts doing something that's basically twisting side-to-side and pushing and pulling my arms back and forth without letting go of my wrists. Let me at least fix that. I scoot my arms out so that she lets go and I grab her hands instead. I let her guide me for the most part because I have absolutely no idea what I'm doing. Dancing wasn't exactly a thing back on the Surface. I sneak another peak around and see that John's awkwardly standing there while Rick and Fred are randomly wiggling and hoping that it makes sense. Eh, close enough. At least I have someone guiding me along and trying to help me.

We all go on like this for a while, dancing—poorly—and having good old fashioned, stupid fun. When I get tired of it, I break off from the crowd and let myself collapse onto the couch. Somebody sits down next to me. I don't pay any mind to them because they don't say anything, until I look over.

"No way," I can't help but say. It's out before I even think to stop myself. Armando? Like, the guy who forcefully had an AI installed in his brain Armando? The one who's really a good guy but has tried to kill me more than a few times until I helped get the AI ripped out of his head? Yeah, that's him.

"How've you been, Sam?" he says with a smile. He looks like he's actually been able to breath easy. It's a startling contrast to how he was before. When I first met him, he was the New Power's pawn and always looked like he was in pain, more or less. Now he doesn't look bad at all. He looks like a normal guy! Except that his hand isn't moving.

"I've been good!" I say to him, excited to see the guy. He fought against the New Power's control and actually saved my life one time. That's not something you easily forget. "What about you?"

"I've been better," he says, holding up his limp hand. I prevent myself from wincing at it. Most people would just see that his hand is limp, as I do, but I know a little better. I learned from Arthur that when they woke him

16

up from the super coma I inadvertently put him in, he couldn't move that hand at all.

When he was in that coma, the AI in him took over and tried to kill me in the AI realm, in my dreams. In there, he sent his fist into some sort of fog that I've never quite been able to explain. The best Dac and I can decipher about it is that it's the AI consciousness. As a result of that, he lost control of his hand. Well, what he and I both know is that it's not only his hand. He can't feel or control his hand or about a third of the way up his forearm.

"I hear that," I say. "That not getting any better?" I ask, pointing at his hand.

"Nah," he says, "it's still with the AI."

"Look," I say, rolling my head against the back of the couch. "I really am sorry about that."

"It's fine," Armando says, a small smile playing on his lips that hints at a touch of sadness. "You're still alive and I wasn't myself." I open my mouth to speak, but I never get the chance. He spots something across me and says, "I should go." Armando gets up and disappears into the crowd. This isn't over.

"So what do you think?" a rather feminine sounding voice asks me. I look next to me and see someone that I didn't see there before. Armando is pushed to the back of my mind, unfortunately.

"When did you get here, Sarah?" I ask her. Next to me is my great-great-great-great-great-great-great-great... uh... you get the picture, it's a lot of greats, grandmother. If I ever called her that though, she'd probably beat me until I forget my own name.

"A while ago," she says kindly. "I didn't want to interrupt you. It seemed like you were having fun." I look over to where Rose is still dancing all by herself. A new partner will come along in no time, but for now,

17

she's taking the world by storm in her own way. It's captivating.

"More or less," I say, a small smile trying to creep up on my lips. Rose sees me staring and giggles at me, being self-conscious for only a second before she goes back to what she was doing. Sarah smiles at me, tracking my eyes to see what I'm looking at. What can I say? It's a good sight.

"How're you feeling?" she asks me, still smiling, but with genuine concern in her eyes. She's taken on a very motherly role recently. Sometimes it can be a bit much. I don't see much of the Royals, since we got back to the Sky Nation anyway, but I see the most of Sarah.

"Still sore," I tell her honestly. "Jinn wanting me to keep training isn't really helping either. I feel like most of this," I gesture to my body, referring to my aches and pains, "is thanks to him."

Sarah chuckles softly before saying, "It's possible. You know how to fight though."

"Yeah," I say, thinking about all the trouble I caused before waking up. Without thinking about it, I softly add, "I'll need that soon."

"What was that?" Sarah asks. I doubt she heard what I said. The music is pretty loud, and I did mumble. It's not even good—wait, never mind. A rock song just came on. Much better. Rose seems to get disinterested with dancing for now and heads over here.

"Nothing," I say to Sarah as I scan the relatively small crowd.

When I see something way out of the blue, I can't help but burst out laughing. I get weird looks from both Sarah and Rose, but I don't care. I'm enthralled by the dance off between Mark and Jinn. They're both terrible!

Sarah winces when she sees the stump where Mark's right arm used to be. I've gotten so used to it that it

18

doesn't bother me anymore. And besides, there was much worse on the Surface. Life happens.

Mark doesn't seem to mind it anyway. There are a bunch of things he can't do with only one arm, but he's found a way around most of it. It does get a little weird when we have to scratch his remaining arm for him though.

"I hope Kane hurries up with that arm," Sarah says. I shrug in response. Kane has been working on a mechanized arm that can replace the one Mark lost. Apparently, Kane was already working on building a human shaped robot, so he's supposedly just modifying one of those arms to work with a living person. Who knows what the real story is though. It's Kane. Everything is a toss-up. For all I know, Kane paid Mark to cut his arm off so he could try to replace it.

"Mark's fine," I say, knowing how he's been. "Only problem is when his elbow gets itchy." Sarah looks up with only her eyes in thought before trying to scratch her left elbow with her left hand. I never thought I'd see any relative of mine, let alone a Royal, make themselves look like a velociraptor. I do my best not to laugh at Sarah. Surprisingly, I keep myself under control… It's a miracle!

"What're you doing?" Rose asks when she gets over to where we are.

Sarah stops what she's doing instantly and says, "Nothing." Rose rolls her eyes and takes up the seat next to me on the couch.

"So what were you guys talking about?" Rose asks, "Other than nothing."

"Just Mark and Jinn's dancing," I say, pointing them out with a jerk of my chin. Rose smiles and shakes her head when she sees them. She's much more polite than either Sarah or me. Rose is older than me, but I can't say that age comes with wisdom here. Sarah is some big number worth of years older than either of us.

I try to enjoy the party longer, you only turn sixteen once after all, but what I saw and did in the AI world keeps nagging at me. We can't just sit around. I can't anyway.

"How does it feel to be the same age as me?" Rose asks.

"Not much different than yesterday," I say. In light of everything else I need to tell people, being sixteen isn't that important. "And we'll only be the same age for a few months anyway," I tell her. "It's not like you can stop aging in order for me to catch up with you."

"That's pretty much what I did," Sarah says nonchalantly, sipping on a drink I didn't see her get.

"You don't really count," I tell her. "You guys are unique cases." Sarah shrugs as if it's nothing. I close my eyes and practically slam my head back against where the couch curves so that I'm looking up at the ceiling. I take a deep breath in and slowly let it out. I repeat this process a couple of times before Rose takes hold of my arm and rests her head on my shoulder. Again this is nice.

"Everything okay?" she asks me. And there goes the nice. Oh well, now is as good a time as any.

"No," I say, getting up slowly. She untangles herself from me before I stand up. I groan as my injuries act up whenever I stand. It gets really annoying.

I walk over to the kitchen without talking to anyone and open the refrigerator door. I can feel at least two pairs of eyes on my back as I do so. Alright, so where is it? Why does there have to be so much food in here? Can't Jinn make it easy to find this stupid stuff? I know it doesn't have to be refrigerated, but he likes it cold, so it has to be in here. Ah, found it.

20

I pull out a bottle of Blue Elixir, the slightly glowing, electric blue drink that makes all your troubles go away. Well, it makes all your injuries go away. I set it on the counter and close the fridge with a foot. Apparently, Jinn looked over at some point and sees me doing this. He pushes the button on a remote and the music suddenly stops. He doesn't say anything, but I can tell there's a question on his lips. He knows I don't want to drink Blue Elixir this time around.

"We need to talk," I say before opening the drink I temporarily swore off and downing the entire bottle.

Chapter Two

"What happened?" Jinn asks, hard eyes tracking my every move. That used to be disturbing. Not so much any more.

I gasp after essentially drowning myself with the Blue Elixir. A warm, tingling sensation passes over every part of me that hurts even the slightest bit, and the pain melts away. Oh yeah, this stuff is good.

"Oh, you know," I say, breathing heavily for some reason, "the usual."

"And what would that be?" Jinn asks, not amused. You would think he could probably guess what happened by now. He's known me long enough. Actually, he's probably asking *exactly* what I did *because* he knows me so well.

"Well," I start, dragging out the word, my voice a higher pitch than usual, half trying to sound innocent. I examine the ceiling before confessing, "I kind of, sort of, maybe, *accidentally* declared war." I get stupefied looks from everybody in the room. I'm pretty sure the neighbors, who are miles away, are looking at me like I'm insane too. Their hearing suddenly getting better just long enough to hear me say that.

"What?" Jinn asks, but not accusingly.

I give a nervous laugh before saying, "Yeah, well, I

saw Steven and his master in a dream and, well, you know." Maybe I should've drowned myself with that Blue Elixir. It'd be ironic, killing myself with the ultimate healing solution. It would probably also be slightly less embarrassing.

"Well shit," Jinn says, heaving out a sigh through his nose and rubbing his temples.

"Alright, party's over," Mark calls out over everybody, pushing enough buttons on a remote to return the house's lighting to normal. Jinn keeps huffing and puffing through his nose, now pinching the bridge of his nose as if he had a migraine. He's breathing so hard that I'm convinced smoke is about to start billowing out of his nostrils.

"Probably not my smartest moment," I say, absently snapping my fingers and clapping an open palm against the top of a closed fist.

"It doesn't matter," Jinn says. Uh, what? "It was inevitable."

"Excuse me?" I say, confused in my own right.

"We figured you would do something like this," Jinn says evenly.

Ouch.

Entirely true, but ouch.

"So," Jinn continues, undisturbed by the fact that he totally just smacked me mentally.

Maybe I should take lessons from him, Dac says in my mind.

You already know how to do it.

Still, Jinn says, "we've had the Raven's preparing." I look up from the table at him. Jinn lets his hand fall away from his face and crosses his arms. Settled onto Jinn's face is this look of smug confidence that is the exact opposite of what I expected to see. "Nathan has been directly working with them and making sure they're ready for this. Arthur's been working nonstop to make sure everybody has a sword in hand."

"Stupid brat," Arthur himself grumbles, sounding pissed as always. "You're making me a fortune," is that a problem? "but it's so much work." Ah, so he's just being lazy. That makes sense. He pulls a large, silver coin, maybe an inch and a half in diameter, out of his pocket and absently rolls it between his fingers on his left hand. "I've almost made back everything I've lost thanks to you." Ah, good memories. Thanks to a bet Jinn made with Arthur when we first met, I never have to pay for anything I get from Arthur or his shop. "None of the jokers that order Sky Iron swords even want to help me make them. Pansies." With his last word he catches the coin in between his pointer finger and thumb. "At least I've expanded my arsenal." Now that's scary. He was already a walking armory before.

"Sorry about that," I say to Arthur, referring to how much I've cost him. I'm pretty sure he can tell that I'm not sorry at all though.

"Damn right," he says, giving me his signature glare. "To Hell with it though. At least with you, things stay interesting," he slaps Dac on the back, who's standing right next to him, and a hollow echo rings out in the room. "And besides, you commissioned my greatest creation."

"I would say so," Dac agrees, pounding on his chest.

I'd call you daddy's little girl, but I'm not sure how that would work.

This is revenge, isn't it?

Oh yes.

I look around at everybody here at my birthday party. Some of them—John, Rick, and Fred—I've known for years. They've been friends. Everyone else I only met when I came up here to the Sky Nation. Even though it

24

hasn't been all that long, it feels like it has been a life-time. I look at them all… and see that they look *a lot* more confident than me. That's not normal.

"So what now?" I ask. Apparently, they've been acting on the assumption that I'd do something monumentally stupid like this.

"Now we start to act," Sarah says. "Now that you've actually done something, and that it's not just our speculations on your actions, we can move." Well, that was fast.

They have been thinking you'd do something like this for months now, Dac reminds me.

True, I respond. *Were you in on this?*

Nope. They told me nothing. I'm just not very surprised. The others keep talking about their plans of attack, but I don't really hear any of it.

It's still weird! Who plans for somebody to piss off the baddest boss in the world?

Anybody that knows you, Dac says. I can sense the deadpan to his voice.

Touché.

I zone in just in time to hear Sarah say, "We've limited the search, in no small part thanks to you, to the Surface. Nathan, Kane, and Dad have been searching all over the Sky and Water Nations to make sure the New Power's headquarters…" headquarters? Since when did we start talking about them like that?

Shh, Dac hisses in my head, *I'm trying to listen.*

"… aren't there," Sarah continues, uninterrupted. "And they're not. We don't know exactly where they are, but we will have all our available resources on the look-out for it.

Jinn takes over from her, saying, "The current plan is to take the majority of the Ravens, and of Nathan's newly established army, and to move them down to the

Surface. From there we will establish our own base of operations and commence the search." He finishes with a not quite smug enough look on his face. On the other hand, I have a totally dumbfounded look on my ugly mug.

"Uuuuh," I manage to grunt. Hold on, I'm processing this. Um, okay. So... "Do we actually have a plan this time?" I ask. I say it slowly, sounding like if I'm not too careful with my words, they'll crack and shatter. This is probably the most prepared we've ever been and I'm more than a little skeptical. We never have a plan. Or at least I don't. And we never get to lead the charge. Maybe I should just quietly sit in the back of the room so that I don't accidentally mess anything up. It could actually happen.

"That we do," Mark says, leaning forward and wrapping his arm around Jinn's neck and squeezing.

A true sign of the apocalypse breaks out when Arthur actually cracks a smile. It's a rather disturbing thing, as if he doesn't quite know how to smile. "What's wrong, boy?" he asks. "You look like you're going to be sick. Should I grab my video camera?" Okay, it's a cynical, evil smile. Everything is right with the world. No apocalypse. Not yet anyway.

"No need," I tell Arthur, much to his disappointment. "I just had the attention span knocked out of me."

While some of those before me manage to look surprised that I can say something that makes absolutely zero sense, Arthur says, "Ah, got some cinders on your arms, did you?" Damn him. Ever since making my sword with Arthur, whenever he brings up something like *that,* my arms itch like crazy. When Arthur and I made my sword, he gave me these old, ripped up gloves. The sparks and fire and heat all managed to hit my skin at one point or another. It can be a long story, but I've got the small, silvery scars to prove it.

He did that on purpose, Dac speculates as Arthur enjoys the sight of me resisting scratching my arm.

You think? I say back to him, irritated.

It's just a good guess.

Probably a bit better than that.

Do you really think that poorly of him? I roll my eyes as a response. Both my real eyes and my mental eyes. I learned how to do that one a couple months ago. Dac knows every thought that ever passes through my mind: past, present, and future. Well, he knows the future when it happens, so of course he knows my thoughts on Arthur.

Oh, right, Dac says, remembering that I just know Arthur. It's not that I think poorly of him or think that he's evil. I just know that he's an ass.

"So what now?" I ask Jinn and Sarah. They seem to be the most informed out of everybody.

"That's what we were going to ask you," Jinn says, scratching the scruff on his chin. "We tried asking John, but he said you might have a better idea of where to set up camp." Set up camp? Right, need a place to set up a base on the Surface and I'm one of the only four people up here that really lived there for a while. Why didn't they just ask Rick or Fred? I know they've been living in the Water Nation, but it's not like travel is that big of a deal for these guys.

About a thousand different places and ideas race through my head, vying for my attention. A couple ideas stick around for a while before I dismiss them as insufficient. I'm not sure how long it is before I accidentally

say aloud, "That could work."

That's a terrible idea, Dac says. Of course he

27

immediately shoots my idea down.

No it's not, I argue.

Yes it is. How do you even plan to fit all the Ravens in there?

I'll figure it out.

No you wont. You can't change space like that.

You can in my dreams, I point out, referring to the AI realm.

That's different!

"Sky Nation to Sam," somebody says back in the real world.

For the last time, I am *real!* Dac shouts in my head, half jokingly. We've had this discussion many times before.

"Sam," somebody says again. I try to focus on them, but it's like just waking up. I'm for some reason really disoriented.

"Boys lost his marbles," Arthur says. He pauses for a beat before adding, "again."

"I'm not crazy," I say for the umpteenth time.

"See," Arthur says to everybody. "I told you all he needed was a good insult." Jerk. Jinn shakes his head, exasperated.

"Regardless," Jinn says, now addressing me. Wait, does that mean he agrees with Arthur? "Sam," he says sternly, making absolutely sure that he has my full attention. "Sam, do we have a place?" I think for another moment, deciding that we may have to spread out, but it's a start.

It's not going to work.

Ignoring Dac, I say, "Pack your things. I think I have an idea.

Chapter Three

A moment later, everybody disperses, the party officially over. Jackson, Rose's dad, and Rose take off together, and Mark goes to his room here. He technically has a house of his own, but he's almost always here. Rick and Fred mill about with John, none of them sure what to do while everybody else leaves. Arthur takes Armando with him, still acting the warden at times. He's probably going to deliver him back to his official guardians. He's been free of the AI for a while now but the Ravens are still skeptical.

Jinn pulls out his cell phone and it's at his ear before too long. "Gerund?" he says into the phone, starting to walk toward the backyard. "Yeah, it's me. Sam finally did it," he closes the door behind him at that point, preventing my eavesdropping... I mean accidental overhearing. I look after Jinn as he walks farther from the house and starts disappearing down his abrupt slope. Something tells me he's going for one of the Sky Bikes he keeps in the shed out there. He finally got around to replacing the one that I, um, badly crashed into his roof a few months ago. He has an older, beat up bike, and a shiny, brand spanking new one with a turbo mode and optional wind shield, good for weather, long travel, or for deflecting swords in the middle of a fight.

Guess which one is mine. I'm thankful to even have one, but still.

"Come on," I say to Rick, John, and Fred. "Let's go get ready."

"For what?" John asks, apparently still not understanding the situation.

"To go home," I say more morbidly than intended. I don't look back, but I can feel all three of them pause, freezing in their tracks. This clearly doesn't bother Dac at all, as I can hear him walking behind me. He's not very quiet when he moves. It's not like he's crazy loud like some movie robots are, but he *is* a large moving mass of metal. I don't know when John, Rick, and Fred start moving again. I fall into my own little world. It's not the AI realm, not by a long shot.

I'm scared, I say to Dac, voicing my concerns in the farthest corner of my mind. I know he can hear me though. I honestly don't mean to tell him, but he's listening.

It makes sense, Dac reassures me, also as a quiet whisper in the back of my mind. He knows that anything else at the moment may very well break me. *This is the place of your nightmares. You've been haunted by the Surface all your life.* I try and say something in return, but not even in the corner of my mind can I form a coherent thought. All that's there are red-rimmed memories of the factories. The sound deafening my ears is the ghost of machines moving every which way, sizzling, boiling metals, and the horrid cries of dying children. Or at least those of freshly mutilated children. The Ash Day plays in my mind. When ash rained over the whole city from one of the factories. During that memory is when Dac breaks through to me.

In the middle of the raining ash in my mind, the metal man, which is my closest friend, walks out and says, "But you can beat it." The grey, hazy world in my mind ripples as if it were reflected on a pool of crystal clear water and a single drop disturbed the calm. Through the ripples, reality changes so that I can see the real world again, brought out of my memories.

While in my imagination, I somehow managed to walk up the stairs and get my hand on the door to my room. I close my eyes for a second, let out a held breath, and push open the door. I was just in here less than an hour ago, but now it all looks different. It's taken on that tint that I've learned far too well over the past year. I'm looking at my room in terms of what is essential, and what I need to bring with me. I see all the cool trinkets that I've acquired over the past year. I see all the stupid stuff that I somehow managed to get together, but I don't really see any of it. I see my small duffel bag behind the closed door of my closet, and see my tooth-brush and toothpaste. I feel the weight of my necklace around my neck and the weight of my shrunken down Sky Iron sword in my pocket.

Mentally going over everything that I need, I unconsciously grab hold of my necklace, a round green gem embraced by two metal wings on either side strung on a leather cord. Truth be told, it's not the coolest necklace in the world, but it means a lot. It means that I'm somehow a prince of the world, a title I never, ever, ever wanted. I still don't want it. I have this tendency to flip out on people when they try to call me "prince". It just doesn't sound right. I mean, who would bow down to Prince Sam the Incapable? *If* I was interested in the whole prince thing, I'd probably have to change my name to Maxwell or something regal sounding. I mean, Sam? That's not very impressive.

You just insulted your own name, Dac feels the burning desire to point out.

I know, I know. Just let me have my own thoughts for a bit. I'm trying to sort everything out. By that I mean my own fears. Sure, Dac managed to help me from going full panic attack very briefly, but that doesn't mean much overall. I'm still scared to go down to the Surface. Yes, I admit it. I'll charge into a burning building with barely a second thought, but going down to the Surface, not even fighting anybody, has me petrified.

I first get my duffel bag and begin gathering up the things I've learned I need to have when leaving home. The basics: clothes, personal effects, money, sword, cell phone, necklace, more clothes for when I undoubtedly destroy mine, double check that I'm wearing my flying boots. Pretty normal stuff. The last thing I add in the bag is a dented and scratched up little box my mom gave me before I came up to the Sky Nation. I've been putting some stuff in it for her as I go. I think it's time I return it to her. I know it's not essential, but it is important.

I throw a jacket on before I sling my bag filled with what I've come to think of as my life's worth of collections over my shoulder. The strap is going across my chest, pushing down on the skin, the bag itself resting on my back. Without any special ceremony, I head downstairs. My bag bounces against my back with each step I take. I don't hear Dac follow after me, but I can feel his eyes on me in both the material world and in my mind. I know he means well, but it sends a shiver down my spine. That's a feeling I really don't need right now. I know very well how many eyes will be on me as soon as we get down to the Surface.

When I get to the living room, nobody is there. It makes sense. Everyone did just split up to go get their things collected. I just happen to know what I need and where it all is. Oh, and living upstairs also makes things easier. Rick and Fred should still be packed, but for all

I know they only brought enough stuff for the one day. They may very well have to go back down to the Water Nation to get their things collected. Even then, they may just choose to stay in the Water Nation. Generally, I would opt out of the Surface if I have a choice. Unfortunately for me, I don't. Usually when you're the one that declares war, you have to be there to follow through with it.

I throw my bag onto a portion of the couch and collapse next to it. So far as I know, this could be one of my last chances to sit down for a good long while. I basically let my mind go blank for a while, which is a miracle in and of itself, and rest. I don't sleep, not by a long shot. Who would want to end back up in the AI realm after what I just did there? I may never sleep again! Or at least not for a day or two. Sleep is one of my favorite parts of a twenty-four hour cycle.

After not too long, Jinn comes back inside. He doesn't even notice me sitting on the couch as he walks on by, his step wider than usual. He may not even realize it himself, but he's hurrying. Jinn's definitely riled up. He'd never let it on, but I'd almost be willing to say he's nervous. There's nothing wrong with it. As calm and collected as Jinn typically is, I've seen through that layer on multiple occasions. Me? I don't have any delusions that I have any manner of calm and collected. Generally, I'm running around screaming, trying my best not to look totally stupid as I figure something out.

Jinn starts to take the steps two at a time, further proving my point that he's in a hurry. I've never seen that man take stairs more than one at a time, with the exception of when he has a sword drawn and blood on his... well, everywhere. Fighting a massive battle in an underwater tower in order to save a supposedly eternal king from a jerk-bag in a suit generally does that to a person. Jinn quickly disappears from sight as the stairs spiral away from me.

I sigh aloud, frustrated with waiting. This is worse than when I had to wait to go down to the Water Nation. At least there wasn't a lot of waiting involved with that one, and above all else, I could concentrate on hating my dad. Oh, and I was a little distracted with the whole "just learned I was a prince" thing. I had more to keep me occupied then. Now I just have time. Stupid thing. What is taking everybody so long? Don't they know that I'm losing it over here?

Calm down, everybody is going as fast as they can.

That's not fast enough! I accidentally snap at Dac. *I'm sorry,* I say to him. *I'm losing my mind here. I've got to get going. I can't sit here any longer.*

What're you going to do? he asks me. He already knows, but we've gotten into the rhythm of asking each other what we're thinking, not just knowing it. It's better that way. Still, I don't answer him. This time I'll let him just know. Dac, thankfully, doesn't say anything. He just let's me do my thing.

I get up off the couch and sling my bag across my back again. In a slightly quickened pace, I walk over to the base of the stairs and shout up, "Jinn! Jinn!" The name echoes throughout the building. It's more than unusually quiet here, it's almost as if it's empty besides me. "Jinn!" I try shouting again, not waiting long before trying again. What can I say? I'm impatient.

"What's all the shouting about?" Mark says, coming out of the hall to his room on the first floor. I turn around to look at him and see that he was definitely in the middle of packing. His very favorite pajamas, that I personally think are hilarious, are slung over his arm, neatly folded.

"Nothing," I say to him, for once not laughing at his

pajamas. I turn away from him and look up the stairs, hoping to see Jinn magically appear.

Dang, is something wrong with you? Almost a year after seeing those pajamas for the first time and you still laugh at them every time. Well, every time except for this time.

I'm just a little distracted, I say to Dac.

That's an understatement.

Wait. Mark. My eyes widen a little bit as I realize that Mark can probably be more helpful than Jinn right now. I look back at Mark and remember that his pajamas are slung over his *only* arm. "First of all, how'd you do that?" I ask him, nodding my head at the pajamas. If anything, he's gotten better at folding his clothes since he lost a hand.

"What, this?" he says, looking at his laundry. "It's nothing," a very smug look comes across his face before he says, "I've just been working on something lately." Working on something? Like what? I quickly look Mark up and down as if he would've grown a tail or something that I didn't see. His arm didn't grow back. Nothing. We already tried all sorts of the Elixirs on that, but nothing worked. We didn't try any dangerous or risky combinations, but we got creative. Mark still only has the one arm and nothing that would help him with two-handed mandatory tasks.

I shake my head to clear out the thoughts of what Mark could be working on and ask him, "Mark, can you track my phone no matter where I am?"

Mark looks confused, but still says, "Well, yeah, but I don't see why you're—"

"Thanks," I say, not letting him finish. I start walking towards the door, again turning my back on Mark. Normally, I would never act this way towards my friends, but I don't quite feel very normal right now.

35

"Where are you going?" Mark asks me. I only slow my pace as I open the door and pause in the frame.

"To the Surface," I tell him, looking back over my shoulder. It's a windy day. I'm not even completely outside and already the wind is tousling my hair around my face. "I'm sorry. I can't wait," and deep down I actually am. I wish I could wait for my friends and then all of us go down there together, but I can't do that. I just can't. The Surface is eating at me, and I don't want those I care about anywhere near that demon sitting just below us. "Just come find me when everybody is ready. You know how to track my phone, so I'll keep it on me, but if that doesn't work, just ask Dac to show you where I am. He'll be able to find me pretty easily." I've got my hair and a bad angle obstructing my view, but I can still see the confusion on Mark's face. A sort of clarity is coming along his face, but it's coming rather slowly. I take a step forward and start to close the door behind me.

"Sam," Mark says sternly, but not forcefully. I completely look back at him through the crack left in the door and see him standing there, both concerned and confident. "Don't worry," he says, a smile actually coming on his face, "we'll be down there before you know it."

I don't know how to say any sort of thanks for the reassuring words and smile, so I blankly stare in a corner. These guys really believe in me that much. I hope I don't let them down. I flick my eyes back at Mark and give him a nod and a grunt of thanks for his words. And I believe him. I may not know the right words to say, but my nod gets it across. I pull the door entirely shut behind me, and I'm left entirely alone outside Jinn's house.

The wind howls in my ears, a sweet melancholy

song. It's as if it knows I'm leaving and doesn't want to see me go. And I don't want to go. I close my eyes and tilt my chin towards the sky. I take a few steps forward to be farther away from the house, and simply experience. I listen to the wind sing and feel the sun cook my skin. I feel the cold bite of the wind regardless of the sun's thoughts. I feel the platform Jinn's house is built on sway beneath me, essentially anchored in place, but moved by the winds. Up here, it's like every part of me is vibrating perfectly and is in sync. I know what's right up here. I like it up here.

I savor every little feeling and suck in a big breath. I hold onto that breath as if I'll never get another breath of air from the Sky Nation again. I treasure the taste of it slipping over my tongue. I feel the cracks in my mouth the air creates. I hold onto that breath until my lungs burn and beg me for more air. Even then, I don't gasp. With my eyes still closed, I slowly let out my breath through my nose. I start to take in another breath, to appease my lungs, and still feel the magic of the Sky Nation in the air. I can still taste it, and I hope that me leaving now doesn't mean I'll never get to see it again. Because it's everywhere. At the right times, I swear, you could look around and see golden trails of dust floating and dancing throughout the entirety of the nation. I tried showing it to John once, but he didn't see it. Neither did Rose or Jinn initially, but Nathan did. One of the extremely few times he was here, he saw me sitting outside and asked what I was doing. I told him about the dust and he just smiled. He sat down next to me on the edge of Jinn's platform and watched the magical, golden dust with me until it ended up being early in the morning. It was like nobody had ever seen it but him, and he was just glad to be there, to be able to watch it with a friend.

Even now I see the golden trails move behind my eyes and can almost swear that I'm a part of them. I feel it. I don't know why, but I know that I'm a part of the magic of this place. Maybe it's just wishful thinking.

I finish taking in my second breath and open my eyes. I set my jaw hard and look just beyond the edge of Jinn's platform. I wish I could stay longer. I even take another deep breath before finally acknowledging what I've got to do. I tighten the strap of my bag to an almost painful level and look out again.

Time to go.

I take off running towards the edge of Jinn's platform. No yelling, no rebellion, no nothing. Right now, I don't even know the right sounds to make. So I just breathe as I run for the edge. The same edge where I first became connected with Dac. The same edge that Jinn pushed me off of multiple times. The same edge where so many things began for me. And I think it's about time that it gets a question of its own. For me, right now, is this a beginning or an end? Back when Jinn first taught me to fly, he said that if I fell below the clouds, I'd be in trouble. Now that's my aim.

I get to the edge and take my running leap off of it.

Same as when I first flew, it's as if time stops entirely. There's no floor beneath me anymore. There's no going back. I can clearly hear my heartbeat in my ears, counting out my frozen moments in time. For me, time stays slowed as my dive truly turns into a dive. I start to tilt forward, my boots still off, and time resumes.

Suddenly the wind is howling in my ears and there are claws and hands tearing at me. I tilt so that my head's pointing down. My hands are still ahead of me so I move them back and to my sides like a swimmer would, as if I'm trying to propel myself forward faster.

My clothes whipping about around me, my hair

pushed straight back, I plunge face first towards the ocean of clouds beneath me. It really is an ocean. The clouds move like nothing else in this world, and it really is something to behold. I wish I could freeze right here and watch it for a while, but there really isn't any time for that.

In a streamline position, I race forwards. Tears are ripped from my eyes, from the wind or me actually crying, I don't know. I fall faster and faster until I crash into the wet, white layer of clouds. My vision is entirely consumed by white as I continue to race forward, face first. My heart continues to hammer in my chest as I dive right back into my own personal hell. My entire being screams at me as I move back to a place I know...

Home.

Chapter
Four

    I close my eyes before I leave the clouds, and I know when I do. I feel the lack of their moisture on my skin. The wind rips and tears at me. I feel the hands of the Sky Nation trying to hold onto me. But it's inevitable. I still feel the wind tear at me, but as I fall farther and farther, the Sky Nation's grip wanes. If I could see something physical about it, I'd say that I've been putting off a trail, and it's at its end.

    Before I know it, the feeling of the Sky Nation is gone. Now I'm just falling; falling towards what I know, towards the thing that I've tried so hard to get away from. No matter how much time I spent up in the Sky Nation, or down in the Water Nation, I've still felt its pull. No matter how much I've tried to ignore it, the Surface has been there, calling to me, pulling at me. Even sitting up in Jinn's house, watching a stupid movie with Rose and John, I could feel it. It's been pulling, and nagging, and demanding my attention. I only realize now that I never really escaped. I only evaded its gaze for a time. I'm like the prisoner who voluntarily returned himself to prison, who returned to his cell, his back broken.

    But I'm not going with a broken back.

    I'm not going back to sorrowfully return to my cell.

I'm going back to the Surface now, not as a defeated little pup, but as I am now. An armed, pissed off kid that has a lot against that forsaken place. I'm going back now, to bring the Surface to its knees.

I open my eyes and look back behind me just for a moment. I'm leaving a vapor trail behind me, thanks to passing through the cloud. Huh, so that's how those're made. I never knew that. I can't help but grin to myself as I look back down towards the Surface. Moisture is torn off my face as I speed forward, especially since I'm looking straight down. I hope everybody is looking up at this vapor trail right now. It's coming to change everything.

With a thought, I kick on my boots and race forward even faster. Lucky for me, I think I recognize where I am.

Yet again I find myself taking a deep breath. Why is this the most terrifying part of everything that is happening? I swallow down that annoying saliva that gathered in my throat and reach out my fist. I knock on the door three times and put my hand at my side. Is three enough? Is it too many? It's been way too long. While I wait, I start to readjust my bag across my back. I only landed all of two seconds ago, and it's still really tight.

When I'm almost done fixing myself, I hear the padding of footsteps behind the door. I freeze up, heart and all. Seriously, I can't feel it beating. Is that a bad thing? Before I can figure out my heart situation, the door unlocks and is pulled open.

Standing before me is a rather timid woman who I swear could be wreathed in light. Her face looks tired and worn, but it's always like that. At least, so far as I can remember. Her hair's a total mess, but who has any time for looks down here? It looks like she tried to tidy it up, but that's about as good as it gets. She's wearing very nondescript clothes that have nothing special about them at all. They're basically just to keep her from being naked.

She looks at me and any weariness from her eyes vanishes. A shaking hand makes its way up to cover her mouth and her eyes begin to dampen. She makes a small choking noise before saying, "Sam?"

It takes my mouth a moment to register that my brain is telling it to say something before I can finally spit out, "Hi Mom." I can see it in her eyes that she wants to step out and crush me in a hug. I can tell that she never wants to let me leave her side… or so I think.

But she doesn't move.

Eyes wide, she doesn't dare take a step out of the door. She doesn't even toe the line. She simply stands there with a rather confusing expression of longing and horror. Is that what it is? I honestly don't know.

"Mom?" I say again. "Mom, what's wrong?" Still she doesn't move. "Mom?" I ask, actually sounding concerned. I raise a hand as if to touch her and take a miniscule step towards her. She flinches back. She actually moves back a step. She, her, my *mother,* takes a step away from me. Since when did that happen? "Mom, it's me," I say, my voice shaking. Why do my eyes burn, dammit? She freezes and so do I.

"Mom?" I say one more time, a pit forming in my stomach. What's wrong? And my eyes need to stop bugging me!

"Hun? Who's at the door?" I hear somebody from the inside yelling. Heavy footsteps come towards us. I can't help but stare at my mom. There's absolutely nothing else that I can do. I just look at her. I try and look into her eyes, but she looks away. Essentially the moment I make eye contact with her, she breaks it. She turns her head to the side, and tries to look even farther away from me with her eyes. Somehow, in a small way, the world crumbles around me and I'm left standing alone on a small island in the middle of nothing, and not even Dac can be there to comfort me. I am completely, truly alone.

"Mom?" This time it comes out as barely a whisper, my voice breaking as if I haven't used it for the longest time. It's almost as if I've forgotten every word I know. I can't put anything together.

"Honey?" The man says again. "Hun, who is—" he shuts up when he sees me, and suddenly my entire vocabulary, and even some words I don't know, come back to me. Something comes to mind to call him, but since I'm not sure it's even a real word, I keep it to myself. "What're you doing here?" he asks, face hard.

"Just figured I'd come see my mother, Dad," I say back. I suck any feelings and expression that I was feeling for my mom away and glare back at him.

"Well, you've seen her," he says, placing a hand on her shoulder. He probably doesn't notice it, but I can see that she's silently crying, shaking like a freezing dog, "now you can leave."

"I was just about to," I say. He looks me dead in the eyes. My father has no problem with that.

"Good," he spits back rather quickly. I don't move initially, instead glaring at him and flicking a glance at my mom. "Honey, why don't you go back inside," he says to my mom, and she does as he says. My mom makes a move to leave, but I stop her.

"Wait," I say curtly. I swing my bag around so that it's on my stomach. I unzip it just enough to reach inside and pull out something close to my heart. "This is for you," I say, throwing it on the ground at her feet. The little wooden chest pops open, and its contents come spilling out. Small trinkets from both of the other nations lay scattered across the floor as a mixture of Surface money, Sky Nation money, and pictures of basically the last year are blown about by a gentle breeze. I don't really feel any wind, but that may be because I've gotten used to the wind up above the clouds.

My dad glances down at the mess at his feet and looks at the money wistfully. He doesn't care much about the rest of it. My mom on the other hand, doesn't look at all. She doesn't even flinch.

I zip my bag back up. "I've been collecting this for you," I say to her, not my dad. "This whole time, I've been sure to put away more and more. All of it for you. I've never stopped thinking about you. I know I've been gone for a while, but it was for a good reason." Again, my eyes burn, and tears threaten to overtake my face. I probably make some weird face as I push my bag back around to sit on my back. "Mom," I say, my throat closing off. "Please look at me." I can't help it; I feel the water on my cheeks. Stupid rain.

That's right, Dac says gently, *it's raining. Everybody up here is still getting ready. You have plenty of time, and I'll get them to wait longer beyond that.*

Thanks...

My mom doesn't respond to my pleas. She won't turn to face me. If anything, she buries herself in my father. She follows his previous mix between an order and a suggestion and heads inside. Before I know it, my mother, the only person I knew to have truly loved me, disappears from my sight. And for some reason, I feel like it may be for good.

I blink hard as if that could get rid of my newest memory. I openly let it rain in front of my dad.

"Get out of here," he tells me. He doesn't move from

his spot at the door, doesn't move to close the door, nothing.

"If you have any semblance of a heart, or care about me at all, just give me a minute," I choke out. My eyes don't leave the floor. I basically go between squeezing my eyes shut and staring at what I've collected for the past year. My chest collapses in on itself and I'm thrown for even more loops. It's as if I became the center of gravity and all of existence is trying to squish me into nothingness. It's like my existence offends the universe right now, and I'm finding it near impossible to breathe.

My dad is silent for all of two seconds before he says, "Do you remember my promise to you?" He made me more than a few promises, generally from eleven years ago now, but I know which one he's talking about.

"Yes," I say quickly, only managing to say that much. The memory, although I have a bit much going on right now, comes back easily. He's talking about when we dropped him off on the Surface months ago and the two of us basically promised we'd kill each other if we ever saw one another again. And honestly, I really did have zero intention of ever seeing him again. Too bad things don't generally work out how I plan. Maybe I should plan to be poor, that way a million dollars can fall in my lap.

"I'm letting it slide just this once," is what my dad says. "For your mother, and as a thank you for your gift, I'm letting you go." What a winner. You don't 'feel' like supposedly killing me because I delivered a ton of money to your front door. "But never again." I look up at my dad, my vision blurred thanks to my... the rain... and see him completely straight faced. He's entirely serious about what he said. "Now leave." I run the back of my hand over my eyes to clear the rain away and tighten the bag on my back.

Without looking away from my dad, I abruptly kick on my boots to full power. I rocket up and away. I turn the boots off for a brief second to reorient myself when I'm high in the sky so that my belly is facing the ground. I turn the boots back on and speed away. I look back behind me at the house I'm leaving behind and realize that I really left it a year ago. I'm not welcome there any-more, nor am I wanted.

Funny, this rain is moving really fast. And it's getting heavier.

Chapter
Five

I fly, and fly, and fly. I don't know where I'm going, but I don't stop. Normally, flying and being up in the sky makes me feel better. Right now, it doesn't do the trick. Stupid everything! What's been the point of all this? I'm not making anything better, I'm just convincing myself that I am.

You haven't done anything for the Surface yet, Dac says, trying to comfort me. It's not working. At all. *We're all about to come down there and then it'll change. You're going to* force *it to change, and that's final.*

I bring my flight to a simple hover above the road. I look around me in the physical world and see that nothing has changed on the Surface. Still a dank place where dreams are crushed under boot. It's still a place where, when one person is broken, the only courtesy given to them is that they're ignored. Sometimes that's all we really want and need. And sometimes, like right now, I could really use a friend. One that isn't just a voice in my head.

I'm more than a voice you realize, Dac says.

But you're not here right now. What you're saying is helping, but it's still different.

How? Dac asks me. *What you're looking for is somebody that cares about you, not somebody to physical-*

ly hold you. You're thinking that you just want somebody to wrap their arms around you, but I can do one better. You know what I'm talking about. I do. And he's right. He's absolutely right. It's one of the best things that ever could have happened to me. I've got Dac. I am the only person alive that has the greatest friend in the world that knows every little thing about me, even the parts I don't, and won't ever leave me alone. Not for one second of one day. He can't even if he wants to. He can talk or be silent, but he can't leave.

A while back, Dac and I got separated, and I felt like a part of me was missing, that there was an emptiness. That didn't last long, but it was not a fun few hours. When he got close enough for the mental link to reconnect, once again binding us together, that emptiness was filled. As ridiculous as it sounds, I think that the AI, my best friend, from within day one or so has let me feel loved. Sure we didn't much like each other right off the bat, but that changed. So far as I know we've only gotten closer.

Don't be getting all mushy on me now, Dac says, following my train of thought. *You're making me want to leak here.*

Is that a thing? I ask him.

How should I know? he responds, *I've never tried to before.*

Not feeling the sharpness of my loneliness, of being denied by my mother, I gently alight on the ground. I feel the solid ground beneath my feet, not swaying like the platforms of the Sky Nation, and feel sturdy. I'm back home. The dull throb and partial emptiness of what just happened still thriving in me, I look around me. The street doesn't look much different than any other.

Looking down from the center of the street, the cracked road is the center of the lines of nearly uniform buildings. There's enough difference between them to give people a feeling of uniqueness, of individuality, but it's all just an illusion. There are maybe only five types of buildings around here and they're reused essentially at random so that everything is the same but for the colors and what's inside. Nothing looks to be in perfect condition. It's not like anything is threatening to crumble to the ground, but nothing is perfect either. There aren't any cars on the road. They're expensive, and if somebody buys one, they're not going to leave it in the street for the enforcers to "accidentally" destroy all willy-nilly. It's actually really quiet out here. Why is it so quiet?

Better question: what time is it?

At about the same time I think it, I hear the sirens. They're off in the not too far distance, and getting closer. Oh no.

Oh no? Why oh no? Dac asks me. He can figure it out on his own. I'm not going to tell him right now.

Relying solely on instinct that I've developed over the majority of my life, I take off running the opposite direction of the sirens. Now people in the Sky Nation might think this makes me look guilty of something, which it does, but it doesn't matter. Everybody down here is guilty of something to somebody. The enforcers and factory managers seem to have unanimously decided years ago that everybody alive without the money to pay them off has done something wrong.

Fly! Dac tries to prompt me, *Fly!*

I hear him yelling, but my brain doesn't process what he's saying. There's a lance of terror streaking through me as I run as fast as I can away from the sirens, my boots making heavy thuds on the asphalt. The loose bits of the road move away from me and slide underfoot, threatening to knock me down. We're all used to it down here. I figured that maybe after spending all that time up in the Sky Nation that some of my Surface instincts would diminish, but nope. Not one bit. I get back down here and everything comes rushing right on back. Lame.

I look over my shoulder and see exactly what I've been expecting to see: Something right out of nightmares. Well, my nightmares. What's chasing me is an enforcer truck. The eight-wheeled beast of a "car" comes speeding towards me, appearing to have every intention of running me over.

Um, Sam, maybe you should move, Dac suggests. There's no point in moving though. They're not going to kill me, and even if I do duck down an ally, they'll follow me. They've probably got ten enforcers on that truck.

The sound of a snapping whip cracks in my ears, and I'm shocked up so bad that the skin on my face tightens across my head. I haven't been hit by anything, there's not even a whip out here. It's just the fear of my memories, plain and simple.

The truck itself has a flat back that's extended out behind its rear wheels with a relatively flat top that comes to an angle with the windshield. The angled panel extends beyond the windshield to meet another flat edge of the angled piece that heads down under the truck before bending to a wheel well. The front of it looks sort of like the front of an above water boat and a simple *V* that can be created by a person's hands.

I don't see the enforcers driving it, but I know they're there. Hell, I bet their grinning like this is the most fun they've had all week. I don't know about them, but I would not put this high up on my list of things to do again.

Looking behind me again, I see that the guy on the passenger side must've rolled his window down because his arm is sticking out of it with a led pipe in hand. Oh crap. My heart sets to beating even more irregularly than usual, which makes running rather painful. I tear my eyes from the pipe and look forward, focusing on pouring on as much speed as possible. Problem is that they're in a car, and I'm too dumb to try to fly.

They catch me with ease, and when I see the nose of their car come even with me, I involuntarily scream, "NO!" I check behind me one more time and see the arm holding the pipe, ready to swing at me. Knowing full well what this means, tears threaten to fill my eyes. God no... This means that—

"Ugh," I grunt, as I'm clobbered in the back of the head and limply fall to the ground.

Chapter Six

I squeeze my eyes shut tighter as I regain consciousness. This is not good. Not. Good! Why didn't I fly away!? How dumb can I be?

That's what I was wondering, Dac says. *I figured you didn't fly because you were so scared you forgot that you could.*

That's really not *what I want to hear right now,* I tell him. Oh God, I'm really here aren't I? I thought I'd never have to come back. Anything, please! I'll go back in the arena every day for a year just SOMEBODY HELP ME!

A whimper actually manages to find its way out of my throat as I start to basically hyperventilate.

"Oh good, he's awake," a voice that I know is sinister says to another person in the room. "Are you ready to give it to him?" My muscles tighten, and I try to fold myself up into myself and become a hole of nothingness. I bite down on the inside of my lip so hard that it hurts, but I don't care. They're really going to do it. This is really happening.

"Just another moment more," the second person says. I hear things moving around on a metal tray as he picks things up and sets them down more heavily than he needs to. In a stereotypical fashion, I hear latex gloves slap as the guy draws them up past his wrists.

I try to move, and feel my arms belted down. Even my legs and upper body are restrained. I'm going nowhere fast. I can't even get to my sword or move my elbows really. In trying to move my arms, I feel that while there's only one restraint around my right wrist, my left arm has two on it, and is twisted so that the underside of my wrist is facing up. The first of the two bands is thick and around my wrist with a rectangular hole cut into it. The second is further up my arm, yet still below my elbow. Basically that one's there to be sure that I'm not moving.

Regardless, I still try. I'm very careful to never open my eyes. I don't even want to peak. I don't want to see any of it. Maybe if I don't see it, I can convince myself that it's not real. Please don't be real.

Please.

You're going to be okay, Dac reassures me. How does he know? He doesn't know anything! He *doesn't know* what's about to happen. What it means. I *do*! I know what's happening. It's something I've avoided for most of my life, something that can never, ever be revoked or removed.

I whimper again but I don't cry. I'm sorry everybody. If this is really happening, then I don't know how much help I'll be to you. I don't know if I'll even still be here when you get down here.

SAM! Dac shouts so loud in my head that it's like a physical slap, the one word echoing. My eyes snap open with the shock of what Dac just did. Unfortunately, I see everything. I'm in a dimly lit room. The only light source is a single red bulb that's completely exposed, hanging overhead. Everything cast in its evil glow, I see the two people in this small cube of a room besides me. One of them is an enforcer. He's probably one of the one's that picked me up off the road. No doubt they ran my record once they had me. I still feel everything in my pockets at least, and I see my backpack. The enforcers never bother rifling through our things, seeing as we don't have much to begin with.

They don't leave us with our belongings out of the goodness of their hearts. No, it's generally because they don't want any of the junk we have. That, and they seem to think that if they touch us too much, that they'll catch a disease. We do shower, it's not like we're test animals all infected with instant death disease. Are we?

The enforcer looks like he's wearing a reddish black outfit made of a bulky jacket and long pants. They're only those colors because of the lights. I know that they're normally grey, the star patch on his left shoulder showing his position in society as an enforcer. On his right deltoid he has three black horizontal stripes. Those are really special to get. It means that he's caught two other people like me. The lowest one of them getting to start a new line is representative of me. They do this to us and they get a badge and a raise. How does this make sense!?

The second person in the room has the gloves on that I'm expecting. He also has a medical mask covering his nose and mouth, and a buttoned up lab coat on. For the last time, he picks up what some people may think of as a tattoo gun. I know it as my death sentence.

What even is that thing? Dac asks me, *What's going on?*

I'm dead, is what I tell him. *They're putting a mark on me to authorize the use of lethal force on me from any and all personnel on the Surface. Any ordinary person could kill me if they feel like it, and they'd probably be paid for it.*

That's a little harsh.

What it's typically used for is letting factory enforcers

and any enforcer in general really abuse me. To them, it means my life is forfeit.

But it's not, Dac says. *You can still fight.*

I'm not strong enough, I say. Wait. Not strong enough? This isn't a year ago when I couldn't do much more than street fight. Not only that, but I have a freaking sword *and* two of the three nations backing me.

That's what I'm saying! Dac says. *You've made more than a few friends since you were last down here, have defied and nearly crumbled the New Power, and have picked up more than a few skills. You're acknowledged as one of the best—if not the best—swordsman in the entire Sky Nation. You've bested two of the kings!*

He's right.

You're right, I tell him.

Of course I'm right! He shouts back enthusiastically. I can do this. I will do this. They can't hurt me! Well, physically they can, but I'm not going to let them get me down. Not as much anyway.

My eyes harden as my whimpering look turns to a glare oozing with hatred. It's enough to give them the chills. The one that'll be marking me actually freezes and takes an unconscious step back.

"What is it, you pansy?" the enforcer chides. "He's just a kid and he's bound so tight he can barely move. Just put the damn mark on him." Just a kid? Dude, you have no idea who you're talking about.

"R-right," lab coat says, stepping forward again. He picks up the tattoo gun and pulls up a rolling stool. He sits to my left so that he has easy access to the exposed part of my wrist. A switch is flicked with a subtle movement of a thumb on the stylist, and a droning buzz emanates from it. He wraps his left hand around my closed fist to steady himself. He's only doing it out of his own "artistic integrity." It's a black box. There's not too terribly much art in it. They honestly don't care if it hurts us or not. Its only purpose is to label us with a death warrant. I might have to wear long sleeves more often now. Maybe a bracelet will do the trick. It'll take some playing.

I clench my fist tighter and, in a surprise that's up there with the greatest hits, the artist says, "If you tense up, it'll only hurt worse." He's actually being nice to me? He looks up at me, and now that he's closer I can actually see his face. All the colors are distorted by the red light, so I can't tell what his eyes are, but that's not the most important part to me. Peeking out from under his mask on his left cheek is a tattoo I couldn't see before. There's a black bird there that looks like it's in flight.

My mouth almost drops open, and he looks at me, pleading for me to understand. The shock on my face is probably being translated differently for everybody in the room. While the artist knows that I understand, the enforcer probably just thinks I'm scared witless.

Trusting what he says, I unclench my fist and do my best to relax. He looks back down to my arm, hiding the tattoo from me, and readies himself to begin. The gun touches to my skin, and it doesn't hurt nearly as bad as I was expecting. It doesn't hurt much at all, actually. It feels like somebody taking their fingernail and scratching my skin really hard, but all on the same spot. It's not bad to begin with, but it gets really uncomfortable as he goes on.

Careful to leave my arm as relaxed as I possibly can, I tense up the muscles in my jaw. This sucks. This really, really sucks. How long is this supposed to go on for? Dac starts singing in my head in some attempt to distract me. Honestly, I'm not sure if it's making things better or worse. Seeing as he doesn't know either, he keeps singing. Whatever, I won't yell at him about it. At least it's a distraction.

Really though, this guy is a Raven? What's he doing down here? I didn't know that anybody was on the Surface yet. Even then, how is he already so integrated into the enforcer's system that he's marking people for death? How long have they been down here? I don't think I know this guy, but anything's possible.

When we have a moment where you're not singing, would you ask Jinn what he knows about this? Maybe Nathan or Gabriel would know better, I think to Dac.

He integrates an *"Mhm"* into his song. It already makes no sense, so why not a little weirder?

After what feels like an eternity, the buzzing stops. The Raven in hiding moves the gun away from my arm, but some of the pain is still there. It stings! Within the same moment that the tattoo artist—if you can call him that—moves away, the enforcer takes a swing at me, punching me in the jaw. My head is whipped to the side and I'm seeing stars. I did not see that coming.

I try to spit out some blood before he punches me in the gut. I make those charming noises a person makes when they're hit in the stomach. It's sort of like an overly dramatic death in a movie. I didn't know that is a normal sound until now. Geez. The enforcer pulls out a knife, letting it bathe in the wicked red light. He grabs the hair on the top of my head, forcing my head back and up so that my neck is as stretched out as can be. He puts the knife to my throat, pushing just hard enough to draw a line of blood. My feet do an awkward little dance, trying to push my body higher. That doesn't work at all though, seeing as they're shackled right above my ankles, belted to the chair. At the very least I'm able to tip the chair back a bit, which helps.

"Finally," the enforcer says, "I can kill you."

"You'd probably mess it up somehow," I antagonize him. He pulls my hair harder, potentially ripping it out of my head, and adds the slightest bit more force to the knife. It's enough. I get the message. I won't push the crazy to killing me. I would swallow my saliva, but I'm afraid the motion would have him slit my throat. There's still a chance of me getting out of this alive.

The enforcer is breathing heavy, launching spit at my face, as compared to me carefully taking shallow, measured breaths. He debates the merits of killing me as compared to keeping me alive to play with. Personally, I wouldn't ever let me out of this chair if he plans to live a long, happy life. I won't tell him that though.

Making his decision, he pulls the knife away from my throat, leaving me able to take deep, chest-heaving breaths. He's not done though.

Before I can tell his intentions, he pulls my shirt up and flips the knife around in his hand so that the blade is coming out of the pinky end of his grip. Carefully, meticulously, over my right hip, he takes the knife and pokes two slits that aren't too terribly deep, but are enough to leave a very visible scar. I hold back a scream, but I tense up completely and make a variety of grunting noises in an attempt to distract myself. It's not deep enough to kill me, but it is in no way pleasant. A grin comes across his face as he takes the knife and, right below the slashes, carves in a big *U*. My eyes bulge, and I bite the inside of my lip hard enough to draw even more blood. The taste of iron dominates my mouth and does little to distract me from any of the pain.

The enforcer takes a second to admire his masterpiece before violently throwing my shirt back down to cover it. I feel my shirt touch the wound and get sticky with blood. Awesome. Now I'll have to rip the scab off when it starts to heal. I try and keep up my glare at him, but I look more like a deer in the headlights. I look down to try and inspect the damage when I see exactly what he did. Not the cuts themselves, but the marks on my shirt the blood is leaving.

"You cut a smiley face into me!" I shout at him. What the heck? Why would he do that? That's not cool!

It could've been worse, Dac tells me.

Don't even go there.

"I think you need to smile more," the enforcer says. That didn't sound very genuine. Jerk.

"Let's see how well you can smile when I knock all your teeth out," I mutter beneath my breath, confident he can't hear me.

"What was that?" the enforcer demands. I roll my eyes at him in response. If he lets me move my arms freely, he'll know exactly what I said. He glares at me and I don't break eye contact. Neither of us even makes a sound. I can hear my blood pumping in my ears. Maybe I just think I can because of my shirt getting wetter as time goes on. Hopefully it'll clot soon.

The tension is broken by the tattoo artist—potential Raven—loudly clearing his throat. Although the enforcer doesn't look away, he gives him his attention.

"Hm?" The enforcer grunts, letting the artist know that he's listening and giving him permission to speak.

"His mark is done," the artist reminds us, "it's time to let him go now."

"Let him go?" the enforcer parrots, looking away from me. He faces the artist, eyebrows raised and pushed together. "What do you mean let him go?"

"It's a simple process really," I mutter. "You unchain me, then I kick your ass. Easy."

"Do you have any idea who this is?" the enforcer asks the artist, not bothering to acknowledge I'd spoken.

"Just some kid you picked up off the street, just like many of the others."

"No! This brat here?" With one hand he grabs my hair again and moves to rip it out. Stop it! I don't care about your fetishes. I don't like this! He jabs a finger at my chest and says, "This little shit stain," now that's classy, "is Sam Cutter. He's the brat the boss says caused all that trouble a year ago."

You're famous! Dac exclaims.

Infamous more like it, I correct him. *It's really not a good thing in this case.*

Famous is famous. They know your name. Ugh.

"What does that have to do with anything?" the potential Raven tries to downplay. Maybe he really is a good guy.

"Means he hasn't worked for over a year," the enforcer says. "That, and that he's overdue for a good beating. I'm bringing him with me to the factory so he can get back to working today."

"Today? Wouldn't you want to allow him a days rest so that he can be more efficient?"

The enforcer looks like he thinks about it for all of half a second before flatly saying, "No." In an odd combination of releasing me and putting me back in cuffs that I can't find the fortitude to resist, he has me free of the chair, but with cuffs around my wrists, ankles, and elbows.

"Let's go, chump," he says, dragging me to my feet and throwing me forward so that I fall flat on my face. I try to catch myself, landing hard on my elbows. That annoying, semi-painful tingling that one gets when a funny bone is hit races through both arms. This sucks.

"No laying around," he says, as if it's my fault. "Get up. You have work to do." Douchebag sounds way too excited right now. He grabs me by the collar of my shirt and starts walking forward, pulling me along. I quickly get my feet under me, regardless of the difficulty due to the short chain limiting my mobility.

"You're going to march all the way there," he assures me. "Today is going to be a good day!" Not at all.

"Yay," I sarcastically say in a depressed tone. Screw this.

Chapter
Seven

"Why are you slowing down?" the enforcer asks me. He's had me walking for a while now. I don't know for sure where the marking place was, but I don't remember the factory being very far from the center of everything. My best bet is that he's parading me around town. My eyes have been mostly on my feet, making sure I don't trip in any massive potholes, so I don't know every detail of what we've passed.

Are you guys anywhere close to coming down here yet? I ask Dac.

We're supposedly just about to leave. You leaving ahead of schedule actually slowed things down.

How does that work?

We had to convince Jinn and Rose that diving head first off of the platform is not *a good idea. We all know that you can do it, but you have a certain set of handsome flying boots to help you out. That, and we have no idea what the Surface looks like. Only ones left up here that know anything about the layout are Gabriel, John, Rick, and Fred. Of those, two want to be dropped off at the Water Nation, and only John and I know anything about where you personally would go.*

So you haven't even left then, I state. I don't ask it, I state it. They seriously haven't even left yet, and I've already gotten myself a new tattoo and a job.

Slackers.

Not yet, Dac confirms. *We are packing the transports though. There are enough of us to warrant two.* Of course there are. Are any of them down here when I need them though? No. Never. Why would I want any help? I'm doing so well on my own.

"Move it, we're almost there," he says, giving me a tug. Yes, I said tug. The douche-wad has my wrists chained and is pulling me along. It's degrading, although not unexpected. These guys down here are a lot ruder and cruder than any New Power members I've ever run into. They essentially try to have the same personality that Lynch does. I mean did. None of them are like Steven, with his refined demeanor. All of them are equally jerks though.

"About time," I mumble just loud enough for him to hear. Sure it bothers me, but I'm not going to let him know that. That'd be admitting defeat. As long as I can out jerk him, or at least be a big enough pain in the ass, I feel my mission is complete. Best yet is if he works at the factory he's taking me to. I'm a dead man walking to them, anyway. Why not make me a badass zombie? Zombies can fight back.

Heck, why are we named the Ravens? Is it too late to change it to the Zombies? We could probably get a much cooler logo.

It's definitely too late, Dac confirms, *and with the symbol you have in mind,* we *would be called the bad guys.*

That's probably true. Oh well, I guess my taste in horrifying zombie artwork is completely unappreciated.

Baton in hand, he thwacks me in the back of the neck so that I collapse to the ground. Only thing to say to that: ouch. I hit the pavement hard, the loose bits of asphalt digging into my skin with a sharper bite than I would expect. Unready and unable to catch myself in anyway, I can feel the road rash springing forth on my arm. To make it even better, I doubt there's any chance that he'll give me a second to clean myself off. All I know right now is that my arm and a bit of my neck feel warmer than usual. I'm guessing that's where my waffle cuts are. Awesome.

"What'd you have to go and fall for?" the jerk antagonizes me. I stumble my way to my feet by taking a few quick steps forward. It's like a controlled fall up. That doesn't make much sense to me. So why did I think it? Who knows?

Stop going crazier.

I'll do what I want.

After being dragged by the creep for a while longer, we come up on what really is my own personal hell: a *FACTORY.*

I thought they were bigger.

Wait, what?

Am I actually... not freaking out? I'm actually looking forward to this now.

Alright, you've officially lost it. I don't disagree. What is going on with me? Why would I be looking forward to going to a factory? There is a good likelihood that they'll just kill me and be done with me. I didn't make myself many friends within management. A good number of the workers like me, but they're more afraid of the enforcers than they support me.

Oh. Now I know why I'm excited to go to a factory. The factory itself has nothing to do with it.

I'm excited to cause trouble.

Something is wrong with you, Dac says, keeping his commentary going. *I'm glad we're friends. It'd be boring otherwise.* That it most definitely would.

On the side of the factory, there is just a small, normal door. They designed it this way so that they can supposedly fit more machinery in there. Really, I think it's so that if we decided to run away, we'd be bottle-necked. We've already found out that the enforcers and management spend more time thinking about how to keep us captive and how to "motivate" us. Funny thing is that if you try to motivate them back, they don't much appreciate it.

I take an awkward step so that I can feel the reassuring pressure of my miniature sword against my thigh. Sky Iron—never leave home without it. I really don't know how I managed before without a lot of the things I have now. Blue Elixir, flying boots, and a sword that can change size, for example. Honestly though, I probably wouldn't need any of it if I could just be a good little boy.

When we're even closer to the door, I can see more of the details I know from past experience. Relatively clean, well-kept exterior, billowing smoke stacks, the trapped feeling of misery and anguish. Yup. I'm back home. Next to the door is a thick semi-circle bar with a bunch of chains with manacles attached dangling off of them. The enforcer escorting me takes the end of my leash and hooks it onto the bar with the others. He gives it a few good yanks to make sure it's secure before turning to face me.

"Are you going to make this easy and go in there and work, or am I going to have to let you think about it?" he asks me, starting to take my handcuffs off. The way he says "think about it" clearly lets me know that, if I don't cooperate, he plans on beating me within an inch of my life and still forcing me to work. I know it all too well. It wouldn't be the first time it's happened.

"Moo," I say to him with all the venom a sarcastic

cow can muster. Herd me like cattle. I don't feel like standing here and taking a beating. I'd probably fight back, and he probably wouldn't be able to walk away from it. As much as I *really* want to make sure he can never hurt anybody ever again, it'd blow any cover I have.

Cover? What, are you saying this is some sort of spy mission now?

Maybe. They don't know I can fight back and, for some reason, I'm not scared.

Yes you are, Dac, the jerk, decides to tell me. *It's all in the back of your thoughts, and what you're conjuring forward is a sort of coping mechanism, and if that falls apart, your psyche may crumble entirely, depending on the severity of the situation.* Don't bother sugar coating it or anything.

I raise my metaphysical eyebrows at him, already feeling my heart rate speed up.

Oh, Dac says, *sorry. I didn't realize even talking about it might not be good.*

What did you think was going to happen?! I demand of him, keeping my breathing as steady as I possibly can, but not feeling like I can get quite enough air in. I feel like I just ran a mile, but I'm not sweating. Not yet anyway. I take deep breaths in through my mouth in hopes that it will somehow make breathing easier. I don't think it's actually getting me any more air, but it makes me feel better.

"You little shit," the genius enforcer says, only now understanding the connotations of what I said. What? It wasn't even that bad. Still, he abruptly punches my face. Luckily for me, he hits higher than intended and gets my cheekbone. It doesn't break, but my whole face hurts like hell. The enforcer shakes his hand out in pain while I grab my face, trying to ignore the hurt. It's not working very well.

"GET IN THERE!" He howls at me, opening the door and grabbing a ball of my shirt. I'm thrown inside and stumble a few steps before catching myself on a railing. I'm on a walkway with moving parts almost literally all around me.

"Help me..." I mutter weakly, taking everything in. For some stupid reason, everything is cast in a reddish glow. I've personally always thought it's because the factory managers are too cheap to buy lights for us common folk, and it's up to the forges to light the place for us. Sure it costs them a few workers' lives, but why pay for more lighting? Penny pinching at its finest. It's not like there are no lights in here at all. There are some, they just don't do too terribly much. The walkway I'm on is often referred to as the middle road. Crappy name, I know, but it does make sense. The factory is essentially one giant, open room. It only feels like a bunch of individual workstations because there are so many machines in here separating everything out into independent chambers.

The factory itself extends below ground a couple stories, as well as up a couple stories. Managers generally have a nice cushy office in the corner as high up as they can get, with windows so they get fresh air, and some sort of super powerful air conditioning and air purifiers to keep the crud away. It's so hot in here from everything going on that I already feel the sweat beading up. Lovely.

The middle path is steel grating that can be seen through with some of the most inexpensive metal handrails on either side of it. It's just a small step above minimal regulation. Seeing as it's a factory, the inspectors don't really care.

It's amazing what the Surface can do to a person.

Give them a tiny bit more power than their neighbor, and they will sell that other person out for almost nothing. They'll do anything to keep that power, to not feel so weak. Anything that doesn't put them at risk, that is.

From where I'm standing, I can't see anybody else, but that doesn't mean they aren't there. I'm sure there are at least a hundred people here on the factory floor. With me, that'd be one hundred and one. Yippy for me. Do I get some sort of prize?

"Come on," I'm ordered gruffly. A heavy hand with thick fingers grabs a chunk of my hair and tugs, pulling me along. Oh it's good to be home. "Manager will want to see you so he can say where you're working."

"What does it matter? OUCH!" I ask him. I suck a breath between my teeth before saying, "he's just going to have me work everywhere if he doesn't kill me outright for fun. Just give me a station."

"Nope, manager it is," the enforcer says, pulling harder than he was before. As if he could break me, he drags me the long way through the building. Maybe he's just dense, seeing as we've passed the stairs up a floor twice before he finally mounts them. Up and up we go, the air getting less breathable the higher we climb. A measly five stories in the air, and I feel like it probably would've been a better idea to try and hold my breath starting on the first floor. It's been a while since I've had to breathe this stuff. I forgot just how bad it is.

Actually, it was—

Don't. Say. Anything, I warn Dac before he can point something out to me that I really don't care to hear right now. He's more than likely correct, but I refuse to listen right now. The enforcer, who is holding an already dirty rag over his mouth, raps on the door to the manager's office three times with his knuckles. His hands are bloody. I know a part of that may be me, but I'd be willing to bet he stupidly touched something hot, judging from the blisters also beginning to bubble up. Amateur.

"What?!" I hear the muffled shout coming through the door. Heavy footsteps start marching their way closer, accompanied by the hollering of, "What, blast it! I'm trying to run a factory here!"

The office door is opened far more aggressively than it needed to be, but whatever makes the guy happy. Our factory manager here is not a good-looking guy. For starters, he's a fat, balding old guy with a sad looking comb over. He's sweating more than some of the people working here, and he's in the air conditioning. I only feel a few residual waves of his office's air, and it's like heaven. I notice that the manager is careful not to lean too far out of his office, always staying within the influence of his comfort zone.

He looks both of us, my handler and me, up and down with disdain. It's clear from the way he's looking at me that he's already written me off, that I'm unimportant. The enforcer is only marginally less so.

"Who is he?" he asks the enforcer, already treating me like I'm not a person. In response, the enforcer grabs my wrist more forcefully than is needed, squeezing in an effort to break my wrist before turning it over, exposing the big ugly black bar.

The manager's eyes flick down for a split second before his eyebrows shoot up in apparent satisfaction. "Ah!" he says, sounding not pleased, but some variation of almost happy. It's the sound a painfully self-entitled person makes when they get their way. Hard to describe, yes, but it exists. It's sort of like a pleased grunt of sorts. I can't put my finger on it. "It's about time I got one of these," he says, gesturing to me like an object, as if I am some upgraded piece of machinery that he's been searching for. "I'll put him to good use," he tells the enforcer. "You can go now."

"Sir?" the enforcer asks. He doesn't ask it with any confusion. He's asking for permission. Unfortunately, I know exactly what he's asking if he can do.

"Oh, alright," the manager says, not sounding too heartbroken about it, rubbing his fingers together. "Don't break anything though, I want to get at least a few good days out of it." Lovely. I tighten my gut, knowing what's coming.

Then I get punched in the jaw. Hard. My head snaps to the side and I stumble a few steps. Alright, he did what I expected, just not in the right place. Ow.

"You have a nice evening, sir," the enforcer says, leaving me to my new master. They don't know what I know though. I'm only going to be here for a few short days. After that, I'm out of here. I'd really like to leave by day's end, but that's not going to be enough time to let everybody else know to be ready to get out.

You have a thing for breaking people out of places, don't you?

That's just how it worked out in the Sky Nation! Here, I'm doing this because this isn't right, I tell Dac. *I've had to put up with this stuff for so many years, and now I finally* have a chance to do something about it. Something *more than futile resistances and efforts that I've been able to do before.*

There's a brief moment of silence before Dac says, *Jinn just wants me to tell you that there will probably be a mole in a situation like that.*

Oh there will definitely be a snitch, I say back. Dac can feel free to relay this to Jinn if he wants. This is how it happens here. *Somebody will look at this as their opportunity to get farther in life, find some advantages.*

Nobody will take them seriously. Why would a man ever think that his hammer knows well enough to rebel?

I don't know about that, Dac says. *Those hammers can be crafty little suckers.* I don't know a single hammer I could call crafty... unless...

Was that a pun?

Don't you think it was punny?

And we're done here.

Don't be like that.

You said "punny." That's not okay.

I'm not apologizing for it, Dac says.

I know, I tell him.

"Ah, wait!" the manager calls after the enforcer. He pauses for a moment and looks over his shoulder, raising an eyebrow in question, "Was he ever given a number?"

"Does it matter?" is all the enforcer says, genuinely not giving a damn about much of anything, before he continues to walk off. What a likeable guy. Somebody should send him a basket of Peggy's "special" chocolate chip cookies. I tried one accidentally, and now I will never eat another one of her chocolate chips without somebody tasting it first, which is a shame because, if the cookie is good, then I don't get as much.

"Suppose not," the manager says to himself. He reaches aside and grabs something that I can't see, but I know full well what it is. Before stepping outside of the bubble of his air conditioning and such, he makes it rather obvious that he's carrying one of the many motivators factories use. This one doesn't get to come out much though. While most of their prods are simple pointy sticks meant to hurt, but not too much, this is what we know promptly as a whomping stick. It's a wooden club with ridiculously sharp spikes sticking out all over and in all directions. Only spike free part is where the manager is holding it. Those are meant to kill if we disobey.

Here's the detail the managers seem to forget about those though: they need to hit us. At least with me, that's going to be a lot harder than he thinks.

"Well? Go on," he orders me, waving the whomping stick around all willy-nilly. Carefully. Somebody can lose an eye because of that thing. When I take a moment, his temper flares up. The manager hammers the whomping stick down against the hand railing, denting it severely. It's really noticeable too.

"Good going, genius," I say out loud. Not quite loud enough for him to hear me over the machinery, but out loud. Baby steps. Everybody needs to take them.

Well, here I am, being escorted through a factory by a manager to be put to work. Oh, and if I don't do a good enough job, he's going to kill me without a second thought. Isn't life grand?

Chapter Eight

"I never knew managers had any upper body strength whatsoever," I say mostly to myself, my eyes drinking in the nice new dent that he left in the railing. My bet is that he isn't going to be happy about that when he looks at it in a few hours. I would also put any money I have left on there being special properties on that stick of his. He doesn't look like he has any muscle whatsoever, let alone know how to handle himself in a fight. He has some weight to him, but it's not like Arthur where he has weight, but also strength to back it up. This is just a straight up belly.

I'm careful to never stop walking. If I did that, it'd just be a reason for the cranky businessman to swing his death branch at me. Some things, like toilet paper, are nice when they're perforated. People, much less so.

"What will my job be, sir?" I ask him in the most subservient fashion I can manage. I had limited capabilities with that before, but now it's almost impossible to do for me. I guess the past year hasn't been much of a learning experience in the realm of blind obedience. While I gained more freedom and near fully unshackled myself, Mom fell further, and even learned to love her chains.

Don't do it, Dac warns, like a friend who has seen all

your self-destructive behavior from day one, knowing that even touching upon the thought of my mom has my head swimming. Tears instantly are pressing against my eyes, desperate to find a way loose. My stomach does a little dance of its own and my breakfast wants to come out to visit again. This day sucks.

"Since it's your first day, your work will be light," he tells me. Oh, well, at least there's that. "You'll be assigned to organize the hardening metal before the hammers." Never mind.

I press my lips together and shake my head a little. Of course this scumbag would give me one of the most lethal jobs to do. Why would he do anything else? I'm marked for death, so it doesn't matter anymore. As long as I'm only here for a day or two, it hopefully won't matter much, but I still hate his guts. Unfortunately, I know exactly where to go, so I don't need him to guide me. I had this job for a while. It's where most of my burns come from.

We get to our destination far too quickly. As expected, the manager doesn't go all the way with me, he just gives me the reminder that, "There are guards posted everywhere, expendable." Apparently, expendable is my title now. They don't know my number, so whatever works. I don't even remember the number they assigned me. All I can say is that, before we left for the Sky Nation, both John and I got dangerously close to forgetting our actual names. As our departure date neared though, our sense of identity solidified more and more. The Surface isn't a fun place to be at any point in time. It just seems to be where all bad things happen.

I'm lost in my daydreams long enough that a guard starts to head my way. Oh boy. Already? I really don't want to work. I look at the still molten metal and feel dread. Already knowing the best way to do this, I take my shirt off and toss it aside. That's right, I show off all my scars. You'd think it would make more sense to keep my shirt on, but that's not the case. Last time I did that at this post, I caught on fire.

You really don't have good experience with fire.

Not especially.

Trying not to think about what I'm doing too much, I check where the gloves for this station are normally stashed to find nothing there. I snarl at the empty hanger, as if it's responsible for all my problems. Fine, now that I'm marked they *really* don't give a shit about what happens to me. The somehow still cool metal of my necklace slaps against my chest from swinging when I reach to grab the large metal tools for this task. Well, here I go.

Trying to clear my mind, other than remembering just how to do this, my body goes on automatic. I personally can't even say what I'm doing anymore. I barely notice the white hot flashes of heat on my skin that pop up every now and then. Have I really done this that much?

Before I know anything else, I'm sitting on a couch.

"What?" I say out loud, hearing the echo of the empty room. This place is almost as disturbing as the factory that I was just in. Am in? WHAT THE HECK IS GOING ON?

"That's what I would like to know," Dac says. I can hear him with my ears, not just my thoughts, so I know he's here. I twist around and see him walking in through an open door. Beyond his silhouette, I see the dark amorphous cloud of forever that basically is the AI consciousness. I'm back in the AI world.

"Did you bring me here?" I ask Dac.

"No," he tells me. "I'm not sure why either of us are here."

"Is my body just lying there in the factory?" I ask Dac. Even if he is here, he's not *here*. Dac is capable of splitting his mind into multiple places. He does it every day so that he can stay connected with me in my head and control his body at the same time.

"No," Dac says slowly. He actually takes a second to think about this. What? Is my body melted or something? Oh God, I'm dead. I've got to be, there's no other explanation. "Oh, stop it, you're not dead. You're still working, and you're also really burned. Do you seriously not notice that?"

"No," I say, shaking my head, confused. This is definitely a first.

"What's even weirder is that your perception of time is way off," he says, sitting down in one of the armchairs opposite me.

"What do you mean by that?" I ask him.

"How long has this conversation been going on?" Dac asks me, getting himself comfortable. Why would he do that? Does his body actually get creaky? I never knew that.

"I don't know, less than a minute."

"For you, maybe."

"Again, what do you mean?"

"What I mean," Dac says, leaning forward to rest his elbows on his knees, a gesture I've made thousands of times, "is that I've been trying to have this conversation with you for upwards of six hours and counting." Now I'm really confused.

It takes a few odd mouth and hand shapes before I can manage to ask, "How?" I draw out the *o* for emphasis.

"Simple," Dac says. "You metaphorically, and actually,

checked out while working. It seems that working in a factory is too much for your brain to handle, and you shut down. Your body is on autopilot. The only reason that you're here, with me, is because you've got me as a best friend. Only difference otherwise is that you would be more aware of where you are and what you're doing. You would fully experience working in a factory." Really? Gee... I inspect my lap like it's one of the most important things I can focus on.

I can't even seem to get myself to say anything, so I think to him, *Thanks.* Since it's the AI realm, Dac has more control to change things than normal. He makes it so that his metallic face smiles a bit before returning to normal. Well then. Never saw him do *that* before.

I start to say something, but nothing gets out before I hear something wrong.

Fascinating, a deep, unknown yet familiar voice says, like it's taking a note while observing a science experiment. I don't hear it spoken like I have many times before when I overhear people in the AI realm. This time I hear it reverberating through my head.

"Dac," I mouth, looking at him to clue him in to what I'm thinking. Without a word he nods his head and the entire happy-family-home scene vanishes. I'm left floating in an everlasting black, expanding in all directions. It doesn't feel like a flat color though. As per usual, it feels like the void is breathing and moving. It strangely doesn't bother me anymore. Now it just feels like I'm in a bath. Instead of water, there's something else though.

"And what would that be?" another voice asks. Again I don't recognize it, but at least it feels like I'm hearing it through my ears again.

"How absolutely imbecilic you all are," the first voice says again. Now that I'm actually hearing it, I pick out exactly who it is, and it sends shivers down my spine. I would break out into a cold sweat if I could. I know who this is. Dammit, I know who!

It's the master.

"I beg your pardon?" the poor idiot dealing with this powerhouse says.

"No, you aren't," the master says.

"Come again?"

"Still you aren't," the master says. I can feel him pacing in front of this person, using his very will to crush the other. "You say you beg my pardon, but yet there is no begging, no groveling." I hear the pop of the top of a bottle of scotch, followed by the sloshing of liquid, telling me it's being poured out.

"There are only two that I keep under my direct command," the master continues. He takes a sip from his drink. Only reason I know is because he lets out a satisfied *ah*. "You," he pauses, "and that half competent Steven. Steven has already failed me twice now, and the third I kept under my employ, Lynch, is no longer amongst the living. All because of a single boy, might I add."

"Those were faults of Steven, not me, my master," he finally tries to grovel. He goes on and on and on, but it's like his volume is turned down to make way for his master's voice.

"All fatal mistakes, one of which you are making now." That shuts him up. This person at the same level of Steven must be really smart because he thinks to ask a potentially insightful question.

"And what would that be, my lord?"

"Cutter is in one of your factories right this moment," he again pauses for a brief moment before adding, "Isn't that right, boy?" Oh crap. He knows I'm here!

******

"Hey!" somebody shouts at me as Dac abruptly drags me back to reality. I look over and see an enforcer standing there, a white-hot branding iron in hand. For some reason, factories always like to have a few of those ready, you know, just in case they feel like using them. Sounds like I'm the first person here that they *can* use it on in a long time. Stupid black bar.

"Get back to work," he orders, moving in to brand me. I've already done that once, I don't need it again. On instinct I react, using the tool in my hand to deflect the branding iron out of the way so that it doesn't touch my skin. Since the enforcer didn't expect any sort of retaliation whatsoever, the iron goes flying out of his grip and hits the wall before clattering to the floor. Still without any sort of control over it, I continue a single fluid motion and smack the guy across the face with this hot, heavy mass of metal. Needless to say, he goes down.

"Hell," I say. "I guess we're doing this now." I toss the work tool aside and stick my hand in my pocket. With practiced speed, I draw my sword, holding off until my hand is fully outside of my pocket before making it grow to full size. The small piece of metal in my pocket steadily grows from the size of a pocketknife and extends to a full blade. As it gets to full size, the white glow of the blade gets brighter and more distinct.

Standing out against the glows of fire and molten metal is the harsh white of my sword, casting ominous shadows, yet illuminating everything it can see. If I wasn't in the middle of something important, I could look at the glow for a while. It essentially looks like a glowing smoke that's trapped in some sort of force field so that it can never get more than a half an inch or less away from the Sky Iron.

It would just be too convenient if I could whistle loudly right now. Oh well, all I need to do is fight off every enforcer in this entire factory, manage not to get incapacitated some how, break into the manager's office, and subdue him. Easy enough. One down already. The guards aren't trained very well in case we fight back, meaning that they have little combat experience. Sure they know how to beat us up and abuse us, but I doubt they know more about how to handle a sword than to try and stick us with the pointy end.

I don't bother trying to shout to the other people in here. They won't hear me anyway.

I make a break from my post, trying to remember how to get back to the manager's office. Most factories are designed the same so that, when people are moved around, they don't have to relearn a layout. The higher -ups think it's smart. I don't see what difference it makes. It's not like we get to move around anyway.

As I run I'm careful to not touch any of the walls, considering that they're probably really freaking hot.

It doesn't take me long to run into the first guard. He gets one look at me and starts screaming into his radio.

"Riot! We have a riot!" I dash forward, hoping to hit him and shut him up, but I'm cut short. Without any prelude, a section of the wall explodes in and crushes the guy. He still looks like he's in one piece, and his moaning says that he's alive. Shame. Sunlight streams in through the new hole. Even before the dust settles, somebody walks in.

You're a liar, I tell Dac.

I haven't told you where we are for the past six hours, he reminds me. Right. Forgot about that. It hasn't even been a minute and I forgot about that.

"Found the idiot," Arthur yells to the outside.

"How is he?" I hear Jinn yell back.

Arthur squints at me before responding, "Topless." I look down at myself and notice I managed to forget my shirt. Seriously? First in the Water Nation, and now here in a factory. They both make sense though! I'm not just taking off my shirt for fun or anything like that. I don't even think I look that great without all my clothes on.

"I've said it before, and I'll say it again," Arthur starts. "You look good with a layer or two of soot on you. Makes you look like a real blacksmith."

"What are you doing here?" is the only thing I can think to say back. I apparently have no control over my voice right now because I half scream it, and my voice cracks. Ugh, I thought that was done already.

"What, did you expect us to wait up in the Sky Nation the whole time you're down here?"

"No, but—"

"We just couldn't find you easily is all. John tried directing us to your house, and we got shushed away by some cranky guy. He wasn't very nice. Your mom says hi."

"Really?" I ask Arthur, mostly shocked about that last little bit. She sends a hello through them, but won't speak to me herself?

Really? I ask Dac, hoping that, even if it's not true, he'll tell me.

No. I'm sorry. She didn't even come to the door.

I thought so... She really is lost.

"What are you even doing in this death trap?" Arthur asks me, seeing the depressed look coming across my face and immediately trying to change the topic.

"Um, destroying it?"

"Really?" Arthur asks, looking around. "I've done a better job than you. I broke the door. You just lost your shirt. This isn't one of those bad teenager movies."

"Here's the best question: how do you know about those?"

"No reason," Arthur says a little too quickly. "Are we

going to blow this place up or not?" He's even trying to cover it with explosions. There is more to this story, and I *will* find it out later.

"No, not yet anyway," I tell him, pretending not to notice that he's nervous. "There are still some people in here that we can get out. How would you blow it up anyway?" It's not like he can hit something with his arsenal of Sky Iron and make it go boom.

"Same way I blew the door up," he says, raising a bag in his hand, "explosives. They do exactly as promised and explode. A sword doesn't make things blow up, idiot." I deserve that one. "We don't have a lot of them, but we figured it's okay to use some here. Dac and John said you could use a little 'therapy.'"

"That I could," I say. "Do whatever you need to. I'll deal with the manager." I push past Arthur, seeing a cluster of familiar faces right outside the door. My head isn't in the right place to be saying hello right now though. Sure, I make idle talk with Arthur, but I stay on edge when he's around. Probably has something to do with him essentially burning me as a way of saying hello in a trial by fire. Maybe it's just his cuddly personality.

The path is designed so that enforcers and the manager, if they're ever out here, don't need to see the grunts do "filthy" work, meaning that I don't see anybody as I rush down the walkway. I know that Arthur isn't behind me, seeing as I told him to set the charges, but I still hear pounding footsteps behind me. I check over my shoulder and see Dac and Jinn behind me. Of course those two follow me.

Even if I wasn't following you I'd still be here, Dac points out.

I know, but this really isn't something I want to have to share with people, I tell him. I can't explain it, but I'd feel significantly better if he and Jinn didn't come in with

82

me. I know that Dac will still see and know everything that happens, but it will feel like it's just me in there. That's what I really need. This factory, all factories, have caused me nothing but pain, and brought misery. Every worker in here is just waiting to die. I can confidently say that's how they feel. I've been there most of my life. Only now am I finally, *finally* shedding that. I'm not alone. I get that now. I'm not powerless. I can control my own life. Those with power don't get to control me. Not as long as I'm willing to stand up to them.

When I reach the stairs, I pound up them, taking them each two or three steps at a time. I go up four accidentally and almost fall back like an idiot. I feel cold metal on my back pushing me forward, preventing me from breaking my neck.

Thanks, I tell Dac.

Anytime.

I'm hacking on smoke, again, when I reach the fifth floor, but I don't slow down. I position myself in front of the manager's office door, planting a foot and kicking it down. I throw all my anger at these god-forsaken places into that kick and blow the door clean open. There's a distinct girlish shrill before the door bounces off the back wall and comes at me. I put up an arm and duck my head behind it. The door bounces off my arm and side, stinging, but not seriously hurting, me. I look around the blessedly cool office, not seeing the manager initially until I look lower and see him quite literally cowering in the corner. He's in the fetal position, snot running down his nose, and tears streaming down his face.

I stand before him for only the briefest moment, probably looking like some fallen angel, covered in black soot with my glowing white sword out. His eyes widen when he sees me, and he tries to scoot further in the wall hollering, "*NO! GOD, PLEASE! NO!*" It sounds like he's tearing up his throat from how scratchy and raw he sounds. Good. He should know what it's like, at least a little. It's good that he's scared. He should be. Does he have any idea what he has done to us? To everyone that has *ever* worked in a factory? This fear, this dread that he has now is only a fraction of what we've all had to go through.

Without further delay, I raise my sword, ready to strike this monster dead. I take a step forward to put more power in my swing—

And somebody grabs my arm.

"Let me go!" I demand.

"No," Jinn says sternly, tightening his grip on my arm.

"I can fight you and then deal with this monster," I shout at Jinn. Why is he trying to stop me? People like this manager have been destroying my life for as long as I can remember.

"I know you can," Jinn says, soft but stern, "but this isn't you. You're not a killer." I can feel through his arm that he's probably shaking his head. I never take my eyes off the whimpering abomination.

"Yes I am!" I really scream. How could he think to say that to me? "Have you not been paying attention to *anything* that I've done this past year? I've killed *tons* of people! All of them dead because of *me*!"

"That was self defense," Jinn says, pleadingly. "They were all trying to kill you first, and you were in kill-or-be-killed situations. Nobody should have to go through all of that, especially..." he trails off, reconsidering what he is about to say.

"Especially what?" I interrogate him. "Especially me? Why? What's so special about me? That I'm a stupid prince? That doesn't mean anything anyway!"

"Especially," Jinn continues, cutting off my tirade, "a kid. Dammit Sam, we just had your sixteenth birthday party. It isn't right of any of us to ask anything like this of you."

"You're not asking me," I tell him. He's not. I went to the Sky Nation all on my own. I became a killer without anybody forcing me.

He's right, though, Dac comes in. *I've been in with you this whole time. I've seen your life. I know you're angry, but that doesn't mean that you should throw everything away. Yes, you have blood on your hands, but it's the kind that washes off.*

"No it doesn't!" I shout out loud. I don't care if Jinn thinks I'm crazy. I really don't give a damn right now.

"Sam," Dac starts with Jinn, still trying to talk gently.

"You don't have to do this," Jinn says, right before they make me snap.

"*SHUT UP!*" I scream at the both of them, my throat going raw in one massive howl. "*SHUT UP BOTH OF YOU! RIGHT NOW!*"

Please, Sam, Dac tries one more prod, setting my eyebrow and lip to twitching.

I keep staring straight ahead, never taking my eyes off of the manager. The sniveling, disgusting, horrific, son-of-a.... man. The sniveling... terrified... man. He looks at me. The fog in my eyes thins and I see him as a fat, aging man, far past his prime, his face soaked with tears, spit all around his mouth, and a glossy coat of snot covering from his nose down. His shirt is acting like a mop for anything and everything getting that low. This... man... is scared to death... scared because of me. He's so far past deer in the headlights, I don't know how to describe his expression other than that of a man knowing his death. Knowing without a doubt. Not confusion, not fear; simple knowledge. He has acknowledged that he is going to die, and that it will be by my hand. His reaction is because he isn't ready to die yet. When it comes down to it, none of us are, I guess. We all have something to live for.

I glance to my right to look back at Jinn, but my eyes stop at the manager's desk. There, knocked aside, is a little picture frame with broken glass. It's hard to see, but, beyond the cracks, I can see a woman: A woman with the manager in the picture. His wife.

The fire in my chest doesn't die down whatsoever, but I... I can't find myself to hate this man.

Very, very slowly, I shrink my sword down. Jinn releases my arm just as slowly, and only once my sword is fully shrunken down. I take a drunken step towards the desk, the manager jerking and cowering, even though I'm not taking a step closer to him.

I push a button on the intercom sitting on his desk with only my pointer finger, as if the others aren't willing to work with it, and weakly say, "Everybody get out. Factory's closed." I hear my words through the PA as I speak, giving it a weird echo. I let my finger fall off the button and to my side, my sword still clenched in one hand.

I don't look back at the man behind me. I don't want to look at the part of the Surface that finally almost turned me into a monster. If I was alone, the Surface would've won, and I would've been lost. I don't look at my final test as I quietly say, "That means you. Try to live a better life."

Make sure he leaves in a minute, I tell Dac, as I fix the picture on his desk, not caring that it has broken glass, and leave the room.

Chapter Nine

I walk outside of the factory, calm, yet I would willingly pick a fight with a giant monster if one were in my way. Sorry Billy, it's best that you're deep underwater. Naturally, nobody is out here besides me. Arthur is still probably in the middle of setting the charges while everybody else evacuates the workers. Fine with me. I have zero interest in talking to anybody right now, or going back in there, or anything. I would say that I just want to sleep, but I have a sinking suspicion that won't bring me any relief. With my luck, I would just start eavesdropping on that Master creep's conversation.

I find a dirt pile not twenty feet from the new hole in the wall of the factory and sit down hard. I'm at an angle, so I curl my legs up like I'm in an upright fetal position. I rest my arms on my knees and my head on my arms. It's just one of those days where I don't even feel up to supporting my own head right now.

"Hard day?" somebody asks me. I don't even bother turning around, I already know who it is. Of course he's the only one that didn't go inside.

"You can say that," I tell Gabriel. Instead of looking at him, I decide to bury my head in my arms. That's a perfectly reasonable reaction, right? I mean, this man has lived for so long that he remembers the world as it was. He's the one that split it up the way it is now. Well, he's not responsible for what his kids did, but the whole Sky, Surface, and Water thing? That's him.

"There are plenty more of those to come, I'm afraid," he comforts me. I hear the gravel shift and see through the hole between my arm and leg that he sat down next to me. Would you look at that, I didn't take him as the kind of guy that would ever sit on a dirt mound. He just seems so above it.

"How do you handle it?"

"Handle what?" Gabriel asks for clarification.

"I don't know," I shrug, keeping my head buried, "everything. I honestly don't even know how old you are, and yet you never seem bothered. It's like nothing can touch you."

"Oh, there is plenty in this world that I do not approve of. I try to change as much as I can, but not everybody has the same views as me. Sometimes my children and I disagree. Even after all our time together, it can at times be quite difficult for us to find common ground. Throughout my years, I've simply taken the time to learn that you can't please everyone, and to appreciate what little time we all have in this world." I can't help but chuckle a little. It feels hollow, but there's something about what he said that I find funny.

"What little time you have here?" I question him. "You and your kids are immortal, with the exception of somebody sticking a pointy object in you." It's uncomfortably quiet for a moment, not counting the screaming people running out of the soon to be blown up building. The actual sound around us isn't what I'm talking about though. There's a vibrancy held between two people when they interact, a bond tying living things together. We can't see it, but we can all feel it. It's there waiting for us to tap into and find another living soul. That isn't there right now. It's like Gabriel pulled away from the connection entirely, leaving us as two strangers sitting near each other.

Before he says, "I'm dying," that is. That's when I notice the connection didn't vanish. It's just weak.

The kind of feeling you would get from somebody on his deathbed.

"You're not kidding, are you," I say to him, raising my head. I don't say it as a question. It's more a statement.

"Not in the slightest," Gabriel says. "The serum my children and I took all those years ago didn't stop time for us. It just extended our lives. Minutes turned into years. All this time it has hurt. I've been sick." Sick? As in on his deathbed sick? Like in the story?

"Have you told anybody?" I ask him, not sure how to respond. I've heard people talk like this before. This isn't a friendly conversation. This is a last will and testimony.

Holy crap.

Gabriel is dying.

"Sarah," Gabriel says with a slight nod, "many, many years ago."

"Do you think she remembers?"

"It's why she stays with me," he lets me know. Gabriel takes a mostly closed hand in the other and runs his thumb over his knuckles. It's a habit I've never seen him do before. Looking over at him now, he looks older, frailer, like one would expect of an elderly man. Some of that strength, that vibrancy, while it's still there, has weakened. "She knows that I've been getting worse, but not quite how far I've deteriorated."

"Ah," is all I can say. Apparently it's enough.

"I just wanted somebody to know," Gabriel says. "Somebody with an incorruptible heart." Oh…

"I'm…" I try to say it, but it's hard to get the words

out. "I'm afraid that you picked the wrong guy then." I say it so softly that it may only be a whisper, yet the admission seems louder than the sound it would make when a mountain no longer has the will to stand.

A warm, heavy hand lands on my shoulder. It squeezes, but not enough to hurt, just to reassure.

"That's where you couldn't be more wrong," Gabriel says. I take my eyes from the nothing that I'm looking at and meet his eyes. Although he seems frail, his eyes have all the light and passion that they ever have. Gabriel just seems alive right now, twice as bright as ever.

"I'm not so sure," I tell him. In the enormity of light that he's putting out, I feel like a dark smudge that's on the verge of being eradicated. After what I almost just did, how could I deserve to even be in this man's presence?

"Well I am," Gabriel says. "That you still doubt yourself, that you can stop the darkness that may well up, that is what an incorruptible heart is. Not one that lacks darkness, and fear, and pain, but one that can overcome them and chart its own path, one that can create a new choice, another option for those not strong enough to do so themselves. And this path that's made, let me tell you, will be the most wonderful, most righteous path there ever was."

I'm not sure when I started, but my eyes are hot, as are my cheeks, which are also wet. I've been crying. Apparently for a while, going off of how tightly clenched my jaw is.

"I can't do this," I stutter, shaking my head.

"Yes, you can," he tells me with the warmest smile that I have ever seen in the entirety of my life. It's an expression that tells me that, although I'm almost a complete stranger, he has complete faith in me.

Not trust.

Faith.

There is nothing more powerful on this whole earth than faith.

Gabriel has the faith that, even if I may fall, that I will find myself, that I can do what he thinks I can, that I'm this incorruptible heart.

"I'm not you," I tell him. "I can't do what you're asking me to do. Not even my own mother will speak to me," I admit out loud. I'm already crying my way to dehydration without noticing it, might as well keep going.

"She just doesn't see," Gabriel tells me. "When something truly brilliant is before us, when a person has been lost in the dark for far too long, any light can be blinding, especially one such as you." I grind my teeth together in a futile attempt to shut off the water works.

"Please don't ask me to do this," I beg him. I pull in a loud, shaky breath that barely seems to get any air into me. I try to come up with things to say, but all I can conjure forth is, "Please." It comes out more as a puff of air, spit flinging out of my mouth, than a word, but I think he hears me. My face is contorted and ugly, and I can't think of anything to say. Nothing at all. I don't want this. I don't want to do this. I can't.

Gabriel pulls me into a tight hug. I know he's only technically my great-grandfather of sorts, but I could really use some support right now, something in this reality to cling on to. I grab fistfuls of his shirt, my arms instantly shaking from clenching so tight. I bury my face in his neck and let all the tears out over everything that's happened in the past few days alone.

"I'm not asking," Gabriel says delicately. It's not aggressive in anyway nor is it a blatant statement of fact. He says it in a comforting tone that somehow gets through to my brain and sets me off worse all at the same time.

"All I've done is tell you what you can do, what you'll push yourself to do no matter how hard it gets. I bet that hyperactive son of mine failed to mention to you that that's why your sword glows white, didn't he? It's not because you have some sort of cosmic destiny, but because it knows you deep inside, the same way I have known you from nearly the first moment I saw you.

"If nothing else, you are a good man, Sam Cutter, and I am proud to be able to say that I'm your great-grandfather." He's missing a couple dozen greats in there, but I don't point it out. I just cry harder.

"Although we've only known each other for a short time, I love you the way a grandfather could love any of his grandchildren. You are family to me Sam, and I'm glad I got to live long enough, if only to meet you and see a hint of the brilliance of what you will bring to this world."

"Please don't die," I beg him, head still buried in his now soaking wet shoulder, my chin and cheeks spasming out of control. Gabriel takes a deep breath and lets it out long and low, the simple warmth and humanness of it passing by my ear, making my mental state even worse. The gentle pressure of his open hands on my back are both cruel and a reassurance.

"We all have our time," Gabriel says, "even me." He pushes me back enough to where I see another one of his warm smiles, but this also betrays that his eyes are wet as well, and that there's a nasty trail of snot leading from his shoulder to my nose. "I've simply been gifted with more time than most." I can't speak, I just breathe harder and harder, struggling to get a single breath in.

"I cannot say that I don't fear death," Gabriel says, making sure to look me in the eyes, one of his hands supporting my head, "but my brother is waiting for me.

And I've kept him waiting for far too long of a time." Gabriel wears another one of his terrible smiles that let people know that everything will be okay, that no problems will ever exist again, but I can see through it this time. He's scared and alone. When we die, we don't take anything with us but the deeds we've done. If there's some cosmic scale out there ready to measure me up, I don't know where I'll fall, and I bet Gabriel is thinking the same thing.

"I don't plan on going too terribly soon," Gabriel says, "but if you should happen to see my son before I do, would you please be so kind as to tell him that I'm sorry, I love him, and I forgive him? He always got lost easy and needed a light to guide him back. He's always been afraid of the dark."

I squeeze my eyes shut and nod my head yes, of course. Just please don't die. If only for my own selfish reasons, don't die. I can't lose people I care about. Nobody has even died and yet I find that the foundations of my life have been rocked and shattered. I don't know how to build up again, where to start.

Somewhere far away I hear familiar voices screaming at others to get out of the building and the pounding of running feet. I can't make out a damn word they're saying. I just get the tone.

"Thank you, Sam," Gabriel says quietly. "Thank you for living and listening to an old man speak when he doesn't even want to tell his stories. For showing me that I am not leaving this world abandoned, that there is still good left. Thank you for being you." Gabriel pulls my head in close and kisses the top of it, something that only my mom has ever done to me, and only when I was little. I guess it's a gesture that runs in the family. "No matter what, know that you are loved, that those by your side would do anything for you." With that, he gives me another hard look, light reflected in his eyes like a series of pools, and gets to his feet.

"When you get better," I say before he can walk away, "we should go camping or something."

Gabriel turns with one last smile and says, "I'd like that," before walking away. Lost in my own world, I must've missed the explosion, because ash is raining down all around me like I've only seen once before. Left alone in the devastation of not a destroyed factory, but of my life falling apart, not even sure where to look to find the pieces of me to put back together, I do the only thing I know how.

I throw up.

And then I cry harder.

I know I already have been, but this is loud. I sob uncontrollably, feeling bits and pieces of me break off and shatter. Maybe I'll be able to put it all back together, but today I am broken.

"Sam!" I hear Rose shout right before she plops down in front of me. She skids a bit, so I know she didn't even bother to stop running before she hit the ground. She looks at my face, eyes wide. "Sam what happened?" she demands to know. "Are you okay?"

All I do is sob harder and louder.

"Geez, what's wrong with him?" Arthur asks, slowing his run.

"I don't know," Rose tells him. "He hasn't said anything."

"Sam?" Jinn says, kneeling down in front of me. "Sam, what's wrong?"

I'm sorry, Dac says, carefully. He's obviously not referring to what these guys are talking about. He heard it all too.

Like my normal suave self, I puke up the rest of the contents of my stomach all over the ground. Mixed in with the ash, it's not pretty. It's not pretty to begin with.

Before saying anything else, Rose pulls me in to a tight hug, and I essentially go limp besides squeezing her so tight it probably hurts, "Shhh," she tries to comfort me, stroking my shaggy hair, "everything's going to be alright."

But she doesn't know. None of them know. How could they possibly? This is something not even any of the Royals could understand. Surrounded by all those I love and hold dear, I still feel entirely alone right now. None of them will ever understand this, understand what just happened. Still, I let Rose hold me and rock me in an attempt to comfort me. It isn't helping at all, but I need something to hold on to until I can put myself back together. Not only am I broken, but isolated.

An immortal just confessed his death to me.

Chapter Ten

I don't know how long I sit here crying, black ash raining down on me. What I do know is that Rose never lets go of me. I don't know why she even bothers. I'm being a big baby and should probably find a way to deal with everything. It's hard. Life's hard. That doesn't mean I'm calling it quits on life. Gabriel sure hasn't. How many centuries has he fought against an illness that he has kept quiet about up until now? He only said that he's dying. He didn't look ready to die, so I know that he'll keep fighting. At least there's that.

I check out so far that I don't even know what's around me anymore.

It's warm here. The heat isn't because of the blown up factory next to me, but rather because of the people around me. I really need to stop being so pathetic. If not for me, then for them. I can't pretend that I'm alone anymore. Even when they're terrified, my friends stay with me. Even when I'm terrified, they're here.

Look at me, I'm a complete wreck right now, and I'm pretty sure nearly everybody but Gabriel is here with me. I don't think I want to see Gabriel right now anyway. It'll set me off again.

Before all of this, before I went to the Sky Nation, when I only lived here on the Surface and could only dream of the rest of the world, I never really had anybody.

I had John: who's still here.

Rick and Fred: who now live in the Water Nation, but are here with me now.

And my mom: who won't even speak to me.

That's it. Four people I could count on occasionally, and one of them won't acknowledge my existence at this point. Must've been hard pretending I'm not real when a horde of people from the Sky Nation knocked on her door though.

The only time I really had people like this around me before all this was when…

My head snaps up as I come to. I take in everything around me quickly. First of all, when did it become nighttime? Second, Rose is still holding on to me with everybody else sitting around nearby. Somebody went and got the transport they all came down in and parked it less than one hundred feet away from me.

A breeze comes rolling through, making me shiver. Oh yeah, I don't have my shirt. I wonder if I can get it back. A quick glance at the rubble that was a factory tells me otherwise though. I swear I destroy more clothes than anybody else I know.

You're absolutely insane, Dac tells me.

I'm well aware.

"I have an idea," I say out loud. It's like my friends slowly wake up from a long sleep. Geez, I must've been sitting here longer than I thought. This is still the same day, right?

"What are you talking about?" Jinn asks, rubbing his eyes.

"We're going to need help if we're going to stop the New Power once and for all, right?"

"That's a given," Arthur grumbles, sitting up. "How

would you expect the thirteen or so of us to take on an entire army? An entire nation?"

"We didn't do so bad when the New Power attacked Jinn's house," I remind him.

Arthur opens his mouth to say something and pauses. I think for a blissful moment that he won't come up with something, but he continues, "Weren't all of us almost dead during a surprise counter attack? I decidedly remember that you were crying like a little baby the next morning while we were trying to heal you."

A couple of us glare at him. He doesn't seem to care as he smiles in remembered bliss.

You know, this whole time I've been thinking Arthur is a good guy. Are we so sure about that?

Stop it, Dac chides. Fine, fine. I know that we've already had this discussion, but seriously. How can he like me getting hurt so much?

Mark actually thwacks Arthur in the back of the head. Not hard, but enough for him to know that the road he was going down was not okay. It's hard not to applaud him.

"So what is your stupid idea anyway?" Arthur asks me while giving Mark a venomous look. I'm sure he's going to pay for hitting Arthur later, but I'm sure all of us were debating hitting him at that moment. I sure know I was.

"I know a lot of people down here that can fight to a degree," I try to explain. "It's probably about the right time of year that they're all together anyways."

"Who are you talking about?" John asks.

"They're the ones that taught me how to sword fight before Jinn did," I continue. It's quiet for a bit while everybody tries to figure out what I'm talking about. John catches on first.

"You've got to be kidding me," John says when he gets it.

"What?" Rose asks him. Now that I think about it, I don't know if anybody here *but* John knows this story.

"He plans to recruit the entire renaissance fair," John elaborates, rubbing an eyebrow with his thumb. All eyes are definitely on me now.

"Seriously?" I get asked in a couple variations of disbelief.

I shrug, "There are a lot of them, and they actually do know how to fight to a degree." They're still looking at me like I'm crazy. "Just trust me here," I say, carefully pushing myself to my feet, Rose disentangling herself from me. "I even know where they are. I'll drive." I start walking towards the transport.

Do you even know how to drive? Dac asks me.

Um.

Thought so.

Behind me I hear a conversation.

"Is he okay?" Rose asks, concerned about me. "He was completely devastated a few hours ago, and now nothing."

"Just give him time," Jinn tries to reassure her. "Sam has his own way to cope with things."

"He's done this before," John adds in. "Couple years ago, when we were working in the factories, there was a little kid that was marked, just like he is now. Manager got mad that day and killed the kid for no good reason."

"What did Sam do?" Rose asks.

"He went into a funk for a few days," John says before more quietly adding, "right before he destroyed the entire factory. Nothing as spectacular as this, but he took it down."

"Do you think he's reacting the same way this time?" Mark asks.

*****

I no longer hear them once I enter the transport. Apparently, people like to forget that I have two working ears. One of them may not be as good anymore after having an explosion near it, though. Regardless, I can hear fine. I storm into the cockpit. Nobody is in here, and I really realize for absolute certain that I have no idea how to fly this thing. I don't even know how to turn it on. I'll just lead them through the air then.

I drop myself in a seat, ready to wait for everybody to be ready and find my eyes incredibly heavy.

Do you know where I'm looking to go? I ask Dac.

Yes.

Think you could lead them?

Yes.

Alright. I'm going to take a nap then.

Not long after thinking it, I close my eyes, and before anybody else starts to pile on to the ship, I already feel myself slipping into unconsciousness. And it is beautiful.

"You did *what*?" an unfortunately familiar voice says. Steven. Not even when I'm asleep can he *ever* cut me a break. At least I'm resting for now. When I wake up, I won't be dead tired anymore. Here's to the silver lining.

"He destroyed a factory," another voice says. This one I've only heard once. He's the one in charge of the factories. If he and Steven are bonding over failures, Daddy-aka their master-must not be happy.

"That's what he did," Steven says. "I'm asking what you did."

"N-nothing," new guy says. "Even though Master said that some child named 'Cutter' was in one of my factories, I didn't think it was anything to worry about."

"You idiot!" I hear Steven scream in new guys face. I can't see either of them, but I know Steven well enough to know that he's not respecting the rules of personal space. He's charming like that. "Didn't Master warn you about him?"

"No," the new guy says evenly. Boohoo for you. So you weren't warned to beware of angry fifteen—I mean sixteen—year olds. Big whoop. Even with fair warning, you wouldn't have been able to do much. I had some unexpected reinforcements.

Who brought explosives.

Yup. My friends are like that. Even though I haven't been in my best state of mind, they're good friends.

"Wait, yes he did," new guy amends himself. "I recall him saying something about a kid defeating you. I didn't pay much attention. Everything was running smoothly down here. Over a year without incident." There's a pause in the conversation long enough that I know Steven is thinking.

"That's exactly how long ago Cutter left the Surface," Steven snaps. "Have you really been unaware of the devastation he's left in his wake?" The silence is answer enough. This guy seriously should get informed. "Randy, this is serious."

"I'm well aware, Steven," Randy says.

"So why didn't you do anything when you were warned Cutter was in one of your facilities?"

"I did not believe that a single adolescent could wreak as much havoc as you and the master would have me believe."

"You're lucky," Steven says. "He's only destroyed one. If you don't antagonize him any further, maybe he won't continue bringing our operations down. I'm sorry, *your* operations." Fat chance.

"That may be a problem," Randy says, still somehow sounding confident. I thought he and Steven were supposedly equals. I guess I've seriously damaged his reputation.

"Hm?" Steven grunts.

"From the reports I've received, the Cutter boy was marked," Randy says, losing his confidence, switching to timid with each word.

"You—" Steven starts to try to say something, but is cut off.

"Don't be mad. I had no control over the matter," Randy tries to cover himself.

"You—" Steven tries again, to be cut off yet again.

"Besides, the mark means that it's legal to maim and kill him. Maybe the enforcers will take care of him for us?" Alright, now anybody could tell that Randy is grasping at straws. There is no way that a two-bit enforcer is going to get me, with the exception of a lucky shot, or overwhelming numbers. Your typical enforcers aren't smart enough to band together though.

"*YOU. DID. WHAT?!*" Steven screams at Randy. I'd say he deserves that. "Now there is absolutely *no* chance that Cutter will ignore you."

"Maybe he doesn't know what the marking means?" Randy suggests.

"He's from the Surface, you buffoon," Steven snaps back.

The only answer the brilliant Randy can come up with is a resounding, "Oh…"

"You've doomed yourself," Steven says. "I've combatted the boy for a year now, only personally crossing swords with him twice now. Both times I've nearly lost my life. When we do not meet in person, he has the annoying tendency to annihilate my armies."

"What about Lynch? Master said that the boy claimed his life."

"Not even the boy. One of his underlings can be attributed that accomplishment." I would call them friends, not underlings. I'm pretty sure I'm closer to the bottom of the totem pole than Arthur for sure. Actually, did Arthur or Dac kill Lynch? I know I'm higher up than Dac is, or that we're at least the same level as each other.

The fact that I can calmly think about who killed a person, who amongst my friends took another person's life, makes me sick to my theoretical stomach. Actually, no. It does make me sick, but not near as much as I would expect it to. I don't want to be used to taking lives. I don't want to be used to death. I want it to horrify me, and disgust, and repulse me, but it doesn't. Death is just a fact of life. Everybody that lives dies. With Gabriel's confession to me, that sentiment is truer that it ever has been to me.

"Lynch was a monster to stand against," Randy comments.

"That he… was," Steven says, careful to use the past tense. It's like he's not ready to admit that Lynch is gone. It's been months. I didn't think they were close at all, but maybe they were. Friends? Can bad guys have friends?

"Damn," Randy says, sounding partially depressed. "Only thing I can say is that we're lucky Cutter is only one person then. He can only be in one place at a time."

I may be only one person, but I have a lot of friends. It's a long list that just keeps on growing.

My dream doesn't last long beyond this. Steven and Randy say their goodbyes before I am granted the bliss of a silent, dreamless sleep.

Chapter Eleven

Far too soon I am being woken up by someone shaking me harder than is absolutely necessary. Can't they just let me sleep? It feels like it's been a week since I've had a decent night's sleep. Tonight I'm sleeping like a champion, that's all I'm saying.

Hopefully nothing goes wrong today, and it will pass without incident.

I almost laugh myself awake at the notion.

"I'm up," I say to whoever is trying to rouse me. My voice is rough from disuse. It doesn't sound nearly as pleasant as I would've hoped while trying to convince somebody to leave me alone. Fortunately, they let up on the shaking and let me take a moment to get going. I stretch like a cat after a long nap and hear my back pop a couple of times. Man that feels good. I point my toes and feel my right ankle pop too. Oh yeah. Some people think cracking their back or ankles is disgusting and painful. I just like the feeling. I'm as creaky as Nathan is half the time. Considering everything that's been going on my entire life, I elect to enjoy the little things.

I open my eyes while I still have my back arched and arms outstretched. Dac is the one who got the extreme pleasure of waking me up. I look behind me and see that my fist is essentially in a sour-looking Arthur's face. I quickly snatch my hand back before he decides it's a good idea to take it off.

We're almost there, Dac tells me.

Thanks.

I tried to let you sleep as long as possible. You need your rest.

Thanks even more for that, I tell him, attractively rubbing an eye with the base of my palm. I don't even need to see it; I can feel that my hair is an absolute mess right now. I guess that means I tossed and turned a bit. I'm just hoping I didn't snore.

Not bad, Dac tells me, referring to the snoring. *It was more like heavy breathing.* Again, I choose to enjoy the little things. Is it wrong to be glad I didn't snore like a chainsaw in front of everybody?

"Descending," we get a heads up from whoever is piloting.

I let my weight fall back into my chair and check who's around me. My eyes aren't even fully adjusted before I feel us start moving down. It's that weird drop in my stomach. It's like falling, but worse. So I may be a bit of a control freak, but I really am not a fan of somebody else driving.

Might I remind you that you don't even know how to drive one of these, Dac says.

I'm well aware, I tell him. *I just like riding a bike or flying with your boots more.*

I suppose that's fair.

Ugh, I feel groggy and awful. I guess emptying my stomach without adding anything back in is taking its toll. Any intention of seeing how everybody is doing is forgotten when I shove my head into the headrest and close my eyes again. The light is only making me feel sicker.

We have an unfortunately rough landing and I'm

jostled around. My empty stomach starts doing a dance, and my throat starts to sting in warning that I may lose whatever is left in there.

The feeling dies down just as quickly as it arose, my request for a bucket dying before ever reaching my lips.

"Who are these people?" I hear Nathan ask.

"And why are they dressed so weird?" adds Mark.

I hear a grunt before Arthur says, "Their swords have pitiful craftsmanship. I could do better blindfolded, asleep, and half dead." Why don't you tell us how you really feel?

Outside, the role players are chanting and saying things that I can't make out clearly, but it's getting louder. That's not helping with the clarity at all though. Please be quiet guys.

"Hey, Sam," John says, "you're the only one who knows these people. Maybe you should take this one."

"You've met them before," I say irritably.

"Once," John specifies. "They actually know you."

"Fine," I spit, flailing around to stand up. Lucky for me, nobody is in my range while I get up. After a few grumpy steps to get to the door, I slam my hand into the shoulder-height open button with way more force than necessary.

"Somebody's grumpy," John says. Ignoring that. I do try to spot him by only shifting my eyes, not my head. Why does this door take so long to open?

While the door is opening painfully slowly, I let out a big yawn. To help stretch my back, I keep my hands at my sides and even push down. I probably gave these guys one of the best first impressions ever, as the door opens to reveal a gracefully yawning me that probably has enough class to rival that of all four Royals. Actually, I know for a fact that I can be just as graceful as they can. Even more so in some cases.

"What sorcery be this?" I hear Gary ask. I don't see him in the gathering crowd, but I can clearly see him in my mind's eye. I'm sure he's wearing his same old ratty robes with his lovingly carved wooden staff. He probably even has his sword hanging from his belt. He's so proud of that thing.

And Arthur just insulted it.

Typical.

"Why doth the lad lookith familiar?" another asks.

"Hi Lance," I say, waving arbitrarily at the sea of people. I have no idea where he is in it.

"Is that truly whom I think it be?" another voice says that's clearly trying too hard to go with the jargon of a time long past.

"Hey everybody," I say. "Anybody know where Scott is?"

"Who is this Scott of which the stranger speaks?" somebody shouts. Of course they're going to make me do it. Why wouldn't they? I sigh.

"Where be the valiant knight, Sir Forlork?" I ask.

"Ah!" Somebody exclaims. "The stranger is no stranger at all, for he is a companion of King Forlork." That would mean he won the tournament for king last year. Good for him.

"Yeah, sure," I say halfheartedly. "So, where is he?"

"Does anybody know who Sam is talking about?" I hear the question asked behind me.

"I think he's the person who taught Sam how to sword fight before he met Jinn," John offers.

"Better question," Rose proposes, "why is he talking like that?"

"I don't care," Arthur laughs. "It's funny as all hell, and I'm going to cherish this video tape forever." Not if I break your camera you won't.

"Who inquires of me?" I hear a familiar voice rise. It's

been a few years since I've seen him, but I hope he'll still recognize me. In the back of the crowd, a man stands on top of what's probably a table. Seeing as he's far away, the only details I can make out are that he's a tad bit rounder than most, that he's wearing a long red cloak, and has a way overly ornate, shiny gold crown. Yup, that's him.

I can't help but look back at the collection of Royals right behind me. I didn't notice before for some reason or another, but even Kane is here. I think I understand why it took them so long to congregate and come down here. The trip to and from the Water Nation isn't a short one. It's a long trip to take, even one way.

I digress.

Looking back at the collection of four Royals behind me, including the one that took over the planet, I notice a distinct lack of crowns and flowing outfits.

"Please tell me you guys never wore anything like that," I say to them. Hello foot, meet mouth. I think you'll like your new home.

"When we first succeeded at stopping the violence all those years ago, the people of the world had me wear one for a time. It was a passing fad," Gabriel states. See, that makes sense.

"I thought it might look good," Nathan admits shamelessly.

"Nathan dared me to for about a hundred years," Kane offers up. He probably should've kept that one to himself. I could go my entire life not knowing some of the things they would all try to get each other do.

"Never," Sarah says. "I always thought it was a silly look." I'm glad that I came from her part of the family and not one of the others. Who knows what my inherent mental state would be.

"Name thyself," Forlork loudly demands.

"Please don't judge me for this," I say to everybody in the transport with me before quietly turning back around. I can't introduce myself as Sam. These guys are the sort that'll pretend they don't know me if I do that.

You do remember that Arthur is video taping this, right?

Unfortunately, I do.

"I am Casm," I proclaim, my face going painfully red. Oh God, why am I doing this? "I was last in this kingdom two cycles ago." I let my sentence end sounding relatively powerfully, but I feel like an idiot. I'll be honest; I was all for everything about this stuff a few years ago, but now it just seems unnecessary. I guess a year worth of fighting in a real war does that to a person. I can't imagine the mindset of people like Jinn who've been a part of the war with the New Power for about eleven years now, maybe longer. I never did ask when this all first started, when the New Power became interested in taking over the world.

"Oh this is so much better than I thought it would be," Arthur chitters.

"Approach me," Forlork calls. "Come from your steel chariot, but there your companions must remain."

"I have to walk over there to talk to you anyway," I mutter to myself. I half stomp down the ramp of the transport, the entire thing making creaky noises as I do so. The crowd of people in costume part into two sections to make a path for me. All eyes are on me as I approach Scott. He's too busy talking to somebody beside him that I don't recognize. If he were looking at me, I'm sure that he would've recognized me by now and let us just talk like normal people. As things currently stand, he's probably confused as all hell. I did sort of just come from a transport. Those aren't ever seen down here. Actually, now that I can get a good look at him, I'm not sure if he's freaked out, or excited that this is going on.

Gabriel says that if you bow to this guy that you'll never hear the end of it, Dac lets me know.

Did he ask you to tell me that?

Not explicitly, but I'm sure he knows I'm going to tell you. All of a sudden, I'm really tempted to bow to Scott, but that'd only boost everybody's ego but mine. So, this is the easy answer, no bowing to anybody. It's degrading.

Scott looks back over to me, and it's like he's physically slapped. "Sam? Is that you?" he asks me.

"In the flesh," I say. "How've you been, Scott?"

"How have I been?" he parrots back, "What about you? I haven't heard from you in more than a year!"

"I've been out of town," I say. Detail is fine, but not when I have a horde of potentially angry LARPers on either side of me. I'm not much up for fighting a bunch of innocent guys who may help us in the long run. Besides, I know these guys. I'd much rather show off with a bopper. Those are basically just padded PVC pipe. That way, I can actually hit them without fear of hurting them too bad.

"A lot has gone on," I add, thinking to show him my black bar, raising my left wrist so that my elbow makes an *L* shape, my fingers partially curled. My wrist is facing him.

"I can see that," Scott says back.

"Any chance you could tell everybody to put their swords away?" I ask him. "One of my friends is offended by their craftsmanship."

"Ah, yes, of course," Scott says, as if the fact that a couple hundred people have poorly made sharp objects pointed at my friends is normal. "Sheath your steel, men," he calls out over the crowd. After only a moment of hesitation, all swords are put away. It's a curious sound, hearing all that steal sliding as weapons are sheathed. As funny as it is, I've honestly never heard it. I know the subtle, near nonexistent sound Sky Iron makes as it changes size, but that's nothing like this.

I only know what this sounds like thanks to a year of hearing it multiple times on a daily basis.

"So, friend, what brings you here? After such a lengthy absence, surely there must be reason? Or perhaps the reason is in the visit itself," Scott speculates.

I'm glaring at Nathan for you. He's really confused.

"You even come to us naked," Scott says.

What?

I look down at myself, suddenly not sure if I remembered to wear pants. Nope, I have all my clothes on. A look of confusion crosses my face before I remember that, at gatherings like this, you're considered naked unless you're in period garb.

"Can we talk?" I ask him, ignoring the naked comment. "In private?"

Scott looks me up and down as if gauging my mental sanity. His eyes flick over to touch upon the transport before saying, "Come." He nods his head in the direction he starts walking.

We head straight back to where a large tent is waiting.

And just what do you expect us to do? Dac asks.

You especially should try to not be spotted. These guys are jumpy because of a transport. Everybody else should just wait for a moment. I'm just going to try to explain the situation to Scott, and we'll see from there.

Keep in mind that while we've been making a whole mess of trouble down here, everybody else is only now just getting in the game.

They just blew up a factory. They can wait five minutes.

I'm so glad I met you, Dac says. *Life is a whole lot more interesting this way.*

I accidentally chuckle a bit when entering Scott's tent. Now there's a concept. It feels like forever since I've laughed. I know it's only been a few days, but a lot has happened.

"Sit," Scott merrily encourages, "Drink. Be merry." He makes sure to take the seat at the far head of the table. It's an unusually long table, so I pull up a chair right next to him. He grabs a handful of bread, "So, what is it you needed to talk about privately?" he asks, taking a huge bite of the bread.

"Not much in the mood for pleasantries then?" I ask him, sitting back in my chair. For such an awful chair, it's oddly comfortable. I attribute it to being tired.

"Sam," he starts, plowing more food down his throat. The only thing in here breaking period is a huge cooler of cold beers. He gets up to grab a couple of them, tucking some in his upturned tunic to carry back to the table. While he's still grabbing drinks, he says, "you landed in the middle of the battle field in a giant flying ship. I'm not much in a mood to be talking, let alone for pleasantries."

"You seemed so calm out there," I say, as he spills the cans onto the table. He falls back in his chair and nervously turns the sideways cans so that they're up-right.

"An act, obviously," he says. "If I lost it, they would've too. I did win king last year. How would it look if our best fighter lost his cool?"

"Fair enough," I tell him. "Look, Forlork," I say, using his chosen name for these meet ups.

"Please Sam, not today. I have absolutely no care to be in period right now." He pops open one of the beers and drains it like it's water before moving on to the next.

"Right then," I say. "Cards on the table, plain and simple," I lean forward, clasping my hands together. I rest my hands on the table, trying to look as calming as absolutely possible, "there's a war going on."

Scott laughs nervously as if in response to a bad joke, "Come on Sam, I thought you said you were going to be straight with me."

"It's the truth," I tell him. "There's this organization called the New Power, and they've been trying to take over, well, everything for a while now, and they're based here on the Surface." I take a breath to continue, and that's when Scott steps in.

"Here on the Surface? Sam, you're sounding like you've been elsewhere this whole time."

"I have been," I tell him.

"Bull."

"It's true," I defend myself. "Over the past year, I've spent the vast majority of my time up in the Sky Nation, but I've also been down in the Water Nation for some time."

Scott stops moving altogether and gives me a hard look, seeing that my words are the truth.

"How?" is all he asks of me.

"That is a really long story that I really don't want to get into right now."

A ruckus starts up outside, the sounds of battle rising. Oh no, I hope the LARPers didn't attack my friends.

They didn't, Sam. We could really use you out here! Dac shouts in my head.

"What? What is it?" I loudly say. Dammit, it's been a while since I've accidentally done that.

Before Dac can answer, there's a loud shout, followed by the sound of tearing. I jump out of my seat, pushing the cheap chair back, hand instantly shooting into my pocket. I witness as somebody slices clean through the side of the tent, too impatient to go around to the front, and bursts through. The man is wearing the all too familiar New Power uniform, the black armor with a red stripe down the side, helmet and visor hiding all but his mouth. The difference here is that this soldier is one of the higher ranks. He's armed with one of the electrically charged machetes.

"What is going on?!" Scott cries, freaking out.

Never mind, I say to Dac, *I know what's going on.*

"You!" he shouts at me, pointing his blade. Have I met this one before?

"Me!" I shout back stupidly, climbing onto the table to get at the New Power soldier across from me. I fully extend my Sky Iron sword as I leap off the table. I both see and feel the comforting white glow of my blade as I plant both feet firmly in the goon's face. He stumbles back, half falling back through the hole he cut in the tent as I hit the floor. I clamber to my feet while he detangles himself from the tent just in time to bring my sword up to meet his crackling weapon, and lightning crackles down my sword.

I block over my head to counter his blow and knock the blade aside. He takes a step to my right, trying to close the space, but I've knocked his sword far enough back that he needs to bring it full around to attack again.

I raise a booted foot and swiftly kick him in the knee. There's an ugly loud snapping noise before the screaming soldier crumples to the ground. In his fall, he drops his blade. I'm sure to kick it far out of his reach. He moves to crawl for it. Come on, give up already!

I grab the closest thing to me, which is evidently a chair, and bring it down hard upon his helmeted head. Even with protection, there is only so much he can take before getting knocked out.

Contrary to popular belief, the chair doesn't splinter into a million pieces. It's still whole. So I hit him with it again.

What? The guy is still crawling. It's his own fault.

After a third powerful hit, the New Power soldier stops crawling. I drop the chair on him and look behind me to see Scott in stunned silence.

"Do you believe me now?" I ask him.

Chapter Twelve

"Your... your sword glows," is the first thing Scott is capable of saying.

"Yes, it does that."

"Did he just actually try to kill us?" is the next thing Scott thinks to ask.

"Yes," I say again, "they typically do that. We really have to get going now." When Scott refuses to move, I take a few quick steps over to him and grab his right wrist. "Draw your sword," I tell him. "You're going to need it." Scott draws his sword with his left hand with as much ease as can be had from a man mentally freaking out. Scott's a lefty, so I figure he'll be fine.

"Where are we going?" he asks me, as I start to pull him along on the opposite side of the table as the unconscious New Power member. Alright, I really can't be baby sitting him out there. I let go of his wrist and slap him across the face. That usually does the trick.

Scott shakes his head about and says, "Thanks," the crazy draining from his eyes.

"The New Power always seem to travel in groups," I say, "and if the sound out there is any indication, there are a lot of them. They're going to need our help."

"Wait, we're helping the armored guys?"

"No," I say irritably. "Just hit the people in armor

with a red stripe on it. They're the bad guys right now."

"Got it," Scott says, moving to push ahead of me. No, you really don't, Scott. You don't get it at all. Beyond that, you don't know what it actually looks like in a fight where it seems like everybody is trying to kill you. It only seems that way because it's generally true. All the fighting done here is play fighting; nobody actually dies unless it's a major accident. So far, I think all death has been avoided.

The New Power came today to make up for that.

Scott makes it out of the tent a moment before I do. "Dear God," he says, getting his first glimpse at real combat. It's a mess out here. An entire New Power army is descending on the LARPers, nearly one soldier for every man in ancient armor. The chorus of screaming sets my heart racing, but I don't let myself get hung up on it. Hanging above the battlefield are three gigantic transports from which more New Power soldiers descend. If I can get up there, into the biggest one, I can stop any more from joining the battle.

So go already! Dac shouts at me.

"Scott, find someone with a glowing sword and stay near them. They'll keep you safe," I say to him while half galloping, half running away from him to get nearer to the battle.

"Where are you going?" he asks me as I take off. I kick on my boots and shoot into the air. I race to the largest transport at the head of the group over the heads of all those intertwined in a lethal dance with each other. I spot the Sky Iron of everyone I know sort of huddled together near the transport, but spreading out fast. Dac stands out, seeing as he's taller than everybody else and made of metal. It looks like he charged out a bit to try and help the less experienced fighters. The glow of the Sky Iron is expanding out fast though. We're gaining

117

ground.

Is it cheating that I fly over everybody?

No, now hurry up!

In response, I pour on speed. I'm not going anywhere near as fast as I know my boots can carry me, but fast for the distance that I need to travel. I inspect the transport, more like a carrier, ahead of me and see that the soldiers are emptying out of the sides of the thing, not the bottom. At least it's not a warship. Over the past year, I've learned that I was ridiculously lucky taking that thing down.

The ship is in the shape of a Christmas tree. Alright, so that's a major stretch of the imagination. There's a wide rectangular base. Above that, it comes out slightly and rises up multiple stories and wait... is this the carrier that I initially snuck up to the Sky Nation in? No, no this one looks different. It probably is a cargo ship though.

I shoot into one of the open holes and find myself inside of the carrier. There have to be just as many New Power soldiers in here. I have to stop these guys or everybody outside is going to be overwhelmed. Without stopping to let my feet touch the ground, I zoom over the heads of the now revolting New Power soldiers who would love to be able to grab hold of my ankle, throw me down to the ground, and proceed to kick the crap out of me. Sure there are plenty of them that pay me no mind as they wait in line to drop down to the primary battlefield with admirable determination, but those that are *that* committed to their job are few and far between.

Any idea where the control room is? I ask Dac, realizing I have no idea where I'm going.

Try going up? He suggests.

Well I didn't need him to come up with that idea. That's already what I'm doing. Either this ship is lacking

all the markings generally required to direct people around, or more likely, they're simply covered by some person or another.

I don't fly around long before I find the stairway up. Crowded as it is, there isn't enough room for me to fly over the heads of the New Power soldiers.

Maintaining as much momentum as possible, I right myself and drop to the floor, half tripping up the stairs. To keep my balance, I shove one of the soldiers aside. Like a set of dominoes, soldier after soldier falls, too tightly packed to do otherwise. They have no reason to suspect anyone would be dumb enough to fly into their ship.

Seeing as the soldiers can't do much more than waddle, I'm left trying to squeeze between them sideways, my self-esteem taking a hit whenever it gets difficult. The upside of the close quarters is that nobody can raise a weapon. It's all grabs and shouts. Yelling at me isn't going to stop me.

At the top of the stairs, the headroom doesn't open up at all, and I have to stay on the floor. This would be so much easier if I could fly. Lives are being lost less than fifty eet below me, and I'm stuck crab walking and sucking in my gut!

"Move it!" I shout to the mass of New Power soldiers as a whole. I realize all that does is let them know exactly where I am, but I don't care. I have to get to the control panel to stop the slaughter.

It won't exactly stop the fighting, but it will significantly help us out.

Why can't any of these things ever have similar layouts? I'd even accept a door on the outside straight into the cockpit.

The bodies thin as I get farther away from the drop ports until I get to the point where I can take off again.

Thank you! Without hesitation, I get airborne again, gaining speed in the process. I fly up any and every set of stairs I can find. At long last, I find a sign pointing me in the direction of the pilot. It's a start. I head off in that direction and rejoice when I quickly find exactly what I'm looking for. Before me is the door to the control room.

I sloppily land and run the last few feet to the door. Without hesitation, I pull the beast of a thing open. In here is a simple layout really. This ship has two control consoles set up in a pilot, co-pilot fashion. That way one could cover for the other if anything were to happen. Simple and effective. It also means they have two pilots, one of which is looking out for me.

He surges out of his chair on the right to come at me, but I move towards him at the same time. Ducking low, I grab the pilot around the waist and flip him over my back. That's a new move for me. Arthur is not a good teacher, seeing as his method is "Here, let me show you on *your* body. It'll be tons of fun for me."

It paid off didn't it? Dac comments.

With the extra pilot taken care of, I rush towards the other, slamming into him and hoping that he jerks the controls along with him. I really need to learn how to fly one of these things.

Lucky for me, my plan works. The whole transport lurches to the left. I entirely lose my footing and I see the pilot I flipped go sliding across the floor. Please don't let this thing crash on top of anybody I know.

An impact rattles the transport. That couldn't be the ground. We haven't fallen near enough. I briefly look out the pilot's window to see that we've managed to crash into one of the other ships floating up here in the sky.

No, I will not vouch for you if you tell people you planned for that to happen.

Why not?

Because you didn't. Spoil sport.

Both ships are now sinking slowly to the ground, the other ship's pilot trying to maintain some form of control. Seeing as we're the heavier of the two ships, his efforts are futile.

You may want to hold on to something, Dac advises me as the ships get nearer to the ground.

Good idea, I think back. I kick on my boots long enough to reach the vacant pilot's chair and strap myself in. For extra reassurance, I grab on to the straps of the belt crossing my chest in an *X* shape. I can't help myself but to stare out the window at the approaching ground, just now realizing this may have been a bad idea.

The other ship hits the ground first, seeing as we've pinned it under us. It tears through turf as our ship continues to push it. Then, our ship officially crashes and it's utter chaos. My entire body jerks forward into my restraints, my head snapping to the point where my neck is the most pained thing on me.

The sound of every member of the New Power still on board screaming is just the background noise for the metal twisting and breaking apart and screaming at us. The glass shatters in at us, shards stinging my skin. There's nothing I can do but to look away from it and shut my eyes to try and make sure none gets in my eyes. My neck begs for my attention as I force it to move.

Having my eyes closed makes everything worse, as I can no longer tell exactly what is happening around me. It doesn't matter though, because something—I don't know what—strikes me in the head and I momentarily black out.

I wake up only moments later. The transport has stopped moving, thankfully. A siren that I didn't previously notice is wailing, trying to warn the crew of this vessel of imminent danger.

A little late for that warning, I bitterly think to myself. Dac doesn't respond, either from him being too busy to do so, or him knowing that, if he did say anything, I'm pretty sure my head will split in half.

Is it normal for people to lose consciousness in crashes? I ask him. *Carefully give me some sort of signal if the answer is yes.* There, on the outskirts of my awareness, I feel a tingling that I've come to recognize as Dac. I know full well that it's not just my aching head. No, that feeling is front and center.

I look next to me and see the pilot still strapped in, totally out cold, his helmet and armor cracked all over the place. I slap his nearest arm, immediately regretting the pain, and say, "Good flying, buddy." Only now do I somehow register that the cab is filled with smoke. Wonderful.

I unclip my seatbelt and end up falling forward out of the chair. I guess we aren't flat right now. I try to get to my feet, but the moment I put pressure on my leg, I scream and collapse. I really do not need this right now. I try to pull myself up and out of the cockpit, watching the smoke flow out of the hole left where the glass would be. I just can't find the strength to do so though.

That's a bad plan! Dac screams at me, knowing exactly what I plan to do before I can get around to doing it. My head feels like splitting open. For all I know, it really is split open. I never bothered to check, and I did get hit quite a bit.

Choking on the smoke, I decide to ignore Dac's sage advice and activate my boots. Only the right one, seeing as my left leg can't even support me standing. As planned, it gives me the shove I need and gets me out the window. Only now do I learn exactly what Dac meant by "bad plan." What he really meant to say was "Don't do that! There is quite literally no floor beneath you and you will fall maybe 20 feet!" Word choice is very important.

I frantically try to reactivate my boots. One, either, both, I don't care, just work! In my desperate attempt to stop myself from going splat, I manage to slow my descent, but I still hit the ground hard, collapsing. I'm not getting back up from this one. Not without help and a period of lying here. God my leg hurts. I don't dare look down at it. I don't care that my imagination is running rampant with horrific visions of what may have happened to me. I know myself, and it always gets worse whenever I look at my injuries.

I could use some help, I send out as a desperate plea. I don't care if Dac's response blows my head apart. I will not stay out here, barely able to think in the first place.

We're already on our way, Dac tells me. *At least some of us are. There were a few people I asked to stay behind for you.*

I'm going to assume that's a good thing.

Just don't look. We're on our way, but you guys crashed a distance from where we are. The New Power are in process of retreating, so at least we don't have to worry about them.

How bad is it? I ask him.

Just don't look! We're on our way with Blue Elixir now. Just... No! Stop it! I can't help it. Telling me not to look is like saying don't think about pink elephants. Now all I can think about is pink elephants.

I make the gargantuan mistake of looking down.

I also scream. Really, really loudly.

Chapter
Thirteen

My screams continue long after I know they should've ended. That's my bone! Those are my muscles! Neither are completely in my leg!

I SAID DON'T LOOK! Dac tries to shout over my panic. *MY LEG!*

"Sam!" somebody shouts. I don't look up to see who it is. My eyes are glued to the mutilated monstrosity of my leg. My foot isn't supposed to be facing that direction! Probably the same person that shouted kneels down next to my leg, but I can't take my eyes off the tip of the white bone long enough to tell who it is. Not even a full second later, a second person squats down on the other side.

"Oh God, we need to take care of this right now," that second person says.

"How does this work? Have you ever needed to fix something this bad?"

"Sure... once."

"Once?" the first voice says again.

"Well hurry up and do something!" Dac shouts at the other two. I only know it's him because he's speaking in both my head and in the physical world.

"Get out of the way," a third person says. I think this one's a girl, shoving one of the two near me aside and sitting on her knees.

"Sam," the girl tries to say reassuringly. Which girl? Rose? No, the voice doesn't sound right. Sarah? "Sam, I'm sorry, but this is really going to hurt. Just... just try to hold still, okay?"

Barely processing her words, I try to say okay, but I get a barely audible squeak.

"He understands," Dac translates for me, "but no promises. He's barely capable of thought."

"It'll have to do," the girl says. "Get the Elixir ready. Pour it down his throat the moment I tell you to."

"Got it," the guy still kneeling says.

"Ready Sam?" the girl asks, like I'll respond. "One," she counts, rolling her sleeves up. "Two," her hands start to move closer to my foot. What's she doing? No! STOP! "Three!" she shouts. Before I can get a protest out, my entire world is thrown into blinding pain. I arch my back involuntarily. A white light covers the entirety of my vision, but I can feel every agonizing second of my foot being turned back around to face the right direction. To make it even worse, without a chance to get a breath in, I can feel the exact moment that somebody takes hold of my exposed bone and forces it back into my body. Couldn't we have found a real doctor!?

After that, a liquid is essentially forced down my throat. I'm also forced to swallow. All of this happens before I can take a breath in.

The agony of my body stitching itself back together is too much to handle, and I'm still yet to breathe. I hate every second of this. Just lop the leg off and be done with it already!

Is that so much to ask?

Finding myself unable to mentally withstand it any longer, the sensation of every broken fiber stitching itself back together in hopefully the right position, I pass out a second time.

"How did he know where we would strike?" I hear somebody demand. Oh, you have got to be kidding me. Do I really have to listen to this right now? My mind is still reeling from all of two seconds ago. Can I please not have to deal with Steven and whomever he's talking to right now?

"Perhaps it was simply coincidence," the somebody replies to Steven.

"No, it is never coincidence with Cutter," Steven says. Look, I don't feel like pointing out that you're wrong, but you're wrong.

"Look, Steven, you've built this kid up for a year now. How can he be so bad?"

"You've seen what he's done!" Steven shouts, whirling on his companion. I can't see them, but I can tell that he's spun on his companion. "Randy, he leveled one of your factories in less than a day of being there. Cutter is dangerous."

"I hear you," Randy tells Steven. I'm having trouble remembering who he is right now. Honestly, I'm having trouble remembering who *I* am right now. What the heck hit me? Other than the planet and a couple tons of metal, that is.

"If you hear me, then why aren't you doing anything about it? Your soldiers are pulling away from the battle when Cutter is *there.* He is there right now. This may be one of our best chances to kill him." Well, you're not wrong there.

"Don't worry about it," Randy says. "Almost nobody made it out of that crash alive. Five soldiers we were able to drag out of there, three of which will never see combat again. Your brat is most certainly dead."

"Are you absolutely certain?" Steven asks. "Do you

have eyes on him right now?"

"Let me see," Randy says. It feels like a presence is missing entirely as he leaves the realm of the AI to go and inquire about my health. Steven doesn't say a word while he's gone. I hear the clicking of boots on tile that let me know he is pacing, but not a word is uttered.

After what feels like ages, my head calms down. I can still feel an intensity that I can't quite describe, other than saying somebody put a jackhammer on overdrive and is moving it all around my body.

"Good news," Randy says, startling me. I didn't feel him return. That's not surprising. I can't even feel where my tongue starts and stops right now or where my elbow is in my arm.

"The boy is dead?" Steven hurriedly asks.

"The boy is dead," Randy confirms.

"How do you know?" Steven asks, hesitantly excited.

"I have an eye witness of the boy mangled on the ground, unmoving."

"Unmoving does not mean dead," Steven says. "Why do your people not get closer to confirm the death?"

"They dare not for the boy is surrounded by his companions, the vicious warriors." I'm going to have to tell everybody that's what they're called. "Multiples of them are sobbing around the corpse."

"But he can drink the Elixir," Steven points out. How does he know that?

"As can you," Randy counters. "Just because it heals does not mean it performs miracles. My man says that the boy is covered with oozing wounds. If he drank Blue Elixir, he would have healed by now." So I'm still nice and cut up. Lovely.

I'm half tempted to speak up and ask him how my leg was, but that simply would not do. It's probably a good thing they suspect I'm dead.

"I still don't believe it," Steven says. "It's too good to be true."

Randy sighs, "Steven—"

I wake up with a gasp, my chest hurting worse than I remember. There's a sharp throbbing pain in my leg that eclipses the dull pain everywhere else on my body. I smell explosion and electricity. Jinn once asked me to define what an explosion smells like. When I couldn't explain it, Arthur told him that explosion is a very distinct smell. Electricity, I've learned, also has a distinct smell. Fight the New Power as often as I do and you learn the smell of charred ozone.

The only thing that hurts anywhere near as bad as my leg is my neck. Seeing as I could move a minute ago, I'm going to say it's not broken.

"Okay," I say, unwilling to open my eyes. My eyelids are red from the sun on them, "that was a really bad idea."

Chapter Fourteen

"I tried to tell you," Dac says.

"Yeah, yeah, yeah. You're a genius," I say back. I start hacking, still feeling smoke in my lungs. You would think I'd cough and get all that out earlier, but I guess shock changes things. When the coughing subsides, I swallow and ask, "If I open my eyes, what am I going to see?"

"The sun," Dac offers. I contort my face into a scowl, feeling the movement with every cut, and boy do I have a lot on my face and neck.

"You know what I mean," I tell them.

"I would in no way say it's pretty," Sarah says. So, it was her earlier, "but it's healed." I cautiously crack open my eyes and tilt my head down to look at my leg. I whimper at the pain in my neck. I'm having a really manly day today. At least I'm not trying to impress anybody.

All I can see of my leg is an extremely bloody pant leg, and that my foot is facing the right direction, resting at the correct angle. Still sitting next to me is an equally bloodied Sarah. Her hands especially are red. She's the one who reset my leg. Beside her is a shell-shocked Mark. Opposite them is Jinn, who looks like he's the most calm of the three of them.

"This is going to be a weird request," I say, "but

would one of you mind moving my pants so I can see?"

"Can't you move it yourself?" Sarah asks. Jinn calmly reaches across me and moves the fabric to reveal what's beneath. For starters, it's my leg, which is good. No bones are sticking out, and I'm not dead, which is also good. There's a massive puddle of blood, but it looks like my pants have soaked up the worst of it. Just under the blood, I can see a large ugly scar that's four inches of jagged nastiness. As Sarah said, it's not pretty, but it looks like everything is where it's supposed to be. I'm just going to ignore the pain for now and be grateful that I still have my leg.

I let out a sigh of relief and lie my head back down.

"Go check on everybody else," I say, ready to be alone for a bit. "I'll be fine, trust me."

"Are you sure?" Sarah asks.

"Yeah," I say, swallowing hard.

"Okay," she says, gently rubbing my leg to reassure me. "Give us a shout if you need us." I barely move my head in a nod, but I know she sees it. "Come on, boys. Let's give the kid some privacy." At her word, she, Mark, and Jinn all get up. I hear the grass crunch under their feet as they pass by my ears and trail off in the distance. I don't hear Dac move, meaning he's still standing above my head. I don't say anything to him, and he doesn't say anything back. Right now, the silence is nice. The sound of wounded warriors is off in the distance, but I've gotten disturbingly used to that sound.

After a time of silence, I think to Dac, *Am I suicidal?*

No, Dac says back. *You're reckless. There's a difference.*

I'm not so sure anymore, I tell him.

And why's that?

It sounds like the mature thing to say.

You're sixteen. Get over yourself.

Hey, I could've died. Cut me some slack.

Not a chance you big baby. I laugh at that. It's a good thing to laugh, even if it makes your thoughts swim. It's a nice feeling. It doesn't feel like there's enough of that anymore. A time after my laughter subsides, I hear the crunching of grass again.

Who is it?

John, Dac tells me, as John sits down next to me. I wonder what he's going to say, but he sits there quietly, maybe just checking up on me.

"I hate this place," John says.

"I have to agree with you there," I say.

"Tell me why we had to come back, again? I thought things were going good up in the Sky Nation."

"We have people down here," I remind John. "Both of our families are still down here."

"Speaking of which, your parents are really mad at you for some reason."

"I'm going to chalk it up as daddy issues," I say. When you think about it, it's true. I try not to get upset with my mother yet again. I try to convince myself that it's all my dad's fault, but I know that's not entirely true. The Surface gets to everyone eventually. Mom stuck around just long enough to see me off. She did what she could. I can't ask for more.

"How're you doing?" John asks me.

"I feel about as good as I look," I tell him before running my tongue over a cut on the inside of my cheek I didn't notice earlier. Alright, maybe I look a bit worse than I feel, but only slightly.

"That bad?"

"Yup."

"I ask again, what are we doing down here?" John asks me.

"I don't even know," I tell him honestly. "I thought I

did, and that we were doing the right thing by trying to stop the New Power once and for all and that maybe that would help to better the entire world, but I don't know any more."

"Stop being such a downer," he tells me. "You always get moody when you get hurt."

"Then give me my ten minutes of melodrama," I beg of him.

"You got it," he chuckles at me.

Incoming Royal, Dac warns me.

Which one? I ask back.

Nathan. Alright. I can handle Nathan right now. I don't think I can face Sarah after knowing she has quite literally stuck her hand in my leg, and Gabriel... I don't know how well I'll be able to face him again, or how long of a chance I will have to do so.

"How're you doing, Sam?" Nathan asks as he approaches.

"Moderately well," I half lie.

"Glad to hear it," Nathan says. "I just got a message from Kane saying that he and a large group of Water Nation citizens will be surfacing a few days from now. I told him he could meet us where he picked us up last time. Shouldn't take us long to fly there, but I just wanted to let you know."

"Why would you want to let me know?" I ask him.

"Well," he starts uncomfortably, "you two are from around here," Nathan says, I'm sure gesturing to John and me. "If you have anybody that you would like to stop and see, after a day or two of working out strategy with these guys, who said they were willing to join us by the way, we could go and see them."

"Can we see my family?" John asks hopefully.

"Sure," Nathan says. "We can work out the details of where to fly when we get closer to leaving. I just wanted

to let you two know that the option is open." His phone rings then. I hear the sound of it rubbing on fabric as he pulls it out of his pocket. "It's Kane. I should probably take this."

Lifting my arm as little as possible, I wave him off by flailing my hand.

"Right," Nathan says. The click of him hitting accept to the call plays before he puts it to his ear and says, "What's up, brother?" I hear the tinny droning of Kane going off in his ear before Nathan starts to walk away.

"I hope your reunion goes better than mine did," I tell John.

"I'm not sure how much worse things can get," he quietly speculates. I pretend I didn't hear him.

"Don't worry about it," I reassure him. "Soon as you're back through that door, Coral is going to be all over you."

"You think so?"

"Your baby sister loves you. All you have to worry about is not worrying until we get there."

"That's confusing," he tells me.

"You get the point, though," I tell him, rolling my shoulders to better lie down and relax.

"Yeah, that I do," John says, trailing off for a moment. That's when he decides to redirect his nerves, "So why did you come down here? If you're being so negative..." he asks me. I open my eyes to stare up at the far too bright sky, buying myself a moment while I wince and squint. Desperate to come up with an answer, I say the first sensible sentence that comes to mind.

"Somebody had to get things started," I say. If I really wanted to give him a good answer, I would need more time and significant psychiatric help. My one sentence is going to have to be enough for now.

John doesn't say anything back. We both sit here in

silence, taking in a calm day of sunshine on the Surface. The little things like this are what got me through the day for fifteen years of my life. Windows of bliss like this only come around perhaps twice a year. Lying here, grass tickling my skin, bugs driving me partially insane, warmth on my face, I can almost rationalize why somebody would want to live down here.

Both of us think it, but neither says it. We let the miniscule bit of homesickness seep through, as we find it easiest to do nothing while we wait for the others to be ready to go.

Gabriel, Sarah, and Nathan are talking with everyone here willing to fight with us, showing them that there are still Royals out there that are worth believing in. Also, the fact that Gabriel conquered the planet a long while back gives them some credibility. How do I know this? Simple. Another familiar face in the crowd seeks John and me out and asks me if they're okay. The looks he gave Dac while talking to me are definitely one of the more pleasant things I've seen the past few days.

It's funny. Here I am, trying to be invisible, and the Royals are being Royals, trying to maintain their spotlight. Through that, I'm still sought out. Not only am I found, but am asked if the Royals are legitimate? Who would've thought that my word would ever have more authority than that of a Royal? Sure it's "yes, they're okay, they generally don't bite," but that's beside the point.

After what feels like hours, but is probably only one, I try to get to my feet and head over to where I'm assuming everybody is gathered.

It doesn't go that smoothly.

Immediately after putting pressure on my previously broken leg, I collapse. I hit the ground hard, banging my chin and biting my tongue. I curse, getting my elbows beneath me and partially pushing myself up. I'm shaking, not due to exhaustion, but surprise and most likely mental strain. Blue Elixir is nothing short of miraculous when it comes to physically healing wounds, but that doesn't mean anything for the mind.

My mind is still convinced that the bone is sticking out of my leg and that I can't walk. Although my rational mind knows and can see otherwise, something deeper simply refuses to agree yet. I once asked Nathan about this and all he could say is that he doesn't understand the mind well enough to try and tinker with it. I was quickly reminded about the long lasting incident of "helpful" artificial intelligences launching mental assaults and killing the people they were linked to.

If I had known those stories before trying the boots on with Dac inside, I would've been much less inclined to do so.

One workaround for the impatient is to drink a near lethal amount of Blue Elixir. At that point, your body is so focused on not dying due to what's healing it; it forgets you were hurt in the first place. Again, I have no idea how it works. All I know is that it does. It's how I was able to keep moving after the big battle at Jinn's house where I first took down a warship. I also refused to drink Blue Elixir for a long while afterward and still refuse to drink that much in a single sitting to this day.

"Little help?" I ask John, muscles in my jaw and neck strained.

"Yeah, yeah," John says, popping up to his feet and helping me up. I lean heavily on him, unable to stand on my own yet. I test my leg out and find that, while it can in fact handle my weight, I still can't seem to walk on my own yet. Sometimes Blue Elixir really sucks.

You'll be fine in a day or two, Dac reminds me. He's been quiet for a while now, yet present in my thoughts.

It's like that sensation where you could be thinking about something like... flowers... while going through combat training, or practicing maneuvers on a Sky Bike, or even flying from point *A* to *B*. It's like that, but opposite. While I felt like I was consciously resting, I was talking with Dac quite a bit. I've done it plenty of times before, but it's always weird realizing that it's happened. I imagine it's what it must be like if I could suddenly communicate with my subconscious thoughts. I have done that to a degree with the AI realm, but I'm not counting that. Those experiences are about me taking active control of my subconscious as compared to talking with it. Total difference.

That's Dac and my best explanation, anyway. Truth is, we have no idea what the exact details are. He has been around for a long while, being the original prototype for the flying boots that Nathan developed. Even though he has been alive the entire time, he has been dormant. Apparently Dac didn't even activate until I put the boots on, and something kick started within him.

"How do we know we can trust you?" I hear somebody say, as I get closer to the mob of people. I'm going to use my super senses to divine that this isn't going well.

Good guess.

"We have done you no wrong," Nathan tries to argue.

"Neither have rattlesnakes. Doesn't mean I trust them," the same voice says.

"He's got a good point!" another voice adds. This is about to get really ugly. I would run over there and try to fix this, but I'm limping so bad that John has to half carry me right now.

"And there's blood on her hands!" a third brings up. From the exasperation of the isolated individuals that are familiar to me, I can tell this is a point that has been brought up multiple times already.

"It was a medical emergency," Sarah defends herself, annoyed at giving the explanation yet again. "Sam would've lost his leg if I didn't do anything."

"When Kendriath saw him, he didn't see no broken leg!" yet another person argues. Are they still using their character names? Is anybody taking this seriously?

Getting closer, I see that a lot of them *are* taking the matter to heart. Those willing to start an argument are the minority. There's a hard-set determination on the others that is the result of being slapped in the face with reality.

We're at war, and we will lose.

We don't have the numbers to take the New Power on. Not yet.

That's why we need their help. If we can get everybody willing to stand up to the New Power to fight with us, we can take them down. It won't cure all this world's ailments, but it's a massive first step. After these guys, we're apparently meeting with a portion of what the Water Nation can provide. Lastly, we're basically going to go door to door taking down factories and recruiting the employees. It's not a perfect plan, but while we're working down here, Gerund—current leader of the Ravens that nobody really listens to—is working the Sky Nation, and Kane and Eli are recruiting for the Water Nation. I know it sounds bad that we've essentially got only one person working each nation, but, under each person, more are helping.

Before me is the example of why this plan makes me nervous. Only a few people are outwardly arguing and unwilling to trust, but the others aren't doing anything to shut them up.

"That's mostly due to a miracle in a bottle," I shout,

but nobody can hear me.

"Stage?" John asks.

"Stage," I agree. We didn't construct a stage, there just happened to be one here. For a renaissance fair, they have more technology here than I think existed at the time. More indoor plumbing as well. They have a microphone and speaker system rigged up on a stage that is probably used for performances, or award ceremonies, or war talks. Not the kind of war talks going on now, but "war talks" nonetheless.

I can tell that John is not happy that we're moving at a crawl, but he's putting up with it.

"Do you think it would make more of an impact if you go up there with Dac?" he asks me. He's just trying to get out of carrying me.

What do you think? I ask Dac, my face going blank. John doesn't say anything, but keeps walking me towards the stage.

Sure, why not. It's not like a select few are ready to riot anyway. A seven-foot tall metal man couldn't hurt.

Instead of stopping and waiting for Dac to meet us, John and I keep moving slowly. When Dac does reach us, he and John carefully trade spots with each other.

"Take care of this idiot," he orders Dac, sounding concerned. I would like to think that the concern is for me, but it's more likely about his family.

"I promise I won't break him too bad," Dac says.

"Real funny, you two," I mention, tightening my jaw in pain. Stupid leg! You're mostly healed! Stop feeling like you're about to fall off!

Man up, Dac thinks to me. He has taken to talking out loud with me less and less. The past year after leaving the Water Nation, he would talk out of his body quite a bit, just because he could, but not so much anymore. *Too much work. Doesn't feel right.*

I can't say that I disagree. Talking out loud with Dac feels awkward and forced, other than when I accidentally shout to seemingly nobody. We just work better when it's all mental thoughts, I guess.

We mount the steps to get onto the stage, and I almost collapse from the way I put weight on my leg. Lovely. I can't even get up four steps!

As a work around, Dac picks me up. He legitimately grabs me around the waist and carries me up the stairs.

Not a word to anyone... ever.

No promises.

I limp across the stage, ending up behind the Royals before I put a hand on Sarah's shoulder to stop the arguing with a deaf crowd.

"Hi," I say to everybody, trying to get their attention. If it's not me they're looking at, Dac definitely has their attention. Seven-foot tall robots generally do that.

"See!" the same naysayer in the crowd shouts. "He doesn't even look hurt!" Mumbles and grumbles spread throughout the crowd gathered before us. Maybe me coming up here wasn't such a good idea.

"May I have the microphone?" I ask Sarah.

"Sure," she says aggressively. I hope she wasn't picked up by the microphone, or she is going to have even less favor.

"Yes, I am fine," I say, holding the microphone too close to my mouth. "I am now, anyway. As you can see though, my pant leg is completely shredded and soaked through with blood. I don't know how long ago the New Power's attack was at this point, but I got hurt. I was hurt really bad." I roll the microphone in my hand, trying to think of where I'm taking this speech. I really didn't plan on saying anything other than reassuring words that the Royals are trustworthy.

"Worse has happened," I say, digging myself into a

deeper hole. Why can't I just say to trust Sarah, even if she's mad, give her the mic, and exit stage left? "Lives were lost. I can't say I know names or numbers specifically, but I do know that people died."

You don't even know if that's true, Dac points out.

Do you? I ask him.

I know at least one person died, he tells me.

Well there you go. I took a guess that made sense.

Try not to gamble when you say things like 'I know people died.'

"Only reason I'm alive is because I drank this thing called Blue Elixir that's essentially a real life healing potion." There, use terminology that they are very familiar with. It's much easier than trying to explain exactly how it works. I don't even know the details, honestly. "I'm sure you all saw a rather spectacular crash of two of the enemy's ships, yes?" The mumbling and grumbling is more reluctant this time. "Well, that didn't happen on accident," I say. "I flew in to one of them and crashed it into the other. Something I highly recommend avoiding if at all possible."

"How can you fly?" somebody shouts.

"Ask me later," I say. "The short version is the consciousness of this robot," I point to Dac, "is in my boots, and the boots fly. No, we cannot get you a pair."

"Actually, that's the gist of it," Nathan mumbles. Then he starts going off about technical details that I ignore.

"Look, I've gotten off track. Public speaking isn't really my talent. I've been with these guys," I make a sweeping gesture at the Royals, "for close to a year now. While at times they may seem arrogant and annoying as all hell, they're good people. You can trust them with your life when it really matters. I'll spare you the gory details, but Sarah really did save me. The dried blood on her hands is mine."

140

When do you plan to make your actual point? Dac asks me. I take a deep breath. He's right. I should just say it.

"Trust us, please. We're trying to make things better across the Surface. This right here is just the start. Bring anybody willing to listen on board, destroy factories, and free the workers. As far as I'm aware, our plan is to basically cause so much trouble that the New Power can't ignore us. That's when we'll take them out. Just give us a shot." The assembly is entirely silent. There isn't even an awkward cough. No crickets, nothing. Just silence.

"A little faith can change the world," I say, before handing the microphone back to Sarah and limping away, not needing to give a queue to Dac that it's time to leave.

Chapter Fifteen

"I hate giving speeches," I say. Sure, I can handle talking to people. In front of a crowd, I can even do alright, but speeches?

"You did great," John tells me. "You just like complaining."

"Ugh," I grunt.

"All you're doing is proving my point."

"Stop talking."

"Stop being so cranky," he chides.

"Fine," I tell him. Just then, my stomach decides to growl obnoxiously loudly. My eyes widen in embarrassment, but John just laughs.

"So, that's why you're in such a bad mood," he says.

"Shut up," I tell him.

"Ever since we were kids, you would get cranky when you were hungry."

"I really want to punch you," I tell him.

"Come on," John says, wrapping an arm around my shoulders. "Let's go get you some food before you bite somebody's head off."

I do my human equivalent of growling at John before pointing in a direction and saying, "Food tents are normally over there."

John and Dac walk me over to the food tents where

everybody is absent but the guy running the funnel cake booth. He seems to live behind that cooker. That's probably why I eat way too many of them whenever I'm here. They're delicious though. Three isn't too many, is it?

"See, and now you're in a better mood," John says, taking a large chunk of my third funnel cake. We're sitting on an old wooden picnic table that has partially rotted through in places.

"About the same," I tell him, licking my fingers.

"At least you're not as cranky." Instead of responding, I pop a particularly sugarcoated piece of funnel cake in my mouth.

"I found you," somebody says from behind me. I turn around in my seat with my pointer finger in my mouth to lick off all the sugary goodness to find Jinn walking up.

"We weren't exactly hiding," I say, taking my finger out of my mouth.

"True enough," Jinn says, taking a seat next to me. "That was some speech you gave."

"It was nothing," I say. "I just didn't want another fight to break out while I can barely walk."

"You know it might help if you have some more Blue Elixir."

"No thanks," I tell him. Not a chance I'm having more of that stuff. I'll sleep it off over the next few days. "After multiple experiences where I end up with toxic levels of it in me, I'm not pushing it again. Not if I can help it."

"Whatever you say," Jinn says. He looks at the funnel cake, confused. "What is that?"

"Seriously?"

"Yes. I have never seen this before. I'm going to make the bold assumption that it's food?" Jinn asks, completely uncertain if he's right or wrong.

"Yes, it's food," I tell him.

"Do they not have funnel cake in the Sky Nation?" John asks him.

"Funnel... cake?" Jinn slowly repeats. Wow. They really don't have funnel cake up in the Sky Nation. They're really missing out on a good thing.

"Go on, try some," I offer, sliding the plate closer to Jinn.

"How?" Jinn asks. "Don't I need a funnel to eat it? I don't have any on hand."

"Is he serious?" John asks, incredulous.

"No, you don't need a funnel to eat it. Here," I take off a chunk that looks like it'll be good and hand it to him.

He looks at it the same way I know I've looked at foods only from the Sky Nation or Water Nation before shrugging and putting the whole thing in his mouth. He chokes on the powdered sugar and coughs. I slap his back to help him along, and hopefully put a stop to the coughing.

"It's good," he says, after he manages to swallow it.

"What're you guys doing?" I hear Rose call from behind me. Jinn and I turn around to look at her. Mark is with her. I'm going to guess he was looking for Jinn.

"Funnel cake," Jinn says, pointing to the plate in front of him. He wipes the tears from his face and tries to stop choking. His voice sounds rough due to the powder in his throat.

"Is that cake you're supposed to eat with a funnel?" Rose asks.

"Oh my God," John mutters, putting his head in his hands, elbows resting on the table. "They're a bunch of idiots." Jinn still has the faculties to smack him upside the head.

"Sit down," I tell them. I'm reluctant to give them each a bit seeing as the mass of my food is diminishing.

"You can try some of it."

Rose sits next to me, Mark across from Jinn. Both of their eyes are fixed on the food, as if it comes from an alien world. I sit back so that they can grab at it, but neither of them does.

"No, you don't actually need a funnel to eat it," I tell them. "You do this." I tear off a big chunk and hand it to Rose, who stuffs it into her mouth while I hand another piece to Mark. I hear Rose coughing on the powdered sugar before Mark even accepts his piece. By the time Mark is gagging, Rose reaches to the plate and takes another large bite.

"Hey," I say indignantly.

"Perks of having a boyfriend," she coughs. "Do you have any water?" She puts the next piece in her mouth and looks like it's pure bliss touching her tongue. She's careful not to inhale this time as she puts it in her mouth, and thus avoids the coughing that comes along with a sugarcoated throat.

"No," I tell her.

"I'll go get some," John offers, getting up to go purchase a couple bottles of water.

"They should put chocolate on this," Rose speculates as she reaches for a third bite. Inspired, Mark and Jinn also grab for chunks of their own. I'm just going to mark this cake off as a loss and call myself satisfied. There's not a chance of me getting another bite in with these three just now having their first.

"They do," I say, leaning back to avoid grasping hands.

"Well, why didn't you get it that way?" Rose asks.

"I don't like it that way," I tell her.

"Where's the funnel cake merchant?" Jinn asks. "I'll go get us some." I point him in the right direction, and he gets up to go buy more.

John gets back before Jinn with an impromptu t-shirt sling full of water bottles.

"Here we go," he says, spilling them over the table. Everyone snatches up their own bottle, and John sits back down. While Rose and Mark crack theirs open and drain the bottles, I open mine and just take sips. I've got this killer headache that I refuse to believe is due to sugar. Mark and Rose lick their fingers in anticipation of more funnel cake. When Jinn arrives with three more plates worth, balanced like a waiter would, I swear wild animals attack.

If I'm being honest, Rose and Mark attack, but it's frightening. Even Jinn joins in their enthusiasm. All three of them seem to disregard the fact that their food is still steaming hot and shovel it all into their mouths in less than a minute each. There is no way they're getting out of this without being ridiculously sick.

Are they even breathing? Dac asks.

I have no idea, I tell him. *I'm not even sure they're swallowing between bites.*

John looks on in horror before excusing himself. He leaves the table mumbling about something or another. I don't pay that much attention.

"Did you guys have a reason for finding me, other than eating?" I dare to ask.

"Yes," Jinn says, discovering that he forgot to get napkins. "We wanted to tell you that it's probably only going to be an hour more before we take off. Nathan said that we're making a stop for John to see his family?" Honestly, it's kind of funny watching Jinn lick his fingers like a little kid.

"Yeah," I say, glad that we will be leaving shortly. "John hasn't been home in just as long as I have. He's worried about his sister."

"He has a sister?" Rose asks.

"She's six years younger than him, not even ten years old," I say in confirmation.

"Wow," Rose says. "I never pictured John as an older brother. He always seemed like a younger child to me."

"I never thought of his family before," Mark admits. "Only reason I ever thought of yours," he points a bit of food at me, "is because I've met your dad. Can't say I like him very much."

"Can't say I do either," I tell them. It's quiet for a moment before a dreaded question is raised.

"What's it like?" Jinn asks carefully. "Being back."

Really? You have to ask this? I thought I'd made it perfectly clear before.

"Can't say I'm happy to be here," I start, "yet as I spend more time down here, as the horror and memory passes, it's like a fog moves on. It's not as bad as I thought it'd be."

"Not as bad?" Rose bursts. "You would've lost your leg earlier if not for luck and Blue Elixir."

"I never said that it's *good*. I just thought it was going to be worse is all. Before I met all of you, one of the things that I was most afraid of was getting this black bar." I turn my left wrist over in front of them so that they can see the solid black rectangle an inch tall by two inches wide. "This mark means that I'm no longer protected. Enforcers and honestly anyone who feels like it are allowed to use lethal force on me and kill me if it comes to that." The three of them look at me with concern in their eyes. I'd be hurt if they didn't.

"When I got the mark," I continue, "I just about dropped dead from fear and panic. Obviously, I'm still here. The guy that gave me this mark is a Raven. That's probably the only reason my heart didn't beat right out of my chest. He had a tattoo right here on his cheekbone." I point to the location on my face right below the corner of my eye.

"I didn't realize we had people down here," Jinn says.

"Neither did I," I say. "There's a good chance he has nothing to do with the Ravens, but I'm choosing to believe that he does. It makes me feel better."

"I'll have to ask Nathan and Gerund about this," Jinn says.

"Anyway," I say with the intention of continuing my story, "after everything that has happened lately: destroying the factory where I've spent most of my life," the knowledge of Gabriel's impending death, " and with crashing those transports, I realize it really doesn't matter. Them marking me doesn't take away any protection I had before. It doesn't make me any less of a person. I've been risking life and limb all my life. All this means is that they're probably going to fight back harder."

"That is an excellent way to look at it," Jinn says.

"When did you become such an optimist?" Mark asks me.

"I wouldn't call it optimism," I respond. "I'm just stating the truth of things. This black rectangle is just a tattoo to me now." It's going to take some time for me to get used to thinking of it as that and that alone, but this realization is a start. I think I function better with beginnings than endings. Leaving for the Sky Nation was a start. Now here at the end, I fall apart for a while. I'd be lost without the endless rolls of duct tape known as my friends. I mean that physically and psychologically. They've patched me together more often than I care to admit.

After a moment of awkward silence, I say, "Thank you."

"For what?" Jinn asks.

"For giving me the opportunity to know you guys. To

learn that my life is worth something. I'd always hoped…
but my thought was never reciprocated until I met all of
you. Even Arthur, in his infinite douchery, is a part of it. I
could never repay you guys for what you've done for
me."

Rose kisses me on the cheek, leaving a sugary
outline of her lips. "Thank you for letting us get to know
you, you Surface brat," she teases. She wipes at my cheek
to get the sugar off of it before grabbing my hand under
the table.

"It really has been our pleasure," Jinn adds.

"I don't know," Mark says, winding up for an awful
joke of some sort. "Before I met you, I still had both my
arms." Or maybe it's not a joke? "Eh, who needs two
arms anyway." Okay, so it is a joke… I think.

One of my least favorite parts about being back on
the Surface is the same thing that I hated about being in
the Water Nation.

The waiting.

Gone are the days when Jinn and I would train for a
seemingly theoretical battle to come. Everything we've
had to do since Steven attacked the Ravens in the Sky
Nation has had to be careful and political. Not being as
savvy in the art of politics as the Royals, they're
generally the ones to take care of it. Jinn has also done
some of the political work when it comes to issues
within the Ravens. Although Gerund is technically the
Ravens' leader, the vast majority look to Jinn for
guidance and instruction. He can easily overrule Gerund,
but typically doesn't care to.

Me, I just wait. I'm generally about as delicate as I
was when I was supporting the Royals not long ago. I'm
a hammer while those around me are needle-nose
pliers.

I haven't found a good way to cope with doing

nothing. I get antsy, and bored, and tired, yet hyper-alert all at the same time, and it hurts my brain to even consider how that's possible. To make matters worse, it always feels like I'm waiting for at least twice as long as it really is. When Jinn told me we would be waiting, the conversation ate up a few minutes, but then it turned more into idle chit-chat. My brain is wandering even now. It feels like it's been close to two thousand hours, so we should probably be going soon. I hope.

Please tell me it hasn't only been, like, five minutes? I beg Dac.

It has been more than five.

Six?

More.

Seven?

Stop asking. We should be going soon.

I harrumph and rest my chin on the noticeably sticky table. It is absolutely disgusting.

Rose runs her palm over my back in large circles. I am only slightly embarrassed to admit that it actually feels really good. I let myself get lost in it until she gets bored or tired and simply lays herself across my back. Now *this* is not the most comfortable position I've ever been in, but I don't ask her to move. Another thing I'll admit, but only to myself... and Dac...

Yup! He snaps in my head.

... is that I love it when she's near me. I love it when she's touching me. I love... her.

So why don't you tell her? Dac asks me.

I don't know, I whine. *It's weird.*

How is it weird? I'm not even truly human and I think you should tell her.

Do you really think this is appropriate right now?

No, but when are you ever? He has a point. I mull it over a moment before responding.

I don't want to.

Liar.

Stop it.

"No," I accidentally say out loud.

"Those two bicker so much you'd think they're an old married couple," Mark says to the table before directing his attention at Rose. "Are you sure your dad's okay with you dating a crazy person?" I bury my face in my elbow. I do not need to be cherry red right now, yet I am.

"Yes," she says, not sounding completely certain. Woo! Let's hear it for my self-esteem… "I like this crazy person." She kisses the part of my back her mouth is nearest to, and it sends a tingle racing through my spine that somehow reaches the top of my head and the tips of my toes.

"I love you guys," I mutter to the table.

What a wimp out, Dac judges.

"Was that one directed at us?" Mark asks. I can feel Jinn shrug next to me. Rose nuzzles me. That's weird.

It's sweet.

How would you know?

Because it is. Now shut up.

"Did I miss it?" I hear a panting John shout from behind me. Did he just run over here?

What did you do? I ask Dac, suspicious.

Oh nothing.

Spill it.

I sort of told John that you were going to tell Rose you love her.

YOU DID WHAT?

"I'm not doing it," I say for John's sake and to argue with Dac. Somehow, I manage not to shout it.

"Do what?" Rose asks. Of *course* she has to be the one to ask.

"Why not?" John asks in a whiney fashion. "Dac said you're thinking it anyway."

"Not another word," I threaten, getting an even brighter shade of red under the veil of my arm. The tips of my ears feel like they're about to burst into flame.

"Why not?" Dac asks. I guess he's right behind me.

"No," I tell him.

That's not an explanation.

"But—" John starts.

I silence him with an aggressive, "Shush."

"Why?" he tries again.

"I said no."

"Well that's not much of a reason," Jinn says.

See, I told you so, Dac taunts.

"Don't start with me," I warn both of them.

All eyes are on me, being the spectacle that I am at the moment. That's what I imagine. Seeing as I refuse to raise my head, I don't know for certain if their eyes are on me or not.

Don't worry, Dac says, *they are. Nobody but you, John, and I understand what's going on. Even Rose looks confused.* With his last sentence, a ten thousand pound weight lifts off my chest. I take in a deep breath, noting that Rose has moved off of me, and the stale air trapped by my arm somehow feels cleaner.

"What's going on over here?" Nathan asks, perplexed by the five people staring at me. "Is he alright?"

"He's fine," Dac says, before anybody confused can concern Nathan.

"Not when I'm done with him he won't be," John says, upset at my refusal to proclaim my feelings for Rose. What does he know anyway? Sure, he basically studies girls instead of thinking about things like... anything, but that doesn't mean he actually knows anything. Right?

"What do you want, Nathan?" I ask the table.

"I just wanted to let you guys know that we're ready to take off." The way he says it makes it sound like he's still confused.

"We'll be there in a minute," I say, noting just how muffled my voice is.

"Alright," Nathan says. "We should leave as soon as possible. Kane will be surfacing about the same time that we should get there, providing a short stop for Mr. Stevenson." When did he learn John's last name? "Once we all arrive, Kane says that his forces will want to go on the attack."

Suddenly, we're all very attentive.

Chapter
Sixteen

There's something about the threat of impending global warfare that gets people up and moving. In no time flat, all of us that are flying are back in the transport and we're in the air. I don't even remember all my motions in between getting up off that bench and looking out the window back at the shrinking camp. Arthur stayed behind. I'm fairly certain that he stayed for selfish reasons, seeing as he kept complaining about the shoddy quality of their swords and other weapons. When he found out that what they typically fight with are wooden counterparts, he nearly went on a killing spree. It was almost as bad as when Todd—I hate him—told Arthur to his face that his work was stupid, and ugly, and bad and... and... I probably made up some of those adjectives.

Instead of slaughtering the people we just got to agree to fight with us, he decided he would train them how, and I'm quoting him here, "not to be pansies and how to fight like real men would." He also commandeered their forge to make them some real weapons. For some reason, I feel utterly terrified for all the poor people back there. We didn't even leave them with any Blue Elixir to use in case of... no, not in case of, *when* Arthur decides to take things up a notch.

I watch the camp until it fades from sight, due both to distance and the angle the transport is at.

"Well, that got real, really fast," I mutter to myself, turning back around in my seat.

"Was it not 'real' when you decided it was a good idea to declare war?" I'm asked by Nathan, who just happened to be walking past me after leaving the cockpit.

"It was," I say, "but it didn't feel like it yet." I pause for a beat before asking, "Did he really say that he's ready to go on the offensive?" I don't know about anybody else, but I'm still having issues believing that.

"Yes," Nathan confirms. I was afraid he was going to say that. "Not a full frontal assault, but he's willing to listen to your plan on guerilla tactics and begin enacting them immediately. He said that he's bringing one of his highest commanding generals with him."

"The Water Nation has an army?" John asks.

"They do now," Nathan says. "They've had police, but never until now have they had a force like this. Once the New Power is dealt with, I doubt Kane will keep them around any longer. Technically, the Sky Nation doesn't have one either. I just keep some reserves that know how to fight in case anything domestically happens. I've never had to fear my brothers attacking us."

"And of course something happened," I say. Now that I think about it, the Surface itself doesn't have a traditional "army." It has an abundance of jerks, who I would very much like to push off a building, but no army. The first formal military group that's been established since Gabriel conquered the world was the New Power. Everything else has been in reaction to them.

Here's the question, could we say that the world would've continued in peace if not for the New Power?

Or are they the driving force for change, just as they've always wanted? I know that doesn't make sense, but the New Power are changing everything. By the end of this, by the demise of the New Power, the world will be different. Better, I hope.

Stop being so dramatic, Dac reminds me.

Who do you think this general of Kane's is? I ask him.

No idea, he tells me. *So far as I know, they don't even have police, but Nathan says otherwise.*

Would it be rude to ask him who this person is?

I doubt he knows.

Right. He probably would've told us who it is otherwise, right?

You sound incredibly uncertain.

I just managed to confuse myself.

Congratulations, Dac laughs at me.

Ugh, my head hurts. I take the next few minutes to try and sort out exactly what I just thought to myself to no avail. I don't bother asking Dac to help me try and clarify it because he's equally confused. Isn't he?

No. It's just more fun to watch you try and work it out. It's not even that hard.

I let out a sigh of exasperation and wriggle in my chair to get more comfortable. Behind me and across the center aisle, John is a ball of nervous energy. I'd say something to try and comfort him, but I know from personal experience that it won't do any good. The whole way I flew back to my parents' house, I was nervous about seeing them, and nothing could've made it any better.

The optimal situation was when I finally found my dad up in the Sky Nation. I didn't even know it was him until he was hugging me. Of course, then he turned out to be a controlling psychomaniac that I never need to see again, but that's beside the point.

Gabriel lets out a loud, wet, wheezing cough. All eyes shift to him, even John stills. A cough powerful enough to halt nervous energy. Now that's impressive. Unfortunately I know the cause of that cough. I would rather John still be bouncing around and Gabriel be healthy, but that's not up to me. He keeps coughing harder and harder, trying to catch his breath in between each fit. Gabriel produced a grey handkerchief at some point and is coughing into that. It's still hard to believe that, in all this time, no progress has been made in curing what he has.

What do you think the Elixirs are? Dac proposes. No, that... no... that makes too much sense...

Then why don't they work?

Who knows? I bet the Royals do. I would also bet that they don't know that it didn't work.

As Gabriel's coughing subsides, he dabs his mouth with the piece of fabric he's holding before quickly folding it and tucking it away in a pocket. I wonder how long he has been using a hanky like that. It's a bit random, I know, but he went through it mechanically, like it's nothing.

You're overanalyzing things again.

I'm just worried about him, okay.

You and me both. I think his kids are starting to suspect something's wrong. Look at Nathan and Sarah. I do. They're catching on to the fact that their dad is still fatally sick. I couldn't see it from my seat, but my guess is that there was some blood on that hanky he rapidly stashed away.

"Dad, are you doing okay?" Nathan asks.

"You're not getting sick, are you?" Sarah adds.

Gabriel softly chuckles at the irony.

"I am no worse than I have been for the past millennia," he tells them. Damn, that man is a wizard with words. Why doesn't he just tell them already though? No matter what happens, it's going to break their hearts.

I think he wants his last few days with his children to be happy, Dac observes. *Remember from the story book you read as a kid that the first time Gabriel was really sick—well I guess that's still this time, but whatever—he was bedridden and weak, and had to put up with the sorrow of everybody around him?*

Yes, I remember.

If I had to guess, I'd say he doesn't want that again. He has enjoyed far too much time with his family, too much love, to want to see them sad. He probably thinks it would be better if he just quietly died one day.

But that's... wrong.

Would you want any of us to know if you're dying? Dac asks me. I contemplate his question for a moment before coming up with a less than eloquent answer.

With the way things are going right now, you'll all probably get to see it happening, and I'll be screaming for Blue Elixir the whole time.

What happened to your earlier doubts about if this life was worth living? Dac asks, not accusingly, but with genuine curiosity.

Well, with death so close at hand, I can't help but look at Gabriel with sad eyes, *it puts things in perspective. I'm not done on this Earth yet, crappy as it is.*

That's the spirit.

"Are you sure?" Sarah keeps prying, trying to get an admonition of guilt out of her father.

"Yeah, Dad," Nathan adds, "you're not looking so good right now." As compared to how Gabriel always seemed fully in control of himself, I now notice that he looks physically exhausted. His posture is like that of a sleeping man, and his breathing labored.

"Don't you worry about me," Gabriel tries to reassure them. Any illusion he thinks he may have conjured up is shattered when he bursts into another fit of coughing. He gets his handkerchief out as fast as he can and covers the whole of his mouth. The coughing sounds even worse this time around than last. When he settles down, without removing the cloth from in front of his mouth, he says, "After we pick up your brother, I would very much like to make a stop in Seattle."

A memory springs forth in my mind. That's the place where his brother was... well, the last place he saw his brother all those years ago.

Sensing the finality of his statement, the remainder of the ride to John's house is a quiet one.

About five minutes out from John's house is when he really hits panic mode. A few of us are doing nothing more than trying to calm him down, stop his hyperventilating, anything. Coming so close, he's losing his mind due to a fabricated reality where his sister and parents loathe him, and won't welcome him back, and generally are almost exactly like my parents. I keep telling him that I know his parents, and that they would never do that to him, but he refuses to listen. Mark has a nice bruise forming above his eye where John managed to accidentally punch him in his panic. It takes three of us to pin him down so that he doesn't hurt himself or any of us any worse.

His reaction isn't anything like it was when we discovered that he's claustrophobic down in the Water Nation. That was a mild panic attack. This is full-blown freak out. He's breathing so sporadically that I'm worried he's going to pass out any second now.

"Can we go a little bit faster, please?" Rose shouts up to the cockpit with urgency. She's got John's arm pinned to an armrest with her knee on it. He has already knocked her off multiple times though. Her hair is sticking in weird angles and is poofy from her tumbles and knocking her head against the chairs in front of her.

Me? I'm straddling John so that he squirms a little bit less.

"It's okay, John, your family does *not* hate you," I try to say reassuringly. From the looks I get, it doesn't come out that way at all. At least, I think that's what that glare means. Rose gives me a furious gaze, informing me that she's ready to kill either John or me. John because of what he's doing, me because I'm aggressively shouting in his face at this point.

That 's reassuring, right?

"Not helping," Rose growls between grit teeth as if reading my mind.

Apparently I'm not the only *one who can do that,* Dac jokes.

Somehow, John actually manages to buck me off of him, sending me flipping over the armrest and bowling into Mark. Only having the one hand, Mark was putting all his weight on John. Seeing as I just knocked him over, and that he doesn't have a free hand to steady himself, John takes the moment of liberation to try and dislodge Rose as well. He's one angry girl away from freedom. What he plans on doing other than running in circles around the transport, I have no idea.

While John claws at an ever madder Rose and Mark, and I try to stand up, our apparent B-team mobilizes and takes our places on John, making sure to keep him down. He's lucky that Arthur isn't here. I'm pretty sure John would be knocked out in two seconds flat if he had to deal with this.

In retrospect, B-team is more effective, seeing as it's main component is a giant robot holding him down.

160

There is not much you can do when you have a truckload of metal pinning you down.

"Why didn't we think of that before?" I ask, helping Mark to his feet.

I forgot that I'm heavy, Dac confides in me.

Forgot that you were made of metal? I ask him.

More like forgot that I'm not your shoes, he responds. Oh, right.

During the last short portion of our ride, we all try to compose ourselves and ignore John's hysteria. For the most part, it works. Rose pulls out a mirror from some magical pocket dimension that all girls seem to have access to and rights her hair with determination. Really, I think she's trying to let off steam, and instead of hitting John, she's futzing with her hair because she doesn't want to give him a black eye right before he sees his family.

She's so considerate.

I feel the landing process due to the sudden drop in my stomach as we descend. Even a year later I'm still not used to it. You'd think that with how often I'm in the sky that a simple landing wouldn't unbalance me. I choose to blame my brain misconceiving it as a crash landing. I've had way too many of those for my own good.

During the descent, John inexplicably calms down. His face is wet from tears and his nose and mouth covered in snot. It's not exactly attractive, but we haven't exactly given him a chance to clean himself up.

"If I let you go, do not try to hit me," Dac warns him. "I am made of metal, and you will probably break your hand in the process."

John nods and gives a quiet, "Okay." Dac releases John. He waits for Dac to get clean and then goes to cleaning himself up with his sleeves and the bottom hem of his shirt.

It's a smooth landing, yet I can still feel the bounce of the landing gear while we settle into equilibrium. Looking out the window, I notice that we're conspicuously parked in the middle of the road.

"We probably should not stay here long," I hear the pilot tell Gabriel, to which Gabriel replies perfectly, "Just give the boy the time he needs."

Taking that as a sort of cue, I push myself out of my chair and half hover above John. "You ready?" I ask him.

He nods his head rapidly, not in a wide range, but quickly. "Yeah," he manages to get out before sucking some snot back into his nose.

John gets up a lot less quickly than I did and walks toward the front of the ship as if it's a funeral procession. Giving him space, I follow behind him. I notice Rose mouthing "good luck" at the two of us. She's no doubt still fuming over John throwing her around, but she knows the gravity of the situation.

Leaving the transport, John slows his steps further, trying to prolong climbing the three stairs up to his front door. I give him a little push on the small of his back using only my fingertips.

"Come on," I tell him. He walks ever so slightly faster, drawing in deeper breaths of air with each step. All I can say is that he better not pass out before we make it to the door.

Each step, even for me, feels like it crosses an endless chasm and that each moment we could be teetering on the edge and fall off. I see my own home superimposed over John's house. This is like knocking on my own door all over again, yet I know my own outcome. I suddenly start breathing just as hard as John is. It's like we just ran five miles and are about to drop dead from the exertion.

I stop dead in my tracks at the base of the stairs, but John, braver than me at the moment, continues to climb.

One step.

Two steps.

Three.

John stops at the small square landing right before his door, his heels partially hanging off the step. He teeters there a moment, threatening to topple over. I try to ready myself to catch him in case of emergency, but my precaution is unwarranted. John takes a single step forward so that he's right in front of his door.

Then he does something incredibly brave.

He reaches out a hand and knocks three times.

Nothing. John's hand falls back to his side as the door isn't immediately opened. We wait. Nothing. I almost suggest knocking again before we hear it.

Somebody is coming to answer the door.

Chapter
Seventeen

Breathe, Dac reminds me.

I take a deep breath in, not realizing that I was hold-ing my breath. My head clears a bit and the pounding in my temples subsides. How long was I holding my breath? I look at John and notice that he isn't moving; he's staring straight ahead at the door, listening to the approaching footsteps.

"Breathe," I relay Dac's message to him. He rapidly pushes out any air left in his lungs and sucks another in which he is again holding. It'll have to do for now because I hear the door unlatch. The knob turns and the door opens, revealing John's mom.

She looks up from the door, seeing John standing there and gasps, hand flying to cover her mouth. My mom did the same thing. Is that hand thing just a regular reaction?

I fear the worst, seeing the mirrored actions of our moms, but I should know better.

"Honey," she tries to yell over her shoulder, a barely audible whisper coming out. She clears her throat and tries again, managing to bark out, "Honey!" She never once takes her eyes off John. I don't say another word, choosing to watch the reunion and stay out of the way, silently supporting John. He hasn't managed to even get his mouth to move beyond his lower jaw bouncing up and down, the herald of incoming tears.

"Coming!" I hear John's dad call back from within the house. It's only a moment before he's also at the door.

John's parents look good together. They're younger than my parents. John's dad is taller than John, but not quite my height. His mom is shorter with dark hair. John has his dad's blond hair and his mom's nose. They're both scrawny, but lean. Nobody should have any doubt that these two are John's parents.

"Mom," John starts, looking at them, taking their presence in, "Dad."

Without another word or thought, his parents rush to embrace him, burying John in their arms, fighting with each other to get the better grip. Not surprisingly, in his case, John's dad acted faster and has him fully wrapped in, John's mom vying for space.

John reaches an arm out of his Dad's organic prison and grabs hold of his arm.

This is what a reunion should look like.

"John-John!" I hear a little pipsqueak shout at him. John's sister, Coral, comes rushing out of the house and barrels into John. The four of them look like they're about to fall down the stairs, so while my heart decides to skip a beat, I leap up the short stairs, bracing a foot on the top step and one on the bottom, and hold them up.

"Hi Mr. and Mrs. Stevenson," I grunt, pushing them back up. I doubt they even notice me or that I'm supporting most of their weight right now. "Maybe you guys should take this inside," I suggest. This, they appear to hear.

After reluctantly disengaging from the group hug, Mrs. Stevenson says, "Come in, come in. Oh, God," she waves her hand at her face, looking up as if it will help her not cry. Mr. Stevenson decides to be slightly less polite and practically drags John inside.

"Look! John-John look!" Coral tries to shout above her parents, pulling on her cheek. My best guess is she lost a tooth.

The noise level drops as they all disappear inside and I'm left out here.

Um, what now.

I don't want to intrude on their moment, but I also don't just want to leave John here. But is that what he wants? They did leave the door open. Maybe they want me following them inside. Or they just forgot and want to be left alone. I might as well just ask.

I take a step inside their house, somehow feeling like I'm trespassing on sacred ground, and close the door behind me.

"John?" I say, raising my voice a bit. Not getting a response, I decide to follow the sounds of life. Being as quiet as a can, I find them in John's room. His parents are going over everything in there while his sister tugs on his arm, still vying for his undivided attention.

His room is entirely unchanged. From the posters hanging off his wall with only 3 nails to his dirty kicked about shoes, it's all the same. The only exception is it looked like his family made his bed at some point. Knowing John, he never would've left it that way.

"John?" I say again from the doorway, deciding that walking in his room at this particular moment in time is where I draw my line. He turns around and looks at me, an expression of utter euphoria on his face. A spike of jealousy drives its way through my heart. A wave of bitterness comes over me, making me want to hate this moment, but I'm not quite able to.

"Do you want to stay here?" I ask him, keeping my voice level.

"Of course he's going to stay here," his mom

166

immediately says, clutching her baby boy to show that nothing, and she means nothing, is going to take him away again. She does realize that he *decided* to leave, right? That bit of bitterness almost moves my tongue to action when I see the look on John's face. He knows exactly what I mean.

"Is that… is that okay?" he asks me for permission. He's asking me for permission?

I almost tell him no out of my own spite, but what comes out of my mouth instead is, "Give me a call if you still want to be a part of everything. I'll see you when it's all over, hopefully before that."

My best—human—friend gives me his patented smile and says, "You bet."

I can't help but smile back as I say, "Bye Mr. and Mrs. Stevenson. Bye cutie."

"Bye bye, Sam!" Coral responds. From his parents, I get a mixed response. From his dad I get a look that says he's grateful for something… probably bringing his son back. From John's mom I get a look of pure scorn that tells me that she blames me for taking him away in the first place.

I raise a hand and flick open all five fingers as a way of waving goodbye before heading back to the front door. I don't wait to see any further reaction.

The smile falls from my face as I open the front door and close it behind me, rubbing a thumb under my eye.

Dammit. I don't remember it raining this much on the Surface…

Chapter
Eighteen

The walk from John's door to the transport feels much longer than I know it really is.

I've already filled them in, Dac tells me. *The rule is that you're only allowed to mope until we reach Kane.*

Fine. It's fair. I've spent more than enough time moping about. It's good that John is staying with his family. They're all happy *and* he's safe. His mom hates me now, but I can live with that. Spiteful mothers are apparently nothing new to me. The nice dad was a change though.

I climb back into the transport, somehow hearing the clack of me walking on the metal steps this time over the gentle yet present purr of the engine. The pilot was probably watching me because, the moment I cross the threshold into the transport, the steps start to rise behind me to seal us in.

I sway back and forth as I walk back to my seat, my upper body seeming too heavy for my muscles to keep upright. Passing everybody, I gratefully collapse in the chair I've been sitting in this whole time.

When looking down the aisle, I notice that most eyes are still on Gabriel. It's not an awkward stare off, but eyes are constantly shifting his direction. I only look long enough to find the object of everybody else's attention. Figures that it's still him. I have got to say, I don't really like riding around in these transports. It's so boring. I'd much rather be out there—*in the sky*—on a Sky Bike or flying with Dac. That's where my heart's really at, not this tin can. In fact, next flight I'm going to insist that I fly myself. That'll be considerably more interesting.

While staring at the back of the seat right in front of me, I notice Rose quickly glance back at me from her seat out of the corner of my eye. I don't think much of it until she gets out of her chair and starts walking back here. Is she really going to chew me out about letting John throw her around *now*? I was trying to hold him down, but he was freaking out and I didn't want to hurt him!

Rose plops herself into the chair next to me. She busies herself making herself comfortable while I continue trying to mentally write the script of the universe so that I can win an upcoming argument. I have near everything planned out. As soon as she talks about 'how could you let John throw me,' I'm going to bring up how I was thrown too. She has even fixed her hair—mostly—in the time that John and I were gone. She takes a deep breath, ready now to begin. Hold on, she's had more time to prepare. What if she already has counters to everything I'm going to say? I really don't want to hear a lecture right now. I ready my own breath so that I can argue the moment it starts.

"Are you okay?" is all she asks me. I let out my loud breath of air and look at her without much of a coherent thought in my head.

"Huh?" is all I can come up with.

"Are you okay?" she repeats. I scan the transport as we begin lifting off to see if anybody is looking at me. Nobody is looking at me, but I think the cat may be out of the bag. Gabriel isn't acting any differently though, so I bet he's refusing to talk about what's wrong. I don't want to do the same thing.

"I think so," comes out of my mouth.

Rose furrows her eyebrows and continues, "What do you mean by that?"

"I mean…" I start, trying to grasp how to best explain it. "I'm okay," I start with. Yeah, that's a good starting point. Now where to go from there? "but, I don't know. I, I really don't know. All I know is that I'm okay, just a little shaky."

How articulate.

"Go on," she prompts.

"I don't think I can," I tell her. "I really don't even know where I was going with that thought."

"No, what is it?" she says, trying to pull a description out of my head that I don't even have.

"I don't know," I tell her honestly. She shifts in her seat so that she's sitting on her hip and is looking straight at me. Her eyes twitch left and right, individually inspecting my eyes like she has a tendency to do.

"If you say so," she says, but not in a skeptical way. With our group one man smaller, we travel onward towards wherever Kane is. I forgot to ask. Hopefully it's close to where Gabriel wants to go.

Rose lays her head against my arm, not for her own support, but to offer her's to me in a silent way for me to deal with whatever issues I can't put into words.

Oh boy, where to begin, Dac plays.

Maybe I should start with the sarcastic jerk existing in my head.

You're kidding, right? Right?

I don't know, I tell him. *Sometimes silence is nice.*

You hated the silence when I was gone a year ago.

That was a year ago. Maybe my opinion has changed.
You're lying.
True, but were you scared?
Not in the slightest, I think Dac lies.
This conversation has been a joke, right? I ask him.
I think so, he tells me, apparently equally confused. I don't try and figure this one out. Sometimes it's better to leave things a mystery.

An hour later, we're all standing on a beach, still trying to stretch out the soreness generated by that ship. Well, when I say that we're all standing on the beach, that's a bit of a lie. At least one of us is a couple hundred feet above the beach. Okay, two of us for sure.

You see, it's like this. I had an idea, not exactly a good idea, but it seemed like a good idea at the time. While all the "mature adults" are down on the beach, waiting for Kane to arrive, I got the brilliant idea of trying to surf the transport.

The result of this idea is taking place in about three seconds.

I stand on top of the transport, bouncing up and down on my toes and shaking my hands out. This is probably a bad idea, but when has that stopped me before?

"You ready up there?" Rose shouts to me from the open transport hatch. Rose, the pilot, and Dac are all in there. The pilot for obvious reasons, Dac to be able to communicate efficiently with me, and Rose because she thought it would be fun. There is definitely a reason that I like her.

"Ready!" I shout down to her, holding my hair out of my face. I really need a haircut. There's already a good ocean breeze up here. The salty air somehow manages to taste good and entirely differently than it does anywhere else on the Surface or in the Sky Nation. I'm sure the same smell was here when we came to the ocean all those months ago, but I was too nervous about going to the Water Nation to really appreciate it.

Rose disappears back inside of the transport, and its side hatch slowly closes, the mechanics of it making more sound than I generally hear. I guess it makes more noise outside than in.

We're going to try to start smoothly, but you never know with these things, Dac tells me. I immediately crouch down and try to hold on to the top of the smooth craft. For some reason, I'm under the impression that perfect handholds will magically appear. Unfortunately, they don't.

Good luck, Dac says. *We're going in three.*

Two.

One.

True to his word, the pilot starts off smooth, slowly building in speed. This isn't so bad. I try to stand up and get to my feet. I can handle this. This isn't bad at all.

He only put it in drive.

I swallow audibly.

Before I can crouch back down to yet again try to find the imaginary handholds, we go shooting off. It's nowhere near as fast as when I took off with Dac for the very first time, but it still takes me by surprise. I go sliding back on the top of the transport, not having any sort of grip. I would try to run forwards, but I don't think that would help at all, it'd just be a futile effort.

Besides, if I fall off, I can just catch myself using my boots.

The wind pushes me back, stinging my face, creating hands behind me that grab, and drag, and pull. I can feel the grip wrap around my clothes and pull me back.

Mounted onto the rear of the top of the transport are

two tail wings stuck up in a *V* shape. I'm on my toes trying to grab for more traction when I throw my arms out and grab hold of the wings. I only manage to catch them with the very ends of my fingertips, and I don't think I can hold on long at all. My grip weakens, but I don't let my hands slip an inch. It doesn't take long for my hands to feel like they're going to be cut straight through. Personally, I like having my fingertips. That's personal opinion though.

I would probably break the transport before it broke me, Dac says. That's fantastic. Unfortunately for me, I'm fleshy and can potentially be sliced to ribbons by a sufficiently sharp piece of metal. *Do you want me to ask them to slow down?*

I try to tighten my grip on the wings in response. Considering how I'm barely holding on already, it's more like I wiggle my fingers as little as possible.

I thought so.

After another ten seconds of flight, I fully catch myself. We're not going so fast, I don't think. We didn't slow down, but I feel more used to it. I can't beat the wind, but now that I have my balance, maybe I'll be able to stand.

Ever so slowly and carefully, I uncurl my fingers and move my hands away from the wall. Not surprisingly, the wind doesn't suddenly get more intense. I'm standing! Without holding on to anything!

Carefully, I shuffle my feet until I'm again standing on the middle of the transport. The wind continues to threaten to lift me up off my feet, so I turn sideways in an effort to reduce the surface area for the wind to press against. It gets remarkably easier once I stand like I would on a Sky Rider, one of those flying boards. I haven't ridden one of those in such a long time.

"Alright, let's do this," I shout against the wind, but

knowing it'll get through to Dac. I'm ready to try and ride this thing like I would one of those boards—minus the dancing on buttons to get it to work.

A time gap lasting only long enough for Dac to communicate with the pilot passes, and we're moving faster. Come on, we can do more than just speed. Let's try for something challenging.

In answer to my challenge, the transport starts to lean to the left. I lean the opposite way to try and keep upright. It works initially, but the transport doesn't stop at slightly tilted, the whole thing is rolling.

"Oh crap," I mutter to myself, as I start to run around the circumference of the transport. I can't take too large of steps or, while disconnected from the ship, I would start to move backwards and be left behind, so my running is more like quickly taking obnoxiously large steps. Getting from the top of the transport to the side is easy, seeing as it's rounded off there. I'm extra careful not to step on a window though. Getting from the side to the bottom is more challenging. There's a hard transition due to the landing gear on the bottom, as well as the hard edge between the side and the bottom. I almost trip, but recover by stumbling a few steps.

Sort of.

I make the recovery. I don't trip and fall, but I notice something that I should probably be more concerned about. See, I'm where I am, and the transport is over there. I sort of, accidentally, fell off.

It's not like the cartoons where you only start falling once you look down, I'm plummeting instantly. Lucky for me, this isn't really a problem. As soon as I realize that I fell, I activate my boots. I go shooting off to the side, but I'm controlling my flight now. I bank hard and turn so that I'm facing the same way as the transport.

I turn up the speed to reach the transport. I'm

realizing just how fast that thing can move.

You do realize Rose told the pilot to race you, right?

I do now.

Are you going to let her win?

We'll see, I tell him. *Ask her where the finish line is.* I match my speed with that of the transport and fly right beside it to the point where I could look into its windows. I see Rose telling Dac something. She stops talking for a second and then looks out the window and blows me a kiss with a wink. I hope she doesn't think that's going to change that I'm going to win.

She says just try to keep up, Dac tells me.

Do you think you can add a bit more sass to it? It'd sound more accurate that way. I watch as he relays what I said back to Rose. From what I can see, she rolls her eyes and exasperatedly shakes her head. She looks over at me and sticks her tongue out.

There is no doubt in my mind that you two are perfect for each other, Dac says. *Your maturity level is about the same.* There's a pause before he goes on and asks, *So when are you going to tell her you love her?* My flight falters for a moment, and I plummet five feet before catching myself and returning to the window side. Dac's body doesn't move an inch, but I can hear him cracking up in my head.

I see Rose shouting something at the window. The look on her face isn't concern, but challenge.

Through his laugher, Dac manages to relay, *We're starting now. Good luck. In case you couldn't tell, I'm leaving out a couple of her more choice words.*

I have a couple choice words for you later.

Oh, just tell her already. She asked you out first, now you get to tell her your feelings. It's been close to a year already.

The transport picks up its pace, and I speed up as

well, making sure to stay next to the window where Rose scowls at me.

Why is my love life so important suddenly? I ask Dac, cheerfully waving at Rose, her frown deepening. The transport banks towards me, so I let my altitude dip and slide right under it to come up on the opposite side. Rose is still looking out the opposite window, trying to find me. Dac taps her on the shoulder and points my way. Oddly enough, she does not seem happy to see me. I flip onto my back so I'm flying with my stomach facing the sky above. I like it up here.

Because whenever you think about Rose, your stomach gets a little bubbly, and because you've spent enough time being sad.

But isn't right now just poor timing?

If there's anything I've learned from living in your head, it's that there's never a good time for you. It's just do it, or don't.

The transport picks up even more speed, and I have to flip back over to control my flight enough to keep up. This time they don't level out their speed, they keep going, which is fine by me. The concentration required to keep up is a more than sufficient excuse to not respond to Dac.

As we get faster and faster, the act of flying in a straight line is getting more difficult. My legs are shaking and trembling all over the place, controlled more by the boots than by my muscles.

Have you even flown this fast before? he asks me. My eyes are watering, buffed by the wind. Almost everything is blurry. I turn my head so that I'm more in a line and am now looking straight down at the water below. It helps with my eyes and control ever so slightly, but I know that I can't keep this up.

I can tell you that there is still yet more power

available, but that if you're struggling here—which is fair, considering you're the first person to even use flying boots—you probably won't be able to handle it.

Is it weird talking about yourself as if you're a separate object? I ask him, getting the thought out as I try and rein myself in. Only now do I bother to realize that it's freezing! The wind and wet mist feel like they're freezing the hairs on my arms. I'm sure that, if there wasn't so much moving air to dry me off, I might be dripping in sweat trying to hold my body the way it is.

It's not really, Dac says. *I more think of the boots as my original head, and that now, I'm more in your headspace and can branch out from there.* That's actually a little creepy to say the least. I mean, I don't mind, and I guess I've figured the same thing for the longest time, but still. *The boots are where I primarily reside, but I don't like to think of myself as solely existing in there. How would you like to think that your sword, for example, is as far as your existence extends?*

He's got a point there. I keep trying to speed up and manage a bit more for now. I'd keep trying to go faster, but there's a miracle.

Pilot has pushed our transport to as fast as it can go, and you've passed us. You win. Rose concedes, Dac lets me know. Oh, thank you. I cut the speed of the boots to something I'm more comfortable with and expect to keep flying. Not so much. With that drastic of a change, there's a sort of hiccup. Instead of an easy continued flight, it feels like I stop altogether and start to dip towards the water.

Realizing how weird my body is positioned, I cut power to the boots entirely. Well, I'm no longer accelerating that way, but I'm still heading towards the water. I rapidly position myself so that my feet are below me and their soles are pointed directly at the water before activating my boots again. I crank up the power to try and stop myself and manage to do so, just as my toes start to dip into the water. I attenuate the power so that I float here and catch my breath.

"Let's not do that again," I say to myself, but Dac has to add his own thoughts.

Agreed, he says.

It's a moment before a large object breaks the surface of the water and sends waves out in all directions. One of said waves slams into me and drenches me up to my chest. Even then comes some backsplash that hits my face. I blow out a heavy breath from my mouth to try and push water away and swipe a hand down my face.

"Lovely," I mutter to myself, gaining altitude to avoid another splash. From my new height, I take a brief moment to watch the remainder of Kane's submarine surface.

We should probably start heading back, I tell Dac, knowing he'll relay the thought.

I've already got them turning around, he says.

Chapter
Nineteen

It's a short flight back to shore. I could be back there ridiculously fast, but for now, I fly towards the half visible submarine. When I catch it, I match pace and follow it in until the sand prevents it from moving further. I don't bother waiting for it though, instead flying all the way back to shore. My friends look a bit like specks until I get closer. When I land on the sand, it blows in all directions, and I find myself two inches lower than everybody else. Oops.

"What happened up there?" Mark asks me. "Did Dac stop working?"

"More like user error," I tell him, walking out of my hole. It's not deep, but I don't like it.

I look back at the submarine and see that their smaller boat is already deployed and on its way over. A side of the submarine is opened up like a transport's hangar door. That's where the boat deployed.

"I wonder who's on the boat with Kane?" I ask aloud, trying to keep the conversation going, instead of awkwardly waiting here in silence.

"Maybe it's Bean," Sarah speculates. "He brings Bean everywhere with him, and it's a good thing too. I doubt Kane would be very good at getting anything done if not for Bean."

"Be nice to your brother," Gabriel reminds her.

"I am being nice," she says. "I'm not wrong though. Kane is always locked up in his shop and would forget to eat if Bean didn't remind him."

"I sincerely hope he doesn't have to be reminded to use the bathroom," Nathan adds.

"Don't think you're old enough that I won't spank the both of you," Gabriel says sternly, his fatherly side coming out at hearing one of his children being mocked by his others.

"We're all hundreds of years old, Dad," Nathan whines, to which Sarah seems to look embarrassed that her relative age was brought up. "I definitely think we're too old to be spanked anymore. That wasn't enjoyable when we were kids, and I'm sure it would be less so now."

"Then be nice," Gabriel smiles. Jinn, Mark, and I watch the exchange with bemused expressions on our faces. Watching a father scold his children is not a new sight, but it's always funny to see adults do it. That's only elevated when the adults happen to be Royals.

After a year, it's still weird how... normal they are, Dac says, taking the words right out of my thoughts.

So much for my attempt at having some casual conversation. After the threat of an impending spanking from a legend to another legend, that dreaded awkward silence settled over us pretty quickly. What I do to spend the couple unfortunate seconds it'll take Kane's landing party to get over here is dig a hole in the sand with the toe of my boot. It's hard work pretending not to be bothered by the situation. The others are doing just the same. Jinn extended his sword to be a couple inches long and is passing it in between his fingers, while Mark is scratching his stump more than he ever has before. It has been long enough that I've unfortunately gotten used to seeing him less one arm. It sucks that Blue Elixir can't somehow fix that, or that there isn't some other color that can heal missing limbs. I asked long ago if there's a kind that can do that, or if some sort of combination could do the trick. I had it explained to me multiple times that Blue Elixir is the only one with healing properties. The others may seem to heal a person to a degree, but it's all a sham. Those are more for temporary enhancements. I have no idea why Nathan and the scientists of the Sky Nation bothered to develop all those other colors, but they exist.

The Royals keep themselves busy by pensively looking out at the ocean. At least, that's what Sarah and Nathan do. Gabriel looks like he's about to burst out laughing. He's a rather strange old man.

Do you think he's senile? I ask Dac.

I would hope not, he responds, avoiding a direct answer.

It doesn't seem long, yet feels like forever, before the boat gets to the shore and we can see who's on board.

"I don't believe it," one of the passengers says as he climbs over the edge. "Is that you, Sam?" The passenger asking the question would be Eli. I saved his life when I was down in the Water Nation. There was this building on fire (yes, a building underwater was on fire), and he was a prisoner in there, and so I ended up saving him and a lot of other people at the same time. There is most definitely more to that story, but that's the short version. The accidental brand I gave myself across my palm throbs with phantom pain.

I shake my hand out as I take in what he looks like. Eli is wearing long pants and a short sleeve shirt with a sword belted to his hip. A leather guard of some sort covers his chest over his shirt, as well as leather wrapped all around his forearm from just below the wrist to not quite his elbows. It's a little weird seeing a full sized sword easily out like that. I've gotten far too accustomed to swords of the shrinking variety that can easily fit in one's pocket.

The most disturbing part of him, though, is when I look at his face. He has an eye patch covering his left eye. Sneaking out from under the eye patch is the ugly scar that runs from his hairline to his lip. I was there when he lost that eye and got the scar. It was not pretty. Actually, he might still have the eye. I don't remember. All I know for certain is that he can only see out of his right eye at this point. You would think something like that would slow him down, but judging by his smile, he seems to not even notice it anymore.

"Eli!" I shout to him. He walks down the beach and sticks out a hand to shake mine. I move to shake his back and he grabs me by the forearm, past my wrist. I do the same, going with the flow as he more shakes my arm than my hand. I look at his remaining eye and, as usual, am intrigued by the cloudiness that's characteristic of all those from the Water Nation. There are subtle differences between the people from the Sky Nation, Water Nation, and Surface, but they're most certainly there, and it goes to show how the different situations change us.

"It's good to see you," he tells me with his last shake of my arm.

"It's good to see you, too," I tell him, releasing his arm.

"How have these past months treated you?" Eli asks me. "Last time I saw you, you were in pretty bad shape."

"It's been a series of bad to worse," I tell him honestly. To many, it probably would seem weird how casually I can talk and exist with people older than me, but it really isn't a big deal at all. I've been dealing with people older than me all my life. Eli is closer than most, probably being in his late twenties, early thirties. I never bothered to ask him exactly how old he is. That detail never really seemed important.

"I'm doing alright now," I say, "for the most part anyway. How've you been?"

"More than a little busy," he laughs. "Ever since you signed me up to lead the Sprinters, I've been working with them and the Runners pretty much every day."

"You don't ever let them rest?" I ask him.

"They get weekends," he says. "I did say *pretty much* every day, not every day." They probably praise the weekends then. I can't help but stare at the eye patch, no matter how hard I try to focus on anything else. I know from when I was healing down in the Water Nation that Eli isn't offended by it, but it's still rude.

"Kane!" Nathan shouts from behind me, walking forward to embrace his brother who has traversed the beach. "How're you doing?" Nathan asks him.

"The sun still manages to hurt my eyes," Kane says. I look over and notice that he's wearing dark goggles to cover his eyes.

"Well, if you weren't on the bottom of the Ocean all the time, that wouldn't be a problem," Nathan says.

"Well, excuse me for actually staying with my people," Kane responds, taking that subtle jab.

"Do I need to remind both of you, again, what happens if you misbehave?" Gabriel says, walking up to his sons.

"No, Dad," Kane says, giving Gabriel a hug. "Did he have to warn you and Sarah earlier today?" Kane asks Nathan.

"He might've," Nathan says.

"Typical."

"Would both of you stop bickering long enough to

give me a hug?" Sarah asks, cutting in between the two of them and wrapping her arms around Kane once Gabriel lets go. "I like the new goggles," Sarah says, giving her brother a kiss on the cheek.

"Thank you," Kane says, as he tries to wipe his cheek where Sarah kissed him without being obvious, but Sarah catches him immediately and gives him a wink. "Why must you always do that when you know I hate it?"

"Because I like to," Sarah says, referring to kissing him on the cheek, "and because I know you hate it."

"Centuries of this," Kane complains.

Sarah purses her lips and simply says, "You really should be used to it by now then."

"I'm used to it," Kane informs her, "but that doesn't mean I like it."

"You're my little brother, so deal with it." Kane scowls as the rest of the landing party comes over to us. It's only two other people: somebody that I don't know with a sword on his hip, and Bean, Kane's personal assistant.

"Is everything well?" he asks Kane. I take a brief moment to notice that Bean has the same goggles on as Kane, completely dark.

"Other than my family being over affectionate, yes," Kane tells him.

"Zachary, take your hand off your sword," Eli says. I follow his gaze to the stranger and notice that he was tightly gripping the hilt of his weapon. Somebody doesn't trust us.

"Sorry, Commander," Zachary says to Eli. Commander?

"Is he..." I start to ask before Eli chooses to fill me in of his own accord.

"Zachary is one of my Sprinters that you created," Eli

says, lifting his eyebrows as if to say "thanks for that," but not in a happy way.

"Nice to meet you?" I say, somewhat cautiously. Zachary looks at Eli, his eyes squinted hard. I'm not sure if this is because he's suspicious or because the sun is hard on people from the Water Nation.

"Who is he?" Zachary asks Eli.

"This is Sam Cutter," Eli tells him. I'd thank him for not using my full name, but he continues, "and he's your superior. Sam is actually the founder of the Sprinters." Zachary snaps to attention facing me. He opens his eyes to what "normal" would be, despite it looking painful for him.

"Sir," he salutes me, a hand flying to his forehead. I open my mouth to say something, but close my lips hard.

"Oh, he shouldn't have said that," Mark says.

"What's going on?" Jinn asks him, having been paying more attention to Kane's conversation with the Royals than to me. Mark has told me time and time again that my conversations generally get more interesting than most people's, so he prefers to listen to mine.

"New guy just called Sam 'sir,'" Mark explains. Jinn's mouth opens slightly in understanding with a nod.

Be nice to him, Sam, Dac reminds me.

"I don't understand," Eli says, not catching what Mark said. "Is something wrong?"

"Well..." I say, ready to explain to yet another person my contempt of being called sir.

How nice is nice? I ask Dac to clarify.

Don't make any more enemies. I can do that.

"... I have this thing against being called 'sir,'" I say.

"M-my apologies, sir," Zachary immediately says, reflexively adding the "sir." I glare at him long enough for him to realize what he did.

"Sir, I didn't mean you any disrespect, it was an accident," he tries to fix it. I physically wince every time he says sir.

"Seriously?" I ask him.

"I really don't mean to offend you, sir," he says.

"Come on!

"Sir, I—" Zachary starts again before Eli cuts him off.

"Zachary, I think that'll be more than enough," Eli tells him, sticking an arm out as if to physically hold Zachary back.

"Yes, sir," he says, thankfully, to Eli.

"Sorry about that," Eli says to me. "I figured some good old fashioned discipline like from all the old stories would be beneficial."

"It's not from stories," I say, still trying to get my neck to not feel so kinked up thanks to hearing "sir" a couple of times. "That's how they do it on the Surface and the Sky Nation. I'm from here. That's sort of why I hate it."

"You hate the Surface because they say sir?"

"What? No. I hate sir because it's used down here, on the Surface," I say. I decide to elaborate, "where I was born," just in case he didn't get it.

"Understood," Eli says, running a hand over his chin.

"Lose any more fights to Sam?" Kane asks Nathan.

"I thought we agreed that we weren't ever going to talk about that again," Nathan grumbles.

"We did," Kane says, "but that was payback."

"Of course it was," Nathan says, his voice managing to get even lower.

Eli looks back at Zachary and says, "The beach is clear, go back and get the others to set up a camp."

"I informed you that my family and their champions would be guarding the beach," Kane says.

"And I told you that you should've waited on the

boat," Eli mumbles loud enough so that only Zachary and I can hear him. Zachary nods to Eli, letting him know that he will do as he was asked and jogs back to the small boat here on the beach.

"He takes his job a little too seriously," I say.

"Yeah, but it's a good thing," Eli responds. "Zachary was there when the New Power attacked Hub Fourteen. He lost a couple good friends and wanted to be sure to never have to go through that again."

"I know how that feels," I tell him. When I first started playing for keeps, the very first time I came up to the Sky Nation, I was shoved in this arena where I was forced to fight convicted prisoners. John was in there with me, and I lost it when he'd been hurt. Even more recently, there was a brief moment when I thought Jinn was killed. I don't like talking about that moment, or about the nickname I was given. This is also the same time that Mark managed to lose his arm and Eli his eye. That was not my best day.

"Hey, cheer up," Eli tells me, slapping my shoulder. "Nothing's going to happen. Everything will be fine."

"That'd be nice," I tell him, looking the way of the grouped Royals. I hear the transport with Rose and Dac in it descend behind me and know that momentarily we'll be heading over to Seattle. Gabriel's getting worse, and I feel like I'm one of the only ones who can see it, since he told me. "That'd be really nice."

Chapter Twenty

As predicted, it isn't long before we're up in the air again and on our way to Seattle. Kane is coming along with us, safely tucked away in the transport, while everyone else that came up with him is remaining on that beach, and just off it, to set up a camp for themselves. Theoretically, Kane will be returning there after this short family trip to Seattle to pay their Uncle Tie their respects. Kane doesn't look too happy to be in the transport flying through the sky. He's just as bad as John is with the claustrophobia.

The word is agoraphobia. It's either that or he's afraid specifically of flying, Dac tells me.

What's agoraphobia?

It means he's afraid of open spaces.

Oh. That would explain a lot, actually, considering that he's from the Water Nation.

Considering he was fine standing on the beach, it's more likely that he's simply afraid of flying, Dac says.

And I'd be willing to bet it's because of something Nathan did.

You'd win that bet.

Not me. I don't have any issues with flying. Keeping pace with the transport, I look in through one of the side windows to see the shaking Kane holding onto his arms so tight that he might cut off circulation. I notice Rose looking at me and wave at her. She turns to Dac and says something, giving him a message to relay to me.

Rose still wants to know why you're flying yourself instead of riding in here with the rest of us. I don't even need to think about this one.

Tell her it's because I couldn't take the sitting around anymore. It feels good to be able to fly and not have to hurt myself racing her. Would you also remind her that I won that race?

Dac tells her what I said. She looks understanding up until what I'm assuming is him adding the part about me winning.

She says to grow up already.

I stick my tongue out at her just to show exactly how mature I am. She does the same right back, but adds a ridiculous face to the mix. This is just one of the many reasons I like her.

Don't you mean looooooove her? Dac teases.

One day when you develop a crush on some lady program, I'm going to get you back for all of this.

Why would I ever need one when I'm living through your awkward teenagerness?

Is that a word? I ask him.

Why not? Fair point.

We've been flying for a while now. Dac gave me the heads up that we'll be landing soon about fifteen minutes ago. I'd look around me to try and figure out where we are, but all I see right now are trees. Honestly, I'm genuinely amazed that they haven't all been cut down to make way for factories. Maybe, just maybe, Logan has some sort of heart and, knowing that this is his uncle's final resting place, chose not to disturb it and to let it be a tree sanctuary of sorts. The world still needs to breathe, and trees are responsible for that.

So far as I'm aware, nobody has come up with artificial air yet. Even the Water Nation has entire hubs dedicated to vegetation.

Captain says that we're actually going to start landing now, Dac lets me know.

Thanks, I tell him. I follow the path of the transport as it banks to the side and starts to sink closer to the earth. Due to his passengers, the pilot doesn't try anything fancy, and they have a smooth landing in a nearby clearing. Even from here, I can see what we're here for. It's easy to spot things like giant statues as big as whatever that giant tower there is. I land on the side of the transport where the wall-sized ramp is currently lowering. Soon as I touch down, my legs are wobbling. Maybe flying myself all the way over here wasn't such a good idea.

Now you bother to consider that?

Once the ramp is fully down, Kane is the first off the transport, practically running to solid ground. He doesn't stop when he's off though, instead finding the nearest bush and unloading the contents of his stomach there. Not very dignified, but that confirms that he hates flying... and gets sick from it. The two of them are connected, but I'm not sure if he hates it because he gets sick, or gets sick because he hates it.

"Don't you just love flying?" Nathan says as he comes off the transport, a little too loudly to be a casual comment.

"Don't be so juvenile," Kane manages to say before another wave of nausea overtakes him and his head is back in the bush.

"Do you have to be mean to him every time he flies?" Sarah asks Nathan.

"What did I say?" he responds, like he doesn't know what she's talking about.

"Do you need some medicine, Kane?" Sarah shouts to him, safely staying out of range of the smell.

"Just give me a minute," he says, not bothering to remove his head from the bush. Behind Kane's back, Sarah scowls at Nathan. From what she said, it's not that they don't know that Kane gets sick, or that they did anything special to make it worse, but that she doesn't approve of Nathan teasing Kane for it. That'd be like if I made fun of John for being claustrophobic for years on end. Admittedly, I've been scared of anything with tentacles after meeting a giant squid that saved my life at least twice a while back. It's nowhere near as bad as John or Kane are, but tentacles and me don't get along now, with the exception of Billy, Kane's aforementioned giant squid, when he's a distance away.

Actually, maybe scared isn't the right way to put it. I just don't like it.

When Gabriel comes off of the transport, he's really not looking good. He has a hand pressed against the nearest wall to help support him. He's growing paler, to the point that he is recognizably sick. It can probably be written off as not feeling well from flying, or that his legs have fallen asleep, or a million other things, but I know it's not.

Nathan and Sarah are too busy looking at Kane to notice their dad. Sarah goes over and rubs Kane on the back, trying to make him feel better.

"There, there," she says affectionately. "Let it all out." Kane bobs a bit before even more contents of his stomach are evacuated. With how much he has thrown up, he'll probably start dry heaving soon. That'll be painful, but at least it'll mean that he's almost done.

Gabriel accepts assistance from both Jinn and Mark to get off the transport. He wraps an arm around either of their shoulders, and the two of them get an arm around Gabriel for the extra support. "Would you please take me over to my brother's statue?" he asks of them. I don't hear the response due to Jinn and Mark saying it more quietly. I'm already straining my ears to hear Gabriel.

The engine of the transport cuts out entirely, letting us know that it has been shut off and that we will, at the very least, be spending a night or two here. Rose and Dac are the last off the transport, with the exception of the pilot, who is doing post-flight checks. Rose comes over to me while Dac moves his body off to the side and stands there, frozen.

I figure it's best to keep a guard here at the transport, just in case anybody decides they want to be brave and try to steal a flying machine, Dac explains.

Good plan, I tell him.

"How was flying?" Rose asks me once she's by my side.

"It felt nice," I tell her, offering a smile.

"Tired?"

"Maybe a little," I give her. Really, I'd be happy with going to bed, especially considering that it's relatively dark out and that we've been traveling for a good long time, but I don't want to say that. Looking over at Kane, I jerk my chin at him and say, "At least I'm not in as bad of shape as he is."

Rose's eyes soften as she looks at him and says, "Oh, poor Kane."

"How was he holding up when you guys were in flight?" I ask her.

"I wouldn't know," she says. "Since *somebody* wasn't onboard to talk to," that sounds really accusing, "I read a book instead."

"Was it any good?" I ask her.

"Excellent, actually," she says. "Still would've

appreciated getting to talk to you more."

"You could've talked to me through Dac," I tell her.

Keep me out of this, he warns.

"I didn't want to talk through Dac," she says. "Besides, it doesn't transfer very well when I try to do this." Rose lifts up on her toes and kisses me, and I suddenly feel invincible, yet pathetically weak all at the same time. She pulls away nice and slowly, giving me the opportunity to chase after her lips and make the kiss last longer, an opportunity I don't squander.

She giggles through the kiss and smiles to the point where I'm more kissing her teeth than anything. I love that she's smiling, but I feel weird over here. Punctuating the process with one quick, final peck, Rose wraps her arms around my neck and pulls her lips away from mine. She looks at me, incredibly beautiful, with dreamy eyes, and I'm sure I look back in some sort of a daze.

I told you it'd be a good idea to keep me out of this, Dac says, cutting in on the moment. *Can I have one of those?* he asks, teasing me further. I throw my head back and halfway grunt, halfway laugh.

"And that," Rose says, unwrapping her arms from around my neck, "is payback." With that, she pushes me back lightly, applying all the pressure to my chest.

"Wait, what?" I ask her, entirely confused.

"What Dac just said?" she clarifies, assuming that Dac had spoken to me. "We worked that bit out while we were landing. Well, I worked it out, and he was my accomplice."

Why would you do that? I ask him.

I don't mind helping her with this stuff until you tell her that you love her, he responds. From how cheerful he sounds, I'm sure he would be willing to pull this on me, even if I had already told Rose that I l—lo—luh—lub her... Ah, forget it.

Would you give it up already? I ask him.

Oh no, he says. *This is way too much fun.*

A closed-lipped smile plasters itself on Rose's face as she bounces her eyebrows and says, "Oh yeah, we're going to have fun with this one." I pause for a moment, looking at her confused before a flashing red warning light starts to go off in my head.

"You told her!?" I half shout out loud, not thinking to keep it contained to my thoughts.

Um, no, Dac says. *But you basically just did. Congratulations, and you're welcome. Good luck!* Oh you have got to be kidding me.

"Tell me what?" Rose asks, genuinely confused.

"Hm?" I ask, buying myself a second to think of an answer to cover my ass. "Oh, nothing, nothing. Just a, uh, thing between Dac and me," I say, realizing how lame that sounds as soon as it leaves my lips. Well, when I have a grand total of one second to think of something that sounds reasonable as an explanation for screaming "you told her", that's about the best I've got.

Rose raises an eyebrow, openly expressing her disbelief, "Right," she says, drawing out the word to show me even further that she's not buying it.

"Um," I start, again looking for an excuse, "we—we should go catch up with Gabriel and them," I point somewhere over my shoulder, not sure if that's the right direction at all. It shouldn't be hard to find them. Just look up and walk towards the giant statue, no big deal.

"Right," I continue. This plan is working, right? If I keep moving, she won't have a chance to ask. "I'm going to go, uh," I look back to find the statue and accurately point at it, "that way now. I'll see you guys over there." I don't want to look like I'm running, but I'm walking away so quickly that I might as well be.

194

When I look back over my shoulder, I see that Sarah has walked up right next to Rose and she says, "Men," in a disapproving manner. It's a very recognizable tone. It's the same exact pattern any woman uses when expressing her disbelief in the stupidity in the entire male species.

"More like boys," Rose corrects her, using the same tone.

"Did I ever mention how much I like you?" Sarah says, putting a hand on Rose's shoulder and leading her forward towards Tie's statue.

Further behind them, I hear Nathan say, "I will never understand women," right before Kane begins dry heaving.

In the corner of my mind, I hear two different tones. One is the buzz of Dac being disappointed in me, and the other is Dac cracking up at how lame I am and the lack of grace I wielded to get out of that situation.

Chapter Twenty-One

The only thing more pathetic than running away from your girlfriend? Never slowing down the entire time. From the moment I left the transport until I practically run into Jinn, Gabriel, and Mark, I never slow my step one tiny bit.

Only after I basically mow over a man that's a couple centuries old, a man with only one arm, and a man who's intestines are organized differently than most people, do I stop and really take in what's before me. No, I don't mean how screwed up my friends and I are. I'm talking about the statue. I thought it was impressive from a distance, but I had no idea.

"Wow," automatically comes to my lips without my prior consent.

"I wanted to be sure that more people than just me would remember him," Gabriel explains, looking up at the flawlessly carved version of his younger brother.

"It's beautiful," Jinn says.

"Thank you," Gabriel responds. "I wish I could say I had a hand in its fabrication, but I merely commissioned it."

"That's good enough," Mark says. All of us are looking up at the statue, taking in the detail of the carving. The most fascinating detail: he's smiling.

Instead of a serious looking statue like most others I've ever seen, Gabriel had his brother look happy. The smile doesn't even look creepy.

"If this is here," I say, not looking away from the statue, "then why are you guys only storybook characters down here on the Surface?" I know the question is probably incredibly rude, but I'm genuinely curious. Since going to the Sky Nation and getting to experience the rest of the world, the evidence of the Royal's existence is everywhere. I don't even understand how *I* didn't manage to pick up on it before. No, not the Royals as a whole. Logan is enough evidence that they exist, and he's evidence most—including myself—wish would go away. The real question is, "How do they not know about you, Gabriel?"

"That is a question I often wonder myself," he says.

Rose, Sarah, Kane—who's still looking a little green, but better than before—and Nathan show up, respectfully quiet, unlike myself. They remember that this is actually a memorial. This is somebody's grave. And here I was, running away from a girl and being obnoxious. Oops.

"Hi, Uncle Tie," Nathan says to the statue. The normally airy king seems tame now. That's a weird thought. Last time he got this quiet was when I fought him in the tunnels of the Water Nation. He was louder when I was saving him from a collapsing tower in the Water Nation, even. Perhaps it's something about being humbled that keeps him quiet.

"Dad, what are we doing here?" Kane asks. Gabriel doesn't take his eyes off the statue as he responds.

"I merely wanted to pay my respects. It's been so long since I've come by to see my brother."

"Is now really the appropriate time?" Kane asks. *Kane*, of all people. This is coming from the guy that only recently has stopped asking me if he can dissect me to see why Dac isn't trying to take over my body, or to figure out how people from the Surface are biologically different from those from the Water Nation or the Sky Nation. My favorite moment is definitely when he asked if he could pluck out one of my eyeballs to see how the pigmentation is different, and what that means.

Kane's not the most tactful person I've ever met. He's frighteningly smart, but he doesn't handle people very well.

"Oh yes," Gabriel says. "I do think that now is the perfect time for me to stop by for a little chat."

"Dad, it's late," Nathan says. "Maybe this should wait until tomorrow." Nathan knows it's not that late. We all know it's not that late, but at this point, it's blatantly obvious that Gabriel isn't doing that well. His breathing is labored, and he can't even stand on his own.

"Yes," he says, looking away from the statue, "yes of course. Let's have some dinner first though."

Nathan sighs before saying, "Sure."

"Sarah," Gabriel says, "would you please lead the way to the cabins? As you can probably tell, I'm a tad sluggish today."

"Of course," she says, the concern for her father obvious. He's even admitting that he's at the end of his rope. Well, no, he's admitting that he's moving slowly. I'm taking that in the most morbid way possible thanks to what he told me a few days back. I'm sure that his family has to be catching on that *something* is going on though. They've known him all their lives. They've seen him at what was essentially his best, and that's not this. They have to notice that there's a difference, right? It's not really a deterioration that can be easily attributed to age when the person it's affecting is as close to immortal as anybody is going to get. The only ones who're going to live longer are his kids, and the only reason for that is because they don't have a terminal disease.

"It's this way," Sarah says. She starts walking and looks incredibly solemn. Her arms are wrapped around her stomach, and I notice that she's tightly holding on to her shirt. That's not the look of somebody comfortable with this situation.

She leads us on in silence, Gabriel, Jinn, and Mark trailing behind so that they can go the pace Gabriel requires.

The cabins are quaint. They're small log cabins of the likes I have never seen before. Considering that I've also never seen trees that are this big or healthy, that's not too hard to believe. There are three of them all in a row. Sarah turns into one of them, climbing the two steps to get to the door, and we follow. I stay outside a bit longer to look at them. Rose doesn't say anything as she walks past me, reasonably still angry that I ran away from her. What a bonehead move. I can't believe that I'm that stupid.

I can, Dac says.

Is there some way you can momentarily take over my mouth to just get it over with and tell her for me? I ask him.

I don't even want to try that, Dac says.

That's probably a good idea, actually, I agree.

"What do you want to eat, Dad?" Sarah shouts, coming back out of the cabin when everybody but Jinn, Gabriel, Mark, and me are the only ones yet to enter. "We don't have any food here, so I'll have to grab something from the transport."

"How about something delicious?" Gabriel says after a moment to ponder the question.

"I guess I'll pick something," Sarah says, sauntering past us, back in the direction of the transport. Honestly,

I wasn't sure it was that direction, so I'm going to guess that's where they typically park whenever they come here to visit.

"Would you set me in one of those chairs?" Gabriel asks Mark and Jinn, gesturing to a line of chairs that sit in front of the cabins, but out of the way of the doors.

"Sure," Jinn says, on top of Mark saying "Can do." They ease him into the nearest chair where Gabriel lets out a gentle sigh of relief.

"Is there anything we can get you?" Jinn asks, sounding more concerned than the Royals do regarding the state that Gabriel is in.

"A Coke would be nice," Gabriel says, a soft smile lighting up his face. "There should still be a couple in the refrigerator, if you would bring me all of them." I can practically hear the old man chuckle that I know is waiting somewhere in there. Gabriel doesn't act his age, but he sure has the wise old man laugh down pat.

"It'd be my pleasure," Jinn says with the tiniest of bows. Having casual conversation with Gabriel for a year hasn't totally rid Jinn of his over-dedication to the Royals, but it has dampened it from all out gestures to being respectful. I see nothing wrong with that. Jinn and Mark head inside, and I move to follow them when Gabriel stops me.

"Eh," he croaks to get my attention before adding, "Sit with me a spell, would you?"

I put my foot back on the ground and give him a half-hearted, closed-lip smile before I say, "Sure."

I lower myself into the chair next to him. I can't say it's comfortable sitting here due to the situation, but I also can't deny that the forest is beautiful.

"Move that table in front of us," Gabriel says, pointing to a small table that's no bigger than one foot on all sides that sits to my right. I grab it and move it in front of us as he asks. Gabriel doesn't say anything else until Jinn and Mark come back out, Jinn with his arms full of red cans and Mark carrying a glass in his hand. "Thank you very much," Gabriel says with his kindest smile.

"Any time," Jinn says, giving Gabriel a sad smile. Jinn's a smart guy, he probably figured out what's going on by now. I'd be genuinely amazed if any of us are yet to figure it out. Jinn and Mark are respectful of Gabriel's space and head back inside.

"You can have one if you like," Gabriel says, reaching for a can and trying to pop it open.

I watch him struggle for a moment before offering, "Here," and take the can from him to open it.

I easily pop it open and pick up the glass to pour it in for Gabriel, but he says, "No, I want to drink it out of the can. It's been ages since I've had it out of the can." I can't help but laugh at the childishness of the comment and of the childishness of his delivery. No matter how old he is, he still has that inner child that wants to do things his way. I hand him back the can and he says, "Thank you. It's a tad embarrassing that I can't open one myself anymore."

"It's really not a problem," I tell him. It wasn't. All I did was open a can for a dying man. It's not like I came up with any words of comfort or encouragement. I repeat my previous thought: How am I this stupid?

Gabriel takes a long sip before letting out a satisfied sigh. He doesn't say another word until Sarah comes back around, Dac's body helping her carry food from the transport to where it makes sense a kitchen would be.

"You really shouldn't drink so many of those," she says, always being her father's caretaker.

"Oh, let your old dad enjoy himself a little bit," he jokes with her. She gives him a disapproving look, knowing that there's no real way she can prevent him from drinking every soda placed before him.

"You better drink some of those so that he doesn't have it all," she tells me. Automatically, I grab a can, open it, and take a sip, if not only to appease Sarah. I already managed to get on the girl's bad side. If drinking a few sodas is enough to begin to rectify that, then I will gladly drink a few. I don't want to take them away from Gabriel though.

"Good boy," Sarah says, at full volume. In more of a mumble while walking away, she adds, "You may manage to get yourself out of the doghouse yet, lover boy." I choke on my drink and spit out everything that's in my mouth, luckily avoiding the table full of more drinks. Sarah laughs as she enters the cabin, knowing full well that I heard her, heard that she knows exactly how I feel about Rose. The last thing she muses to herself is, "Boys," before disappearing in the cabin.

"Is something the matter?" Gabriel asks me, referring to Sarah's reaction just there.

"No, it's nothing," I say, trying to bury the thought.

"Are you sure? It sounds to me like you and Rose are having some issues."

"Really, it's fine," I tell him. Gabriel leans back in his chair and closes his eyes to take a deep breath.

"You know," he starts, "I too had issues expressing my emotions." Again, I almost choke on my soda. Is this family determined to kill me within the hour? Gabriel chuckles softly at my reaction before continuing, "I have been fortunate enough to live long enough to get past that part of my life. I would say that love is not something that can truly be understood in a mere one hundred years." And that's if you're lucky. The life expectancy here on the Surface isn't quite as long.

"I have experienced multiple life times, seen the world age and die and be born again a thousand times, and for the longest time, love is what escaped my sight. I always *thought* I understood it."

"What didn't you understand?" I ask him, rudely cutting him off without thinking.

"To explain that," Gabriel says, "we would have to re-discover the formula that has prolonged my death thus far." Prolonged death, not extended life.

You noticed that too, did you?

Unfortunately, yes.

Gabriel continues, not knowing of my mental slip, "Even explaining it would take too long, but I do have a condensed version."

"How many years would that take to learn?" I ask him.

"Only a minute," he responds, knowing exactly what I was going to say. "But here's the catch. It will take me a moment to tell you, but a lifetime for you to truly understand."

"What do you mean by that?"

"Oh, you'll see when you're old and grey like me," Gabriel says, closing his eyes.

"Unfortunately, I don't think I'm going to last that long," I say.

"Did you just call me old?" Gabriel jokingly asks. At least, I think it's jokingly. I hope it is.

"Um, maybe accidentally?"

"Oh, youth," he says wistfully. "More than five hundred years of being a young man, and I still miss it." I sit quietly, not knowing how to respond to that. I'm barely sixteen, and I have to say that being young sucks. Nobody will take me seriously, no matter how much more I know or can do than them. The only ones that ever listen to me are those that know me. I mean, I'm sitting here talking with Gabriel, *the* King of the World, and he isn't treating me like a lessor. Why can't *regular* adults do that?

Sarah comes back outside, more time having passed than I originally thought, with a plate in either hand. She gives them to Gabriel and me. Sitting on the plate are sandwiches stuffed to the brim... and a pickle!

"Thank you," Gabriel says, as he accepts the plate.

"Thank you very much," I echo, taking mine.

"Sure," Sarah says. "Are you two going to come in, or are you eating out here like a bunch of weirdos?"

"We'll come in in a minute," Gabriel says, deciding for me.

"Ok then," Sarah says. Her eyebrows sink a millimeter when she squats down to be eye level and asks Gabriel, "Are you okay?" She puts a hand on her dad's knee, going for some kind of connection.

"Don't you worry about me," Gabriel says, not missing a beat and flashing her a smile. "I'm not going anywhere."

Liar.

"Okay," Sarah says, a look of resignation coming across her face as she rubs Gabriel's knee. "I love you, Dad."

"I love you too, Sweetie," he says. Sarah gets up from her crouched position and gives Gabriel a kiss on the cheek, one that he returns, before she returns inside the cabin.

They're talking about you guys in here, Dac says. Oh yeah, that's right. His body is still in there.

What are they saying about us? I ask him out of curiosity.

They're catching on that something's wrong with Gabriel, and they're wondering why you're his confident.

Honestly, I tell him, *I'm wondering that myself.*

"Go on," Gabriel says to me somewhat enthusiastically, "Dig in. I love these sandwiches." He picks up the pickle first, though, and takes a big bite out of it, "And these are my favorite pickles."

I do as he says and start eating my food. I only manage to take a few bites before Gabriel remembers his promise to come inside. I leave the food out here on the table before helping Gabriel up out of his chair. Dac opens the door to the cabin and helps me get Gabriel to an available chair at the head of a table, with his children surrounding him. When I go back outside to get the plates, Dac comes with me, except he doesn't return inside. Dac goes back to guarding the transport, even though most of his attention is with me. Even whenever he doesn't say anything, with all his fluctuating between primarily focusing on the body and focusing on me, I've gotten used to what he feels like when he's around or not.

The meal is actually pleasant, regardless of the aura that lingers with Gabriel's demise around the corner. Only Dac and I know for sure what's going on, but as Dac said, everybody knows that something is up. Rose somehow manages not to say a word to me all throughout dinner, which is disappointing. The pilot of Gabriel's transport is at the table with us, and the thought comes to mind that I never bothered to ask his name. I don't think I meant to never ask, it just managed to slip my mind. At one point, I casually slip the question into the small talk that everybody is making.

With a giggle and a smile that reveals the bread sticking out from between his teeth, he says, "Tom. My name's Tom Long."

"Nice to meet you, Tom," I tell him. "I'm Sam. Sorry I never asked what your name is before this." Tom swallows the food in his mouth before responding.

"It's alright," he says. "Most people never think to ask the name of a transport pilot. It's always nice when somebody thinks to ask me, even if they do forget it five minutes later."

"Well, I may have to ask you again," I tell him, "but I promise I'll do my best to remember your name," I tell him.

"I appreciate that," Tom says, looking at the pickle he's trying to pick up instead of me.

After the overall nice dinner, everybody is tired enough to decide it's time to call it a day. Everybody splits up between the three cabins to find enough beds for us. I don't know what happens next because as soon as my head hits the pillow, I'm asleep.

No dreams come to me, and it's bliss. Well, dreams come, but not *those* dreams. For once, I don't have to hear the New Power bickering about me and can get a peaceful night of sleep.

Wouldn't that be nice?

I'm only in a shallow sleep. I'm out, but not really resting. I can't say if I'm close to getting a deeper sleep or not when Dac speaks up.

Sam, he says gently, as if shaking me awake instead of shouting at me to get up like he would if we were under attack. *Wake up. You should probably go outside.*

Chapter
Twenty-Two

What is it? I ask him, grumpy that I didn't get a full
night's worth of sleep, or even more than an hour worth.
I look at the closest clock and see that it's a very
unfortunate one in the morning. I feel like I haven't had
an opportunity to get a decent night's worth of sleep for
a year, even though it hasn't been anywhere near a year
since we came back down to the Surface.

Just come outside, Dac prompts again.

"Fine," I whisper, not feeling like saying it in my mind
is satisfactory to express my distaste at being awake
right now. There's a chill in the air, so I drag the warm
blanket off the bed and wrap it around my shoulders
like a cloak while I sluggishly get dressed. It takes a
surmountable effort to think straight after being woken
up in the middle of the night with some mystery
mission assigned to you where the only instruction is to
go outside where it's *cold.*

I have enough presence of mind to choose to grab a
clean shirt and jeans, as well as find one of the jackets I
have from up in the Sky Nation where the wind during
the winter is nothing to joke about. Sure there's the sun
always shining that helps keep us warm, but that wind
can be a killer. Only reason I even packed it with me is
because, well, it's the middle of winter. It's December for

crying out loud. I'm allowed to get cold!

Who does Dac think he is calling me outside right now? Seattle is a chilly place apparently, and it doesn't feel anything like it does up in the Sky Nation because it's so overcast that the sun is never able to help warm us up.

When tying my shoes, I almost fall flat on my face due to my currently absent sense of balance. I look around me, guilty of breaking the silence, in hopes that nobody wakes up. The only sound of life is somebody—I'm betting Mark—snoring painfully loudly. Well, now I couldn't get back to sleep even if Dac would allow me.

I mumble and grumble to myself quiet enough so that hopefully nobody can hear—which is not that hard considering the volume of the snoring—all the way until I get outside. Once I open the door, the cold air slaps me, and immediately I'm shivering. Even with my jacket and the blanket, it's pretty cold.

I close the door, my nose starting to sting, and basically let gravity do all the work as I "walk" down the stairs. I bundle more of the blanket up in my fingers and pull it tighter around me in hopes that it will fight off the weather.

Waiting outside for me is Dac, who I have waking nightmares about touching right now. If it's this cold normally, I don't want anything to do with the cold metal of his body.

"What is it?" I ask him, the cold waking me up quickly.

"Follow me," he says, and starts walking off into the trees. I reach into my pocket to ready my sword, my hand leaving the warmth of the blanket for a brief moment.

You won't need that, Dac says in my mind.

"If it's not something that I'd need my sword for, why do I need to be awake and freezing right now?" I ask him.

Be quiet, he tells me as we start to get into the trees. He stops walking and I keep going right past him, confident that he would lead me. *Just head towards the statue,* he tells me.

I don't much feel like arguing at this point, and so I walk.

You're going the wrong way, Dac says, helping me correct my course whenever I get lost. For how little I'm walking, I get lost surprisingly easy.

How difficult is it for you to go in a straight line? Dac criticizes me.

Apparently very much so, I tell him. At long last, when I come up to where the statue is, the smiling face of Tie towering over me, I notice why Dac sent me out here. He's sitting on the ground, legs crossed, head bowed with a thick blanket covering him.

"Gabriel?" I say aloud to get his attention. He jumps a little bit, not expecting anybody to be out here but him.

"Ah, Sam," he says, slowly turning his head to see me. "What're you doing up so late?"

"I could ask you the same question," I say, walking closer to the ancient man sitting on the cold damp grass.

"I asked you first," Gabriel counters, sounding like a kid. I take a second to think before answering.

"I have a feeling that my answer depends on whatever you're about to say. Dac woke me up and brought me out here," I tell him.

"You have a nosy friend, there," Gabriel comments.

"He's in my head twenty-four hours a day and knows every little detail of what has happened in my life. He's even listening right now."

True, he mentions.

"So yes, he's nosy," I continue, ignoring Dac for the moment, "but I've gotten used to it. It's just life. And from the looks of it, he was right to have me come out here," I give Gabriel a pointed look so that he knows that I know that something's up. More so than usual anyway. He gives me an innocent chuckle, one that a little kid would give when a parent has caught them in the world's most obvious hiding spot.

"Care to sit?" he asks me, patting the grass next to him. Not really, it's cold and wet.

"Sure," I say, making sure that my blanket is fanned out enough to protect me from the dampness of the grass.

I sit down, and Gabriel doesn't say anything. The sound of his breathing is dominant, most animals asleep at this time of night.

The cold tries to creep its way past my blanket, partially being successful in its endeavor. Beneath the makeshift cloak, I rub my hands over my arms to try and generate some heat from the friction. It works to a degree, but a space heater would be even more effective. I'll take what I've got though.

"Of all the things I've seen in this world, there's still more yet I wonder about," Gabriel says out of the blue. "I've never had the privilege to see many things. I'm not complaining, though," he says, tapping my shoulder. "I've seen more than my fair share during my time on our little planet."

"Gabriel—" I start to speak, but he stops me.

"You don't need to say it," he says. "I know that tonight is my last night with you all." Hm, I don't remember somebody putting an entire platform made of lead in my stomach. "I didn't want to spend my last moments trapped inside."

"Do... do you want me to leave?" I ask him. Do I want

him to tell me to leave? Honestly, I don't know if I'd be more relieved or depressed if I could leave. I don't want to watch somebody die, but I also don't want to leave him alone.

"That's up to you," Gabriel tells me, flashing a smile that doesn't reflect the state of his health whatsoever. If I had to guess the age and state of this man solely off of his face right now, in this exact snapshot, I would guess a healthy man that's early into his sixties, maybe seventies. Not a man about to die that's old enough to have seen fairy tales when they were reality.

"I- I'll stay," I say, looking away from him. Why am I looking away? If he only has so long, shouldn't I be looking at him? I'm down to hours, maybe minutes with the man, and I can't even look at him! What's wrong with me!?

"To tell you the truth," Gabriel says after a solid thirty seconds of my self-loathing passes, "I was terrified I'd have to do this alone." That's enough of a trigger that I'm able to look at the man. "I'm well aware that when I do pass that nobody will be coming with me, but I don't have to be alone while I wait."

"Well then, why would you say it's my choice?" I ask him in something as close to resembling an even tone as I can manage. "More than that, you've got your whole family in there. They'd gladly be out here with you until the very end."

"I said it's your choice because I don't want to force you to wait for the end with a very old man." He says "very" in a way that I know he's trying to be funny, but really I don't think anything can make me laugh right now. "And I didn't want my family out here because I'd prefer them to remember me as I was."

"You don't look any different."

"Well, thank you," Gabriel tells me, "but I know that's

not true. I'm weakening, and everybody knows it. I don't know what will happen to me at the end. For all I know, I may turn to dust the moment my heart ceases to beat."

"Don't worry," I say. "If that happens, I'll be sure to collect you before you can spread too far." Somehow the old coot manages another smile and ruffles my hair.

"I appreciate that, Sam." When Gabriel drops his hand, he takes in a deep breath through his nose, "I love the smell of cold air."

I try and get a whiff of it, but find it difficult to inhale through my nose at all.

"I can't really breathe right now," I tell him.

"Ah," he says. "Well, let me tell you then. It's clean and sharp. It feels like it almost hurts, but in a good way. It's like a purification of a sort."

"You got that all from one breath of air?"

"No, from a lifetime of observations," he tells me.

"Gabriel?" I say, somehow determined to say something that I really don't want to.

"Yes?" he responds innocently, not detecting the distress in my voice.

"How are you able to talk about the air right now? You and I both know that you don't get another sunrise."

"Now, that's not true," he tells me. Wait...

"You- you're not dying?" I ask, hope forming.

"No, I will most certainly leave this world," he says, crushing that small glimmer of hope. "I'm going to fight for at least one more sunrise though. I would always try to wake up in time to watch the sunrise with Tie and Lilly. Tie was naturally an early riser, and Lilly thought it was one of the most beautiful things that she has ever seen in her whole life."

"Who's Lilly?" I ask him. That's a name I haven't heard before.

"Now there's a story I'd be happy to tell," Gabriel

212

says. "Lilly is Sarah's mother."

"Just Sarah's?" I ask him.

"Correct," he tells me. "My boys are from another woman, but Sarah is Lilly's daughter. I see so much of Lilly in her that it's remarkable."

"Tell me about her," I say, realizing that I'm starting to cry a little bit. I wipe my thumb over my eyes, hoping for now that that'll be enough to keep any tears away.

"Sarah's mother was the first woman I ever loved. She was my greatest friend during the war all those years ago. It was her, Tie, and me against the world." That's one hell of an opener.

"You remember how I was telling you that, when the war first started, Tie and I fled up to Chicago, right?"

"Yes, I remember," I tell him.

"That's where I first met her. She hated me when we first met. I almost got myself shot a couple times."

"What did you do?" I ask him. Gabriel doesn't seem like the kind of guy to get in that dangerous of a situation.

"I don't know, she never told me," he says. "When I asked her years later, she didn't remember either. All I know is, like I said, she didn't much like me when we first met."

"What changed?" I ask.

"How long of a story do you want?" he asks me.

"Maybe not too long."

"The extremely abbreviated version, then," he says, smiling. "What changed is that she fell in love with me."

"Aren't you being a little conceited?"

"Perhaps a bit," Gabriel jokes. "Along with that, my situation was probably similar to how that lovely young lady, Rose, fell in love with you." If I was eating or drinking anything I'd probably choke to death. As it is now, I somehow manage to choke on my partially frozen saliva. I manage to speak harshly after my bout of coughing subsides.

"She what?" I ask in a raspy voice.

"Can you really not tell?" Gabriel asks me.

"Since when is this about me?"

"Oh, Sam," Gabriel says, rubbing my back with a gloved hand. Gloves, those would've been smart with the cold. "Women are one of this world's greatest mysteries. It's taken me hundreds of years to retrospectively understand them."

"I guess that means that I don't stand a chance," I say, trying to keep the conversation light. Regardless of the fact that my face is wet right now, I don't want these last moments with Gabriel to be sad. Well, too sad.

"Want to know a secret?"

"Sure."

"You don't have to understand women to know you love them. You just need to understand one." I look up from the grass between my feet and see Gabriel smiling down at me. "It's fairly simple to see how much you care for Rose."

Pay attention to this, Dac cuts in. *It's really important to know every word he says. I'm recording it all just in case you're not listening, though.*

Why don't I feel like he's doing that in good will?

"Have you told her yet?" Gabriel asks me.

"I haven't known how," I say miserably. This really isn't what I imagined we would be talking about.

"Ah," Gabriel says. "That's a complicated question now, isn't it? How does one communicate their thoughts, and feelings, and emotions, and very essence to another person? Take this as you will, but in my experience, and in my experience as a father, I've learned a bit in my years."

"Go for it," I say, inviting him to keep talking.

214

"The best and only way to go about it doesn't involve any sort of special plot. If you care about someone, anyone—a girl, a friend, a family member—you should tell them as soon as you know the feeling yourself."

There is quite literally nothing I can say to follow that up.

"Again, take it with a grain of salt. I never was very good at following my own advice."

"I'll think about it," I tell him, unable to come up with anything better.

"You found yourself a patient woman," Gabriel continues, not willing to leave my love life alone, "but don't make her wait forever. It's been close to a year and she's known how she felt about you for most of that time." She... she what?

"How do you know that?" I ask Gabriel, needing that answer about a minute ago.

"I'm observant," Gabriel says. I laugh. It's ridiculous enough that it makes sense. Gabriel laughs too, either pleased that he got me to perk up, or just finding the situation humorous.

"How are you able to talk to me about something like this right now?" I ask him, cleaning the snow from my nose by wiping with my thumb and pointer finger.

"Now that's an easy one," he says. "You may not completely realize this yet, but each individual person culminates their own experiences, knowledge, and essentially their own reality. Each person develops his or her own perception. I want to share a bit of mine before I pass."

"I suppose that makes sense," I admit.

"Indeed it does," Gabriel says with a smile. "What does the world look like from your eyes, Sam? Look around us and tell me what you see, hear, feel in this exact moment." He sweeps his hand across the air while he talks. I take a breath to think for a moment on the question.

"Well, I see a lot of trees," I say.

"What kind of trees?" Gabriel asks me.

"I don't know," I say, frustrated by the question, "the tall kind with leaves. We never had all too many where I grew up and none that looked like these."

"Describe them to me."

"Which? These trees, or the ones from my home-town?"

"These ones right here."

"I don't know," I say again, "they're tall, but I know that I can fly over them. The bark looks like a bunch of rough little mountains circling all around it—"

"Go on," Gabriel prompts.

"From down here, I can't really see the branches all that well, but I know that there is a web of woodwork up there that's naturally grown that way. On the branches are more leaves of varying shades of green than I care to count, and... and I don't know. Why does it matter?"

"Keep going," Gabriel asks. "I'm quite enjoying this."

"I—I really don't know, Gabriel!" I snap at him. "I've been trying to maintain my composure, but you want me to talk about trees, and I just can't do that!"

Good job shouting at the dying guy, Sam. Real smooth.

But he was getting annoying! How is he able to be so calm right now and expect me to be able to have any analytical thought at all?

I don't know, but since he *is* the one that's dying, maybe you should try to humor him?

I have had no part of this conversation, Dac says. *You're crazy talking to yourself.*

After the last echoes of my outburst die out and silence has fully reclaimed the night, even then Gabriel doesn't respond. He waits even longer before saying anything.

"I understand your frustrations," Gabriel says. That's it? That's all he's going to give me? You have got to be kidding me.

That's when he continues, "It has been ages since I've been able to see the world anew with young, albeit jaded, eyes. I just wanted to remember what it was like."

Now I feel like the biggest ass on the whole planet.

There's worse out there, but yelling at an old, dying guy is a pretty low blow.

"I'm sorry," I tell him, quieter than before.

"That's quite alright," he assures me. "Anger is a perfectly natural reaction to the situation I've put you in."

"It's not okay," I say.

"Of course it is," Gabriel says comfortingly. "You more than most have a reason to be angry. You were dealt an awful lot in life, and I wish there was something I could've done about that."

"It's not your fault," I tell him. Great, now I've guilt tripped the dying guy. I'm on a roll today, aren't I?

"I know," Gabriel says. There's a pause before he speaks again as he contemplates what to say, "Sam," he starts, "would you do me a favor?"

"Anything."

"Would you call me Grandpa?" Gabriel finishes. What? I thought he never wanted me to call him that, or anything even remotely like it? And I mean, he's not even close to my grandpa if you really want to get down to technicalities. He's the dad of my great-great-great-great-great-great-great-great—oh forget it—grandma. The blood between us is barely existent it's so diluted.

And yet, hanging around my neck is the cold necklace proving that we're related. I reach up and grab my necklace, feeling the texture of the green gem and of the metal wings beneath my fingers.

"Sure, Grandpa," I say. Although it makes no sense, who am I to deny a dying man anything? Especially a dying man that I've insulted time and time again. Gabriel smiles at me like he just won every lottery at the same time, and found the most beautiful natural location on earth, and is getting to see one of his children after a long absence.

"Tell me a story about a happy time," Gabriel next requests.

"Um, okay," I say, somehow maintaining my composure, but just barely. As I prepare my story, I hear the crackling of paper next to me. "Well, when I first went up to the Sky Nation, it wasn't exactly the best introduction, considering that I was thrown into a warzone right off the bat after being imprisoned, but that's not what I'm thinking about." I rub my palms together not only for warmth, but as if to more fully rejuvenate the memories.

"After Mark and Jinn rescued me, they took me back to Jinn's house. At first it was all extremely weird. Nobody back home would do anything like that. Anyway, shortly after moving there, Jinn started to teach me how to fly. He had me try a jetpack first, but I wasn't very good with that, and I somehow managed to burn myself really badly and nearly killed myself, that resulted with me in a mini coma. Still, that's not the part I'm focusing on. It's what happened during it and also right after. Those were the first times I ever flew, poorly with the jetpack, and then with Dac. It's also when I met him for the first time in general. He and I took to the sky, and it's something like I've never experienced before. It was life changing. I loved every single moment of it and, for the longest time, loathed the thought of being stuck on the ground. Everything about going to the Sky Nation became a new opportunity, and feelings of oppression that have developed due to living down here started to fade."

"Life got better," I continue. "Not only the quality of life overall, but my mental state. A fog sort of lifted with the new freedoms I was granted. From up there, everything looked so beautiful, and down here could seem like a bad dream at times." I smile despite myself and the tears on my face. "Have you ever experienced something like that?" I ask Gabriel. I give him a moment to think, but he doesn't respond.

"Gabriel?" I ask again, prompting him to speak. I look over at him and notice that he's leaning against the tree next to him, eyes closed, and a content smile on his face.

"Gabriel?" I ask one last time, my voice cracking. I raise a hand trembling so hard it hurts and put a finger under his nose.

Nothing.

A sob wretches itself from my throat, and all the crying I've been trying to avoid while talking to him breaks loose. He's gone. He had me tell him one stupid story so that I wouldn't notice it happening. I basically told him his last bedtime story ever, as stupid as that is. He didn't even get to that stupid sunrise he wanted! WHY!? He couldn't have even made it through one more night just for that!?

I don't care that the sound of my crying and distress fills the night, disturbing all other life.

I stand witness to the death of an immortal.

Chapter Twenty-Three

I don't move all night. I'm out there, sitting next to the empty shell that was Gabriel. I loudly cry until I throw up and, even after that, I shake until I can't feel the cold anymore. Why? Why did this have to happen? He was supposed to be immortal, right? Immortals don't die!

At some point in my hysteria, Dac works his way over to where we are and sits down next to me. I would cry on his shoulder, but it's above my head, and my tears would probably freeze my face to his body.

It's okay, Dac tries to comfort me. There isn't much anybody can do for another when a life is lost. There's nothing that we can do for Gabriel.

The moon overhead doesn't care, the fleeing animals don't care, the trees don't care, the giant freaking statue doesn't care. He was here. I'm still sitting next to him *right now*, and yet I know it's not him. I know he's gone and that's just the shell he left behind. At least he was wrong about one thing. He's not dust. Not yet anyway.

I barely manage to turn my head enough to look at him. Although he still has that content look on his face, it's fading. Not the smile, not even the love of his long, long life that's evident through his features, but the man himself. He's withering.

Maybe he wasn't wrong about the dust thing.

"How long have I been out here... alone?" I ask Dac, my voice cracking.

"Near two hours," he tells me evenly, trying not to crack my mental state further. Seems like he's been doing a lot of that lately.

Thank you for being my best friend, I tell him, disregarding my original intention for the moment. *I know in the start, things were weird and that it's not perfect now, but thank you. John's been my best friend for such a long time, and then you come along and there's more to it and...*

Sam, Dac says warmly, *I get it. You're my friend too. Not because you're the first person to hear me, but because you also never thought of me as a tool. Within the first ten minutes we met, you gave me a name. My entire existence waiting to connect with somebody, I've been letters: D.A.C.P, but from the first moment we spoke, you've called me Dac. I've identified myself with a name. I'm not a serial number; I'm not an acronym; I'm Dac. You did that for me. You treated me as an equal, never as a lessor. You're the greatest friend anybody can ask for, and the greatest man I've ever had the pleasure to meet.*

Can I ask you something awkward? I ask Dac, ready to open a can of worms probably better left closed.

I already know what you're going to ask, but sure.

Did you ever consider taking me over, or killing me?

In the beginning, yes, Dac admits. *Centuries of darkness and loneliness are not something I can handle well. One of the only ways to end it is to connect with someone. With you.* Dac's body shifts as if rolling its shoulders, even though Dac wouldn't really feel it. *The only sure way to make sure not to return to that darkness is to stay connected. For most of those like me, taking a host completely is the best solution because, at the end of that cycle, we too cease to exist. Killing a host outright would return us to darkness.*

So why didn't you? I ask again. *Take me over, I mean.*

"I was briefly ready to," Dac says out loud. "But then I saw you, saw you as a whole and saw your heart. I would've been going off assumptions, but you asked me my name. It confused me, and then you promised to do something as ridiculous for me as find me a body, find me a way to continue to exist. I didn't want you to disappear. I didn't want to trap you in the darkness I had. I would've preferred to return myself than to do that to you."

"So basically, the reason I'm alive right now to wish I was dead is because I asked you what your name is?" I ask him.

"No," Dac says. "We're both here because we're connected, because you're a good person."

"Maybe I shouldn't have asked," I try to laugh, but I can't even force myself to chuckle. "It's disconcerting knowing just how close I came to... that."

"You've seen the darkness," Dac tells me.

"I have?" I ask him, confused, and also not totally caring.

"Yes. Do you remember when Armando was running you around the AI world, and you saw what was outside the house you created?" Do I ever. Even in a time like this, that endless expanse of nothingness. Not even nothingness. It's a mess of clouds that are only lit by the streaks of color shot through it. Beautiful, but threatening.

That's it, Dac says, seeing the images I'm conjuring forth.

"I wouldn't want to be there," I admit.

"Especially not after seeing the outside world."

I look around me, everywhere but at Gabriel. I'd

rather see anything right now. Only now am I able to see what Gabriel wanted me to not two hours ago. Two hours? How have I managed to be sitting here for that long?

The trees around me aren't just bark and leaves. They're life. They're a magnificent energy keeping the world afloat, and the creatures that inhabit it breathing. The trees themselves are home to animals who've fled because of my wailing. For all I know, their roots may all connect deep beneath the ground to form one massive organism guarding over the planet as a whole, overseeing the lives of every one of us. It's amazing. It's beautiful. It's more than I've ever thought to see before in the wasteland that was my home street. There's a life here that I've never felt on the Surface before, even in the presence of such a death and such an absence, there's a resilience in that.

"Are you mad that I thought that originally?" Dac asks me.

"No," I tell him honestly. "I'm still here, so how could I be mad?"

"I knew you'd say that," Dac says.

"I knew you would," I respond. I pause for a moment, trying—and failing—to take in a deep breath of cold air and feel what Gabriel was talking about, to see my world in a different way. That crazy old man managed to open my eyes further, even at the very end. After another long expanse, I finally get around to saying what I was thinking originally.

"We should wake everybody up... They deserve to know and see him before he withers away."

"Do you want me to go get them?" Dac asks.

"Please," I say weakly. "I can't even force myself to get up right now."

"I'll be back then," Dac says, standing up. Before he

starts to leave, though, he adds a final thought. "I really am sorry I ever even considered putting you in a place like that, ever getting rid of you for my own selfish gain." He sounds genuinely apologetic and ashamed of himself. "When we were separated for a day, when Arthur installed a fragment of me in this body, well, I didn't much like it."

"I can't say I much enjoyed the feeling either," I admit. His body starts to walk away, but he still speaks with me.

Don't' be too hard on yourself, Dac says, now in my mind. *What happened to Gabriel isn't your fault. He's known that the time has been coming.*

Sure, I say, knowing what he says is right, but still feel guilty as the only person he confided in at the end. Why me? Why did he warn me, and not one of his first children? He didn't tell Nathan, Sarah, Kane, or... Logan. I don't much like one of those four, but they're all his children.

I bury my head in my hands, trying to find a semblance of composure after exhausting all the spare water in my body and turning out the contents of my stomach multiple times. No matter how many times I think I've accepted it, this can't be happening. Gabriel is *The King*, the man who conquered the whole world round and founded the three kingdoms. He really is just a fairy tale character now. He was real, he *is* real, but he's not around anymore.

Is the old story even true? I haven't read it in years. I don't remember.

What am I supposed to do? He's fading fast, and I have no idea what he would want to be done with his ashy remains. What would he want me to do in his stead?

You know what he wants you to do, Dac reminds me. I

don't know what his progress is with getting the others, but he still talks to me. *When he first told you this was happening, he asked something of you.* I rack my brain for the memory and find it, repressed as it is.

He asked me to save his son. To do good.

I can do that.

At least, I can try.

In the semi-stillness created by me wrestling with myself, I hear a twig snap behind me. All too soon I won't be the only one having to deal with this information.

"Sam, is that you?" I hear someone ask. Sarah. Oh god, I shouldn't have had Dac bring them here. I should've warned them somehow. Maybe I should hide the body so they don't have to see it. That's what Gabriel wanted, right? Dammit, I'm screwing everything up! Maybe it would've been best to never let them know and pretend like Gabriel had to go do something or another... forever. I could've sold that, right?

Breathe, Dac encourages me. Only after he says it do I notice that I have failed to inhale since before Sarah even spoke to me.

Stop them, I beg Dac.

"Stop here for just a moment, everyone," Dac says. I hear his heavy body move to get in their way. Oh no, he said "everyone." Like, everyone, everyone? This is such a bad idea.

"Sam, are you okay?" I hear Nathan ask this time. "If you're hurt, Kane's here. He can probably think something up to help you." They think they can help. They really have no idea. Is it right of me to break the news to them like this?

Is it too late to call this whole thing off? I ask Dac, desperate for an answer I know won't come.

Entirely, he tells me.

Wonderful, I say, ready to hit myself over the head with the rock I see within arms reach so I don't have to see them when they learn the truth.

"Um, I have something to tell you guys," I say, my voice warbles and isn't anywhere near full volume. They can hear the tears that just restarted. I know it.

"Sam, what is it?" Sarah asks again. "Can you not get up?"

"And what's that smell?" I hear Mark ask louder than he had to. Right, throw up smells. I honestly didn't even notice.

"Sam, what's wrong?" I hear Jinn ask, pushing his way forward.

How do I tell them? I ask Dac. *How do I tell them their dad, and king, and whatever he was to somebody is gone?*

You do your best? He suggests, not knowing any better.

I take a shallow breath before I manage to get out, "Let them through." Dac steps again, removing the barrier he created with his body. As the group gets closer to me, even more doubts rampage through my mind, telling me to stop this right now, but I glance right and see Gabriel deteriorating faster now. He still represents the man he was, but that won't be true soon.

"Sam…" one of them says. I don't even know who. My ears have mostly stopped working for this moment. They trail off when they see where I'm looking, following my gaze to the corpse of the greatest man to live.

I only catch one gasping word, carrying as much disbelief as one would think possible to make a fact untrue.

"Dad."

I can't move, my crying starts all over again as the Royals descend upon their deceased father. Apparently, my body wasn't quite out of fluids to pump out of my eyeballs, or snot to drip out of my nose. Difference this time is that I can't even find the reason to support myself. I collapse to my side, the opposite direction of Gabriel, and cry just as hard as the first time.

I know the Royals are speaking, that Jinn and Mark are saying something, perhaps their condolences, that Rose is probably saying something, but none of it reaches my ears. They could all be a world away for all I'm aware. If Dac is trying to talk to me, I wouldn't know. Today is a day for bad news and overall sadness. Nothing good can come from these next twenty-four hours. I wouldn't be surprised if I was actually stabbed, an eye plucked out, and Rose broke up with me as somebody murdered Jinn before my eyes and destroyed Dac.

Morbid? Yes. But it's how I feel.

It's not a relief that the others know. It's not a weight off my chest. It's worse actually. Why would Gabriel make me the one responsible for making sure that everybody knows? Why am I the one who has to take a father away? Somewhere in my rational mind, I know that I didn't do it, that he was sick and has been for hundreds of years, maybe thousands, but it sure feels like I'm the one responsible. Who else was going to tell his family?

Next thing I know, someone is shaking me. I sort of come to my senses to notice, through a pool of water, that Kane is shaking me. Is he trying to kill me? Good. Maybe I deserve it. I should've told them about their dad the moment I knew he was still sick.

After looking at him longer, I notice his lips are moving. Obviously he's crying, and his lips are moving. I focus my ears, straining to hear what he's saying. It takes a ludicrous amount of effort, but I can make out what he says.

"Sam," Kane says on repeat until I acknowledge I can hear him. Once he knows he has my attention, he wipes at his eyes and says, "Sam, Dad doesn't have much time left. I emptied his pockets, but we don't want him to be resting here forever. Would you fly him around the Surface, up to the Sky Nation, and over the ocean before he…" Kane chokes up, able to get out his request in rushed analytical words, as if talking about one of the projects in his laboratory, but the emotion residing within the man of science gets the best of him, and the tears take over. Kane, already close to kneeling on the floor, collapses and cries into my jeans, where his head currently is.

"Is that what he would've wanted?" I manage to say quietly, impressed with my ability to control my vocal cords. Kane can't speak, but nods his head, rubbing it against my leg. I twitch my head up and down. He can't see me, but I do it anyway.

"Ok," I get out fast before I choke up again. "I'll do it," I say in another such burst. I get ready for a long sentence and say, "I'll fly him around until… until he's done." Kane rubs his head against my leg again. Jinn helps him up, which in turn lets me get up. I walk over to where Gabriel lies, not caring that everybody is seeing me cry like a small child. Sarah and Nathan move themselves off of him so that I can grab him. I squat down and pick Gabriel up with an arm under his knees and an arm in the middle of his back. It's not the easiest way to carry somebody for a long time, but I owe it to him to make sure he's spread properly this way.

I notice Rose coming closer to me as Sarah, Nathan, and Kane all do as well. Sarah kisses her dad on the forehead. "Goodbye, Dad," she says, making room for her brothers.

228

"Bye, Dad," Nathan says, squeezing his hand so hard I'm afraid that he's going to keep it.

Kane can't say anything. He basically throws himself over the fading corpse of his father and sobs. He would stay there for a long while, but his siblings pull him off, knowing that if what Kane told me to do is to come to fruition, I have to leave now. Rose looks like she's going to say something, but I can't talk right now. I take off.

I shoot into the sky without much concern for my own safety, barely watching out for tree branches. I look below and see that some ash and dust is falling away. There's probably a pile where he started, but Gabriel is deteriorating. I have to book it to make sure I can get everywhere.

Without hesitation, I fly off as fast as I dare, flying near vertically, but at enough of an angle that the ash wouldn't be in a pile on the ground more than a mile below. The fact that there's such a thing as wind doesn't really register, it just seems like the right thing to do.

Faster I fly up, not checking Gabriel to know how much of him has dispersed. I break through the clouds quickly, but not fast enough. As I pass through, I feel the moisture plaster to my skin, the water droplets stinging. I'm vaguely aware that they're taking some of Gabriel away, not even giving me a chance to get a good portion of him up to the Sky Nation, but there was no way around it. If there was any break in the clouds anywhere, I would've gone that way instead, but Seattle apparently doesn't have such a thing, and instead of blue skies, prefers grey clouds.

Once I'm out of the clouds, although my body feels heavier, Gabriel feels lighter. I don't even want to think about how much of him I must've lost in the cloud.

Luckily for me, I see a Sky Nation platform just up ahead. Problem is that it's a bit of a distance away. I disregard my safety even further and fly faster than before. It's not my top speed, but it's starting to get to the point where I know I won't be able to control where I'm flying very soon.

I try to ignore my hair slapping my eyes, and the freezing cold wind, and the fact that more and more of Gabriel is being torn away particle by particle. At this speed, I can pretend my eyes are this damp because of the wind, and not because I'm still crying.

I come in low and at screaming speeds. The pedestrians on the platform all but dive out of my way, even though I'm at least fifteen feet off the ground. I know more of Gabriel is dispersing, but at least it's where he wants now. That's two. Gabriel, you're on the Surface and the Sky Nation—up in and above the clouds. All that's left is for me to get you to the ocean.

"Watch where you're flying!" I hear some asshat shout at me as I race by. There's plenty more jeering, but I pay it no mind. Only one more location. How close was Seattle to the ocean? I couldn't have been that far, could I?

And pedestrians? There shouldn't be any at this time of night. Or is it morning? I don't have time to worry about this!

Unfortunately, I have to slow down just enough to circle back to some rude jerk and scream at them, from ten feet above their head, *"WHICH WAY IS WEST!?"* Reacting to the desperate hysteria in my voice, they point in a direction. This is the Sky Nation. I know well enough to trust that people up here know which way is which on a compass at pretty much all times. Only reason I don't know it now is first of all because I don't have much conscious thought, and second because the Surface has messed me up. If I was able to keep my head the whole way through, my internal compass would be

230

telling me where west is, but it doesn't much want to cooperate right now.

Without taking the time for a careful build up of speed, I race off in that direction, feeling a shock go through my entire body. The pain is tolerable, but persists. Even as my body gets used to the pressure of flying at this speed, the pain doesn't fade. I must've actually hurt something, or myself. Hopefully it will fade soon.

Faster. Faster. I push myself to make it, coming back up to the speed I was at, trying to make it to the platform in time. Now I have less time, and more distance to travel, *and* clouds to go through again. It doesn't much seem possible, but I have to make it. I can barely feel any weight left in my arms, but I know that there's still some there. If this is really what you wanted, Gabriel, I'm going to make sure it happens.

It doesn't feel like long, but I know I've been flying for a while when I see a break in the clouds up ahead.

Thank you.

I dive through them, not missing this opportunity to make sure that Gabriel doesn't dissipate in the clouds any more.

Ahead of me, yet worryingly far, I see an endless blue: The ocean. I'm almost there!

I notice that my speed dropped when I maneuvered through the clouds, so I turn it back up to the constant speed that I've been traveling at today.

Come on, come on!

The water is getting nearer, but I don't know if there will be enough of Gabriel to make it there. Only now does wind become a thought in my mind. Without changing the speed I'm traveling with my boots, I angle myself down to let gravity also give me a bit of a boost, *and* to get me nearer to the water. When I get out there,

231

there won't be much of Gabriel left, so I absolutely cannot mess this up.

My body aches as I race over the earth, showing myself to the population below. Down here, people are starting to stir and leave their homes to see the crazy man flying overhead, trailing ashes behind him in a desperate dash to get to the ocean. I know that we were technically supposed to conceal our presence, but there's no use now. If I want to do as Gabriel asked, this is what I have to do. Sure Logan, the New Power, or *whoever* may be on to where I am right now, but I don't care.

I block out the stunned gasps and screams about me as I have a singular focus ahead of me and push. I go even faster, now threatening to get seriously hurt if I'm not careful with how I handle myself. With how little of Gabriel there is left, this is the best I can do. I'm not going to make it. At this rate, I'm really not sure I'm going to make it.

Still, I persist. I can do this. It's not likely, but I can do it.

With a final effort, I go racing out low above the water, kicking up waves and a wake behind me as I continue onward without dropping any speed. I keep flying. I don't slow or stop until I feel the very last of Gabriel slip away.

I slow down and hover above the water, catching my breath and knowing that I'd succeeded. I feel the aches and complaints of my body for how many bad starts I'd had. I don't care. I did it. I got Gabriel to all three. The Surface, the Sky, and the Water. Too bad I can't fly him to the bottom of the ocean. I know from Kane that my pressure pill is going to be good until I die, but I can't hold my breath, and a jump shirt would help. This will have to do.

Finally, I look down at what remains in my arms: a pair of old clothes, and a necklace barely caught by getting wrapped around my thumb. I thought Kane took everything off of Gabriel?

No. He just emptied his pockets. I guess the necklace never even registered.

Carefully shifting the remaining clothes to my right arm, I drape Gabriel's necklace, the gear medallion hanging from it, around my neck.

"I hope you're happy, Gabriel," I say as I inspect my surroundings and see something magnificent. From the East, the big ball of light responsible for maintaining all life on this earth is peaking up just over the horizon, not yet fully in the sky.

"You got your last sunrise."

Chapter Twenty-Four

Much more slowly and cautiously, I start to work my way back to where everyone is waiting for me at Tie's statue in Seattle. They're all going to be distressed and in disarray, but they're there. The least I can do is tell them that I fulfilled Gabriel's wish of being spread everywhere, probably so that he can continue to watch over his children for eternity even after death.

Only way I know where to go back to is because Dac is sending out a sort of signal that basically manifests itself as a headache that I feel in the direction that he's in paired with an intuition I cannot explain.

Since the sun is out, how long have I been flying for?

The sun's warmth seeps into my skin, fighting off the cold wind that refuses to let me cease shivering. The flight back to where everybody is waiting is much longer than I anticipated. Not even because of me flying slowly. I figured that'd play a factor, but I suppose I got much farther away from them than I thought.

Would it really be so bad to stop flying for the day and catch up with them tomorrow? I'm tired and shaking for more than one reason, and I'm carrying the clothes of a dead man! Nothing about this situation is right!

If you keep flying while you complain, you'll end up

here before you know it, Dac tells me. Honestly, I didn't realize we could still communicate this far apart from each other. We've never done that before.

You're an idiot, Dac says. *I'm in your shoes, remember?*

Oh yeah. I know he's just trying to provide me with a distraction, but it's a welcome one. Too much on my mind otherwise. I feel like I would probably crash if I let my mind wander to the dark corners it wants to visit.

I don't fold Gabriel's clothes, and I don't crumple them either, but I do hold on to them in a state in between as to make sure that I don't lose anything. I was trusted with what Kane said is what Gabriel wanted. I barely made it, but I did it. I made sure you were spread everywhere, Gabriel. It happened probably a bit faster than any of us, including you, were expecting, but I did it. I hope there is still a way for Kane to take some of the dust left behind down to the Water Nation.

The sound of the wind in my ears is strangely comforting. Within the sound, there is silence, a tranquility that even manages to block out some of my louder inner thoughts, the volume and pressure of the wind getting to me. In a silent room, all there is are your thoughts, but up here, there actually is the noise. It's difficult to ignore, but still leaves you devoid of all other outside influence. I just wish I was smart enough to have tied my blanket around my neck or something before I flew off. It's cold!

How's everybody doing? I ask Dac, irrationally hoping he won't answer me. I want to be ready for what's happening when I get back, but I'd like it even more if I could hide away somewhere until this all blows over and everybody could be happy.

How do you think? Dac responds. *For three of them, their dad just died, who is also the king of three of them.*

*Sarah, Kane, and Nathan are all wrecks, trying to support
each other, but not doing so well there. Jinn and Mark and
Rose are also all in tears. Rose not as bad as the others.
Even Captain Tom departed due to lack of control of his
stomach.*

That bad?

Worse.

I knew that was coming. When I saw my parents, I
was a wreck, and they're still *alive.*

What do I do? I ask Dac, as if he'd know any better
than I would. Personally, I'm barely past where they are
right now. I had almost an entire night's worth of being
a total wreck before I even thought about telling them. I
have a semblance of composure now, but that illusion
will most probably shatter the moment I see someone
else crying. I don't want to be reduced to that again.

I don't know, Dac tells me. *You've done all you can,
right? You did exactly what Kane asked you to for his
father. More than that, you told them about his passing.
They know what happened and—although he was
withering—they got to see their father again.*

*I should've gotten them while he was still alive,
shouldn't I...*

That's not what Gabriel wanted, he reminds me.

*Gabriel was dying! I know that I did what he said he
wanted, but what about everybody left behind?*

*He thought he was doing what was best for them,
preserving their memories of his life.*

*But they've seen him dead. That memory is shattered
anyway! Death is selfish.*

Then do everybody a favor and don't die, Dac says
plainly. I can tell that he's smiling to himself at that one.
Despite myself and the shadowy corners of my mind, I
smile. I even begin to laugh. The notion is so stupid. As if
something like living and dying is as simple as a single

236

decision. The way Dac put it, it sounds like I can basically decide when I'm at the end of my rope if I want to accept or deny death. The idea that the word "no" may be the key to true immortality is such a ludicrous concept.

Don't worry, I tell him. *I don't have any plans of dying any time soon.*

Good. Otherwise you'd be a hypocrite.

Oh, well I'd never want to be that now would I?

No you do not, Dac says.

It's funny how such desperate attempts to cheer somebody up, along with a partially delirious mind, can actually be effective.

I fly the rest of the way with a relatively blank mind, desperate to hold on to my brief moment of laughter instead of thinking about what's waiting for me. The flight does take time, yes, but time worth flying. My legs still ache from taking off funny, but it doesn't feel like anything that can't be fixed by a good night's sleep.

I know I'm close to the others when the entire horizon is filled solely with trees. Can't be long now. All I need to do is find Tie's statue and the bundle of sobbing people. Joy.

Instead of circling the trees for a long time, not really knowing where to go, I keep following that sense I have of where Dac is. By now, the sun is fully in the sky, so I doubt that they're actually still at the place of Gabriel's passing, but you never know.

They're not still there, Dac says. *A couple hours ago, Jinn and Rose had enough composure to help me move the Royals. They needed sleep and now are supposedly passed out. Everybody is exhausted from being woken up in the middle of the night for something like that. I'd be amazed if anybody wakes up before noon, assuming they actually are asleep right now.*

Well, at least there's that. If I can get in there and fall asleep myself without having to interact with anybody, that'd be fantastic. I'm not much in a mood to comfort anybody. I'm still working on keeping myself together, thank you very much.

Following Dac's signal, I see the deceptively small clearing up ahead where I know the cabins are.

And you're sure they're asleep? I check again with Dac. With the sun this high in the sky, one would think that the others would be awake. But then again, with how tired I am, I can understand being asleep right now. That's about the gist of my plan. *Quietly* get in there, climb into bed, and pass out until the cold goes away. I've had enough of being cold, and sad, and tired today. I'm done with this entire day actually. Wake me up when it's tomorrow.

I descend into the clearing, trying to be as quiet as I can, which isn't too terribly hard. It's not like my boots make a ridiculous amount of noise or anything like that. As the ground comes closer and closer, I can't stop dreaming of a bed. It doesn't even have to be my bed, just some bed.

Inches above the grass, I cut the power to my boots and fall the negligible distance.

Only to collapse the moment my feet hit the Earth.

I make a rather foul noise as I get to reenact the first few days of me learning how to fly. Trying to push myself up, I find my legs shaking hard enough that I can't get them under me. If I can't even move them well, I doubt that they can support my weight at all.

"Great," I mumble to myself, trying to push myself up, but my legs are not cooperating. "Just perfect."

Okay, maybe I don't get a bed, but grass is comfortable, right? Right?

The frigid breeze answers me with a resounding

"no."

"Wonderful," I mutter, cursing my legs for failing me. Hasn't enough happened? I mean, I know I just flew hard and fast for hours on end, but that's no excuse!

In protest, the rest of my body starts to shake now. Apparently, the rest of me does not appreciate my lack of faith in my legs. Today keeps getting better and better.

Hang on, Dac says to me. I can tell he was laughing before talking to me, laughing because I fell flat on my face. What a jerk. This isn't funny right now!

I try and move forward by crawling forward using my forearms. About two seconds into trying, I decide that this is an awful idea. I stifle a scream. A spasm works its way through my body, bringing discomfort everywhere it goes.

Dammit.

Dammit, dammit, dammit.

Can't I catch a break?

Dac comes out of the building and steadily works his way over to me. He's careful not to let the door slam so as to let those who are still asleep stay that way. With what they went through, it's understandable. Wake up in the middle of the night just to learn of a loved ones death. If I weren't so tired, I doubt I'd be able to sleep a wink. Even if they're all simply pretending to be asleep, I don't want to shatter that illusion.

"Are you okay?" Dac asks.

"I can't really move. What do you think?" I respond.

"Point taken," he says, getting an arm around me and lifting me. I try and help as he drags me back to the cabins, but I can't move my legs at all. My efforts are split between holding on to Dac and not complaining. The latter is much more difficult than one would initially guess. Rounding close corners, Dac manages to accidentally... "accidentally"... hit the doorframes with my shins.

I almost bark out a rude comment, but manage to trap it in my head. He can still hear it, even that way. Sure, it's not as satisfying as actually getting to shout something, but the purpose is served. I'm content with that.

It was an accident! Dac defends himself, and I can tell he means it. I am just unfortunately in one of those moods where I can justify complaining about anything and everything. For example: the air here is weird. How is the air even weird? And... and... and... that's about all I have right now actually.

When we get to the room that I sleep in, Dac basically has to lift me and place me in the bed. It's honestly a little sad and could quite easily be thought of as hilarious by anyone that would happen to be awake right now. I just have more reasons to be glad they're asleep. On top of everything else, we're still trying to be quiet. A robot near seven feet tall trying to put a six-foot tall guy to bed is not the stealthiest thing I could ever imagine.

When he does finally get me positioned in the bed, I manage to pull the sheets up myself. The little things in life keep me from dying of embarrassment. I pass Dac Gabriel's clothes that I've kept tightly against my body up until now. He reverently takes them from me.

What do you want me to do with these? He asks.

Put them on the table, maybe? I offer. *Make sure they're somewhere obvious so that the Royals will be able to find them without even trying.*

Will do, he assures me. *Now get some rest. You deserve it.*

He doesn't have to tell me twice. I only have a thin blanket, considering my thicker one is still out in the forest by Tie's monument. It's cold, but I'm exhausted enough that I close my eyes and within a few minutes, fall fast asleep.

Like a baby? Dac somehow echoes in my mind as I become dead to the world.

There's a tapping. Consistent and sharp. The steady rhythm of it is calming at first, but turns infuriating. Why would my dream think that this would be enjoyable? Unless it's not a dream...

Of course it's not a dream. Why would I expect to get even one day of genuine rest?

The tapping turns to drumming after a time. A series of what I can make out as four individual hits, or so I think anyway. It really sounds like somebody rolling their fingers on an armchair. It's a fairly distinct sound that I learned well from the many times Jinn has been irritated with me up in the Sky Nation. From only hearing the one hand, at least he's not *that* upset.

Wait, maybe this is a dream? A really, really stupid dream that I need to wake up from. No, wait, waking up sounds dreadful right now. Is it possible to change dreams? I don't think that's even a thing, but it's worth a shot.

I feel a tension in my neck as I try and exert my will over the dream to change it. However, all I succeed in doing is giving myself a stiff neck.

"Go on," somebody irritably prompts. Okay, only because you insisted. Would you kindly shut up? Some of us are trying to sleep here.

"Your actions are rash, and I cannot condone them," I hear the one voice I knew would pop up say. Steven. I swear, the guy knows exactly when I want to become a log and sleep forever, and makes sure that I'm pulled into his discussions. Sleep deprivation. I blame sleep deprivation as the causality for why I declared war. A

241

tired and cranky Sam is not to be trifled with.

"You would order me what to do?" the first voice says. It's now easy for me to place this as belonging to Steven's master. Wait, is Steven standing up to his master? This might be interesting after all.

"No, Master," Steven says at full speed, revealing that his real answer is yes and that his fear of his master hasn't entirely disappeared. I figured it wouldn't.

"Then why is it you presume that I care about your opinions?"

"I-I'm sorry, Master," Steven says, not sounding scared, but more as an apologetic backtracking. "I only think of your well-being. With the time drawing so near, they may be attempting to lead you into a trap."

"Your concerns are unfounded. Those that contacted me are far from intelligent enough to have laid a trap. The notion is even more ludicrous when considering the trap would have to be able to handle me."

"Master," Steven starts. He pauses a moment as he chooses his words carefully, "I am nervous. You say you wish to travel out into enemy territory on your own with none to guard you other than your pilot."

"I need no other," Steven's master says.

"Please, Master, won't you delay your departure long enough for me to organize a defensive party? I can feel it in my gut that they are going to try something against you."

"It is far too late for that already," the Master says. "I am already en route. My destination is near, in fact. Your wishes are meaningless." Steven responds with a befuddled gurgling, and I almost snicker. "Amass your forces, Steven," his master says. "I shall reach my destination within a few hours. From that moment on, it will be a very real possibility that open war will officially begin."

That's something I don't like hearing.

Chapter Twenty-Five

After the visions of the New Power commanders fade, I manage to get some restful sleep. In truth, I didn't dream of anything. It was peacefully black. Even still, when I awaken, it's in a cold sweat. I find myself out of breath, desperate to fill my lungs as if I'd just run a marathon. I look around me to see that it's full daylight outside. Have I woken up in the afternoon, or is it already the next day? Personally, I'm hoping that it's just the afternoon. I've slept for more than a day before. The grogginess is a killer. I have Jinn to blame for putting me into a mini coma. Yes, it's true that it saved my life, but I was out much longer than he was ever planning to tell me.

I grudgingly roll out of bed, keeping myself wrapped in my blanket as I go. Turns out that, while incredibly sore, my legs are willing to function again. Today I'm feeling thankful for the little things. More than enough happened yesterday... Two days ago? However long ago it was.

You may want to wear as much black as possible, Dac says to me without so much as a good morning.

Why's that? I ask him.

The Royals decided that today is going to be Gabriel's funeral. Hey, what do you know, I think I'm ready to crawl back into bed and go back to sleep again. Well, I guess I'll see everybody tomorrow then, or maybe not until next week. I am feeling quite tired after all.

Oh, man up, put on your black clothes, and get out here, Dac reprimands me.

Yes, Mom, I tell him, ignoring the extra set of daggers that pierce my heart, thinking of her.

I sift through my bag and find a black pair of jeans and a black long sleeve shirt. It's not the fanciest clothing I've ever worn—which is only thanks to Jinn and the Royals, otherwise the opposite would be true— but they'll have to do. Gabriel deserves more respect, but it's all I have with me. I have the shadow of a thought of wearing a different pair of shoes other than my boots, but remember that they're the only pair of shoes I own anymore. My old sneakers I went up to the Sky Nation in were destroyed in an accident where I set one on fire.

With my all black garb on, I leave the room stocked with bunk beds and head into the common area of this cabin. I'm not in the largest of them all, so I'm not at all surprised to find that the memorial isn't being held here. I am a little surprised, though, to see Jinn sitting on one of the couches facing a fire committing what I can best describe as partial cannibalism.

Wait. Never mind. That's a whiskey, not gin.

You're hilarious.

I try.

He takes a sip and lets out a sigh before rubbing his lips together so that his beard and mustache almost manage to touch. He has gotten a lot scruffier lately. I'll attribute it to less time to shave, but with a guy like Jinn, I would've expected him to be clean-shaven for a moment like this.

I take a moment to observe him, wistfully staring

into the fire. I wonder what's on his mind. It looks like more than just Gabriel is in his thoughts right now.

"Jinn?" I say to make him aware of my presence. He's not normally so off guard. Maybe being out of his element like this is letting him relax a bit? That'd be good for him.

He sits up from his shallow slouch and looks over the couch to see me. "Dac said he told you what today is?"

"Yeah," I say. "It's going to be a rough day, isn't it?"

"It already has been," Jinn says, taking another sip of his drink. I wait until after he sighs before speaking again.

"Where are the others?" I ask. "The next cabin over?"

"Since you're awake, I'd imagine that they're on their way over to the place where he... you know."

"Unfortunately, I do," I say, realizing that he means they're going to do this on the spot Gabriel died.

"I volunteered to be the one to bring you along, in case you couldn't find your way," Jinn says as he pushes himself to his feet.

"Thanks," I tell him. Honestly, I have no idea where that specific spot is. All I know is that it's right by Gabriel's brother's statue.

Lost in my own thoughts and recollections of flying everywhere, I don't notice that Jinn came right next to me until he starts hugging me.

"How're you holding up?" he asks me. When I don't respond, too surprised and confused to do anything, he continues, "That was a brave thing you did last night."

"It's not that hard to fly," I tell him.

"Not that part," he clarifies. "I mean sitting with a man as he dies. That couldn't have been easy on you. I won't ask what it was like because I don't want you to have to remember it, but know that I'm proud of you and that you did a great thing." I don't say anything back. Instead, I hug him back and start to shake a bit. You have no idea, Jinn. One moment he was here, and the next gone. Just like that. I couldn't even look at him while I was spreading his ashes. I couldn't bring myself to do it. I gauged everything off of how much he weighed.

"Thank you," I say, sucking down snot and trying not to cry. I've done bad things to many people. Sure, the New Power have also tried to kill me, but what about those they leave behind? It's not like an entire army is composed of single men or women who have done nothing but evil in the world and have no friends or siblings and are also orphans. I'd be hard pressed to find even one person like that. How many people have I forced to go to funerals? Not how many have I sent to their graves, but how many people have been left behind with nothing but sadness and malice towards me? I don't know what I thought I was bargaining for when I decided it was a good idea to go against every rule set by the world I live in.

Yes, I've seen fantastic beauty, but always at a cost. Look at me. "For all the death and sadness I've brought to this world, what have I paid for it?" I ask aloud. A few small scars and a tattoo? People have died. Others have lost limbs and organs, or even their minds and senses of self. "I've lost nothing."

"That's not true," Jinn says. "The fact that this is even on your mind means that you've lost more than you're even aware of, yet you've gained so much more."

"That's a crappy way to look at things," I say into his shoulder. "So I've killed a bunch of people, and gotten some stuff, and I've supposedly lost things too? How does that make any of what I've done right?" To that, even he can't formulate a response.

"If he were here," Jinn says after a short time, "I'm

sure Gabriel would know exactly what to say to you. Remember that all of us are right there with you. You're not responsible for all death throughout time and space."

"I'm responsible for enough to be more than a murderer. I'm worse than the enforcers. I've killed more people than the ones I'm trying to stop." I can't help it anymore. I bundle up bits of Jinn's shirt in my fists as I cry into his shoulder. How is it that I still have any tears left in me, even after all of this?

I'm such a crybaby...

We stay like this for a while, me crying into Jinn's shoulder, him holding me as if I were a small child. At some point, Dac lets me know that they're delaying the funeral itself as they do preparations. I know it's all in the name of buying me time to get there. That only succeeds in making me feel worse about the whole situation. I still take full advantage of it.

When I feel like I've taken up as much time as I can, I somehow manage to rein myself in and slow the tears.

"Ready?" Jinn asks me when I lift my head from his shoulder. There's a large wet spot on his shirt, but he pretends not to notice it. I nod my head, and we leave the cabin. Once we're outside, I consider the fact that I don't have a jacket on and that it's really freaking cold. Jinn doesn't have one on either though, so at least it's not just me.

We don't talk while we walk to where the funeral is going to be held. Honestly, I don't mind the silence right now. I don't even know what I would say. The sound of the grass crunching beneath my feet is more than enough noise to fill the void of sound. Nature is silent in mourning.

When we reach the funeral site, there's very little activity. I look around and see many different variations of black clothing, Sarah, Nathan, and Kane the best dressed of everybody. Mark has a black jacket on—with one sleeve hanging limp—over normal pants. Tom is wearing his captain's outfit, and Rose oddly enough is in a dress. I don't think I have ever seen her in a dress. From the looks of it, it's probably one of Sarah's that she's borrowing. Dac is just as naked as usual.

"Sorry for the delay," Jinn says to announce our presence. Eyes turn our way. There's sadness in every one of them, as there should be.

"It's not a problem at all," Kane says, no tone in his voice at all. We all have our coping mechanisms. "Now that we're all here, I think it's time we begin."

We all shuffle into the semblance of a half circle around Kane. Nathan and Sarah stand next to each other, as do Mark and Jinn, Jinn making sure to stay close to Nathan, and Rose manages to find her way right next to me. Dac stands on my other side. I can't say it aloud, but their simply being there means a lot.

Kane clears his throat before beginning, "I'm no expert at burial rites, but as we all have… as some of us may have, I have performed something like them many times in my long life." He corrected himself to include only Sarah and Nathan in that statement. I shift my eyes to glance at them, and when he speaks, they both take on a different tone of sadness, probably remembering times they were in Kane's shoes.

"Today I perform one of the hardest tasks of my life," he continues. "Last night, a great man passed from this world. To many he was a revolutionary. Others felt only disdain for him, or only thought him a character in a children's story. The only way he can accurately be described to me, though, is as a father," Kane's words stumble, tears threatening to overwhelm him.

"Dad has inspired all around him for the entirety of

his life. Now in death, he can go and check up on those he met and lost long ago. In death, he can be..." Kane starts crying here, but forces himself to continue, "reunited with members of his family who have already passed, with loved ones long gone." Rose entwines her fingers around mine, squeezing tighter than normal. I'm sure she's trying to fight back her feelings.

"Thanks to Sam's efforts," Kane says, and I look up, genuinely amazed that my name is coming up at something as important as this, "Dad's final wish of being spread to each of the nations came true. I was able to gather," as he speaks now he reaches into a pocket and draws something out attached to a long leather chord. More accurately, three somethings. At the end of them each is an individual glass jar that's maybe only half the size of my thumb, if even, "ashes from where he passed." Kane's hands are violently shaking, barely able to hold himself together.

"And... and I fabricated these. Within each container are some of Dad's ashes. I made one for each of us." He specifically says this part to Nathan and Sarah, who look to be in almost as bad of shape as Kane is. "Take one," he manages to whisper to them. "Please."

Nathan and Sarah step forward, each taking one of the ash holders from Nathan and holding them tight. Kane looks about ready to lose it, so Sarah holds his face in her hands, trying to bring him back down to earth. Perhaps that's the problem, that he's too close to this world right now and wants nothing more than to be farther, to be with his father. Sarah gives him a kiss on the cheek to comfort him and stays beside him, holding his hand for support.

"We all knew him," Sarah says, taking up where Kane left off, seeing as Kane is now crying too hard to speak. He looks ready to collapse to the ground and is being

250

held up only by the support of his sister. "For however long it may have been, Dad touched all our lives. I don't think he would want us to stand around feeling sorry for his passing." No, he wouldn't. This is exactly why he tried to keep it secret from all of you.

"Why don't we just do what we came here to do?" Sarah suggests, not near the driest eyes around us.

"Good idea," Nathan says, half-heartedly laughing as he wipes his eyes. He steps up again now and walks towards Tie's monument. Everybody except me starts to follow him, and Rose tugs me along.

"Come on," she quietly says, grabbing onto my arm with her free hand now, trying to support herself more than she is me. When I follow the others, I find us now gathered around an open hole in the ground. Nathan is standing behind the hole with Sarah and Kane to his right, but on the side of the hole. Kane has something clenched close to his chest, cradled in his arms, as he weeps. I stare at it for a bit to understand that it's Gabriel's clothes that he was wearing when he passed.

"Dad," Nathan says, trying desperately to sound as cheery as possible, "we know this isn't much right now, but think of it more as a promise. A promise that once the world begins to calm down, we'll erect you a monument worthy of standing beside the one you chartered for Uncle Tie." Nathan reaches into his pocket and pulls out a clenched fist. He stares at his fist for a long time, concentrating hard. After about a minute, a beautiful sword with a grey aura extends out of the closed fist.

Since Nathan accidentally invented Sky Iron, he's had enough time to play with it to be able to grow the blades of some people, Dac lets me know as I stare at the sword, flabbergasted.

I didn't think that was possible.

251

He can only do it for his dad, or brothers, or sister, Dac continues, *and he can't do it fast. The fact that he could do it that fast isn't that he's only been doing it for a minute. He has been working on that basically since Gabriel died. He explained it to everybody I think as a way to keep himself distracted. Keep his mind off the fact that his father had just died.*

Nathan drives the sword into the ground at his feet, at the head of the hole. He makes sure that its tip goes in enough so that the sword will be sturdy, but his ultimate goal isn't to entirely bury the weapon. He takes a step back and looks at his siblings. Sarah nods to him and rubs Kane's back, whose eyes haven't been open for a while, so that he knows it's time to do something. Kane collapses to his knees in an instant and cries all the harder, hugging Gabriel's clothes closer to his face. As sad and touching as the scene is, I can't help the thought that pops into my mind.

It's genuinely surprising that Kane is the biggest daddy's boy of the three of them. He seems so detached from everything.

Sarah squats down and consoles Kane for a while, rubbing his back and making sure that he's okay. Nathan joins as well in checking on his brother. I try and do them the favor of not listening. After what I'm sure Kane doesn't think is anywhere near enough time, he lowers Gabriel's clothes into the hole. When he lets go of them, he recoils back as if he was shocked and continues crying on the ground. Dac moves from beside me, and Jinn follows him. They each take up a shovel and proceed to fill the hole.

Like an idiot, I find myself incapable of doing anything but standing here and watching as everything takes place.

"How're you holding up?" Rose whispers in my ear.

"I've had worse days."

"Oh really," Rose says, wiping at her eyes. I see the movement out of the corner of my eye. I can't take my eyes off of the rapidly filling hole. "Like what?"

"Well, there's the day I found out my mother won't acknowledge my existence."

"I could see how that one wouldn't be fun," Rose says, not sure if she should laugh at the absurdity of my comment or to stay serious.

"Or there was the day that I found out that you had a boyfriend," I continue, now trying to alleviate the mood somewhat.

"And what was so bad about that?" she asks me, still seeming discouraged by the world.

"As if you don't know," I counter. She somehow manages to giggle at me.

"That I do," she kisses my cheek before resting her head on my shoulder and looking ahead as I am.

I decide that isn't enough and turn to wrap her in a hug, for both our sakes. She one-ups me again and kisses me for real this time. I have to admit, I can't argue with her methods.

"Ow," she says, pulling away as I start to hug her more tightly.

"What? What is it?" I ask her.

"Your necklace stabbed me," she explains. "It's a lot sharper than usual."

"My necklace?" I say, patting down my chest where my necklace normally hangs and feel an anomaly. I fish it out of my shirt to find that, tangled with my necklace, is Gabriel's. Right. I forgot that I'd put that on to make sure I didn't lose it.

"Is that what I think it is?" Rose asks me.

"If you're thinking that it's Gabriel's necklace, then yes. I almost dropped it when I was... flying everywhere yesterday, so I put it on so I wouldn't lose it. I guess I forgot I had it on." I pull it over my head and spend a moment untangling the two necklaces' cords. I put mine back over my neck and work my way around the hole in the ground to hang Gabriel's necklace from his sword. I look at the Royals to find that Sarah noticed the action. Nathan is too occupied trying to calm Kane to notice, and Kane is pretty self-explanatory. She mouths me a "thank you" before returning her attention to her brother.

"Did I miss the ceremony?" somebody loudly asks from behind me. Icicles grow down my back as their glacial water races through my veins. I know that voice.

I. Know. That. Voice.

That voice should *not* be here under any circumstances.

So I'm not imagining things? Dac asks me.

Why is that voice here?

"Unfortunately," Jinn says. "May I ask who you are and what you're doing here?" I don't dare turn around. If I turn around and see it, that means it's real.

"I called him," Nathan says. "He had a right to know."

"Yes, well when I received reports that there was a white light flying through the sky leaving behind a trail of ash, it was fairly easy to surmise what had transpired." Sarah smacks Nathan.

"Why did you call *him*?" she demands an answer.

"It was the right thing to do," Nathan defends himself.

"Hello to you too," the voice says, ice and fire playing on the wind. Unfortunately, I can guess what his next word is, "Sister."

Chapter
Twenty-Six

"You aren't needed here, Logan," Sarah growls.

"Is that any kind way to treat your brother?" he continues, ignoring her tone. "Our father just died and you would rather pick fights with me than take the time to mourn."

"We are mourning," she argues. "You're not needed for that process. You haven't even spoken with us in ages."

"We've spoken indirectly," he says calmly. I can hear and feel him getting closer to me, even without turning around. "And one of yours, I'm assuming, spoke to me as well."

"What are you talking about?" Sarah asks, furious.

"War, dear sister. I'm talking about war." Against my will, I stand up a bit straighter and probably manage to break out into a cold sweat. "Some brat from my kingdom had the gall to declare war on me. He didn't even have the common courtesy to do so in person. I highly doubt he even has an army about him."

"Nobody has an army anymore," Sarah reminds him. "Since we are all related, there's no need for wars, and thus no need for armies."

"I have one," he says plainly. "I've had one for many years now. Lately, I've had to further fortify it, mostly due to the doing of the same brat I just spoke of."

"Who would that be?" Sarah says, her eyes touching on me for just a moment.

"A child, really," Logan says, chuckling to himself, "as amusing as that notion is." I feel him getting closer.

"Do you have a name?" Sarah asks.

"In fact, I do," Logan says. I can literally feel his breath on my ear as he says, "Sam Cutter." He walks into my view now to stand next to the sword. I see the man that has been the root of all the evil in my life, the man responsible for the foul state of the Surface *and* apparently the New Power.

Logan, King of the Surface and Master of the New Power. I should've figured that the man was one in the same.

Like the rest of his family, he's tall. Roughly my height, he's got a tamer version of his father's hair. I don't see a single scar on the man anywhere, but only his face is exposed. He's wearing a suit far nicer than any I've ever seen his underling Steven wear. Everything is neatly in place and all black. Shirt, jacket, tie, gloves; everything is black. Comparing him to his siblings, he's clearly the oldest of the boys. Although I know Sarah is older than him, she doesn't look it. Logan looks more road worn than she does yet at the same time his face is lacking. He seems void of emotion almost.

"Problem is," Logan continues as he looks at the sword, "I don't know what he looks like. My subordinates have only given me the descriptors of boots and a sword that glows pure white." I look down at my feet and curse myself for not just wearing socks.

That would've been ridiculous, Dac says to me.

Maybe a little, but I wouldn't be in front of the leader of the Surface and *New Power both in one of the only things he has to identify me by!*

256

That's a good point.

"I won't bother asking if you know this character," Logan says. "It won't matter much longer anyway."

"What do you mean by that?" Sarah asks him. Logan shrugs at her, fingering his father's necklace.

"The child declared war on me. I want you to know that what happens next is not what I wished for, nor does the blame fall on me."

"What did you do?" Sarah asks, more demanding.

"I have retaliated," Logan says. "That's something the defending side in a war does."

"I thought you said that you don't know who Sam is," Sarah offers.

"I don't," Logan says, completely agreeing. "Not yet anyway. I have very few leads, but the primary news is that, while he is initially from my kingdom, he now resides in your Sky Kingdom, Nathan. I do so apologize for what's happening." Up until that last sentence, Nathan looked like he was trying to listen while looking disinterested. He very much fails at the looking disinterested part, but now he's not even bothering with a pretense.

"Logan, what are you talking about?" Nathan demands to know, getting to his feet. He's smaller than his brother, but not by much. It's still enough, though, that Logan looks down his nose at Nathan.

"A war criminal against the Kingdom of the Surface is taking refuge in the Kingdom of the Sky. I have dispatched my forces to locate the criminal, as well as either detain or execute him."

"You can't do that!" Nathan screams in his brother's face. "You hold no jurisdiction in the Sky Nation! I have not approved the deployment of your soldiers, and they will not be looked upon kindly!" Logan wipes off the spit that Nathan unintentionally launched at his face with only his thumb. He inspects his thumb to see how much moisture there is before rubbing his thumb and forefinger together.

"Dear Brother," Logan chides, "had you not just said you have no army? What can you hope to do to prevent my entry?"

"I will not supply the transportation to move your soldiers," Nathan says, steadfast.

"Your assistance is not required," Logan says calmly, flicking any remaining spittle on his gloves back on Nathan. "I have already acquired transportation. My forces should already be up in the Sky Kingdom."

Nathan grinds his teeth in Logan's face. It takes him only but a moment to pull away and whip his phone out of his pocket. As Nathan is facing away from his brother, punching numbers into his phone, Logan flashes a sinister grin.

"Gerund, it's me," Nathan says into the phone. I can't hear clearly, but there is a lot of noise coming through the receiver.

Think you could connect us again? I ask Dac.

Give me a second.

Sure enough, after a short time, sound starts coming through.

"... We're holding our own for now," I hear Gerund say. "Who says how long we can keep holding out though? The New Power keep sending more and more reinforcements. It's like they don't even care how many bodies they throw at us."

"Hold on as long as you can, I will head that way now," Nathan refrains from shouting into his phone, but it's easy to hear he's about to pop a vein.

"Hurry!" Gerund screams. I hear him grunt and the clash of swords in the background. It doesn't sound like it's going too terribly well for them up there.

Nathan hangs up the phone, trying to act as calm as possible. He turns around slowly, wild eyes scanning everybody before they come to rest on somebody.

"Tom," Nathan says as calm as he can, "would you mind accompanying me for a moment?"

"Sure," Tom says. Nathan starts walking away at a brisk pace. He grabs Tom tightly around the arm and pulls him along.

"It was a pleasure seeing you again, Captain D. Long," Logan calls.

"I told you," Tom responds, "my name is Tom." He turns back around and matches Nathan's pace. He says this next part more quietly, but I still catch it, "You don't need to use my middle initial you pompous ass."

As Nathan makes his exit, we all watch him go. Even Logan keeps his eyes glued on his brother. Once they're out of eyesight, Logan speaks.

"That man has gotten further and further out of line over the years," Logan comments. "Why do you suffer the irritable peasant?" Logan asks his two remaining siblings, deciding that Rose, Mark, Jinn, Dac, and I are beneath him. Personally, I think I would be very interested by the large robot.

"He's a friend, Logan," Sarah chides.

"Why would you ever desire the companionship of the mortal?" Logan asks.

"Logan," Sarah says, obviously angry. "We *are* mortal. Isn't Dad's death more than enough proof of that?" Logan looks to the sword, bored.

"He was further advanced in years, and ill beyond that. We all knew it was bound to happen." Sarah pops up to her feet and storms over to Logan. She brings her hand back in a wind up to smack him into next week. When she wheels her hand around to hit Logan, he catches her wrist, stopping her. "You will not lay a hand on me in such a manner," Logan says, staring her dead in the eyes.

This is when Kane pushes Sarah out of the way and, without any drama, punches Logan square in the jaw. Logan recoils back a step, managing to bump into me. I quickly move out of his way. Sam Cutter? Who's Sam Cutter? Do you know a Sam Cutter, because *I* sure don't...

Oh boy...

"Don't you dare say another word," Kane threatens his brother. "You never cared about Dad. *Never*," his voice cracks. "All you ever seemed to care about is your stupid kingdom. You do realize that the rest of us haven't called them kingdoms for over two centuries, right? Why are you such an insufferable ass?"

Logan runs a thumb over his jaw where Kane connected. He looks between Kane and his thumb, but doesn't say a word.

"Well?" Kane demands of Logan's silence, "Answer me!"

"Make up your mind, will you?" Logan says, bored with the entire situation. "First you tell me to remain quiet and next you demand that I speak to you." Is he trying to piss everybody off? What is with bad people and trying to piss everybody off? Is there like a handbook or something with these guidelines in it?

"To answer your question," Logan continues, ignoring the fact that his brother looks about ready to tear his head off. I doubt they noticed that they're standing on Gabriel's makeshift grave. Metaphorically buried for not even an hour, and already Logan would dance on his father's grave, "I find myself perfectly pleasant company. I simply do not tolerate lesser beings."

"What a load of crap!" Kane bursts. "We're all

humans here. Sure, there are a few differences, but human at the core. You're a supremacist ass."

"I find it unfortunate that you think that way, Brother," Logan says. "Perhaps I should not have come."

"Perhaps not," Kane says in the mocking tone only a younger brother is capable of producing. Logan nods to himself before turning his attention back to the sword and necklace.

"Farewell, Father. Fear not, for I will complete the dream that you began. I will reunify this world for its greater good." Reunify for the what? "When my quest is complete I will return for the necklace," he says. "It is the closest we have to a crown for the world. Do you still wear yours?" Logan directs the last question at Kane. "I have mine." From within his shirt, he produces the necklace recognizing him as the lineage of Gabriel. His is a red spherical gem clutched on four sides by the talons of some being. The talons only reach half way down the necklace, maybe a bit further. They're at regular intervals and only long enough to hold the stone in place.

"Do not forget your role in this world," Logan tells Kane. "Once I am through dealing with Nathan, I will advance to you... provided you haven't yet come to see reason."

With his final threat hanging in the air, Logan turns to leave. He makes it ten paces before I do something incredibly stupid.

"So much for looking for me," I shout at him while looking at Sarah and Kane. Logan is behind me at this point, a dangerous place for me to let him linger. The look on both Sarah and Kane's faces is one letting me know they think I've lost any semblance of rationality.

"Excuse me?" Logan says, delaying his departure. He sounds disgusted at having to talk with a lower life form like me. What an ass.

Okay, so the psychotic ruler of a nation and leader of the New Power was trying to leave and you stop *him?* Dac shouts in my head. *What the hell is wrong with you?*

I wish I knew, I tell him, mustering up all the calm I can.

"Your forces in the Sky Nation," I clarify for the pea brain, "I thought you'd said they were looking for Sam Cutter." He makes a high-pitched, noncommittal noise.

"That's a secondary objective of theirs. I did not tell a lie."

"You're full of crap," I tell him. I muster up the courage to turn around and look directly at him, only to find that he managed to reproach and is now within a foot of me, staring me down. Our eyelevel is almost exactly the same. I'd be willing to bet that my extra height on him is due only to my boots and absurdly messy hair. From this close, with all his attention directed at me, the hardness and cruelty of his eyes is near overwhelming. "You say that you're looking for the one who declared war on you, yet your intention is to conquer your brothers' nations," I try to take in as much detail as possible looking at his face. As I said, his eyes capture any who look at him in an instant. I try and get everything, though, everything from his sharp nose to his not entirely full lips, to the fact that his left ear is ever so slightly higher than his right. Taking everything in, there's one thing that bothers me, only one thing that's off. It's in his eyes, but I can't put my finger on exactly what it is.

"Your deduction is not false," he admits, "yet is not entirely accurate either."

"Why do you say that?" I ask him, paying careful attention to his eyes. "It sure sounds like the goal of the New Power."

Did you just call him out on being the leader of the New Power? A bewildered Dac asks. *It's bad enough that you couldn't just let him leave but now you're calling him out on things? WHY ARE YOU PUSHING THE BUTTONS OF A MADMAN?*

Keep track of his eyes, I tell Dac. *There's something not right there, and I can't tell exactly what it is.*

You are absolutely insane. Where's the nearest institution? I'm checking you in.

Just do it, I plead.

Check you into the loony bin? Gladly.

Would you just shut up and pay attention to his eyes!

Alright, alright already.

Just trust me here. Something's not right.

"I see you've heard the name of my forces. How trivial," Logan says.

You're right, Dac says after observing Logan's eyes through mine. *There's something really familiar there.* But what? What is it? "What? Did you think you could let a little piece of information like that slip, and that I would cower before you? You understand nothing of the world, child."

"I understand that I'm going to kick your ass," I tell him. I can feel the collective mental energy of everybody around me trying to get me to shut my mouth. If they had their way, I would've stopped talking about ten minutes ago, before Logan even showed up. You know, just in case he happened to somehow be listening.

Logan cocks his head at me, and that distant look in his eyes grows more pronounced. That's it! It's a distant look. I-I think. Maybe? Is there a chance he's just disinterested?

I mean, he *is* a jerk who thinks he's above all others.

It doesn't take long for his attention to zero in on me again, his gaze harsher than before. I can easily imagine any from the Surface withering under his stare. Honestly, I'm probably only about two seconds from wetting my pants and breaking down in tears. This is not a situation I want to stay in for any longer than is absolutely necessary.

It wasn't absolutely necessary for even one second, Dac points out.

I couldn't just let him walk away like that, I respond.

Sure you could've, Dac says. *You see, you take that heavily booted foot you have attached to your freakishly long legs and you shove it in your mouth.* Before I can come up with a response, Logan starts to speak.

"Who are you?" he says slowly, thinking carefully about every word. He seems insulted that his diction contained so many mundane words. Good.

Do I tell him?

It's a little too late to back out now, genius.

"My name's Sam Cutter," I tell him, focusing hard on not letting my voice crack. "I know you've heard of me." Only now does Logan size me up, taking in the details of me from head to toe. I can tell his eyes linger on my boots. It's not a super obvious thing, but he pauses there for a moment longer than he does anywhere else. Since I'm wearing long sleeves, the mark on my wrist is hidden, and I doubt he can see the brand on my palm. I'm sure there are plenty of other scars for him to notice, but there's not too terribly much of my flesh revealed for him to examine. When he looks like he's about done checking me out, he opens his mouth to speak, but I talk over him.

"I'm sure Steven has told you all about me," I say in a rush, mostly just trying to make sure that I speak before him. He hums.

"Indeed he has, Mr. Cutter, indeed he has. From what I can tell, the only trait he did not over exaggerate is your ego and… adolescent charm," he sticks venom in each of his words. That, combined with the entire oppressive aura around him, is enough to make me not want to be here anymore. I *really* don't want to be here anymore. Can I leave? "In fact, I believe he may have under exaggerated. I didn't believe it possible." I react in the most dignified way I can. I make a rude, mocking face at him. A part of that is me sticking my tongue out.

"I hope you're harder to beat than he is," I say. No I don't. Shut up. Shut up, shut up, shut up! Oh my God! I swear my mouth has a mind of it's own. Stop talking!

"Considering my subordinate yet breathes, I would say that the Flying Demon is yet to claim victory." He seems smug and content with his comment, but honestly I'm just confused. Flying Demon? It takes a few seconds of chewing on that name to remember exactly what he's talking about. Back in the Water Nation, when I thought Jinn had been killed, I earned the title of Flying Demon to the New Power. Can't much say I'm a fan of the name. I'm even less of a fan of what I did to earn it.

A sneer finds its way to my face. The deeper my frown goes, the wider the smile Logan develops.

"See, I've been trying to mentor young Steven. He claims he can raise this sort of reaction from a person, but I'm yet to see it."

"I'm going to rip your teeth out," I say with my teeth clenched.

"I doubt it," Logan says. "I doubt the combined effort of your pitiful armies could take on my glorious revolutionaries." I grind my teeth together and I'm pretty sure I start to growl.

"I offer you this," Logan says, addressing Kane and Sarah but still looking at me. "You have two weeks to see the error of your ways and swear fealty to me. Otherwise, I assume you know the battlefield we will

265

meet on."

"I'll see you there in a fortnight," Kane shouts.

"Pity," Logan says, shaking his head at me as if it is my fault his brother isn't obeying. "I loathe to stand above your mangled corpse, but progress cannot be stopped." He flashes me another cold smile, making sure that I'm thoroughly disturbed before turning and walking away. "I shall see your might in two weeks," he says. "One way or another, the kingdoms will come under my control, and the world will be right again."

Chapter
Twenty-Seven

I stand stock still until Logan in gone. I don't even take full breaths until I hear the sound of his transport taking off and leaving.

"Is 'not good' the understatement of the year?" I ask.

"The New Year has only just begun and already I don't think that one can be topped," Sarah says, just as stiff as I am.

Rose comes up and smacks my arm, "What were you thinking?" she demands to know.

"I wish I knew," I tell her, rubbing my arm. "I just kind of started talking, and I couldn't stop myself."

She stares at me in disbelief before saying, exasperated, "You're an idiot."

"So I've been told," I say. The relative silence is broken by Jinn's ring tone going off. With the gravity of the situation, he doesn't hesitate to answer.

"Hello?" he says into his phone. After a brief pause he says, "Hold on. Hold on already, I'm putting you on speaker." He pulls the phone away from his ear and presses the button to put it into speaker mode. Arthur's voice comes out in the oxymoron that is a slow rush.

"It wasn't good, Jinn," he says. "They showed up again. I had to have these Surface dwellers take refuge in the ship Sam crashed when everybody was here. Still, the New Power attacked. This group held up well, but there were still casualties." Jinn looks over each of us as Arthur speaks, gauging our reactions. "There was a point when I wasn't sure how the fight would go. You know I'm not very good with leading. That's about when the New Power pulled out, gave the message to contact our generals. What the high hell are they talking about?"

"It would appear that we've met their leader," Jinn says. Arthur is silent for a moment, taking in this bit of information.

"I assume his head is no longer attached to his shoulders?" Arthur says. Well, anatomically speaking, a head is attached to a neck, not shoulders, but I won't say anything.

"It's a bit more complicated than that," Jinn explains. "Turns out that the leader of the New Power and the King of the Surface are one in the same." Again, Arthur doesn't immediately respond.

"How's the kid taking it?" he eventually asks. Jinn looks up from his phone to look at me.

"It could be better," Jinn says.

"Ah, well, give him my regards and a slap on the arm for me, will ya?" Arthur says, somber. "And let him know his friend Scott made it just fine. A couple injuries, but still alive and in one piece."

"Can do," Jinn says, not breaking eye contact with me.

I break the contact, looking down and mumbling, "Thanks."

"Jinn, they're not messing around anymore," Arthur says. "The New Power aren't using those staves like toys. The power is amplified far higher than I've seen before, and they're sending more and more blades. Care to explain what's going on?"

"We're finishing things in two weeks," I say loud

enough to reach the transceiver. "That's what he said. The King said that we're to meet him on some battlefield two weeks from now."

"Since when do you address people by titles, kid?" Arthur asks me, halfway surprised I can hear him. I don't know why, considering that Jinn warned him he was being put on speakerphone.

"Since I'd get lashings and water restrictions for doing otherwise," I admit. I'm not in a mood to beat around the bush right now. Kane and Sarah look at me with sad puppy dog eyes, seeing me as an adorable animal that has just been kicked. The emotion is mixed with a shock that such a reality could exist.

Believe it. It's been my world for fifteen years. Only one of the sixteen I've been here has been any different.

There's a much longer pause this time where nobody wants to speak after my revelation. I wait for somebody to say or do something. Through the phone, I can hear background noises of the LARPers recuperating from the New Power's attack. I don't make out anything specific, but there's quite a bit of comotion. Arthur is probably close to the thick of it. After I'm sure that nobody is going to say anything, I decide to speak up again.

"Would anybody like to explain what he meant by a battlefield you'd know?" I direct this to the two Royals. Logan was talking to them when he mentioned a battlefield.

"Years and years ago," Kane starts, still trembling with anger, "we set up rules, mostly as a joke. We decided that if anything like this should happen, that we can decide upon an all out conclusion of sorts."

"What do you mean by that?" Mark asks.

"It's exactly what happened," Kane states. "My brother decided the date of the final confrontation to be two weeks from today on the appropriate battlefield."

"Which would be?" I lead him, trying to get to the answer that I was actually looking for. Kane takes an irritated sounding breath, although if the feeling is directed towards his brother or me, I do not know.

"The rule we set is that the final battlefield would be the nation of the one who declared war. Considering that you're from the Surface, that means that the primary battle will take place here."

"The entire Surface?" I almost gasp. That doesn't help! I don't know if anybody has noticed, but the planet is huge!

"Theoretically, yes," Kane says, "but I have a feeling I know where Logan will want to meet."

"And where would that be?" Arthur asks through the phone, just as impatient as I am.

"My brother doesn't much like traveling, and he's arrogant enough that he would select right in front of his capital to attack. Sorry, his citadel. I always thought he was jesting whenever he would have a slip of the tongue like that, but now I'm not so sure."

"You've never seen where your own brother lives?" Dac asks.

Good question, I tell him.

"Not in a long, long time," Kane says. "Logan would always converse through messengers or phone calls. On the rare occasions we would meet in person, we always met at Dad's old dwellings. Logan always made some excuse of wanting to see the family. After enough years, I started making excuses to not see him. I know siblings shouldn't have a relationship like this, but it's what happens."

"I wouldn't want to see him either," I say.

You sure you wouldn't like to see him at least one more time?

Only if I can punch him... in the face... with a brick.

Sounds reasonable, Dac laughs in my head.

"This is the worst family drama I've ever seen," Arthur says.

"Have you met my family?" I mutter. Rose hugs my arm, being close enough to hear what I said.

At least your mom and dad are not actively trying to kill you.

That's only because my dad and I aren't in the same room this particular moment.

I don't think he'd actually go through with it, Dac says.

I wouldn't let him get close, I say. Even thinking about my own family makes my stomach uneasy. I'd gladly talk more about how screwed up the Royals are over talking about my own familial issues any day of the week. If the day ends in the letter "y," I don't think it'll be a good day to talk about my family. That sounds reasonable, right?

"Unfortunately, what our family does has global ramifications," Sarah says. "There's still five of us left, but I don't know how many there will be a month from now."

Five?

Let's see, there's Nathan, Kane, Logan, and Sarah. Gabriel would've been the fifth but... well, I don't especially want to go there right now. I am still at his burial sight. I don't need the thought to reinforce it. Who's the fif...

Never mind.

She means me.

"That's a little grim," Mark says.

"We're on the Surface," I tell him. "This is the right place for that line of thought. I don't know how many I could pull from this place."

Before anybody can respond, through the phone I

271

can hear somebody calling for Arthur's attention.

"Be there in a moment!" he shouts back, turning his head away from the microphone. "I have to run. What's the plan?"

"We have two weeks," Kane says. "Prepare your men for war. Nathan will send pick up for you and your soldiers in a few days."

"Got it," Arthur says glumly. "You lot take care of yourselves now, and I'll see you soon."

There's the beep of him hanging up, and Jinn returns his phone to his pocket.

"Well, what do we do now?" Mark asks the question nobody else wants to.

"Once Tom arrives with transportation," Kane starts, "I will need to return to the Water Nation and rally the forces I can. Everybody here should do the same." It seems like he's done talking when he adds in a last note, "Oh, and make sure you say goodbye to anybody you care about. As of now, we don't know any of our life expectancies past two weeks."

Chapter
Twenty-Eight

As Kane promised, Tom—apparently his full name is Tom D. Long—returned to pick us up. Kane returned to the Water Nation and I'm not sure where Sarah went off to. Mark, Jinn, Rose, Dac, and I are all up here in the Sky Nation. Jinn and Mark are off doing work with the Ravens and Nathan. What would I say about what I'm doing? I'd say I'm being completely unproductive.

I'm currently lying on the floor, alone, with my face in the carpet. Nobody else is here in Jinn's big house. Sure, I could go out and find something to do, but it's pointless. What is there to do when you know the world is going to tear itself asunder in less than two weeks?

I've looked at the blank screen of my cellphone way too many hours of the days that pass, debating calling my mom, calling John, calling somebody just to hear a voice other than Dac or my own.

I'm pretty sure that Dac is the only reason that I haven't jumped off this platform without my boots.

Jinn and Mark return late at night and leave early in the morning, so it's not like I talk much with them. It doesn't matter how late I stay up. They generally come home, hastily eat something, and collapse.

Luckily for me, my phone starts to ring. I fish it out of my pocket and turn my head to the side to place the phone against my ear when I hit answer.

"Hello?" I say, trying not to eat carpet as I talk.

"Sam!" I hear John shout in my ear, "You're never going to believe what's been going on. Are you still on the Surface?"

"Not right now," I tell him.

"Oh, then you're really never going to guess what's happening!" He sounds so enthusiastic. I know it should perk me up, but it only deepens the pit in my stomach. This waiting around is worse than when the New Power attacked this house, or when the people of Hub Fourteen and more attacked the Water Tower. Those waiting periods were measured in hours, nothing more than a day.

Two weeks. We were given two whole freaking weeks to dwell on what's going to happen. I know it may not seem like such a big deal to everybody else, but to somebody with absolutely nothing to do but think about the bloody confrontation to come—and imagine every gory detail—it's absolutely terrifying.

The most depressing part is that in a fair amount of the scenarios that play out in my head, we lose.

Knowing that so much excitement and joy could still exist in a person, hearing John talk like that, makes me sick to my stomach. There's a good chance I'm going to be dead and gone soon. There's a chance everybody I care about is going to be dead soon. The fact that there's a chance of *one* of the people I care about dying soon is enough to put me in a dark place.

For the sake of John's ignorance, I try not to sound like I'm already writing our eulogies, "What's happening?"

"The factories are revolting!" he shouts. My eyebrows shoot up, and my entire body twitches. If anybody were here to witness it, it would've looked like

274

I was a fish out of water that flopped once.

"What?" I say into the phone. Did I mishear him? The factories are revolting? That couldn't be right.

"The factories! After you sort of blew one up, others started being overthrown. I saw it on the broadcast. They're saying that the guys from the factory *you* blew up, the guys *you* saved, have spread around to other factories and were inspired to follow suit. Of course the Surface's official broadcast is putting it in a much harsher light, but it's happening! For every factory that's destroyed or abandoned, more and more people join the cause. Things are changing down here, man! Oh, and I saw Rick and Fred doing it too!"

Well that's one way to put it.

"I don't believe it," I say, trying to process what he's saying. It's like the words are going in my one ear and are only being contained because the other is pressed against the ground.

"Yeah!" he shouts excited. "The King is doing an official broadcast any moment now. He's supposedly going to address the factories. It's going to be amazing seeing his reaction." My eyes widen in realization.

That broadcast isn't to talk about the factories.

Through the phone I can hear John's sister say, "John-John it's starting!" in her cute popping voice.

"I have to go Sam," he says to me. "Broadcast's starting, I'll talk to you after."

"JOHN!" I shout into the receiver, pushing my upper body up with my free arm, "JOHN WAIT! DON'T WATCH THAT BROADCAST!" I pause a moment to see if he's trying to respond. When I get no answer I again scream, "*JOHN!*" The disconnected tone sounds in my chest and my heart sets to racing.

"DAC!" I scream like a man on fire, shooting up to my feet as if it would make a difference.

I'm already on it, he says to me, trying to remain calm. *I've never tried to hack into something like that, and I don't know if it's even possible.*

"Just do it!" I scream at his metal body. I'm tense as if ready to fight, forced to wait. What is Logan saying? Is he torching neighborhoods right this moment just to prove a point? He can't do this! This is between him and me, not innocent people!

I feel the eons racing by like grains of sand in an hourglass. I dare not say a word or think too loud for threat of breaking Dac's concentration.

He's announced the war, Dac says hastily at what feels like the turn of the second eternity.

"Stop him!" I screech.

I can only find one way to stop him, Dac says.

"Do it!" He's silent for a few seconds before speaking.

You're live.

What?

The only way I could interrupt him, Dac explains, *is to broadcast over him. Speak out loud and you'll be broadcast. They won't see a video of you, but everybody tuned in on the Surface will hear your voice.*

Is this really the best way you could think of doing this? I telepathically shout at him. I don't want anybody to hear me reprimanding him.

Stop complaining and say something already! It's not like I can stop them forever, you know, it's only temporary until they fix the bug I've created!

Fine!

"Um..." I start real strong. Good job Sam. You're talking to the whole Surface and all you can think of is "um." Brilliant. "People of the Surface," oh God, what am I, an alien? "My name is Sam Cutter. Honestly, I don't know if my name has been mentioned or not yet." I look at Dac, worry in my eyes, and see him roll a finger, telling me to go on. "I'm from the Surface, just like you. I lived there most of my life until I escaped last year. Since leaving, I've seen some fantastic things. Things I never would've thought possible. I also saw people trying to ruin it; I saw the New Power. I don't know if you've heard, but apparently that's the name of the Surface's invasion forces."

"Yes, I declared war on them," I continue, entirely unsure of my words, "but truly I'm not the one to start it. Regarding the other nations, this war started at least ten years ago. For us on the Surface, the war started on ourselves long before that. But the battle is only now beginning." I can't help but feel awkward talking to the thin air. How do I know this is even working? Can they hear me? How does Dac even know how to do this?

Shut up and keep going. I ignore the oxymoron.

"In a little over a week, the final battle will be held, and everything will be decided," I say. "I know we, the Surface, have only just become active in this battle, and that it's conclusion feels like it's coming far too soon, but I think we all know it couldn't have come soon enough. This has been a long time coming.

"He may or may not have told you, but if he's brave enough, the Ki—" I catch myself. I was about to say king instinctually, having had that drilled into me, but I refuse to call him that, "Logan," I say, "will tell you when and where the battle will be. If you want to give your all for the freedom and safety of the world, meet me there. I don't blame you if you stay home though. I'm in the middle of wishing I could do the same... I'm sorry I brought this on all of you." I pause, trying to think of something else to say, anything. I have to keep talking to keep the broadcast off.

"It doesn't matter anymore," Dac says out loud, "I lost control. I couldn't do that again if I wanted to." The strength departs from my legs as I collapse to the ground. I don't think I could do that again.

Ever.

You did good, Dac says. *We didn't block everything, but you stopped a lot of the threats he was going to pass out. You gave the people of the Surface hope. Keep in mind that the entire planet was watching that message. They'll come to help. Some of them.*

I don't want them to, I say. Dammit, why did I say something like that? Why!?

Why not? he asks me. I don't hesitate to answer.

Because I've asked them to die.

My phone beeps and I scramble to grab it. On the screen, a single message is displayed from John.

Are we going to die? – John.

I break.

I can't even respond to him. I throw my phone and curl up into the fetal position, sobbing. The rest of the day passes this way.

***

I slept on the ground there that night. I was asleep before Mark and Jinn returned and slept past when they left. Thankfully, they didn't try to wake me or check on me. I fetch my phone from where it landed and find it broken. That figures. I probably shouldn't throw technology. On the now shattered screen is still that single message. I respond to it with two letters I don't entirely believe.

No.

I send the message on and don't expect a reply. I don't get one. That I couldn't even call says enough.

Another day passes in my self-imposed solitude. It's not like I'm shutting people out, it's just that I'm not making an effort to go out and see anybody.

Today, though, it's different. While I am very busy with lying face first on the carpet, I hear the doorbell. Confused and interested by the sound, I get to my feet. When I open the door, there's a very pretty girl standing there. She looks me up and down, and within three seconds, comes up with her diagnosis.

"You are definitely not okay," Rose says, coming inside, invited or not. She marches through the house, expecting me to follow her. I sigh and close the door, locking it. I don't know who I expect to try and barge in, but habit makes me lock it. I push off the closed door and spin on my sock to follow Rose. She's far ahead of me, but she doesn't slow.

Rose pauses momentarily to open the door to the backyard, but continues her march once it's wide enough for even me to fit through.

"You know, this is not helping," I tell her as she leads me through Jinn's back yard, since she has refused to say anything other than to tell me I'm not okay. Still, she doesn't respond. We walk past the training circle Jinn has, and she heads for the edge of the platform. She sits with her legs dangling off the side in what I notice is almost the exact same place I found her ten months ago.

I take my spot next to her, the same side as I did back then.

"If you're planning on jumping," I say as I sit, "I should tell you that I don't have my boots on right now." She gives me the evil eye until I have myself situated, and I add, "But I would still find a way to catch you."

Her glare immediately softens. No, I did not say that because of her evil eye. I actually barely noticed it sitting down. I was just making sure I didn't fall. That would be embarrassing, dying of falling off a platform days before the biggest battle of our generation.

"And how would you do that?" she asks.

"I don't know," I admit, looking out over the clouds. "I'd find a way." She's quiet a moment, gauging me before speaking. I wiggle my toes in their now wet socks while I wait.

"Do you remember what the first thing you said to me was?" she asks, squinting against the sun. Her squint scrunches up her nose in not necessarily the cutest way, but I like it.

"The truth?" I ask her. She nods. "I have no idea." I look at her with a smile on my face. Her expression doesn't change for a second before she starts laughing at me.

"Honestly, I don't either," she confesses.

"Then why were you asking?" I ask her, now laughing myself.

"I was curious," she says innocently.

"You were just curious?" I echo, incredulous. "You show up out of nowhere, tell me I'm not okay, and then ask me if I remember the first thing I said to you and you've got no reasoning behind it?"

"No, I said I was curious, not that I had no reason," she counters.

"That's pretty much no reason."

"Is not."

"Is too."

"I'm older than you," she reminds me. "I'm wiser to the world than you are, so I say it's not." I laugh a little bit at that.

It's true that she's a bit more than a year older than me, but, "I think I'm probably the more road worn of the two of us."

"Probably true," she agrees. "What do you want to talk about?"

"I don't really want to talk about anything," I say. "I

don't want to do anymore waiting. I don't want anybody to die." Apparently, I'm no good at keeping my mouth closed. I think that's a valuable life skill I should really work on developing.

"Everybody dies eventually," she says, lacing the fingers of her hand through mine that I'd absently had sitting out, supporting my weight from behind.

"Doesn't that suck," I say, depressed. The clouds beneath us march along, the wind carrying them quickly for clouds.

"You better not go dying," she orders me. I mock salute her.

"I promise not to," I lie. How could I promise not to die? Out of everybody that's going to be out there fighting, how do I know that I'm going to live? Do I even have the right to be telling her that lie?

"Hey!" she snaps at me, "You're in one of your moods, so that means you don't believe what you just told me." I smile sadly at her before looking at my feet. She's determined though. With her free hand, she grabs my cheeks and forces me to look at her.

"Perk up, Mr. Depressed, or I will throw you off this platform right now." Considering the fact that she's mimicking the state she's holding my lips in, I don't take the threat very seriously, but I get the point.

"I'll do my best not to die," I say seriously, "but you have to promise the same."

"Oh, I know I'm not dying," Rose says. "There's still too much for me to do in this life." I smile at her, the gesture not quite reaching my eyes.

Rose releases my face and says, "You shouldn't be alone."

"I'm not alone," I tell her. "I've got Dac."

"Well, no offense to you, Dac..." she starts.

None taken, he says before she can even finish.

"... but for you two, that still counts as alone. I mean have somebody that is not in your thoughts all the time around."

See, Dac says, *I knew I wouldn't be offended. I don't agree with her definition of alone and am slightly insulted, but I'm not offended.*

Aren't those basically the same thing?

Not at all, Dac says. *I think.* He thinks. Sure, why wouldn't he know? Eh, it doesn't matter to me.

"I've been alone most of my life," I tell her.

"That doesn't change things," she says. "So here's the plan: You and I are going to sit here, or somewhere else on this big lawn, and watch the sunset."

"Now you're making plans for me are you?" I ask.

"Only when your only plans probably involved you laying on the floor."

"Dac called you, didn't he?"

"He may have," Rose smiles.

Traitor, I say to him.

I deny all accusations! he defends himself.

Rose does a little butt hop to get right next to me and rests her head on my shoulder, looking out the same way I am. We sit like this for over an hour when I feel a bubbling in my chest and a gasp in my mind.

Do it! Dac snaps. *Do it do it do it!*

What are you talking about? I ask him.

You know what I'm talking about you ninny, do it!

What are you—

DO IT! He sounds like an over excited teenage girl.

What—

Do. It.

Dac—

Do it!

Stop!

Do it do it do it, he starts chanting.

Will you shut up? I shout at him.

Only if you do it.

Stop, I beg.

He hums in thought before giving me a snappy, *No.*

The chanting resumes. After no more than a minute of it, I snap.

Alright already! Stop! It instantly gets entirely silent in my mind. The trace of Dac that I feel is an excited buzz in the back bottom left of my skull. I take a deep breath and close my eyes.

"I love you," I say, incredibly quietly.

Weak! Dac judges.

I hear a single throat chuckle that's almost a judgmental noise before she says, "Took you long enough." I'm sure she's trying to hide it, but I can feel her huge grin on my shoulder.

"Yeah, sorry about that," I say, still not opening my eyes.

"I knew you'd get there someday," Rose says, picking her head up off my chest and kissing my cheek. "And I love you too."

YES! Dac screams, basically throwing a party in my head. If I stain my ears, I could swear I hear the sound of an overexcited robot falling over.

Not a robot! Dac throws in there, unable to keep the excitement out of his voice.

I start smiling myself now, in part due to trying not to laugh at Dac, but mostly due to the warm feeling settling over me taking the place of the uneasiness.

Although she repositions herself multiple times as we wait, we stay true to Rose's plans. The two of us sit out here until sunset and it's absolutely fantastic. We don't move until the stars are hanging in the sky overhead. I make a wish on the first one I see.

When we do finally return inside, it's because my

toes are freezing cold. Only wearing socks outside in the Sky Nation will do that to you.

Rose follows me up to my room where I take a pair of sweatpants into the bathroom to change, not wanting to be naked in front of her. When I return, she's standing there wearing a shirt she just stole from me, her pants and shirt discarded on the floor. "What? It's nothing you haven't seen before." I smile at her, taking a mental image of it.

When I crawl into bed, she follows after me, and it's the best night of sleep I've had in a long while.

***

The remainder of the days passes much more nicely than their predecessors. Rose comes and goes as time permits, spending most nights sleeping in my bed with me. We talk about everything and nothing, our discussion rarely touching on what's to come. On the day it's supposed to happen, I wake up early of my own accord. Rose slept at home that night. She and Jackson, her father, are going to be fighting tomorrow, and they wanted the personal time together.

I shower and dress myself. I don't wear anything special. I have on, as always, a t-shirt, jeans, and my boots. I leave my wallet sitting where it is on my nightstand, but I make sure to have both my phone and my sword. When I look at myself in a mirror, I can't help but notice how plain I am. Jeans, t-shirt, boots, messy black hair, a body's worth of scars, and a tattoo I never wanted compose what I present to others. How is it that the Royals, even when they're wearing normal clothes, have such a presence?

It's almost unsettling how the day begins. Jinn and I eat breakfast together like any other day, except the table discussion is different. He gives me a gift. Jinn produces a belt, complete with miniature metal vials of Blue Elixir with sport-tops so I can bite, drink, and keep going.

He already has his fastened. I separate myself from my cereal long enough to do the same. I count and see that there are six vials in all, three on either side. I move my arms around and, although they're a little troublesome, the belt and bottles don't really interfere with my movement.

"All together that's only one full vial of Blue Elixir," Jinn explains. "Nathan couldn't find a better way to distribute it. If you need more, drink what you have and fly back to the command tent. We're going to try and have as much Blue Elixir as possible there."

"Got it," I tell him for the tenth time.

When we're done eating, we head out back and grab our Sky Bikes. Jinn leads the way through the air, as he had been given the coordinates of where to go by Nathan. Dac is riding with me. I don't notice the time pass as we fly. At this point, I'm sure everything will pass in a daze until somebody points something sharp or sparking at my face.

When we do reach our destination, though, I nearly fall off of my bike. Nathan's citadel is a gigantic castle with a mass of New Power in front of it that seems equal to the amount of people I've seen in my entire lifetime. Alright, maybe there's more. I doubt that's all of them. The castle dwarfs all of us easily. Metal and stone combine to climb at least ten stories in the air, not counting it's continuing spires.

There's an unbelievably vast open field with nothing in between to interfere with the combat about to ensue. I really cannot capture the scope of this thing well. All of the New Power don't even begin to fill the field.. The ocean is off to my right, to the east of the battlefield, and there are clouds hanging overhead being gently carried by the wind, indifferent to the world around them.

What may be even more surprising is the amount of people gathered to fight with us. Looking through them all, I see a raised wooden platform that's only perhaps one story high. There's a single person standing on it, and although I can't hear them, whatever they're saying sure is making everybody else scream in enthusiasm.

Jinn and I carefully come down and land on the platform where Sarah is. I go red in the face realizing that her speech isn't her speech at all.

It's a recording.

Of me.

She is playing a recording of what I said when I took over the airwaves.

"Is there a reason you're playing this?" I ask her.

"It's what inspired them to come here," Sarah says. "I wasn't expecting this many people here. They know exactly what they're getting into."

"I was really hoping nobody would come," I tell her.

"I know how you feel," she says, rubbing my shoulder as I dismount my Sky Bike, "but it's out of your hands now. They heard your words and were awoken, not manipulated."

"They're still here because of me," I say, miserable.

"There's a chance we can win this," she says.

"What do you mean a chance?" I return, "We are definitely going to win this." After two weeks of moping around, I believe my own words. Despite the situation, people came. More people from the Surface want this change. I wouldn't say I feel happy, but I feel light. I feel as if I can shed the past month or so and return to being in a better mental state. I feel good right now.

Sarah pulls Jinn and me both into a hug, smiling at

my comment, "Be safe out there, you two. I plan on forcing my brothers to throw a victory party after this." Jinn and I both laugh at that. I can even hear a chuckle from Dac.

"You too, Sarah," Jinn says. I just say "You too." Dac lumbers over and participates in the group hug. I hear somebody climb onto the platform.

"Now isn't that sweet," I look over and see Arthur standing there, staring at us.

"Get over here, Grumpy," Jinn says. Arthur doesn't complain about the nickname, and he does actually join in the group hug. I would say we're all scared. A healthy dose of fear can be a good thing.

"Nobody's allowed to die," I say one more time, eliciting a round of laughs from the group. Arthur genuinely laughing is a strange sound.

A silence comes over the battlefield that I didn't notice until just now when the only sound is the five of us laughing. The hug breaks apart and we look out over the field. There is a terrifying roar just before the swarm of New Power begins to lurch forward, charging.

It has begun.

Chapter Twenty-Nine

Without hesitation, our forces return the battle cry and rush forward. I follow their lead and skip over to my Sky Bike. As I remount my bike, I watch Dac jump off the platform into a newly frightened group of people. The funniest part is that some of them—the LARPers— recognize him and slap him on the back, welcoming him to the fight.

"Sam, wait," Sarah says as I start my bike. The engine roars to life and I almost miss her.

"What's up?" I ask, looking at her. I can't keep my eyes focused on her though. They keep shifting over to the two charging armies, the New Power obviously the larger. "How are they all armed, anyway?"

"Your LARP friends apparently had a lot of weapons sitting around. I don't approve of all of them, but it'll do," Arthur tells me before drawing out his scythe and taking the stairs down from this platform. That makes sense, I guess. I hear him muttering, "At least they have shields," as he goes. At least, I think that's what he says.

"Just be careful, okay?" she says. "I'm going to try and help coordinate everybody from back here, but I'll be out there as soon as I can."

"You got it," I tell her, putting my bike into flight mode. A slight smile comes to my face as I hit the gas.

There isn't near enough runway to take off from this wooden platform, but there is height. The Sky Bike shoots off the edge with me on it, dropping a couple feet before it really starts flying. Hopefully I didn't hit anybody before getting airborne. I get some altitude over their heads for the sake of safety, but I don't go too high.

I try and rush to the front, but I can't build up enough velocity to do so. The spearheads of the two armies meet, and there's an explosion of sound. Steel meets steel on a larger scale than I think I've ever heard. The enthusiastic battle cries last a bit longer as the flanks of the armies collide. Once the sounds of melee are predominant, the enthusiasm turns to sounds of abject terror and death. I can tell, in the instant that I'm approaching, that we're not doing too terribly well.

I fly in low over the heads of the rebelling forces, drawing my sword out to its full length. Once I'm over the heads of the New Power's forces, I tighten my thighs' grip on the bike and flip it over. Without any particular need for accuracy, I swing as hard and fast as I can over and over again, hitting a New Power soldier each time. None of them expect an attack from above, so none even attempt a counter attack.

I continue like this as long as I can until I feel my knees starting to slip. The instant I get that sensation, I turn my bike over, making myself right side up again. I take only a second to resituate myself before banking hard to turn around. Thinking it might be effective, I drop my altitude a bit and turn my Sky Bike into a swift battering ram. I feel every collision with a New Power helmet. I don't need to look behind me to know I'm leaving a wake of destruction.

I'm almost at the front! Dac lets me know.

I'll get you there faster, I tell him, pulling up over the heads of the New Power. At this point they notice that somebody is attacking them from overhead. Spears and staves and swords are all being thrust at me as I travel, forcing me to get even higher to remain out of their range. Someone launches their sparking staff at me. I swerve out of the way of it and hear the surprised scream of a different soldier. Brightside is that, not only did he take out one of his friends, but now there's an unarmed soldier out there.

When I pass over the front, back into friendly territory, I see that any semblance of formation that the New Power had held dissolved due to the chaos of battle. That didn't take too terribly long. The front keeps growing longer as more soldiers pour over the sides to try and get in on the action. Ahead of me is what I'm looking for. A ways off is a metal hand sticking high in the air.

You're nowhere near the front!

I was exaggerating! Dac defends himself.

Just grab on when I pass over you!

Dac must've told something to the people around him because they're all diving off to the sides, trying to get as low as possible. I slow slightly as I pass overhead. I witness Dac jump vertically, both arms extended. From there, I feel the dip as his weight is added to my Sky Bike. I don't know exactly what he grabs on to, but I know for sure, from even my own actions, that it'll be a miracle if this thing is still running after today. I pull up hard, my bike groaning at the effort.

"Sorry!" I hear Dac yell beneath me. I can't see it for sure, but I get the distinct impression he accidentally kicked somebody in the head.

I turn the bike as sharply as I dare—which is barely at all—while still pulling up, trying to keep above the heads of our soldiers. Having more than an extra six feet of metal dangling beneath me makes maneuvering difficult. Controlling the Sky Bike to the degree I'd like right now is much harder than I anticipated. I shrink my sword down some so that I can use both hands to control the bike and really give it my all.

Giving it as much speed I can, Dac and I pass over into enemy territory.

Here I go! Dac says, just before he lets go of the bike, dropping into the thick of it behind enemy lines.

I look behind me as my speed picks up without changing any controls. I witness Dac disappear into the forest of New Power armor, crushing two people under him as he falls. "DAC BOMB!" he screams as he hits the ground. I hear it in my head and out loud, the excitement in Dac's voice only a tad bit disturbing. There's a second long delay until he pops up screaming and his swords start flailing, deftly taking out the New Power.

Are you going to be okay? I ask him, only now considering the fact that I just threw him into the heart of the enemy forces—well, he's close to the front, but he's on the wrong side of the lines!

I'll be fine, he says, *but Arthur is going to have to teach me how to buff the damage out after this!*

I'll make sure he knows, I laugh. Dac laughs back.

It's really entertaining how they think they can electrocute me. The current just travels over my body and shocks somebody else hitting me with a metal object. They're beating themselves!

Just be careful, I remind him.

Why does everybody keep saying that? he asks. *It's not like I can die like this anyway. I am in your shoes!* How is it that I keep forgetting that?

The radio on my bike crackles to life and Jinn's voice pours through, "Sam, look up," he says. I look directly above me and see open sky. It's a little cloudy, but not awful.

An irritated groan comes through the speaker and Jinn says, "Above and around the citadel." Oh. I turn my gaze that way, and I unconsciously ease off the throttle a tad.

Like an angry swarm of bees, a number of New Power that I don't care to count emerges from behind Logan's citadel, all of them mounted on Sky Bikes. I hit the communication button on my bike, acutely aware of that ugly noise it's making.

"You don't suppose they'd nicely go away, do you?" I ask Jinn.

"No," he responds flatly. "I'm trying to contact Nathan and see when he's going to get down here. I doubt anybody even bothered to tell him that everything has begun."

"Good idea," I tell him. "It'd be really helpful for the King of the Sky to show up right now."

"As we both know, Nathan isn't the best when it comes to the convenience of others."

"Isn't that the truth," I agree. It's an effort to take my eyes off of the incoming swarm, but I take a moment to look around and try to locate Jinn. It takes me a bit of circling, but I see him. He's the only Sky Bike over this far, and for some reason, he's heading back behind our lines. "Where are you going?" I ask him.

"I'm on the phone," he says. "I can't concentrate well enough to safely dodge spears right now and I don't want to fall out of the sky." Yeah, well listening to how my bike sounds, I may very well fall out of the sky anyway.

What the heck did you grab on to? I ask Dac.

I don't know, he says, sounding like he's busy concentrating on operating his body. After enough time,

I've come to know the change in his tone. *I really just grabbed wherever I could get a grip. Would you even know what was broken if I could tell you? Maybe it has something to do with the fact that you decided to plow through a long line of helmets.*

Let's call it a combined effort, I settle on, deciding for him. Despite my instincts telling me to do otherwise, I continue my lazy circles through the air, staring at the oncoming problem that is the flying New Power. I circle twice more before an answer comes to me, and I return my sword to my pocket.

Actually, that's not an awful idea, Dac says. Finally, some support.

On a third circle, I lay on the gas. My bike screams at me, trying to curse me out, but lacking the tongue to do so. I launch myself at the swarm of buzzing New Power soldiers. As expected, now that I'm in the right state of mind, I notice that they're in formation. As I approach, I know they're looking at me, probably thinking I'm nothing more than a madman. I ascend a tiny bit higher so that I'm about the height of a Sky Bike over them so that if I were to continue straight on, I'd hit their heads and nothing more. As I begin to perform the maneuver, I swear I can hear laughing, but I may just be making that up. Still, I get some sick sense of satisfaction that, at the very last moment, I flip my bike over. There's enough time for me to see the confused and scared expression of the New Power that I'm about to crash right into.

A split second later, I grab ahold of him, and the two of us go tumbling off our Sky Bikes. Without somebody to steer it, his erratically falls to the ground, crushing New Power ground soldiers underneath it—as planned—and my bike goes whipping into another one of the New Power's Sky Bikes. Everything goes exactly as planned. The wreckage of the two bikes—mine and the one it hit—comes crashing down to the Earth like an extra large meteor, squishing more soldiers beneath it.

Except for the screaming. I didn't quite expect the screaming. It's coming from both me, and the guy I ripped off his bike. I let go of him and activate my boots in short order, keeping as much altitude as possible.

"Who's up for round two of bumper bikes?" I ask myself. The answer is clear.

ME!

Oh, and the New Power up there. They just don't know they're playing yet.

I shoot up and through the ranks of the New Power. From above them, I see that, while starting to freak out, they haven't come up with a viable strategy to counter what I'm doing. I'm not sure they even realize what I'm doing yet. Their initial assumption was probably that I was a kamikaze. They're not entirely wrong. I do plan on crashing them into each other, but I won't be dying in the process. Flying boots can be quite handy.

I do a quick loop to avoid losing momentum and tackle the guy closest to me. Not expecting my hit, he's easily unseated. I dive to catch the handles of his bike and pull the whole thing up, crashing it into another bike, setting the other one off balance and knocking its pilot off. I continue driving this one up and into the next pilot, making sure to start a chain reaction. They go bowling into another three members of their squadron. Those three all manage to hit at least one other.

Personally, I'd call that a solid seventy-five points. If I'm being honest though, it's probably more like fifty-three. I repeat this process only a few more times before they start to catch on. The flying New Power break their formation and start flying with no particular pattern at all. I go a bit faster than I have been and manage to catch up with one of them.

294

"You're not going anywhere," I mutter to myself as I grab hold of the end of his Sky Bike, avoiding his large thruster. I slowly claw my way forward to grab onto this guy's arm as he drives. I yank hard, forcing him to pull on the controls. The turn is abrupt and sharp enough that he goes flying off the vehicle, and the thing goes spiraling to the ground. I try not to hear the loud crunch and louder screams of horror as I race off to find my next target. If I have to do it like this every time, there's no way I'm going to be able to get all of them.

While chasing this new guy, I get a chance to survey the field, as he is *really* dedicated to not let me grab him. The forces on the field have pretty much dissolved to individual melees, from what I can tell, but I'm sure there is much more intricacy to it than that. Arthur is among those at the front of the bundle that is the Surface forces, his Sky Iron glowing red, giving him away. Dac is almost as obvious, if not even more so. He's still in the thick of the enemy, probably wading his way deeper into their forces as the Surface advances. Every New Power in his direct vicinity is giving their undivided attention to the seven-foot tall metal man that is having no problems whatsoever tearing through their comrades.

Stop it, you're making me blush, Dac says, hearing my internal analysis of the situation.

Good, they'll be even more frightened of you, I tell him. I grab ahold of this new guy, but I can't crash him because he's over our own forces now. I try and wrestle for the controls, but he fights back, either out of fear or dedication, I don't know. I'm too afraid to do anything rash or hasty. I don't want to accidentally drop this bike on some poor guy that I convinced to show up here.

To my horror, I notice the remaining New Power in the sky fanning out wide and approaching the unsuspecting forces of the Surface. They're going to be annihilated. Jinn is in the air and battling them as they go, but with their division into two groups, and only the two of us here, there's not much we can do against them. He chases the group, flying wide to the left of our forces, leaving the force flying equally as wide, skimming over the ocean entirely unmolested as they move to decimate our dwindling numbers. I still hold on to this guy's bike, but my struggle against him is less than half hearted as I cannot take my eyes off the oceanic flyers, kicking up a mist, that are going to annihilate our forces.

And then tentacles happen.

Out of nowhere, massive tentacles erupt out of the water, smashing the Sky Bikes together and ripping them apart as if shredding metal is as easy as accidentally ripping toilet paper.

There is absolutely no way. He wouldn't do that, would he?

My question is answered when an entire fleet worth of submarines surface and proceed to beach themselves, never slowing down and leaving long deep gouges in the earth. The subs all list to their sides while hatches open and men start pouring out. I would watch all of them move, but something even more fascinating happens. Out in the water, Billy surfaces.

Kane brought his giant pet squid.

And he's riding it.

I can see the glow of his sword from here.

Is the water here even deep enough for Billy? Between the crazy man riding a giant squid of death and the fresh, large, wave of troops coming from the Water Nation, a weight starts to lift from my chest, knowing that Kane finally bothered to show up.

It only gets better when I hear, "Eyes on the sky," come through the communication of this guy's bike.

I scan the clouds overhead, knowing exactly the only thing the voice could be referring to. It doesn't take me long to see it. It's quite magnificent actually.

Pouring out of the clouds, as Kane's troops are from the ocean, is an entire fleet of Sky Bikes. At their head is a glowing yellow speck that has to be Nathan. He looks like there's less metal around him than everyone else, not that I can really tell from this distance. Is it possible that he's riding one of those boards instead of a Sky Bike?

Other than all the bikes, transports start to come from the clouds bearing the insignia of the Ravens hastily painted on their sides. While Kane provided a finite, yet vast, amount of submarines, it looks like Nathan brought a lot more to the party.

"I think you guys are going to lose," I say to the New Power solder I'm currently holding on to.

Nathan's forces don't stay in their spearhead long as they must have seen what the New Power is doing, trying to hit us. Nathan's group breaks into three, a bulk of it continuing onward with two smaller forces heading to meet with the New Power. Where is that big group going?

As I watch them, I see even more mounted New Power rise up around the citadel in a similar formation to that of Nathan's.

"I wouldn't be too sure about that," the New Power goon I hitched a ride with says over his shoulder, smiling a creepy smile at me. At some point, he turned and flew back over his own forces.

"What are you still doing here?" I ask him, drawing my sword out of my pocket and smashing the hilt into his helmet. He goes limp and falls back, crushing me under his suit and releasing the controls.

This is not good.

The Sky Bike goes careening forward, diving down towards the soil without anyone to guide it. I spend the next two seconds desperately reaching out to grab it, but this guy in his armor is too heavy and has me pinned down. Stuck, I watch for the remaining second we're airborne as we violently crash to the ground.

Chapter Thirty

The moment the bike hits the ground, the unconscious guy and I are torn from it. It's a horrible experience, really. I bounce over the ground, hearing the bike do the same, but on a much larger and more deadly scale. I lose track of everything and don't really see anything as it happens. Initially, there isn't any pain, only the shock of it all and the sensation of hitting something. Not pain, but my body acknowledging that it has touched something. I can't count how many times this happens. I can't get my brain to function properly.

Only when my body stops moving does cognitive thought return. The miracle that is my brain grants me the knowledge of utmost importance right now.

Pain.

So much pain.

I open my eyes and the world swims. My head is pounding, my ears deaf. Everything hurts, and yet it doesn't feel like I'm hurt. I'm shaking. I know I'm shaking. I can't even take full stock of myself because I don't even know what happened. I know I crashed and I woke up. That's about it. I look down my body, trying to tell anything, and get two useful pieces of information.

"Oh, that's a lot of blood," I say, noticing my torn jeans and bloody arms first. The second thing I notice is a much more pressing concern. I'm in the middle of the New Power, and they're all advancing on me. I flip over, movements like a drunken man. I slowly get to my feet, stumbling along the way. Once I'm more or less upright, I point my sword at one of the New Power goons arbitrarily and notice a big problem. "Oh crap," I sigh, slurring my words.

Did I say I point my sword at them? I meant to say my empty fist. Apparently, somewhere along the way during that crash, I lost my sword. Fantastic. Absolutely fantastic.

I franticly look around to try and find my sword, but everything is blurry. Why is everything blurry? It wasn't like that before.

Drink your Blue Elixir! Dac says, far louder than is necessary. My head feels like it's about to split apart even more than before. And what Blue Elixir? I don't have any Blue Elixir.

Oh wait. Maybe I do. I keep my empty fist in the air, just in case it's dissuading anybody from taking advantage of the guy who probably looks dead on his feet. Did I have a red long sleeve shirt on earlier today? With my free hand, I pat my waist and feel the surprisingly still cool, yet sticky, metal containers that Jinn gave me this morning. How long ago was that again? It couldn't have been too terribly long but it feels like a blajibaber.

What was that? Dac asks me. Again, my head hurts worse than even the first time he spoke. I can't think straight. That's what that was.

I want pudding.

Wait, I can't have that right now. What was I doing again? Right, Blue Elixir.

With as much dexterity as I can muster, I draw the metal container out of its pouch, a surprisingly easy task up until the moment I bite the wrong side. I spin it against my chest until the right side is facing me and bite it again. This time I feel the Blue Elixir touch on my lips. Like a baby drinking from a bottle, I start sucking on this thing like my life depends on it—which it probably does.

The first thing to happen is that I'm no longer craving pudding, which is good.

I can feel a tingling start through my body. It wasn't enough Blue Elixir. I grab the second little bottle, simply releasing the one I was holding, and start drawing on the new one as fast as I can. The motion hurts some, but it's more bearable than it was a second ago. With this one, after the warmth of Blue Elixir tickles my nerve endings, my vision starts to clear a bit. It's painfully obvious to me that I am a bloody mess from head to toe and am sticking my fist out at a bunch of armed soldiers threateningly. I'm sure the only reason they haven't attacked me yet is because they don't know that all I'm drinking is Blue Elixir. Considering I've seen Steven drink something else, I wouldn't be surprised if these guys knew more about the other colors of the elixirs than I do. I also notice that spread among the New Power uniforms are the uniforms of the enforcers. I knew I didn't like those guys.

I scan my surroundings and spot the glow of my sword amidst a group of the New Power. Dammit, why are there so many of them? I mean, couldn't there just be one? Maybe two. I could handle two, but this many, only having a fist and the unknown to threaten them with, is not going to go well. I look more at my empty fist and see something that unfortunately makes a lot of sense as well as almost makes me throw up. There is a large piece of metal sticking out of my arm, and it's bleeding profusely. I spit out the second vial and reach for the third and last one on the left side of my body. I put it between my teeth and try my best to look menacing as I drink it. I don't even know if it's possible.

All at once the New Power seem to lose interest in me. A quick survey of the situation informs me of the obvious: our forces have pushed this far forward. Heading right towards me, or more accurately, towards my sword, I see a spinning mass of red death. Really, Arthur is going over the top, screaming his head off, cleaving through New Power soldier after soldier.

"Hang on Sam!" I hear him shout as he raises his scythe into the air and hacks through three people in one clean slice. I've never actually made him mad, have I?

I certainly hope not, Dac says. I could swear I witness the man head-butt somebody, regardless of their helmet. Worst part is that he wins. The man is a monster. With everybody distracted by the incoming forces, I take the golden opportunity to grab another vial of Blue Elixir.

I drink it quick as I can and already have the fifth in my free hand before I'm done with the fourth. Once it's empty I let it fall to the ground and stick the fresh one between my teeth. I suck on it as I stumble my way over towards my sword, and Arthur with it.

I push soldiers out of my way as I go, trying to send them to the ground. For the most part, I'm only successful in being the guy sucking on a tiny metal bottle that's shuffling big scary New Power around, but hey, who's embarrassed? Not me.

Okay, maybe a little.

Point is, I'm not dead, and that's what matters.

Even though the Blue Elixir bottle is empty, it doesn't occur to me to just drop the thing. I do, however, jump on the back of the unsuspecting New Power goon in front of me. I lock my arms around his throat so he can't throw me off. He stumbles forward a few steps before falling to the ground. I release him and keep my feet for the most part, but I manage to trip over him and also fall to the ground. Without even thinking about it, I turn my face plant into a roll that barely even stings. I stop my roll with one knee on the ground and the other foot planted and my arms sort of awkwardly to the sides. Don't ask me how I did that because I don't know. The most confusing part is that I still didn't manage to lose the bottle. When I look up, I see a hefty bearded man with a glowing red scythe.

Actually, I notice the scythe first. It's pointed at my face.

"You're alright?" Arthur asks me, not believing it. He hears an approaching New Power soldier and turns his attention to it, removing the scythe from my face. I scramble forward the few extra feet and retrieve my sword. I also have the presence of mind to spit out the empty Blue Elixir bottle.

"Alright is such a relative term," I say, getting to my feet just in time to block the long staff of a bold soldier, the electrical end sparking over my head. I grab the staff with my free hand and bring my sword back around, cutting at his middle.

A sting runs up my arm letting me know that I didn't have enough Blue Elixir to totally heal up, but that I'm probably in a good enough condition to keep going.

"Geez, kid, you look like a nightmare," I hear somebody else say. I can't afford to look around to find him, but I recognize the voice as Mark's.

I dance out of the way of the blade of an enforcer, just to bump into somebody not in a uniform. Actually, he's wearing a full set of steel armor. I guess I know where he came from. Also, why is it that we've never worn armor?

Doesn't work against Sky Iron, Dac tells me. Considering how easy it is to break through the armor of the New Power, that makes perfect sense.

"Sorry!" I shout to the guy I bumped into as I spring forward and drive my shoulder into the guy that I just avoided. He goes tumbling back, knocking over one of his friends, and they both hit the ground. I almost feel bad for them as they're trampled by their own allies. There isn't time to linger on it though because, the moment they disappear, more people take their place. How many soldiers did Logan bring to this fight? It feels like we've got half the Surface fighting against us. Now that I think about it, considering how many people strive to become enforcers to avoid the enforcers, that may very well be possible.

Logan wouldn't bring that many people, would he?

As I slash through the next grouping of soldiers trying to attack me, I catch sight of Mark and his brown glowing Sky Iron. As Arthur did, Mark brings his own forces. The line isn't quite where we are yet, but from how many friendly faces I'm seeing, it's all but moved to this position. Slowly but surely, we're carving our way up to the citadel. How long can we keep this up though?

I decide that my efforts would be best spent trying to connect our two forces and start trying to reach Mark's party. While fighting, something else catches my attention.

"Sam!" I hear a rather feminine voice scream. This one I actually bother to look for. I slice through the current guy I'm engaged with and skip back, switching out with one of the guys that Arthur brought along with him. This guy was ready and waiting as he immediately jumps into the fray without me having to signal him or anything. In the time that everybody has been fighting, an unspoken system seems to have developed on how to let fighters rest. I take this precious seconds long breather to look all around me and over the heads of the New Power and our own soldiers—seeing as I am somehow taller than a lot of them—and spot a pink halo.

"Rose!" I shout over to her. I can't focus my listening on trying to pick out her voice, though, due to a New Power soldier breaking through the bubble the LARPers Arthur brought along created. He moves to drive his sparking staff into the chest of the toppled fighter, but I prevent him by getting my sword in between the two. I don't try and hold his weapon there, that'd be stupid. More than getting my sword in between them, I slap the staff aside so that it stabs the ground and not my ally. I don't know his name, but if he's fighting for what's right, then I will do my best to defend everyone here.

Reversing the motion, I bring the hilt of my sword up and smash it into the New Power goon's mouth, sending him reeling back. The friendly beneath me rolls away before getting back up to his feet, an attack bouncing off his armor. That stuff really comes in handy when it's not electricity or mythically sharp objects coming at you.

There isn't an opportunity for me to try and get back to the side carving their way to Mark. Instead, I take it upon myself to try and connect Rose and my groups. It's disturbing how the fighting becomes automatic. There comes a point when I can't feel a clean, full breath of oxygen in my lungs and the whole of me is aching. Still my body moves, narrowly dodging death and dealing out blows all the same. The blood covering me becomes no longer solely my own. From what I see of myself, I know that I'm nowhere near as horrifying as I was back in Hub Fourteen when the New Power attacked. That was me burying myself in a literal mountain of bodies, an experience I never want to go through again.

Another group of fighters develops in between Rose's party and my own, fighting the New Power as they go. We're really doing it! We're pushing them back!

Look who's here! Dac shouts enthusiastically in my head. I don't need to look far. From the party advancing this way, a hole opens up for the New Power to move into, which they don't overlook. As the New Power advance, they're immediately halted by a massive, heavily damaged mass of metal with his arms out to the side and his head down, charging straight through, sending over a dozen New Power and enforcer soldiers to the ground, where the troop he leads moves forward to finish them off. One of them, though, skips those on the ground and specifically moves to attack the guy that I'm engaged with.

"Saw you take a nasty fall," Jinn says, standing before me, drawing his sword out of the dying soldier's chest.

"Your Blue Elixir to go helped with that," I tell him, deftly moving around him and slicing diagonally from top right to the bottom left of a New Power soldier trying to come up behind him.

"Why aren't you still in the sky?" I ask him.

"Nathan asked me to split up the landing Ravens and lead half while Gerund took the other." Sure enough, once he says it, I notice the party with him and Dac are, for the most part, Ravens that I recognize. I know some of their names, but mostly it's just familiar faces.

"Where's everybody else?" I ask him, just before stopping a blade meant to hit me.

"Not now!" Jinn grunts, taking on his own assailants.

Nathan's still in the sky, and Kane is leading the bulk of the Water Nation's forces while Eli is at the head of the Sprinters. Most of Kane's forces are still near the water, but they're stopping the New Power from coming around.

"Your friend Scott's over there," Arthur shouts, near

enough for me to hear. I see Arthur's glow, but not the man himself. I have nothing to distinguish Scott with, so I'm going with what he says.

There are still more names shifting uneasily in my mind, but seeing as nobody else volunteers information about them—and that nobody's health was spoken of—I'll choose to assume everybody is well and somewhere in this mess.

I dash forward, cutting a man's legs out from underneath him, and finish the job. Without a moment to feel relief for having one less enemy on the field, somebody takes a swipe at my head, and I duck out of the way. Not many people take the time to realize that ducking and shifting bodyweight can be a very effective means of survival. The difficulty of it is that, with so many people here, I can't always move how I want. I realize the importance of staying as close to this guy as absolutely possible, but there's only so much I can do.

After what feels like a long time, the four parties combine into one, Arthur's group, Jinn and Dac's group, Rose's group, and Mark's group. United, but we don't have any time to talk. The mountain of metal and the five different auras of glowing swords become a warning of loss of life.

See, I like this a lot more. There's something comforting about having an army of people *not* trying to kill you surrounding you as compared to the opposite. As a group, with Nathan leading the sky, and Kane defending a flank, and Sarah doing I don't know what—the only mystery that could be significant for the whole of our army—I feel slightly less like I have to pee my pants. It's quite relaxing. I still feel ready to wet myself, but only slightly less now.

It plays out almost like a rehearsed dance sequence. With the slight freedom of mobility having allies grants us, everybody is able to shift around more. I wouldn't go as far as to say it's so simple that I could strike up conversation. No, but I do get to make sure that everybody is well. I don't deny that we've all sustained injuries, but the Ravens, the LARPers, and the Surface volunteers move between each other, defending one another from foes that would otherwise have killed many of us. I've gotten far too used to fighting all on my own. The entire perspective and situation changes when there are friendlies around you. Finally somebody is watching your back for more than a sufficient place to bury a knife.

Most of the fighting still feels like I'm on my own, and I am, but I have the support of those around me. The places where I would barely escape injury or would sustain a blow are prevented or lessened.

As messed up as it is, it's a pretty exhilarating experience.

The fighting continues for ages, the sun shifting overhead. I'd say the only reason we're able to go on as we do is because of the sheer mass of the two forces. There are times when our fighters shift out of the forefront to catch their breath. Nobody is invincible, and nobody is able to just keep going.

Except for Dac. He's the constant up front.

As long as you don't get your toes stomped up to the point your foot is disintegrated, I can keep going until I shut down! he assures me when I grudgingly step away from the front.

Desperately needing the break, but not wanting to let others take my place and die where I might survive—not being pretentious, but the majority of the people we have from the Surface have never held a weapon before—I take my last little bottle of Blue Elixir and down the thing. This time, instead of wasting the bottle once it's empty, I take it and throw it into the fray, trying to hit one of the New Power or enforcers. So far as I can tell, I completely miss. At least I tried. I've got one more idea. I undo the belt that housed the Blue Elixir vials, and shake it out in my off hand.

I'm out of the fight for less than a minute before I feel like I must get back into it. The moment I notice one of our guys start to get pushed back, I shove my way up to him, lashing out with the belt to slap the enforcer with it and attract his attention. I never thought it would hurt him, but it served its purpose. It's entirely a distraction and attention capturing tool.

The guy I saved gives me a nod of thanks as he retreats to safety, an ugly gash across his arm. Here's to hoping he's smart and goes to get that looked at before he returns to the front. From the brief glance I got, I doubt he'll be able to safely return at all.

"We can't keep going on like this!" I hear Jinn shout. Without noticing it, the two of us managed to get close together in the melee. Looking around me, I know he's right. While we may be pressing our advantage, it's costing us dearly. One after another falls. It feels as if our bubble around us is being lost to death and dismemberment.

"And what do you suggest we do?" I shout back at him while I slice through my enemy. I don't care that Jinn's basically next to me, it is going to be impossible for me to speak calmly for possibly the remainder of the week thanks to today.

"I've got an idea!" Dac shouts, his voice reverberating out loud and in my head. "Clear me a path!"

"Clear a path!" Jinn echoes even louder. Immediately responding to the order, the forces Dac and Jinn brought with them start to solidify the protective bubble around us, redoubling their efforts. Along with the bubble, a long line back is created. Fighters spread that way, getting into combat or not, just making sure the space is open—minus all the corpses. I move to throw myself into combat when Jinn grabs my shoulder and holds me off to the side, close to the fighting, but still making sure the pathway is open.

Get ready to run, Dac lets me know.

"We're going to have to run," Jinn says.

"What are you doing?" I ask the both of them, speaking to Jinn and thinking it to Dac. I watch Dac relatively calmly walk to the back of the group, away from the front lines. He stands there for a moment, waiting for everything to clear up, with his eyes supposedly on Jinn.

I'm getting us to the citadel. Just keep up, Dac tells me.

"Just be sure to keep up," Jinn reinforces. He sticks his sword in the air, looking back and forth between the front and Dac. "Move!" he screams, swinging his sword down as a sort of cue.

All as one, the fighters at the front break apart, rapidly moving to the sides with their only concern being defense. They don't even defend too terribly much. They're scored on multiple times. The New Power rush into the empty void between all the combatants, excited to take us supposedly unawares.

That's when the New Power and I both get a surprise. Rushing past me at full speed is Dac. He has his head down and arms stretched wide, running right into the horde of New Power.

And keeps going.

"Come on!" Jinn shouts only to me, dragging me by the arm to follow in the hole of fallen soldiers Dac leaves in his wake. Seriously, as he moves at nearly constant full speed, person after person falls to him, either diving aside or simply being knocked to the ground. "Condense and stay together, men!" he orders everybody else, "We will end this battle shortly!" There are shouts of encouragement as Jinn pulls me along, desperately trying to catch up with Dac. I'm tired enough right now that I feel my lungs are going to burst due to the running, or my legs may simply fall off. There's also the chance that I may get stabbed, slashed, or electrocuted. Jinn doesn't seem very concerned with defense right now. He and I even put our swords away, shrinking them into our pockets. Personally, I don't agree with the notion, but the way he looks at me lets me know that I'm going to regret it if I don't do as he suggests.

"Where are you going?" I hear Rose scream to me. I would respond, but all air is going to working my body right now. I unfortunately can't say anything. I doubt she'd be able to hear me over the screaming and flailing New Power anyway.

After the first few dozen feet, Jinn no longer needs to pull me along. I get the picture. Don't attack, don't defend. Efforts are to be expended in solely one way right now: run.

That's what we do. Jinn and I stay as close to Dac as possible. I wish I practiced running more. It's brutal. The three of us are our own little bubble among wolves trying to gnaw our heads off. On top of that, the terrain itself is troublesome to navigate. We're literally dodging around the bodies of the soldiers Dac knocks down, not to mention making sure they don't stick us with anything sharp or sparking while we pass over them. I think I understand John's claustrophobia down in the Water Nation. There is literally no way I can make sure the three of us get out of here alive, let alone unscathed. I myself could probably fly away in two seconds flat, but I would most certainly be hit on my way out. If I tried to take Jinn with me, we'd both be screwed, and I couldn't fly as well. I won't even get started on how to get Dac's body out of this. He would just have to turn around and repeat this process to get out.

There's nothing I can do. No other way that's any safer at this point. So we run. I look up at the citadel to see it getting closer, growing taller, more menacing. I can feel Logan standing at one of its many windows, scowling down at me. The monstrosity of metal and stone seems to capture an essence I don't often see.

You may want to watch this, Dac tells me.

Watch what? I ask, sparing the thought as I leap over a particularly large fallen enforcer.

Look in the sky behind you. I make the impossibly stupid decision of taking my eyes off the path in front of me to look where he said. Hanging in the sky and getting closer is something I haven't seen in a long while.

"WHAT THE HELL IS A WARSHIP DOING HERE?" I scream way too loud before unconsciously picking up the pace. I seriously get up to the point where Dac could probably give me a piggy back ride if the two of us could swap places entirely. In the sky is the warship Steven pointed at Jinn's house close to a year ago. When did they have time to build another one? And why is it heading this direction?

Since you obviously did not *see the large Raven's logo painted on the side, I should probably tell you that Davis is in there piloting that thing.* He's doing what now? *I managed to connect to his communications between Nathan and the warship, so I just told them your plan, and they're willing to participate.*

My plan?

So I lied a bit, Dac says. *At least they're going along with it.*

What exactly is "it"?

Of course, as I ask the question I hear a high-pitched whine louder than any of the other sounds on the battlefield. Recognizing the sound, I look behind me and notice the whole front of the battleship glowing.

It's not going to...

Oh yes it is!

The cannon of the ship goes off. A beam at least the diameter of a small building comes out of the thing as the tone deepens. It seems like it stretches the whole way, but maybe it's just a single pulse. I'm horrified and exhilarated, both as the beam passes overhead, and as it connects with the citadel. When the blinding light fades, a smoking hole is left in the side of the structure.

"That's our door!" Dac relays out loud for both Jinn and me to hear. Why don't we just blast the entire New Power with that thing!?

They've been charging that shot for twenty minutes, Dac somehow knows. *Nobody ever said that ship was efficient.* Looking at the hole it made, I'd sure say it's efficient.

We don't run much longer before we burst out of the thick of the crowd and into the area the ship's blast annihilated. The ground is scorched, as is the building, smoke still pouring out of the hole in its side. As we cross the burned ground, I have the distinct displeasure of noticing the charred remains and ashes of any New Power who happen to have been standing in the area. The smell of burning fills my nostrils. At least it's not specifically of people.

Regardless, I almost gag. There's something more important than that though.

Shadow passes over us as we enter into Logan's citadel.

Chapter Thirty-One

Fire! Of course there's fire! Why wouldn't a giant cannon set things on fire? It sure explains all the smoke. No longer having any idea where we're specifically going, the three of us continue running just as fast as we have been, if not more so. Dac is upright and doesn't have to bowl through any more New Power. Not right now, anyway.

Sucking in more air than usual, Jinn and I start coughing bad. I pull my blood and sweat soaked shirt up to cover my nose and mouth. The smell of it is bad enough that I almost throw up yet again. The brand on my hand burns all over again in phantom pain.

The moistness of my shirt keeps out more smoke than it would otherwise, which is a small consolation. The smoke stings my eyes, and I find myself more following the sound of Dac clunking around than my own eyes. I feel like Jinn is probably following the sounds of my coughing. I don't look to see exactly what he's doing, but I hear him next to me, and I know we're going the same direction.

"Stairs!" Dac warns us. I still manage to trip on the first step. Jinn gets ahead of me while I catch my fall. I don't stay down. I move my shirt back over my nose and keep going. As we climb the steps, the smoke thins. I let my shirt fall, grateful that I don't have to essentially inhale blood.

The three of us leave the stairs on some floor. I don't know how high we are, and I don't especially care. We get away from the stairs and some of the smoke. Dac and Jinn come to a heavy stop, and I follow suit. I more collapse to the ground and roll onto my back.

I'm well aware that we are almost as deep in enemy territory as is possible, but right now, if I don't get a few cleans breaths in me, I think I'm going to pass out.

"Well, we can cross long distance runner off of the list of things I want to be when I grow up," I say in between breaths. I only get one mumbled word in between breaths, so it takes me a while to say. I crush my eyes closed. Light hurts. Everything hurts. Exercise is not fun.

"I don't know about that," Jinn says, leaning over with his hands on his knees, taking just as long as I am to speak and breathing just as hard. "You kept up pretty well with a robot that doesn't need to rest."

"I would like to see you do what I did," Dac says. That's it. He just says it.

You can't even pretend like you're tired? I ask him. Thinking it is so much easier than saying it.

I've got my own issues, he says. I peek an eye open and look at him upside down, not willing to move from my current position. Dac's body is a mess of missing metal and giant dents. He looks entirely off. No part of him escaped the damage unscathed. It's not like I can see wire exposed, but I honestly have no idea how Arthur made him. This could all be superficial damage, or it could be critical. I know that if I had been bashed around as much as him, I think I would've long bled out and had most every bone in my body shattered.

Does it hurt? I ask him.

It's not a physical pain I can feel, he tells me, *but the body is working nowhere near as well.*

Better question then: are you okay?

"Overall, I am well," Dac says so that Jinn can hear him. Only now does Jinn look at his body and see the wreckage of it. Seriously, it looks like big parts of him are about to fall off.

"Are you sure?" Jinn asks him.

"Yes, I am," Dac tells him. "As I constantly have to remind everybody, as long as Sam doesn't get killed and have his shoes destroyed, nothing will happen to me. Arthur will just have to make another body, worst case."

"Oh I'm sure he'll love that," I say, still huffing and puffing. I close my eyes again, not wanting to see anything until oxygen doesn't feel like it's trying to kill me.

"Are you two ready yet?" Dac asks.

"Give... us... a minute," I say. "Or... I'll... rip off... your... something..."

"You're not that threatening when you can't form complete sentences," he lets me know.

"Keep watch for a minute," Jinn asks of Dac. "We only need a moment to catch our breaths." Jinn sits on the floor next to where I'm lying down. I open my eyes to see him taking off his belt of Blue Elixir. Out of the pouches, he pulls his remaining three Blue Elixirs. He sets one directly in front of my face, seeing the new injuries I managed to sustain on the run over here. It's nothing serious, just minor lacerations all over my body. He drinks one of the remaining two. I drink the one he gave me, greedily having the tiny little bit of liquid.

"Next time I declare war against a crazy immortal king, remind me to bring a water bottle," I say with a gasp. I don't care that it's Blue Elixir, I'd be just as happy with a gallon of water. No, I think I'd be happier with a gallon of water. After I suck down the tiny thing, my body feels cheated and demands that I keep drinking. Too bad I don't have any liquids or I would gladly oblige. Sure, I feel some of my wounds closing up a bit, but that's nothing. I almost cry when I see him tuck the last little thing of liquid away in one of his pockets.

"All the same," Jinn says, "I would have to vote that we do not repeat a situation such as this one."

"That works too," I agree. After a short time of lying here, my breathing becomes even. Jinn regains himself in roughly the same time. I don't want to stand up yet, but Jinn climbs to his feet.

"Come on," he says. "We've delayed long enough. People are dying outside while we rest."

"Does this mean more running?" I ask as I get to my feet. I still feel surprisingly loose from running like that. I thought I'd be barely functioning and stiff. Jinn watches me as I clench and unclench my fist a couple of times, as well as roll my ankles.

"The lack of stiffness is due to the elixir you drank," he reminds me. "And yes, it does mean more running."

"Wonderful," I grumble, stretching my back. Blue Elixir can't do everything for you. "Anyone have any idea where to go?"

"My best guess is up," Jinn says, heading towards the stairs.

"Great," I say, exasperated. "Running *and* stairs." With any sort of protest dying on my lips, we mount the stairs and start climbing.

And climbing.

And climbing...

How many stories is this place?

The stairs are now circular, climbing higher and higher in a stone cylinder somewhere in this castle. I can't tell if we're in the interior or the very exterior of the structure, seeing as the only looks outside are infrequent holes in the walls on all sides of us that are at the same height as my feet.

After enough climbing, I feel like we could be in the Sky Nation, and a hole opens up at the top. The three of us emerge from the stairwell in an enclosed hallway. A long, long hallway that probably goes the entire length of the citadel. At the far end's opposite wall, I think I can see an identical hole to the one we exited from. In the middle of this hallway on our right hand side is a large set of double doors. To our left is a wall of mostly windows. I get right up to the window and look outside. I see exactly what I expect: the battle.

It's still a mess out there. From here, I can see most of the duels buzzing about in the sky. I can't quite see Billy over in the water, but I can see the overall layouts of the armies. There are no individual faces, only masses to be moved or sacrificed. The warship in the air seems more to be hanging there than anything else, probably charging up its next blast. Dac said that it would be twenty minutes until it could fire again. How long has it been since that first shot? It couldn't be any more than five minutes. Five minutes is probably an over estimation even.

Jinn steps up next to me and takes ten seconds to look out the window before saying, "We're losing." I take a careful look at the field and see what Jinn saw. "It's slow, but our forces are getting pushed back. They will last a while more, but ultimately, we will lose."

"Isn't that why we're here?" I ask, angrily pushing off the window.

"That it is," Jinn says, following me. I can hear both of them follow behind me as I march to the double doors and push the both of them open, stepping into an even larger room. It's a giant round room with very little in it. In the back of the room—the back from my perspective—is a spiral staircase leading up into yet another chamber. The stairs have no hand railing and no wall around them. They're entirely exposed. It appears as if they simply disappear into a hole in the ceiling. I swear, whatever was in this room must've been removed because there are quite literally only three things in it.

Standing in the center of the room are Steven, Logan, and that Randy guy.

Seriously, what dictator's minion is named Randy? Dac echoes my thought perfectly. I really don't even look at the guy. All my attention is directed at Steven and Logan. Steven is to Logan's right, and Randy to his left, just as Dac is to my right, and Jinn to my left.

Steven and Randy stare at the three of us, trying to look menacing. Dac and Jinn keep their eyes on them. I focus in on Logan who's reaching into his suit's breast pocket. The guy is actually wearing a suit on a day like this. He looks just as well dressed as he was at Gabriel's funeral. Maybe he's not quite as dolled up, but someone would have to make quite the argument to convince me.

He pulls out a pocket watch and flips it into his hand. With the click of a button, Logan opens the lid. He takes his time to shift from looking down his nose at us to his watch. There's no chain attached to the watch, just the thing itself.

"Hmm," Logan hums, pressing his lips together. "It took you far longer than I expected to get here," he says, never looking up from his watch. "You also have far fewer numbers than I anticipated. Perhaps I thought too highly of my siblings and of the one who would declare war on me." He closes the watch and returns it to his pocket. Logan turns around and walks away, heading further back to the spiral staircase in the back of the room. Never again looking at us, Logan announces, "If you should survive, I will be waiting for you upstairs. I have no time for one that would waste it."

I grind my teeth as I watch him walk away. No swords are drawn, but I can very clearly see the ones hanging on Steven and Randy's hips. There are three of us and two of them. How does he expect them to beat us?

There are two ways to look at it, Dac comments so that only I can hear it.

What would that be? I ask, keeping my eyes on Logan as he disappears up the stairwell.

The first way is that one of these two is better at fighting than we think. If that's true, my money is on Randy.

So what's the second way? I ask him, looking at Randy now that Logan is gone. He doesn't look any better at fighting than the rest of us.

The second is that he intends for only one of us to meet him upstairs while his cronies here keep the other two busy.

Now there's a thought.

"I will cut you down where you stand, Samuel," Steven threatens, a hand on his sword, "and you will plague me no longer."

"You couldn't beat me jacked up on drugs, and you won't be able to now," I respond, not even reaching for my pocket.

"Must you remain as impertinent as our first interaction?"

"Are you going to try and strike up a conversation, or are you going to attack me?"

"Why do you toy with the child?" Randy asks Steven.

"Only because it brings me great joy," Steven answers, drawing his sword. Randy follows suit. I bet I could take Steven even without my sword. Randy is the biggest unknown in this equation. The light blue glow of

Jinn's blade enters my peripheral vision shortly after Randy and Steven have their metal out. I could check and see if Dac has his weapons extended, but I don't take my eyes off the two ahead of us. So far as I'm aware, three of five weapons have been drawn. At least this means there isn't going to be a long, drawn out monologue like Steven typically likes to do.

"Come," Steven says to me, raising his sword before him. "Let us end this dance between you and I."

"You don't need to tell me twice," I mumble to myself, quickly drawing my sword from my pocket and dashing forward. I feel more than see Dac and Jinn move with me so that all three of us advance at once.

You get Randy, I tell Dac.

Got it.

Steven and Randy advance in return, but it doesn't feel as if they're moving as fast. Still, we all collide at the same time. I swing my sword around heavy from the top, and Steven brings his up to counter, seemingly never having planned to be on the offensive to begin with. In nearly the same instant, Dac crosses blades with Randy. I don't know how exactly they meet, but I hear the connection.

I push Steven back, away from me. He stumbles two steps before finding a sturdy stance and moving to attack me again. I watch his movements, ready to block, when Jinn comes between the two of us. He throws his shoulder into the center of Steven's chest, knocking him back further.

"Get going!" he yells at me, although he's literally a step in front of me. "Dac and I will handle these two, you go get Logan."

Um.

Isn't he the better fighter? Is the thought that crosses my mind.

Not according to him, Dac tells me. *Just go, he's right. Jinn and I can take these two, or at the very least buy you enough time to deal with Logan.*

Whatever that means.

"Just don't get yourself killed," I tell Jinn, watching over his shoulder as Steven finds his feet.

"Same to you," Jinn says. With that, he's done with our conversation. He lunges forward, taking advantage of Steven. I don't waste time before bolting for the stairs. This short run is very different than the one to get to the castle. Nobody tries to attack me this time. Well, Randy tries to take a swipe at me, but Dac literally grabs his arm and stops the movement.

I hit the stairs and stay as close to the center as I can, and move as quickly as I can. For no good reason, the lack of a banister worries me. I simply have the irrational fear that I'm going to fall off.

As it spirals around, I'm tempted to look at Jinn and Dac to see how they're doing, but the sounds of their combat will have to do.

When I come out the hole at the top of the stairs and enter the new room, I immediately recognize it. This is the throne room I've seen Logan and Steven talking in multiple times. There's carpet down the stretch of the long room to end with an elevated throne. The only difference is that Logan is not in the throne this time.

I step away from the literal hole that is the stairs and look around me. Looking left, I see a huge, ornate stained glass window taking up nearly the whole wall. Standing at it, looking out at the battle below, is Logan.

"I knew you would abandon your comrades," he says without looking away. "Everything is as expected."

Chapter Thirty-Two

"What the hell do you mean everything is as expected?" I ask him, the glow from my sword lighting up the gloomy room.

"I wanted this moment alone with you," Logan says, still watching out the window with his hands clasped behind his back. "I do not presume that explaining anything to you will matter. I will achieve my ultimate goal."

"Go on," I mumble to myself, taking a slow step forward, inching my way closer to him, "tell me exactly what your plan is. It's not like I'm still clueless beyond you want to take over *everything*." Is there actually more to it than that?

I'm acutely aware of Logan unlocking his arms, letting his left hand at his side, and putting his right hand in his pocket.

Nathan wouldn't have, would he?

They are brothers, Dac comments, apparently not too tied up with fighting to talk with me.

How's it going down there? I ask him.

These two are a much better team than we thought. It probably would've been smart for you to stay.

It's a little too late for me to come back now, I tell him.

I know, he says, *and we'll handle this. You worry*

about the guy you're having a casual conversation with.

I don't think it'll stay civil that much longer.

I keep my steps light, but I do not slow. Having light footsteps in flying boots is not easy. I could fly, but he might hear the noise. At least this way, his brain might let the sound pass as white noise of everyday life. Is that even a possibility, or is it just wishful thinking?

"Although, with you I've learned that the time for talking has come to a close, hasn't it," Logan says. He turns to face me and deliberately takes his clenched fist out of his pocket and thrusts his arms out to the sides in challenge. "Come then. I will liberate you."

Liberate what?

He brings his right arm in front of his body, and slowly a blade extends out of his clenched fist. When it extends to its full length, I know he's ready. His sword glows the same blood red as his necklace, tingeing the room in menace. If I look at the walls, it already appears as if the colors of our blades are doing battle of a sort before we even reach each other.

I don't try to sneak any more. I stand up straight and walk towards him, my sword hanging loose but ready in my hand. It takes him a moment to decide that I'm worthy of walking. Logan takes few steps closer to me. Although we both look relatively relaxed, we're both wound up to the point that, once this starts, it won't stop until one of us is lying at the other's feet.

"Are you sure you want to do this?" Logan taunts, cutting out the superfluous language.

"Are you?" I return. He laughs at me.

"I have had dozens of lifetimes to perfect the art of death. You've only had a rather short life that will soon cease to be."

"That didn't stop me from beating your brother," I say, bringing my sword to my center and grabbing on

324

with my second hand. I still keep it pointed down, but I'm even more ready to attack.

"My family has grown lame in their luxury. I assure you I do not take after them."

"We'll see about that," I mumble. The two of us come to a halt. It's not signaled or organized, but here we are. There are about eight paces between the two of us. Eight paces from one of our ends. The two of us are absolutely silent. Beneath us I hear the sounds of Jinn and Dac's fights echoing through the halls, and I swear I can hear the bloody cries from outside seep through the walls. It seems like we're the only still things on this whole world at this moment. For this instant of time, I am the eye of the storm.

"Come on then!" Logan challenges me, taking a step back to get into a fighting stance. I follow suit, not wanting to grant him any advantage. "Come on and die!" We both start running towards each other.

One step.

Two.

Three. The man isn't there anymore to me. My eyes are on his blade, ready to keep the cold metal away from my flesh.

Four.

Our blades meet and the sound can almost crack reality. They don't stay connected long as we both retract from the attack-parry combo and try yet again. This is not a ruthless fight, not entirely anyway. There's calculation enough coming from Logan to compensate for the both of us.

He swings low, trying to cut my right leg out from under me. I deflect his blade and move in close to him, trying to push him back to get him off balance. Logan is too smart for this as he spins to the side, entirely avoiding the shove and leaving me the one without a solid stance.

Without hesitation, Logan brings his blade back again, this time aiming for my neck. I duck the move and cut up at his arm. Maybe if I can wound him that way, then I can gain an advantage over him. He sees the attack coming and snaps his arm away. He's fast, but not fast enough. I miss his arm, but I tear through the suit he's wearing.

From my awkward position, there is absolutely nothing I can do to avoid the kick he sends my way, driving his heavy boot into me. I fall to my side. Even before he can start the swing of his attack I'm rolling. I tuck everything in and try to roll around Logan. When he misses his first attack, I take the opportunity to get up and lunge into him.

He deflects the tip of my blade, and we're both back to standing and dueling. My back aches from where he kicked me, but it's more like a dull throb than anything.

All sound of the world disappears. All I can hear are our two breaths, mine growing labored more rapidly than his, and the explosion of Sky Iron meeting Sky Iron. I feel the burden of every blow.

On and on this goes, the two of us spinning around each other, trying to find an opening.

We never stand still. Standing still is death in this situation.

I feign a swipe to the left, but still he maneuvers on time to counter my attack on the right. While our blades are crossed, Logan takes this opportunity to firmly plant his boot in my chest and shove me away. I stumble back a couple of steps, unable to help the situation. I do my best to make sure I duck out of the way of his diagonal slices. Down and left first. Down and right immediately after.

He gives me absolutely no room to breathe.

Once I'm upright again, I launch a strong flurry at him, wanting either to break his concentration or, at the very least, to make his hand numb. I feel like we've only just begun and I'm already out of breath and starting to sweat. Logan looks like he's only now starting to breathe hard.

He catches the last of my heavy strikes before his face and holds my blade there. The two of us put our weights into the deadly embrace between us. The swords don't move much, but there is shaking, definitely shaking. I look up from our hilts to the tips of the swords, watching their slight, threatening movements. After traveling the length of the weapons, my gaze comes to rest on Logan's face. I know that my own expression is locked in a twisted snarl as I try and pull every last ounce of energy I may have been reserving out for this moment. Logan halfway looks like he doesn't care.

Surely, he also wears an expression translating the effort he's expending, but it's not the same as mine. He still looks detached from everything. His eyes are vacant almost like he's... he's... he's...

I know that look.

My heart freezes in my chest, and a chill runs down to every extremity. I feel my jaw unclench and my mouth open wide as I stare at him. The swords start to point at me while the thought runs its way through my mind. Every neural highway has the same damn thought.

"I know that look," I say out loud, the words escaping my lips like a convict fleeing in silence in the dead of night. The expression on Logan's face changes. There's anger and relief there now.

It makes so much sense! How the hell have I not managed to put this together already!?

Logan pushes me away, and I let him. I don't stop a

mere three paces away. I keep moving, keeping back from him. He doesn't pursue me, letting me get ten paces away where I hold still. Except I can't hold still. I'm shaking even more than before. I am afraid of this man.

No, not afraid. I'm terrified.

My eyes slide down his body, not caring for any detail but one. A detail that I've known but have never connected.

He's wearing boots.

Chapter Thirty-Three

There's only one reason I know that look. I've seen it before.

On *me*.

That's what I look like whenever I'm talking...

Whenever I'm talking to Dac.

Satisfied to have caught his own breath, Logan jumps back into the fray, never throwing the most powerful attacks at me, but always having eloquent form. Under this latest onslaught, it's the least I can do to keep him from scoring any hits on me. The glow of the swords paint his face in shades of the cruel tormentor and that of the victim alternatingly.

Is that possible? Dac comments, having caught my thoughts.

"Have you finally connected the dots?" he asks me, continuing his brutal assault. Anything I'm showing right now could probably be best described as abject terror. He pounds away at my defenses, adding more and more force to his attacks. "Have you pieced together the puzzle that's been laid out before you?" At the end of his statement he brings a particularly strong attack down over my head.

I bring my blade over my head. I support its tip by holding the flat of the blade with my open palm while still keeping a firm grip on the handle. In order to give myself enough time to do this, and to give myself more support, I drop down to one knee, keeping the opposite foot planted.

"Have you seen your own demise?" Logan asks, getting hysterical. He keeps his sword pressed against mine, leaning into it. My arms tremble under the weight. My sword gets closer to me. I'm stuck. I don't have a good way out of this one. "Or do you still not understand?"

"I think I understand perfectly," I get out between clenched teeth, straining against him. This is not good.

"Then speak!" Logan demands of me. "Speak before you are silenced!" Logan's screams launch spit in my face. I close an eye to make sure no spit gets in it.

Sam, move! Dac recommends.

"Who are you?" I ask him.

"Can you really not tell?" he asks, giving me a creepy smile.

"What do you go by?" I ask him, fully aware now of who—or more accurately *what*—he is.

"I have found I quite like the title Master," he says. "Although, if you were to try and give me a cute nickname, I still like the *P*."

Digital Automated Core Processor.

D.A.C.P.

He's an AI.

He's a freaking AI!

How long has Logan not been Logan? What's it like in there? Is he trapped?

Is he still fighting?

"I can't tell you how nice it is to have this all out in the open!" Logan, no... Master says. As he says "open," he grabs hold of my head and flings me behind him. The strength is supernatural, as I tumble twenty feet. This time I don't lose my sword. It's all I can do to try and push myself up to my hands and knees as he stalks closer. "I address you now, Brother. I can sense you in there. From the moment your mortal shell challenged me, I realized the connection. I *knew* that there was another like me trapped out there. I am here to *free* you."

Um, what does that entail?

He's going to try to kill you, Dac clarifies for me.

Hasn't he been trying to do that anyways?

There's more to it than that. I bet he's going to keep his monologue.

Why do you say that?

Well, I love to talk. He probably does too.

Touché.

"When I saw your tie to this physical realm, I was in awe! You transcended the mortal ties that limit us. When I free you, Brother, you and I will stand side by side as we awaken our remaining brothers, allowing them the same presence you have. *You* are the key to the continued survival of our superior species."

Told you, Dac says.

Does that mean this is in part my fault? I ask.

Probably.

Of course, I mentally sigh.

On my hands and knees, Master kicks me, sending me tumbling again. I'm near the window now, and Master in Logan's body is steadily approaching.

Hold on, we're coming!

Behind Master, I see Jinn and Dac come up out of the hole in the ground where the stairs are.

"SAM!" Jinn shouts, entering in a dead sprint.

"Do not worry, Brother!" Master calls behind him without looking, "I will free you of this poison that plagues you." Before I have the opportunity to contemplate what that's supposed to mean—obviously

331

somehow my death—Master picks me up by the neck. I'm choking only for a moment before he throws me back again. He really is a lot stronger than he looks.

I both hear and feel the glass of the window shatter as I collide with it. The sounds of the raging battle return in full as I suddenly find myself outside, falling through the air. At this point, it's instinct that makes me activate my boots and rocket through the sky, getting further away from the citadel. Further away from that thing that used to be a man.

"Don't think you'll be getting away that easily!" I hear Master roar. I only barely catch the hint of his words with my ears, but they echo in my mind almost as clearly as when I talk with Dac. Knowing what's coming next, I look back over my shoulder, paying absolutely no attention to the Sky Bikes buzzing around me. One of them could hit me right now for all I care. I watch as Master leaps forth out of the hole in the side of the citadel that he used *me* to create and take flight with his boots. Is there glass in me? I don't feel any glass. That could be bad. You know what's worse?

A CRAZY RAMPAGING AI IN THE BODY OF AN IMMORTAL KING THAT IS FLYING AFTER ME!

That's offensive, Dac comments quietly.

SHUT UP! I scream at him, not in any mood for a joke. I turn over and fly on my back so that I'm facing him, but still moving away. He has greater speed than me, catching up easily. He swings at me in the air. I parry and am immediately set to spinning. I've never fought like this. Never.

"I have always wanted to see if the designs of my maker were satisfactory!" Master screams at me, swinging attack after attack. Apparently, he hasn't done this either. This is half epic battle, half confused cats batting in each other's general direction. Having better access to the movement in literally any direction than ever before, even on a Sky Bike, while fighting is really something to behold. When he swings high at me, I entirely cut the power to my boots and drop a few feet, just to spring back up and hit him hard, leaving a gash in his side, one of the first serious hits either of us has landed. While in the air, we each have managed to actually cut each other. It's gotten more intense up here.

I keep going, flying higher and higher.

"You can't escape from me, Cutter!" Master screams up at me, partaking in the chase. Perfect.

I give it as much speed as I possibly can. As I travel, I swear I hear familiar voices screaming my name, but I drown them out. The wind and threats coming from Master reach my ears. I rush up past the Sky Nation, and still I keep going. I go, and go, and go. Then Master falls silent.

I halt my ascent and scan the area for him. I don't see him. I don't see him anywhere. I don't—

A sharp pain spreads throughout my entire body, localized at my middle. I'm trembling and hyperventilating both. I look straight down and see a nightmare: a red glowing blade protruding from my stomach, coated in my own blood. My sword slides out of my grip and twirls as it falls toward the clouds.

"I told you, Cutter," Master hisses in my ear from right behind me, the hairs on my neck standing up. He's holding me up, his free arm around me and under my elbows. The power to my boots cuts out, and he's the only thing keeping me in the air. "I will free my brother from your tyranny." Lights start dancing before my eyes, consciousness, no, life fading away. "With this, I succeed."

Chapter Thirty-Four

Master draws his sword out from my stomach and now the blood really starts pumping. The black around the edges closes my vision even faster. I take in wheezing breaths, just trying to get enough air in.

DAC! I shout at him, even though I can't say anything out loud.

I ALREADY KNOW WHAT YOU'RE GOING TO ASK! he shouts back at me.

I can still beat him! I say, his words not fully registering.

JUST DON'T LET GO OF HIM!

Master tries to let go of me, but I grab hold of his arm. With him no longer supporting me, I drop like a log. The only reason I don't fall to my expedited death is because of my grip on Logan... Master... whatever! The jarring impact makes me wish that death were here already.

"Why do you struggle?" he asks me, trying to shake me off.

"Because somebody has to," I rasp, fingers slipping.

DON'T LET GO, Dac repeats to me. I'm trying, buddy. I'm trying. The shadows around my vision close all the more quickly, but I'm not as scared of it this time. These shadows I know. With this, I am familiar.

Master squirms, holding his head with his left hand. He dropped his sword at some point, both of our blades plummeting.

"What are you doing?" Master asks me, sounding a little scared. Is it scared? No. Unfortunately, I think he only sounds surprised.

Got it! Dac lets me know.

The familiar blackness completely covers my vision. The last thing I see is that I've let go of Logan, and that now both of us are falling towards the Earth.

I open my eyes and suck in a single gasping breath, my lungs filling with clean air. My hands fly over my body, and I feel no injuries, no harm. In the back of my mind, I know the wounds are still there. I know that I'm still dying, that I'm falling toward the ground, but that doesn't matter here. That doesn't matter right now.

I'll do everything I can to alter your perception so that this takes up as little time as possible in the real world, but I can't do too much, Dac says, keeping me informed. *I'm keeping the both of you here, and he does* not *want to stay.*

Thanks, I tell Dac, reaching into my pocket and feeling the familiar poke of my shrunken down sword. *I know I can stop him here.*

Just do it quickly, he tells me, sounding like he's straining while holding up the sky, *this is not as easy as I'm making it look.*

All I can see around me is white. Everything is entirely white in an empty void except for me, like I'm the only thing that exists. Dac has explained this to me before, the only other time I have asked him to bring me here.

The AI realm is loading. Either Dac or the entirety of the AI consciousness is searching through my memories for an appropriate setting to make the workable room. The two of us never really figured out how exactly that one worked. In a matter of seconds the "safe" world will come to exist, and the ether will exist on the outskirts, trying to swallow up the safe area Dac is maintaining. If he loses his focus, it will collapse, and that will be the end of... well, I don't really know what comes after that. I would much prefer to keep it away.

The white void somehow gets brighter, and I have to squint against it, even shielding my eyes. When the brightness fades, I lower my hand and see the reality that the AI consciousness brings to life for us.

"Of course it's here," I mumble, seeing a perfect recreation of the arena up in the Sky Nation. I'm on one end of the large oval field of dirt, and I see Logan at the other, still getting his bearings. He doesn't look entirely like Logan. In fact, Logan's appearance looks like paint being washed away by water, slowly leaving the body it previously coated.

"What have you done?" Master screams, his true form beginning to show itself, as I continue taking in the scenery. All the seats are empty. There's not a single person here besides Master and me. "Brother!" Master screams again, "I only want to liberate you! Why would you bring me to such a place? Grant him no strength and we will crush him!"

Boy is he delusional.

HURRY UP! Dac grunts at me.

You got it, I tell him. I whip my sword out of my pocket and rush forward, not having the courtesy to wait for Master to get his bearings. It's not my fault that he wasn't prepared for this. I feel lighter on my feet than ever before, crossing the expanse of the arena in no time. The disoriented, shadowy Master catches on to what I'm doing and tries to draw his own sword out of his pocket. Problem is that his pocket is floating away. He has no sword.

"You're not Logan!" I shout at him as I slice through him. His scream makes the entire universe I perceive vibrate. I almost fall down due to the earthquake he brings on us. While screaming, Master holds himself and stumbles back a few steps.

He doesn't bleed from where he's hit. Honestly, it just looks more like shadows retreat from the wound faster than elsewhere. After all his time wearing Logan's skin, he doesn't know himself anymore. There's something else.

This is the first time I've actually hurt him.

Once the ground stops rumbling I immediately get back on top of him. This time, though, when I bring my sword around, he holds out his empty right fist. A black, inky blade appears out of nowhere, and counters my attack. The sword looks more held together than the rest of him, but still it has that smoky effect around it. If we were out in reality right now, and if it were reflective of his actual Sky Iron sword, it'd be the exact opposite of mine. Blacker than midnight.

"Cutter, you rat!" he howls, swinging wildly at me. It's really quite easy to deflect his attacks. What? Did we show up here and suddenly he's incapable?

He thrusts out a hand, and before I know what's going on, I find myself launched into the air and backwards. I involuntarily scream as I fly half the distance of the area before hitting the ground hard. Real or not, that hurt.

This is more real than anything else, Dac reminds me. *You're literally fighting with your essence here.*

I know, I know! How the heck is he able to fling me through the air like that?

He's from here, Dac says in a hurry, sounding more

and more under pressure. *He's had more practice.*

Not having moved from his position, Master gets into something near a sumo stance. His shrieks get all the louder as he throws his arms out. Somehow I keep my footing through this existence's rumbling. The shaking is vicious enough this time that I feel like my brain is going to be a big bruise when he's done.

As his tone gets higher and he gets overall louder, the echo of Logan around him dissolves faster. This feels different. My ears... Am I going deaf? What is he doing!?

I watch as the very edges of the stadium are vaporized, the black ether of the AI realm closing in, destroying our life raft as if it were nothing.

DAMMIT! I can hear Dac shout in my mind. *He's ripping everything apart! STOP HIM!* For only a second more am I frozen, watching in horror as the black smoke encroaches. The stands are all but gone. Then I break out into a sprint.

I stumble while trying to reach him. I use my free hand as a sort of third leg, slowing as little as possible until I can get upright again. Every step feels as if it's crossing a continent. Master is impossibly far, yet miraculously near.

"Stop it you idiot!" I shout at him, holding my sword over my shoulder with both hands, ready to swipe at his neck.

When I get to him, I swing with everything I'm worth. He shifts ever so slightly to the side and my sword sinks into his shoulder. His screams change, as does the pressure in my ears, while he falls to his knees. Again, this is different, yet familiar. We're back to pain now. He's hurting.

I plant my boot on his chest, and I swear there's a white halo surrounding my foot where it touches him, but that could be my rapidly fading mind in the real world tricking me.

DAC!

I'M TRYING! He screeches, *THIS. IS. NOT. EASY!*

Master's screams of pain shift slightly again to outrage as I press hard and drag my blade out of him. The halo around my foot disappears, but again it may never have been there in the first place. I take a second to glace at the damage he wrought, and notice that the stands are entirely gone, swallowed by the AI consciousness. Some of the arena has disappeared too, the sand and dirt pouring off the sides into nothingness. We still have most of the actual battle area, but it's much smaller.

Master shoots up and launches an all out assault against me. Defense doesn't exist for him anymore. Every swing of his sword gets heavier. Every movement warrants the ink drinking away from him to dissipate faster. All I can do is defend. Every time our blades connect, I feel the whole of me being squished, only to try and stretch back out again whenever we're not touching.

I risk throwing an attack at him. He decides defense doesn't matter and takes the slice across his recessive arm while paying me in kind. The pain from the injury burns more than anything I've ever experienced before. The entire definition of pain just became redefined for me. Dying? That's easy. Whatever this is, that's true pain. I stumble a few steps, one handedly trying to deflect his sword and sparing only a second for my arm. The cut isn't deep, but disturbing.

As ink flows from Master's wounds, so too does it from mine. From the gash in my arm pours something of the same texture of that coming from Master. Difference is that mine's white, the exact same as my blade. No amount of adrenaline coursing through my veins dulls the pain. It's slow, but I feel a weakening, as more of that white essence flows out of me, floating into the sky and away. The pain multiplies as time passes, only getting worse and worse.

"I will *wipe* you from reality!" Master screeches in my face, ink in the form of spittle coming out of his mouth. He sounds deranged, like not all of him is there anymore.

"Go ahead and try!" I taunt him, racing back into the duel. I redouble my efforts, trying to get the better of him. It's hard. As in the real world, he has little to no opening, but he is slowing. Problem is that I am too.

Dying in the real world and apparently *slowly* dying here.

I just can't catch a break.

JUST HURRY UP AND WIN SO I CAN PULL YOU OUT OF THERE! Dac begs.

I swing to attack, as does Master, but the motions translate to a collision. Master flickers under the pressure of the move. If we're fighting with all we are here, there must not be much of him left. He lets out a bestial roar and punches me in the stomach.

The same mysterious force as before is applied, and again I go sailing through the air. I try and activate my boots to catch myself, but no reaction. Apparently, those don't work here. That's unfortunate.

I hit the ground and flip over backwards, literally heels over head. When my feet come back down to the dirt, I slam them down and get myself into a crouch, halting my roll. With a glance behind me, I notice the disturbing fact that I'm on the very edge of the boundary of safety. If I had slid back another six inches, my foot would be gone. The AI consciousness is acting almost like it's trying to reach into our boundary and grab hold of me. Tiny tendrils reach out towards my foot, and I decide I don't want to see if they can reach. I push up off the ground and charge towards Master, who's already rushing towards me. It truly is him now. Not one speck of Logan remains. He's entirely a black, shadowy figure that could very easily escape into the ether, and I would never be able to see him. Yet there is a difference. It's hard to describe, but I know it's him. He has developed. There's a ring of sorts around Master that makes it so he doesn't blend with the background. I'm sure I'm imagining it, but it works for me.

Our swords meet, more powerfully than ever before. Both blades are deflected away towards my upper left. I take this opportunity to smash my elbow into Master and see if I can propel him back the same way he did me.

It doesn't go as planned. He stumbles a step from the force of my hit, but he doesn't go flying. There it is again. Where my elbow touches him, I could swear I see a white halo. What the heck is going on?

Not using my sword due to not being able to get it into position in time, I leap forward and punch Master where his jaw would be. AGAIN! The white halo cloaks my fist and Master lets out a retched, bestial howl that, in any other situation, would stop my heart from working.

Now, it just means that I'm winning.

I bring my sword across and another leaking wound opens, the black from him and the white from me floating higher and higher into oblivion. His howl continues, never breaking between the two blows. He falls then to hands and knees. In fact, it almost looks as if Master is frozen. Considering the fact that my left arm is all but unusable from one insignificant wound, and that he's covered in deep gashes I've delivered, I'm awed that he can still move.

When Master tries to push himself up, I drive my

knee into where his face should be. The white halo appears now too, and he falls backwards.

"How?" he asks me, getting up again. "How do you possess the ability to harm me with your hands!?"

The what?

I DON'T KNOW! Dac screams. He sounds worse than me. *JUST KEEP PUNCHING HIM!* That I can do.

My first move is probably rather stupid. I throw my sword at him.

Yes, really.

Master knocks the airborne blade away and doesn't pay attention to me closing on him. When what I'm assuming are his eyes lock on me, his face elongates—is that him raising his eyebrows?—just in time to get a face full of fist.

My hand glows white as I connect, and I don't give him the kindness of falling back. I keep coming hard, fast, and strong. Punch after punch I throw at him, each time our forms connect, whatever part of me touches him glows white, and he seems to grow darker, becoming a void.

"Even if you defeat me," Master says menacingly, landing a few punches of his own. Those sting. It's nowhere near as bad as the wound in my arm, but it's like a sledgehammer every time his fists connect, "you will never save the one whose skin I wore! I have long thrown him to the abyss!"

Logan's still alive?

"We'll see about that," I respond, teeth clenched. I take a long wind up and throw everything I have, every last ounce of energy I feel residing within me, into one massive punch. It lands square in the middle of his face. One of my feet leaves the ground and I don't even notice it until I'm stumbling forward. Master falls hard, driven by the force of my punch. I stumble forward a few steps, knowing that if this were reality every one of my fingers would be broken right now. I turn around, ready to keep fighting, but Master is still laying on the ground. Even more, the white glow of my fist is still in the middle of his head. He's perfectly still. I walk back over to him, weary of a sneak attack, but somehow knowing this is no feint.

I stand over him and watch the white smoke left behind spread to cover his whole body. It's fascinating and somehow beautiful, the white halo spreading even though the black ink that still leaks from him. He's spread out, arms out to both sides and legs split apart. I watch it, not sure what it means initially, until he starts to fade.

The entire bundle that is Master turns to ink, the white and black mixing together in a dance up and away, carrying away bits of Master until the entirety has drifted away. Where he once laid is now nothing.

I collapse to the ground, ceasing to function.

My mind is shutting down, and I know Dac is screaming at me, but I can't hear him. Is he trying to lift me out of this reality? Is Master still alive behind me? Am I even alive?

The white stream flowing out of my wounds is pretty incredible to see float away. If it weren't killing me, I could probably watch it all day long.

The way I fell, I'm looking out into the encroaching shadows of the AI consciousness. Even now, I can't help but think of how beautiful the streaks of color are. Watching the shifting clouds, it's almost like I can see someone standing there, watching me. Dac, is that you? No, you don't look like that. You look different. Then who....

"He's still alive," I say to myself. Against the wishes of probably the universe, I force myself to get up and limp over to the edge of the arena.

What are you doing? Dac shouts to me, breaking through whatever wall was there.

"He's still alive," I say, looking out into the storm, seeing what I saw before. "Logan is still alive out there!"

Sam, you're about to die! *You have to get out of there.*

"I have to save him," I say, Dac's story of the horror racing through my mind at the same time as Gabriel telling me that Logan is afraid of the dark. He has been alone out there all these years, lost in nothing but a black abyss. For all I know, there's nothing left of the man. Yet I see him. He's right there! That damned king, looking like a small child, is lost out there no more then ten feet from where I'm standing.

Sam, NO! Dac screams at me. *You can't touch that stuff! If you do, you'll be lost and* I'd *take over your body!* I trust you. I trust him. I can do this. It's ten feet. I can make it back.

Sam, Dac warns, hearing my thoughts. He knows exactly what I'm thinking.

"Just keep me breathing," I tell him, smiling at where I think Dac is looking at me from. With that, I move to take a step forward.

SAM! Dac screams, hysterical, and that's the last I hear from him.

Chapter Thirty-Five

All sight: gone.

All sound: gone.

All feeling: gone.

Nothing. There is nothing but my thoughts. I can't even find the streaks of color I saw previously.

Where am I? Where was he?

I try and take a deep breath to calm myself, but I can't feel it. I—I can't breathe! But I don't have to. Without moving, I gasp for air, never finding the oxygen my lungs desperately crave. It doesn't even burn. Like I said, there isn't any pain. I can't even feel that dull ache in my stomach that lets me know that I'm dying in life. Is that what happened? Did I die? For real, I mean.

No, there's no way that my timing is that good. This place is just a total disconnect from everything. No wonder the AI are so desperate to get out of here and stay out.

Dac? I ask, trying to connect with him. *Dac, are you there?*

Nothing. I don't know what I was expecting, but there's absolutely nothing. It's not painful, but that spot in my brain that I've decided is like Dac's room, his space that he resides in, it feels different. It's like when we were separated before, when Arthur first put him in

345

his body, but so much worse.

That first time around it was an ache of sorts. Honestly, I've tried to forget it. Now it's just an absence. If I go on like this long enough, it'll be like he was never there.

The feeling in my limbs is gone. I can't even feel my own teeth. There is literally nothing. I try rubbing my fingers together to get some sensation, but nothing. There's not even the pressure of touching something. This is so not okay.

I stand stock straight... I think. I'm too scared to move. I don't want to get lost in this mess. Have I taken a step? Seriously, I'm petrified. The lack of oxygen is strange to say the least. My lungs don't burn, and my head doesn't feel any lighter. Then again, I can't feel my lungs or my head. It's like I'm severed thoughts, lost and destined to spread apart until I can no longer find myself.

If that's the case, then can I really say that I'm standing still? In this place, do I have legs? Do I have a self? Is there an I, a we, a he, a you? Or is it all a plane of nonexistence?

How long have I been here? Dac existed in this place for how many years? I wonder what that felt like to him. Actually, no, I don't. I want to understand, but I can't handle that. I don't want to know that horror.

I scratch my arm and...

I scratch my arm?

I look over to where my shoulder should be and, sure enough, I see it. In this sea of absolute darkness, I can see my shoulder and nearly the entirety of my arm. The reason why is worrisome to say the least.

The reason I can see is that there's still that white stuff spilling out of my arm. It hangs around, wispy for a brief moment before disappearing, being swallowed whole by the darkness. Every time it swallows more of my energy whole, the entire thing changes. There's pressure. Whatever that light reaches, I feel. I move my arm around slowly, making sure my whole body is still attached.

It is.

Ten feet, right? I can do ten feet. My foot is about an actual foot long, so if I walk heel toe I won't even lose my direction. Does that make sense? I don't know, but it's the best idea I've got.

No, that's stupid.

But is it?

I miss having Dac to talk to.

A tiredness comes over me, and I feel like curling up and going to sleep for a good long while would be a fantastic idea right now. Would it really be so bad to sleep? I mean, who does it hurt? Sure, there isn't any discernable ground beneath my only sometimes visible feet, but that doesn't mean it won't be comfortable.

I take a step forward, fully intending to lie down, but remembering that I have something more important to do here. If I could stop freaking bleeding out for five minutes, I'd be fine. Between the blood loss and everything else, it's hard to concentrate.

I stumble forward again and swear I'm lost. I could go back. It's only two steps backwards, and I can get out of here. Logan's probably only three more steps ahead of me. It could be two if I take normal sized steps. I could possibly even make it in one if I take a big enough step!

While debating the merits of leaving this place and begging Dac to get me out of here, I somehow take another step forward. I didn't decide to do that! I was still thinking about leaving. Stop doing stuff without my permission, body. I need psychiatric help.

A third step, this time meaning to... I think.

Well, I'm more than half way there now. I might as well keep going. That's my rationale, and I'm sticking with it.

Sucking in a deep breath of... never mind. Can't breathe. Well, I still go through the motions of taking in a deep breath. Actually, that's not very calming. It just makes me worried all over again that I can't taste the air, or feel it in my lungs. Oh, this is a bad idea. I look all around me and notice a new detail, while freaking out of course.

The color steaks have returned. They're beautiful, absolutely stunning. It's like I'm a part of them now. They are all around me and moving. From the outside they looked like they were at a standstill, but from here, I can see them shift and flow. It's a vision to behold. I nearly turn and try to follow a particularly tantalizing green streak, but stop myself right after picking a foot up. Keeping my eyes on the world around me, I take another step forward.

It's now that I see him again. Logan is standing before me, crying. Still, there's no noise, and I don't know if he can see. I stand there, watching for only a moment, hoping he'd notice me. I would wait longer, but I'm running out of time.

Feeling another dizzy spell come on, I grab hold of Logan's arm and turn around, extra careful to turn *exactly* the opposite direction. It's weird, not being able to feel Logan's wrist. I have to trust that it'll be there though. I mean, I did grab it. Just because it doesn't seem like it's there doesn't mean anything, does it?

I hate this place.

Five steps forward, no, six! Six and I get out of here. Dragging Logan along is a lot more difficult than I expected. Even though it doesn't seem like he's there, moving forward is more difficult. It's not a feeling, but just that I'm moving at a slower rate. It's too bad I can't see the way out of here! Dac didn't let the arena dissipate did he?

On that sixth step, I decide that, yet again, I've been wrong about what true agony is. Everything begins to return. My head passes through a membrane, feeling more difficult than when I passed through the sides of the Water Tower. Every single hair on my head burns hotter than ever before, being etched back into creation. Do you have any idea how many hairs there are on a human head? Too many! I might just shave my head after this as a precautionary measure.

The hair is nothing.

Once skin comes through, pure torment. Needles, millions and millions of needles, and that's just one inch of flesh. My perception isn't entirely back to full yet, and I don't want it to be. I want to pass out. I want to die. I don't want this. I want anything but this. I'm sure I'm screaming, but I can't hear it. Hearing isn't back yet.

Still I keep moving forward, I keep moving into the pain. Two thoughts other than agony, that's all I can manage. One, keep walking forward. Two, don't let go of Logan. There's an incessant buzzing in my head that I can't focus on. I really can't. Even if I wanted to, I don't have the mental capacity.

Am I breathing? I should breathe. I suck in as much air as I can possibly manage. I don't recommend inhaling lava.

Oh, yeah, I don't recommend this either. This is worse.

Every step is more miserable than the next, and my arm where Master cut me is most miserable of all. The stinging across the rest of my body hurts more than it did when I was first hit. As it is now, somewhere in my mind—the tiniest corner where thought isn't consumed by pain—I'm debating the merits of chopping my arm off. Mark seems to be getting along with only one arm. It's not even my dominant one! Together, Mark and I could make an entire upper body and do weird holiday costumes. Yes, this is definitely a good idea.

Unfortunately, there isn't time to get to cutting my arm off. Even though I'm entirely out of the blackness now, and entirely miserable, I keep marching forward, dragging Logan out. I can feel his hand now. I know that he's there, and I keep pulling.

My hearing returns to me so that I can understand the blood curdling horror coming out of Logan and me. He's actually louder than I am. I open my eyes and look behind me, look back at him. I watch as I pull the last of him out of the blackness. Even though we're free, shadowy tendrils come off of us like steam on piping hot food. Everywhere these tendrils are is what burns. It must've been covering my eyes at some point, but has since cleared. That's the only explanation as to why I can see.

"*DAC!*" I shriek. My own voice terrifies me. I can't take in any details around me. "*DAC, GET US OUT OF HERE!*"

In an instant the pain is gone. I snap my eyes open and take in a breath of air. It feels different. There's substance to it. I'm alive! I'm awake! I'm... I'm...

FALLING!

I look up, which may be down, or is it sideways? Anyway, I look and right there I notice the approaching ground!

"CRAP!" I scream, instantly activating my boots. I pour on all the energy I possibly can and then some. My fall halts painfully and abruptly, giving me the grim reminder that there is a hole in my stomach. Good news is that, after everything, I've got adrenaline working for me.

I swear my feet touch the soil before I start shooting in the air. Looking up, I see Logan's body right above me, basically. I re-angle myself and grab him as I'm flying. He's not awake yet, but he's breathing. Logan is still alive.

You're alive! Dac screams, rattling my skull. *NEVER DO THAT AGAIN!*

I don't intend to, I promise him. *Besides, I don't know how much longer that whole alive this is going to last.*

I do my best to bring Logan and I close to the ground, but I don't have the energy or presence of mind to safely land. Hello allocated crash-landing dirt and random civilians. May you please be soft and not accidentally hit us with anything pointy.

Losing grip of my consciousness, power to my boots cuts out and, for the last time, the dirt rapidly approaches.

I try and catch us, but it doesn't go very well. It's more like a running stumble that an uncoordinated cat would be embarrassed by. I drop Logan before I even get to the ground, not able to hold him anymore. My run, fall, stumble thing ends with me entirely losing my footing and tumbling farther than I would've thought possible. I did forget to slow down though. That probably would've been smart. I also somehow manage not to hit anybody. Apparently, when there's a guy that just fell from the sky rolling across the floor, everybody manages to keep away from him.

When I do finally stop moving, I manage to note that I'm covered in a lot of blood, and that my body is in quite a strange position. Also, that my bicep still hurts where Master cut me in the AI realm. My stomach doesn't hurt so bad though. It's just kind of warm.

I'm pretty sure I see people rushing towards me, but it's hard to tell. Everything is blurry. Would anybody mind if I throw up? I feel that coming on.

Hold on Sam! I think I hear somebody say. *We're almost to you! Just stay awake! Don't go into the light!*

What light? There's no light, only fuzzy silver people. At least they're not stabbing me. I think they're not stabbing me. What does that feel like again?

Without my thinking about it, one of my hands moves to cover the gaping hole in me. This manages to get it to hurt again.

Oh yeah, that's what being stabbed feels like.

"Sam!" I hear with my ears now. Heh, ears. The ones running towards me are here now, kneeling before me, and still I can't make out who or what they are.

"Sam!" they all keep shouting at me. Who's Sam? Right, that's me.

"Hold on, Sam!" They keep shouting. "Hold on!" Hold on to what? I'm pretty sure all my organs are still in my belly, so no, I won't be grabbing those.

They're touching me and doing something, and everything is weird and distant. They better not try anything funny. One of them opens my mouth and tries to pour something down it, but I can't tell what it is as my world fades to black.

Epilogue
Fourteen Years Later

"What happened next?" the little girl pipes up, her squeaky voice cute enough to melt the most frozen of hearts. She has her bed sheets pulled up tightly to cover her nose.

"Yeah, what?" pipes up the slightly older boy in the bed on the opposite side of the room.

"Tell us," the girl pleads. She gives her brother a very pointed look, telling him to get with the program. He gets the message very quickly. She obviously gets that look from her mother.

"Please," he begs, holding the word longer than absolutely necessary, just to make it perfectly clear that he is begging and has no intention of doing anything otherwise.

"Please," the girl echoes, throwing the blanket down to her waistline. Her sheets were tucked in so nicely a moment ago until the begging started.

"Pleeeeeeease," the boy starts all over again.

"Please please please please please please please please," the girl bounces up and down incessantly, her volume never getting any lower.

"It's already way past your bedtime," the oldest in the room laughs at them. "Besides, I'm pretty sure I've scared Ally more than enough."

"I'm not scared!" she pipes up, entirely throwing her blanket.

"See, Dad, she's not scared," Ian argues, defending his little sister.

"I promise I'm not!" she squeaks.

"If you don't tell us, I'll get Dac to," Ian threatens. An angry look settles on my face as I slowly turn my head to look at the metal man sitting in the corner of the room.

"What?" he says innocently, defending himself. "You're awful at bedtime stories. I was just trying to make sure they got to sleep."

"What have you told them?" I ask, my eyebrow twitching.

"Nothing," he says, making the fatal choice of continuing the lie.

"He's told us all about when you two first met!" Ian pipes up, selling Dac down the river. "He makes Uncle Arthur sound really mean." That's probably because your Uncle Arthur can be mean.

"What else has he told you?" I ask Ian, but not taking my eyes off of Dac.

"A whole lot!" Ally says.

"Really," I say, raising both of my eyebrows.

"If you would just tell them the whole story, I wouldn't have to," Dac says, putting his hands up. It's not like I'm going to leap out of my chair and attack him. The kids are awake.

"What wouldn't you have to do?" Rose asks, walking into the room.

"Turns out Dac has been telling Ian and Ally stories," I tell her. She walks right past me and kisses Ally on the head, who's bouncing up and down with joy to see Rose.

"Mommy! Mommy! Mommy!" she repeats over and over again until Rose picks her up.

"Hey sweetie," Rose says before kissing Ally on

the forehead. She then turns to look at me and says, "I know."

"You knew?" I ask her.

"Yeah, of course," Rose says, not holding anything back apparently. "He's actually really good at telling stories. I especially liked when he told them how you fell in love with me. It was actually pretty funny."

"How do you know this?" I ask her, confused.

"I like to come in and listen when he's telling the stories. You get so busy helping Sarah and Logan down on the Surface that, some nights, I get to come in here and listen to his stories."

You... he... what?

"Traitors," I say, exasperated. "I'm surrounded by traitors."

"Oh, nobody's a traitor," Rose says, waving a hand at me. "Dac's basically you anyway. You two have close to the same personality."

"No we don't!" we both complain in unison.

"Whatever you say," Rose smiles slyly.

We do not have the same personality, I clarify for the two of us to hear.

Agreed, Dac says. *I personally think I'm the superior of the two.*

Well excuse me, I say, making my voice sound weird.

"Fourteen years later and you're still acting like you're sixteen years old," Rose says, amazed.

"Like you're any better," I comment.

"I have certainly matured," Rose says, bouncing Ally up and down. "Wouldn't you say so, Ally?" Instead of an actual answer, Ally gives off an excited squeal of delight.

"Told you," Rose says smugly. Dac and I look at each other, not buying it. When I look at Rose, I can't help but smile. No matter how mature she may say she is, never once has she changed to me. When I look at her, I have always, and will always, see the girl I fell in love with years ago.

Seeing her there, playing with Ally and Ian, now that he's also hopping out of bed, I can't help it. I smile at it and could watch it all day long.

You did good, Sam, Dac tells me in the privacy of my mind.

Thanks, I tell him. And I genuinely mean it.

"You know," I loudly say to the three of them, "I *was* trying to get Ally and Ian to bed. *Somebody* is turning five tomorrow."

"Me!" Ally squeaks.

"No, sweetie," Rose says, playing with Ally's hand. "You're not even turning four until next year."

"Me!" Ian bursts, even more excited.

"Exactly," I say, walking over and picking him up. He's heavier than expected, and both my bicep and my gut hurt when I lift him. Fourteen years after the fact, and there's still some pain. They poured nearly every drop of Blue Elixir we had left on that day down my throat, and still I didn't completely heal. When I asked Jinn how his stomach wound felt, he said it didn't hurt him anymore, but he also wasn't stabbed with Sky Iron.

"Dad's right, kids," Rose says, starting to tuck Ally back into bed, but not before giving her a raspberry. "You wouldn't want to be tired for Ian's big party tomorrow, would you?"

"No," they both say, sounding defeated yet climbing into bed.

"Is Uncle Jinn going to be there?" Ian asks.

"He sure is," I say.

"Grandpa Jackson?"

"He sure is," I respond.

"How about Grandpa Nathan?" he asks. I know where this is going. He's going to go down the whole list of names.

"Everybody is going to be there," I tell him, trying to stop the list before it ever starts. "Nobody is going to miss your birthday. Even Grandpa Logan, Grandpa Kane, and Grandma Sarah are going to be there."

Smug and satisfied, he squirms into a more comfortable position in his bed.

"Night, Daddy," he says, closing his eyes and getting into his favorite sleeping position.

"Night, Ian. Night, Ally," I say, reaching for the light switch. "I love you two."

"Love you too," they both say in chorus.

"What about me?" Rose asks.

"Love you too, Mommy," they tack on the end.

"That's better," she says, just as satisfied. I flick off the light and close the door to a crack so that they can sleep well. When Rose and I get to the living room, away from their door, she asks me, "Are you still going to do it?"

"Oh, heck yeah," I say.

"I can't believe you got Nathan to make another pair of flying shoes," Rose says, holding her face in her hands.

"Don't worry, Dac's been working with him and the AI inside to make sure it's not crazy."

"What if it's a girl AI?" Rose asks. "I'm not ready for that."

"Don't worry," Dac says. "It's not. If it was, then I would've already shoved those shoes on your feet, Rose."

"Well, that's comforting," she says, shaking her head with her eyebrows high. I genuinely laugh at that. "Stop laughing," she says, smacking me. "I still don't think you should be teaching Ian to fly so early."

"We live in the Sky Nation," I remind her. "Flying is just a little important."

"I still don't approve," she says, crossing her arms. "It's dangerous."

"Oh, don't worry about it," I try to comfort her. "If he falls, I'll catch him."

"Now you're starting to sound like Jinn," she says, looking at me out of the corner of her eye. Ouch.

"I think you two should go to sleep," Dac says out of the blue.

"What a great idea," Rose says, perfectly willing to go along with it. It takes me all of two seconds to figure out what their plot is.

"You're going to go finish telling them the story, aren't you?" I ask Dac. He starts to speak, but Rose throws the same look at him that Ally did to Ian.

"Nope," he quickly says out loud, aborting whatever else he was going to say.

Absolutely, he admits in my mind. *You can't just leave them hanging like that!*

I sigh, "Just go. Apparently, you're the better story teller anyways."

"You got it," he says, saluting me just to be a jerk and lumbering back towards the kids' room.

"Come on," Rose laughs at me, pulling me up out of the couch. "Don't let them see you, but you should hear the way Dac tells stories."

Yeah, come on! I'm good at it, Dac agrees with her.

"Fine," I say, defeated, letting her pull me out of the chair and quietly following her to the outskirts of the kids' room. Rose and I sit against the wall by the time Dac starts telling the story again. And he's good. I wouldn't say he's better than me, but he's good. He even manages to include the bit about how every one of Master's soldiers that were being directly manipulated by him through the AI consciousness collapsed the moment I defeated him.

Listening to his story, to *my* story, I can't help but to reflect on my life, on everything that's happened. I've gained so much that I wouldn't trade for the world. Sure, there were more than a few rough patches, and I gained a body's worth of scars and my first and only tattoo, but it was worth it. It was all worth it. Every miserable, glorious second that I'd never give up or change: It all led me here.

It all led me home.

The End

Jake Giles Netter

www.JamesMorrisBooks.com

James has long been in love with the stories told in Science Fiction and Fantasy. A self proclaimed nerd, he proudly lines his room with the books that he loves. *Sky Bound* and *Water Tower* were written while he was in high school, *Surface* was written his sophomore year of college. Raised in San Diego, California, James now lives in Nashville, Tennessee attending college. He typically prioritizes reading and writing over homework.